Titles by Susan Plunkett

REMEMBER LOVE
SILVER TOMORROWS
HEAVEN'S TIME
UNTAMED TIME

UNTAMED TIME

Susan Plunkett

JOVE BOOKS, NEW YORK

TIME PASSAGES is a registered trademark of Berkley Publishing
Corporation.

UNTAMED TIME

A Jove Book / published by arrangement with
the author

PRINTING HISTORY
Jove edition / February 1999

The Penguin Putnam Inc. World Wide Web site address is
http://www.penguinputnam.com

ISBN: 0-515-12447-8

A JOVE BOOK®
Jove Books are published by The Berkley Publishing Group,
a member of Penguin Putnam Inc.,
375 Hudson Street, New York, New York 10014.
JOVE and the "J" design are trademarks belonging to
Jove Publications, Inc.

PRINTED IN THE UNITED STATES OF AMERICA

10 9 8 7 6 5 4 3 2 1

For Michael, Steven, and Kari, with love

UNTAMED TIME

Chapter 1

A FAT SNAKE slithered across Captain Raford Stricter's shoulder and down his torso. Burrowed in a shallow trench covered by dirt and humus, Rafe eyed the slithering viper examining his boot. The pungent tang of the jungle floor stung his nostrils. Overhead, the shrill call of birds punctuated the drone of insects thriving in the dense vegetation.

Through the external assault on his senses, he thought he caught the mellow laughter of Staff Sergeant Craig Blackstone. After three covert missions together, they knew one another as well as they knew themselves.

Rafe remained frozen, watching the snake, not daring to move until the creature moved on in search of better prey.

Rafe squinted in Craig's direction. The way Craig's brown eyes glittered in the thick shadows assured Rafe that he was indeed quietly laughing. "Your hide is too tough to be tasty," Craig said.

An animal in the jungle canopy shrieked a strident warning. The high branches rustled. A dozen birds took flight.

Something or someone was moving.

Rafe slowly surveyed their surroundings and listened carefully. Within minutes, he heard the unmistakable sounds of men. Twigs snapped. Branches whipped the air. A small rodent darted for cover on Rafe's right.

The enemy reconnaissance team was returning on a path that brought the flank man within a yard of the vegetation hiding Rafe's feet. Adrenaline shot into his bloodstream, the heady infusion preparing him for combat.

He lay still. Through half-closed eyelids, he studied the passing mercenaries. The smell of perspiration filled his nostrils. The proximity of their labored breathing spoke of how quickly a mission could go wrong. One twitch, one nervous trigger finger would end it right here.

The sixth and final man passed the snarl of vine-choked saplings a few yards left of Rafe's position.

The mental sigh Rafe allowed eased the battle-ready tension coiling his body. Listening to the men move farther into the jungle, he doubted if any of them knew what they had sold their services to protect. But Rafe, a career soldier, held no qualms nor accepted any responsibility for the pending fate of the opponents of the missions he undertook.

The sophisticated laboratory the mercenaries guarded was the team's objective. Within the secret facility carved into the mighty Andes, a radical political faction prepared to manufacture a stolen formula. In aerosol form, it could render an unprotected population immobile for up to thirty-six hours. The aftereffects caused no permanent harm. However, where heads of state and governments were involved, a coordinated, bloodless junta would change the balance of power in South America.

The first warning of heavy rain rumbled overhead. Within minutes, fat rain drops splattered on the greenery.

Leaves performed chaotic dances in the otherwise still air. The moisture gathered on the lofty canopy and spilled in a shower of miniature waterfalls.

Familiarity honed during their three previous missions brought Rafe and Craig from the jungle floor in unison. Rain carved rivulets through the mud, humus, and bits of jungle coating their filthy fatigues and skin mottled with jungle paint. Rafe turned his face to the greenery overhead. Even the rain sluicing through the layers knitting the trees together was hot.

They examined their weapons, then rechecked their gear. Each man withdrew an electronic signaling device from his pack and slid it into a readily accessible pocket.

Their target was close enough for Rafe to sense changes in the jungle. Close enough for his keen sense of smell to detect the faint odors of food, chemicals, and fuel running the generators secured in the rock forming the Andes peaks.

"If we run into trouble, activate your beacon," Rafe murmured. "The lab has to be in the valley below." He glanced in the direction the patrol took earlier. Using a circular search pattern, he and Craig had taken an arduous nine days to zero in on the location.

"I didn't crawl through this mosquito-infested jungle to do this halfway," Craig said in hushed words. "Let's bring the Tomcats right to the barnyard door."

Pride in the young sergeant he had trained and walked the razor edge of danger with filled Rafe's chest. Craig was the best of his men, one he relied on without reservation. Damp debris fell from Rafe's camouflage-painted face when he nodded curtly. "I'll take point." Out of habit, Rafe assumed the most dangerous position.

"Still don't trust me, huh?"

Rafe started walking. It wasn't a matter of trust. As the leader, he sought to protect anyone with him. This time, it was just him and Craig, under the belief that two men could find the target, set a beacon, then get out. Maybe.

The plan still bothered Rafe. The timing seemed too tight, but they couldn't afford anything short of complete success.

Cautious determination marked their progress through the vine-laced jungle. The rain became a torrential downpour. The poor visibility offered them protection, but posed an equal hazard. The safe paths of the earlier patrol dissolved into spongy humus. Once again, they studied every step for traps and detection devices.

Rafe froze, then cocked his head. The momentary glance he afforded Craig conveyed the urgent message his hand enforced with a familiar signal. *Hide. Quickly.*

In a silent flurry of motion, both men melted into the jungle. Sweat mingled with the rain running down Rafe's hair. Prepared to defend himself, he kept his weapon aimed in the direction of the threat.

Four men hurried toward them through the downpour.

As soon as the mercenaries disappeared into the dense growth, Rafe checked his watch. "Not a regular patrol," he said softly.

"Yeah, and going somewhere in a helluva hurry." Craig's brown eyes almost disappeared amid the mottled camouflage paint covering his face. "I'd sure like to know where and why."

"It doesn't matter as long as they don't get in our way or come back too soon." Rafe took a final look over his shoulder, then brought his weapon around. "Let's get in, get out, and haul ass to the rendezvous."

The two Rangers picked up the fading path the enemy had made in the soft jungle floor.

Elation swept through Rafe when they located their objective. The success dancing in his bones emboldened him. Protected by long shadows and heavy rain, he and Craig penetrated deep into the armed perimeter guarding the entrance to the underground compound.

Satisfied they were indeed at the "henhouse door," Rafe nodded at Craig. Both activated their electronic signals, then dropped them into the vegetation. The simple act ensured the total destruction of the compound.

Rafe checked his watch. He held up four fingers, the number of hours they had to reach the rendezvous point. They hurried back the way they'd come.

In a high orbit above Earth, a satellite registered two signal bursts originating in the mountain jungle of Bolivia. A tight military bandwidth relayed the signal to a tiny pinpoint in the Pacific Ocean one hundred fifty miles off the coast of Peru. The countdown started.

The Rangers moved with more speed and less caution. Neither worried about tripping an electronic warning device. They watched for the traps designed to maim or kill. Intense training and experience had honed their survival instincts. They had memorized the location of the physical hazards and traps lying in the path of their retreat.

Adrenaline propelled Rafe down the rain-soaked ravines and up the jungle slopes. Sharp, wet leaves grabbed at him. Determined to make the rendezvous point, he pressed onward.

Rafe checked his watch again. The seconds seemed to fly faster than his feet, which raced across the rugged terrain.

By now, the *USS Abraham Lincoln* had launched the strike force of F-14 Tomcats loaded with enough ordnance to level the clandestine lab. He signaled Craig to quicken the pace. Damn, the timing was tight. Unless they got a break in the weather, and soon, they would go to hell with the chemical-mixing terrorists they just delivered to the powers on high.

Running, slipping down a rain-rutted slope, they fled as though Lucifer himself breathed fire down their necks.

The staccato of gunfire shattered the dense shadows. Rafe dove for cover. A tree whined and groaned overhead, then splintered. A severed branch tumbled through the mesh of vines, then caught. It swung, falling lower with each arc.

Craig breathed a soft curse in the cacophony of screeching birds taking flight. A waterfall spilled from the snarl dangling overhead.

Rafe rolled for the nearest cover, Craig beside him.

Each man watched the hundred and eighty degrees directly in front of him, and relied on the other to cover his back. The rain slackened, leaving them exposed to enemy eyes.

"Think they saw us?"

"Don't know. They shoot at anything that moves. We take no chances." Rafe took his bearings, then glanced at his watch. "We can't wait more than another minute."

"Hell of a choice, isn't it?"

"Beats no choice." Rafe didn't need to review their options. It made no difference whether an enemy bullet or friendly fire got them. Dead was dead. The firestorm he and Craig had summoned would reshape this part of the Andes for better than a three-mile radius.

Rafe nudged Craig, then nodded toward a narrow opening carved through the vine-webbed trees. Overhead a brightly colored bird squawked as it took flight.

On his right, a man moved through the brush.

Rafe slung the Winchester Viper over his shoulder, withdrew his knife, and slithered into the jungle. Hand over hand, he crawled soundlessly toward the spot where death awaited them unless he struck first.

A few feet ahead, a soldier dropped onto one knee. In the same motion, he aimed an AK-47 in Craig's direction.

Damn, he'd seen Craig. Did Craig see him? Rafe willed Craig to shoot. Noise be damned.

Urgency surged through Rafe. The second he needed to bring his Viper around was too long. Rafe's entire body coiled, then sprang at the mercenary.

A single shot rang out. Within the same heartbeat, Rafe neutralized the threat with a stroke of his knife.

His chest heaved with anxiety. Breathing quietly through his mouth, his sharp senses analyzed every sound.

The coppery tang of blood mingled with the earthy smell of the jungle.

When Rafe glanced at Craig, he met brown eyes set in resignation. Craig didn't move. Anger, frustration, and an acidic sorrow tightened Rafe's gut.

Rafe slid his knife into the scabbard strapped to his thigh, then raced to his buddy.

Craig shook his head. "Keep going, sir. Make the rendezvous."

Damn it, they'd come this far together, they'd reach the clearing, too. "I will, and you're going with me." He dropped to his knees, picked up the Stevens 12-gauge shotgun, and shoved it into Craig's hand. "Hold on to your weapon, Sergeant."

"You can't make it with me on your—" A sharp hiss whistled through Craig's teeth as Rafe hoisted him from the ground.

The distinctive sound of an AK-47 chattered from the downside of the slope.

With Craig draped across his shoulders, Rafe skirted the pitfalls lurking in the thick brush and among the fallen, decaying hunks of jungle. He avoided a hidden trap, and kept moving. The problem was, the presence of his enemies forced a course parallel to the escape route. He felt like a quarterback holding the entire team on his shoulders and racing across the field instead of toward the goal line.

Rafe changed direction. Two nights earlier, they had taken shelter in a cave well hidden by heavy growth. He headed for it now. If he couldn't outrun the mercenaries, he might hide long enough for them to pass.

The seconds ticked away.

The sporadic gunfire drew closer. Whatever the destination of the four men who hurried from the compound in the driving rain, they had found company. From the sound of the gunfire, there were at least six, maybe seven, soldiers in the jungle.

Lungs screaming, legs and shoulders burning, Rafe panted with relief at the sight of the crumbling granite outcrop. Ten more yards.

At the cave, he eased Craig free, then steadied him against his shoulder before groping through his pack. He retrieved Craig's jacket and wrapped it around the wound leaking over them both.

"Can't leave a trail," Craig rasped, helping Rafe stanch the worst of the blood flow.

"Can you make it inside on your own?" Rafe gingerly lowered Craig to the ground. One look at the sergeant's face told him they had reached the end of the road. Craig would bleed to death before they covered another mile. Fortunately, shock dulled the full impact of the bullet's trauma. Soon it would wear off or pull him deep enough that he wouldn't care what came next.

Craig nodded.

"You have point, Sergeant. Check it out before you go in."

"Yes, sir." Craig grimaced, lowered his head, and began crawling through the brush toward the narrow opening in the rock.

Rafe backtracked a hundred feet. He erased the signs of their presence, carefully checking for blood spatters that might betray them now that the rain had stopped.

Shouts and the sounds of men crashing through the jungle came from all directions. A burst of gunfire was followed by another, closer series.

Scooting on his belly, he wormed his way backward, concealing, blending the jungle floor until every trace of their trail disappeared.

Once inside the dank shelter, he spied Craig curled against the wall. The pronounced rise and fall of his buddy's chest conveyed a grim agony in the faint light seeping through the small, low opening.

With an eye on the entrance and a hand on his weapon,

Rafe shucked his pack, then gingerly removed Craig's pack.

"Get the hell outta here, sir." The effort of his raspy plea tightened the grimace etched into his shadowed features. "You don't have much time."

Rafe dug his medical kit out of his pack. "Where the hell do you suggest I go, Sergeant? I estimate at least half a dozen guerrillas are prowling around our doorstep." He pushed a morphine tablet into Craig's mouth. They weren't going anywhere for a while. The sooner the pain-killer got into his system, the better.

"Time's running out." Craig lifted his shoulder, then exhaled with a groan. "You can slip through 'em, sir."

"Like hell I can." The edge of his knife slit Craig's shirt open. Rafe shifted, allowing the scant light to illuminate Craig's side and back, then swore softly. The bullet had ripped through the flesh near Craig's left kidney. Damn it. Craig's life was spilling onto the ground. He had to stop the bleeding.

Rafe cleaned the wound quickly, then spread a fine layer of skin seal over the gory hole. Patching the leak was the best he could do under the circumstances. It wouldn't be enough. As an afterthought, he shoved a second morphine tablet between Craig's teeth, then handed over his canteen.

"Drink. Swallow." When Craig hesitated, he added, "That's an order."

Craig swallowed. "I'll never pass a piss test now."

A lopsided smile curled Rafe's lips. "You already passed every friggin' test the Rangers have, Sergeant. Your conduct is better than satisfactory."

Some of the tension ebbed from around Craig's brown eyes. "Yes, sir," he whispered.

The sound of gunfire drew closer.

Rafe hurriedly bandaged Craig's wound. It never occurred to him such an act smacked of futility. If they eluded the guerrillas, the firestorm on the way from the

Abraham Lincoln would obliterate them all.

Captain Rafe Stricter knew about failure, loss, and defeat in his private life, and that's where it stayed. As mission leader he had made sure defeat belonged to the enemy. Not him. Not Craig. And the day was not over. He would think of something.

He glanced at his watch while helping Craig get as comfortable as possible.

Sixty-five minutes until zero hour.

Bringing their ammunition and both weapons, Rafe took up a position at the mouth of their shelter. While he contemplated a way out, no one was coming in.

SIERRA NEVADA, NORTHERN CALIFORNIA, 1847

Lorilie McCaully should have known better than to check on the bear cubs. The route to the den had taken her too close to the Ketchums.

Disappointment in her well-intentioned but reckless action spurred her to outrun the consequences. She would try until her lungs burst. But outrunning the powerful horses the Ketchums rode was nigh unto impossible.

The land rose sharply. The men on horseback would have to ride around the steep rise.

Lorilie scrambled around stately pines and thick scrub, her gaze darting to the top of the slope. Loose rock bit into her hands and bounced against her shins. The soles of her boots slipped on clusters of dead pine needles caught on the crags. Her breath came in hard gasps. Still, using every piece of scrub and rock available, she climbed.

Panting, she reached the top. Her limbs ached. The stitch in her side wound tighter, threatening to double her over.

"We'll run her to ground this time. Hal, you go around

the right. Bobby, take the left. Cyrus, you stay here and grab her if she tries anythin' tricky.''

Lorilie's thundering heart lurched. The steel in the orders old man Gaylord Ketchum barked carried a determination as strong as hers to thwart them.

There was no time to hurt, barely time to think. Desperate, she drew pine-scented air into her burning lungs, then took the only direction open.

The Ketchums followed wherever she led. They had no mercy, only fear of what they did not understand. And power. And brutality.

She snagged a low tree limb and propelled her body at an oblique angle. They had not caught her yet.

The mix of alder, knobcone pine, and scrawny fir trees thinned. Granite slabs worn smooth by wind and weather stunted the growth of white-flowered syringa.

As she reached the top of the incline, she offered a prayer of apology to her deceased grandfather. When he lay dying, she had promised she would be more cautious and attentive to the danger posed by the Ketchums.

The land gradually sloped downward. The angle helped her gain speed, though her legs felt like weights.

A lapse, a tiny lapse. That was all it took the Ketchums to find her. Again.

The prospect of escape turned grim with the thunk of shod horses on granite. Movement on the right caught her attention. She stumbled, recovered, then waved off a large gray wolf watching from a cluster of boulders. If the Ketchums spotted Loner, they would kill him, or at least try, after they caught her.

A shout and the hesitant clank of horseshoes on the unyielding stone sent a final spurt of energy through Lorilie.

''We see you, girl! You won't be gettin' away this time.''

She halted. The escape route had run out. Two feet ahead, the land fell away as though a great talon had swiped through the rock when it was soft and pliable. Chest heaving, lungs burning, she massaged the stitch in her side. Fifty feet below, a mighty river carved a deeper bed into the stubborn mountains.

Lorilie lifted her chin. Beads of perspiration ran down her neck and slipped between her breasts. Dark, damp splotches grew on her red-and-white shirt. Determined to persevere with dignity, she faced her pursuers.

Four men on horseback approached cautiously. The sun caught the silver in old man Ketchum's scraggly beard. The brim of his weather-beaten black hat shielded his eyes glittering with triumph.

"Looks like we got you, girl."

Lorilie retreated half a step. Bits of loose rock trickled over the granite lip behind her.

Below, the swollen river roared a steady warning.

"You ran yourself into a corner. Are you ready ta come with us peaceably?"

Keen anguish pierced Lorilie's aching body. "So you can kill me like you did my grandfather?" She spat the words like bitter venom.

"The choice was his."

Fear melted into rage. Her fingers curled into fists at her sides. "Choice? You gave him no choice. What could an old man like him do to you? Trip you with the crutch he leaned on because the leg you broke was still mending?

"You killed my grandfather! An old, helpless man—a man who helped you without asking anything in return except for us to be left alone."

"Don't get snippy with me, girl. If your grandpa did what I asked, nothin' woulda happened." Old man Ketchum patted his mount's neck.

"You had no right to ask him for anything. You knew he would die before he gave what you wanted." A gust of wind rose up the face of the cliff behind her. The perspiration soaking her shirt created a chill against her heated skin.

"And so he did. Now I've got you." Thin lips spread across yellowed teeth with a gap just left of center. The wind plastered gray-white strands of his beard against his sinister grin. "You give me what I want and I give you what you need. A man. Seems Bobby's the only one willing ta take you on."

"I refuse to be anyone's whore," she snarled. She dared a glance at the noble Bobby Ketchum. Her stomach cramped at the thought of having him within an arm's length.

"What you want don't matter now."

Hal Ketchum leaned forward in his saddle. "It never did, witch."

Old man Ketchum glared his eldest son into retreat. Hal had the good sense to mutter an apology while he examined the smooth leather along the top of his saddle horn.

"Let's end this, girl. You're gonna give me what I want, then belong to Bobby and work your witchery for us. That's the way it's gonna be. We're willing to let bygones be bygones. We're a long way from other folks. There ain't much sense in your carrying on this way."

Anger washed through her, sending her onto her toes. "Bygones? Was it too much to leave us in peace, the way you found us?"

Old man Ketchum crossed his forearms over his saddle horn. "Now, girl, we might have done just that, if the old coot wasn't so selfish. And you—you sent them damn wolves ta kill our stock. We can't abide such actions."

She glared into his flinty, unfeeling eyes. "Use your head. If I had sent the wolves after your livestock, they would have slaughtered everything on four legs. You care nothing about truth. All you want is a convenient excuse to justify your vile deeds."

As though weary of the conflict, old man Ketchum shook his bowed head. Slowly, he straightened in the saddle. "Bring her along, Hal. Enough of this sass. We're goin' home."

Hal reached for the rope tied to his saddle.

"No!" Lorilie's protest reverberated into the abyss. "I'm not going anywhere with you. Ever!"

"Yes, you are, witch," Hal sneered.

"We're doing our Christian duty." Old man Ketchum adjusted his hat. "You ain't gonna survive next winter out here by yourself."

If Bobby intended his picket-fence grin to soothe her, it did just the opposite. A shift in the breeze wafted his sour body odor in her direction.

"Christian duty? Since when did any murdering Ketchums acknowledge Christian duty? Christian? You lack any reverence for the sanctity of life. You call me a witch, try to force me into being a whore for Bobby. Is that your notion of Christian duty?" She retreated half a step, the inner rage heating her cheeks and neck. Her heels hung over the precipice. She felt a small stone dislodge, and gripped the insides of her boots with her bare toes.

"Careful there, girl," Hal warned, lifting the rope away from his saddle.

Lorilie glanced at the air beneath her heels. With a sinking feeling, she weighed her options. She lifted her chin. "I will have nothing to do with you. Not now. Not ever. If the river is the my only choice 'tis far better than submitting to the hell you have waiting for me."

She bent her knees, spread her arms, then pushed off, praying she arced far enough to avoid the jagged rocks below the surface. She might survive.

Maybe.

Chapter 2

RAFE GAUGED THE locations of the mercenaries from bursts of gunfire. The enemy was looking hard, taking no chances, believing they had the rest of the day to flush out their quarry. Crouched low against the unyielding rock at the entrance, Rafe waited with a patience as old as the Andes.

"Capt'n?"

He afforded his sergeant a quick glance, hating the agony cratered in the dusty smile lines around the young man's brown eyes. When the hell was the morphine going to kick in?

"Give me my weapon and get out before they find—"

Sensing movement outside the cave, Rafe stiffened, silencing Craig. If either man feared dying, he hid it well in a brief exchange that communicated volumes.

A shout rose from beyond the heavy growth hiding the narrow opening.

The tension inside the small cave stretched. In the ominous silence, the rapid clack of a large beetle hurrying toward the dank interior sounded like a drum roll.

A flurry of bullets strafed the ground just outside the opening. Bits of detritus became missiles bouncing off the walls and Rafe. A razor shard of rock stung his forehead above his left eye; another grazed his upper left arm.

Still Rafe did not move. The man outside was probing, testing, hoping to draw them out, too lazy or scared to get on his belly and confront his suspicion.

Leaning closer to the opening barely large enough for a man to crawl through, Rafe took a long, slow, deep breath. Through the miasma of potassium nitrate, powdered granite, and freshly pulverized leaves, he caught the acrid scent of the other man's sweat. The mercenary knew he was close; the possibility of confrontation terrified him.

Rafe listened while outside the cave the man assessed his options.

The clank and roll of metal on stone sounded loud in the small cave.

''Shit.'' Rafe balanced his weapon into his left hand.

In a smooth motion, he swept up the grenade, then tossed it outside the cave. Continuing the motion, Rafe twisted his body over Craig's.

The explosion fractured layers of calcium deposits from the cave walls. Smoke and powdered rock filled the air. Pieces of the ceiling cracked and fell like hail, covering them with a thin layer of debris.

The Rangers lay motionless for what seemed a small eternity.

Outside, angry shouts penetrated the lingering cloud of destruction ringing in their ears. Rafe pushed off Craig and swung his weapon toward the opening.

For a moment, he thought the dust too thick to see daylight. He bent low, eyes squinted against the stinging grit suspended in the recess. Relief and dread tugged at his inner calm.

The opening was gone. The explosion had brought down enough rock to seal them inside the mountain.

He listened as the men in the jungle cursed the remnants of the dead grenade tosser.

If he understand the mercenaries correctly, the rock barricading the exit hid them without entombing them. He couldn't have planned a better concealment.

Gradually, the sounds leaking through the stone barrier faded. The tentative splatter of rain offered a false tranquillity.

Rafe pushed into a sitting position in the utter darkness and groped for his pack.

The dust-filtered beam from his flashlight danced along the wall before illuminating Craig.

"How much time, sir?"

Rafe didn't need to look at his watch to confirm that it wasn't enough for either of them to escape. "Forty-one minutes."

Avoiding the contrition in the sergeant's eyes, Rafe rinsed his dry throat with a swig of water from his canteen. He lifted Craig's head and tipped the container to his parched lips.

Panting, Craig grimaced when Rafe settled his head on his pack. "At least we're going out with a bang, sir."

"That we are, Sergeant."

"No telling how many lives we're saving."

Rafe preferred silence, but he wasn't the one needing a distraction from a fiery, gaping wound in his side. "More than a handful. Maybe whole damn countries."

Blessed silence settled over them. Rafe had never feared death. Life offered worse consequences. Before each mission, he contemplated the manner in which death might take him or his men. He did not dwell on such matters, but considered them a part of the whole mission. A good combat leader understood the consequences and prepared himself and his men accordingly.

All in all, dying with Craig in a shallow cave seemed better than most of the alternatives he had examined before this mission. At least this death would be quick—a few seconds of awareness followed by obliteration. He'd seen far worse ways of dying.

"The brass wasn't shitting us, were they, sir?"

Doubts. Not good. Must be the pain. "About what?"

"What's inside this mountain."

Rafe drew a heavy breath and let it out slowly. "No, Sergeant, they were not. The product is exactly as advertised."

Craig relaxed. "Helluva drug lab."

"Definitely not your standard garden variety," Rafe mused, recalling the intelligence reports and videos. "Addictive only to the power-hungry dispensers. The world's goin' to hell."

"Guess we are, too." Several minutes passed before Craig spoke again. "You leaving anyone behind?"

Impulse cried out *Yes.* He caught the answer on the tip of his tongue. Craig didn't mean the Rangers he trained or the men who planned the covert missions he executed with the steady-handed precision of a brain surgeon. "No. No family. Jennifer . . . she married and has a daughter. I doubt she'll miss me."

Pebbles grated as Craig shifted. "You were married, sir?"

"No. Came close, though. She wanted to, but I never got around to asking. A man like me has no business getting married."

"Yes, sir."

"You leaving anyone special behind, Craig?"

"Just my ma."

Rafe swore under his breath. Christ, he'd forgotten about Clara Blackstone. Who would tell her? Worse, what would they tell her? Not the truth. No one learned the truth about the casualties of a covert mission.

"She'll twist whatever they tell her to fit her beliefs. I've been dead to her for a long time. Guess that's not too bad." Craig's voice assumed a thin, raspy quality. "Ma's a Rapturist."

"Rapturist?" What the hell was that?

"They're a strict religious sect . . . sort of a cult in South Dakota."

"Oh." There was no accounting for why people chose the paths they took. Rafe accepted the end of his chosen road as inevitable.

He gazed down at the sergeant who had become his closest friend. The realization that Craig would never see his twenty-seventh birthday knotted his gut.

"Having something to believe in that explains whatever happens isn't too bad, I guess."

"No. Maybe not too bad at all."

Craig groaned.

Rafe shone the light on him. Whether from the morphine or raw pain, Craig found a respite in unconsciousness.

He turned off the flashlight and leaned against the rock wall. The hot, thick darkness posed a lesser threat of suffocation than the memories evoked by Craig's innocuous questions. Perspiration soaked Rafe's clothes. He pulled the bandanna from around his forehead and mopped his face.

The black foil of the cave made it unnecessary to close his eyes. Jennifer glowed in his memory. Competent, independent, she possessed a sense of humor that always found the bright side. She could make him laugh at damn near anything, even himself. He'd loved her; in retrospect, he had not loved her wisely. He hadn't asked her to marry him. He hadn't asked her to come back even when he knew she would.

He had chosen the Rangers over her and the family they once dreamed of raising.

At the time, her accusation had evoked an anger that sought a vent. He had none. All he had was grief. He worked through the familiar stages. But it was different from losing a man during a mission. Jennifer was still alive. She had moved on and he had gone back to training special recruits.

Rafe snorted in the dark.

Helluva choice he'd made, this black hole instead of Jennifer and kids.

Hindsight clarified a man's stupidity with glaring precision. If he had it to do over, maybe he'd make different choices. Maybe not. However, life, like the missions he led, offered no do-overs, no time-outs, only consequences.

There was no accounting for luck. It didn't always ride on his shoulder. Sometimes it shone its fickle smile on the opposition. Like today.

A familiar sound leaked from his pack.

He flipped on the flashlight and dug out the emergency radio.

"This is the Chicken Coop." Colonel Livingston sounded calmer than usual, meaning he was worried.

"Mother Hen." Rafe glanced at Craig and found quiet acceptance in the brown eyes looking back.

"The Farmer's going to market," Livingston said.

"He'll buy a fat pig."

"The nest is waiting. The Cats are holding."

Rafe never expected it otherwise. The Rangers took care of their own. The helicopter would wait at the rendezvous point until the F-14 Tomcats ordered it out. "Mother Hen and her chick are deep in the barnyard."

He met Craig's pain-glazed eyes. Resignation softened the youthful face beneath layers of dust and camouflage paint. Craig nodded slightly.

"Release the Cats into the barnyard," Rafe said in an even tone, his gaze never wavering from Craig's.

"Confirm that, Mother Hen." The slight crack in Colonel Livingston's voice conveyed deep emotion.

"Drop the eggs, Chicken Coop."

Silence filled the link.

"They know Mother Hen is in the barnyard and the foxes are hunting. Close the gate. Make it count. The chick and I are ready. Don't be late.'' Rafe switched off the radio.

For a long moment, he stared at the cave wall. The grenade explosion had released layers of calcification and revealed more rough granite.

''They'll strike on schedule,'' Rafe said.

''I reckon they will, sir.''

''We've been on what, three missions together?''

''Yes, sir.''

Rafe managed a lopsided grin. Damn, he didn't want to die with his best friend treating him with the same cool formality as he would any other officer. ''I'd say we've dated long enough for you to call me by name.''

Craig shifted slightly, then groaned. ''I don't reckon rank has much privilege in death.'' He brought his left shoulder up an inch, then winced. ''I'll call you by your mother-given name, but I damn sure won't let you kiss me, no matter how often we date.''

Rafe chuckled, enjoying the tease. Goddamn, but he liked Craig. ''Not even on our last date?''

''Shit, no.''

The last vestiges of a feeble, forced smile melted from Rafe's face. This was the last mission. As the minutes ticked by, he realized the odds he'd beaten long ago had finally caught up with him. Seemed a man ought to live longer than thirty-two years.

''Are you a religious man, Craig?''

''Getting more so by the minute.'' Craig shifted again, then moaned.

Rafe glanced at his watch. ''Start praying.''

When he looked down, he realized Craig was doing just that. Rafe wasn't sure he knew how to pray anymore. He gripped his Viper with his right hand and rested his left on Craig's shoulder for reassurance. The sergeant was the closest thing he'd known to a brother. If fate could grant him a final wish, it would be for Craig to survive.

Rafe had chosen this life and squandered all chances

of being something other than a finely tuned, instinct-driven predator. He was committed to the path he'd chosen for his destiny. Craig wasn't. Craig hadn't acquired the callousness wrought by years and practice. He hadn't learned to look at the atrocities of the strong and powerful perpetrated on the weak and innocent without being deeply affected. Craig still had a few untarnished parts of his soul. A man so full of life and promise ought to have a real chance at living it.

For Craig, Rafe did something he hadn't done since before his parents died when he was eighteen. He closed his eyes and prayed.

He begged God to have mercy on Craig and let him live. Show him another sunrise. Maybe let him find the right woman. Just a small miracle. He'd never asked God for a miracle before.

He didn't believe in them now. But just in case God was in a generous mood, it wouldn't hurt to ask for one for Craig.

The first rumble reverberated through the mountain.

Every bone in Lorilie's body rattled in the chilled river. Her instincts for self-preservation catapulted her to the surface. Gasping, coughing, she swam with the current. Instinctively, she reached for the shore. The frigid water carried her over a swell, then slammed her into a trough. Through the hair plastered around her eyes, she caught sight of another tumultuous trick of the current. Kicking hard, she skirted the worst of the vortex.

The strong current swept her downstream, swamping her, denying a lungful of precious air. The weight of her shirt, trousers, boots, and even her hair, worked against her. The power of the river roared in her ears along with the rush of her blood. Intent on surviving her folly, she concentrated on staying on the surface and using the powerful current to carry her to the shore.

She desperately grappled for one overhanging rock after another, only to have patches of crumbling cliffs break off at her touch. The opportunities slipped away.

Angling toward the side, kicking with every bit of strength she possessed, she rode the fringes of the current eddies. Unexpectedly the torrent propelled her toward the cliff face.

Ahead, a portion of the cliff had fallen away. The current swirled in the fresh recess. Through the spray of hawkish water and her own wild hair, she saw her chance. Determined, she swam with desperate strength.

The river caught her in a whirlpool at the base of the crumbling mountainside. She grabbed a dangling tree root and held on. The weathered bark bit into her hands. The river pulled, reluctant to give her up.

Kicking, circling with the current, she inched hand over hand up the sturdy root. Her arms strained in their sockets. The pain made her try harder. When exhaustion threatened to drop her into the unrelenting river, she thought of old man Ketchum and the putrid Bobby.

She refused to give them the satisfaction of committing suicide—even unintentionally. On the other hand, she hoped with all her heart they believed her dead. Maybe then she could live on the mountain in peace.

The farther she emerged from the river buffeting her lower body, the heavier the weight on her arms grew. Her durable boots became anvils shackled to her ankles. The saturated fabric of her baggy shirt and grandfather's woolen trousers felt like a hand reaching from the river and dragging her down.

She grappled for a hold on the cliff face and tried to shove away the hair hanging like broken slats across her face. With the aid of the dangling root, she climbed using any rock or scrubby growth the cliff afforded. The breeze off the river caught her loose clothing and slapped her tingling skin. Her shivering fingers and toes slipped, then grabbed again. Her knees and elbows banged and bounced against the unfeeling rock as she pulled herself up.

Near the top of the escarpment, she crouched on a slender ledge nestled in a shallow alcove to rest. The long shadows of dusk rode the land, and so might the Ketchums.

I've learned my lesson, Grandfather. I will be responsible and vigilant. I will practice good judgment and caution.

Lorilie wrapped her arms around her legs. Weary, chilled to the point of numbness, she rested her forehead on her knees. Torrents of loneliness filled her soul, leaving her as cold inside as outside.

Guilt assailed her.

Years earlier when the Ketchums entered the mountain valley, she had watched from a distance. Strangers were rare and always a threat to the diminishing numbers of the Gifted people. Since Lorilie began roaming the forests as a small child, the Gifted scattered along the mountainside had disappeared. Some had died. The rest had departed in search of other Gifted enclaves or to the anonymity of the cities. There seemed no middle ground between total isolation and complete absorption into society. The latter ensured the demise of their talents in future generations.

Over a year earlier, Lorilie had broken an unwritten law when she saved two of the Ketchums from the wrath of a mother grizzly. In truth, she had had no choice. As one of the Gifted, her reverence for life disallowed turning her back when any life was threatened.

At first they had been grateful for her intervention. Later they had become fearful. Accusatory. Vengeful. Greedy.

Soon, very soon, she and Marica the Healer would leave their beloved mountain. In the lowlands, it would be warm.

Huddled on the ledge over the river, the only warmth came from the tears flowing down her cheeks.

A wolf howled at the top of the cliff. Lorilie lifted her head, listening.

The howl sounded again.

Loner. Ever-faithful Loner.

The expectations of her companion forced her to take a deep breath. Carefully, she straightened her shivering legs. The fragile perch beneath her toes seemed to have shrunk. She was close to the top, just a few more feet. Trembling, dirt-crusted fingers grappled for the next hold. As she stepped from the small ledge, rocks and dirt clods slipped away and joined the rushing river.

Lorilie climbed as the last strains of light vanished in the western sky.

When her head rose over the top of the cliff, Loner's fangs clamped on to the back of her shirt. The big wolf tugged, hauling her over the edge. She pushed, trying to help, and lacked the strength to do more than protect her face when he dragged her toward safety. Panting, tired beyond belief, she rolled onto her back. She wanted to sleep for three days right here.

Loner's cold snout nudged her shoulder. His gray-white coat glistened in a shaft of fading sunlight. Expressive eyes spoke to her heart.

"In a moment." She hated his unease, and wanted to reassure him.

As her breathing stabilized, the night chill seeped through her wet clothing. The cold nipped harder the longer she lay on the ground listening to her heartbeat. It settled into a rhythm harmonizing with the fierce river below.

Jumping into the river had smacked of foolishness. If she had entered the water a little to the right or left, the rocks just below the surface would have broken her bones. She had been lucky. Once again, the land chosen by the Gifted had favored her.

Determined to survive the impetuous folly Grandfather had chided her for on numerous occasions, she rolled to her feet. The aches in her legs reminded her of how many rocks the river had bounced her off.

Thoughts of the warm, safe place she now called home filled her mind. The river had carried her several miles. In the gathering darkness, the land seemed steeper, the distance greater.

Each time she tripped during the long trek home, Loner either nudged her upright or positioned himself to break her fall. The stumbles grew more frequent as the night aged and a gibbous moon crept through the stars.

The ebb and flow of the sounds of the river on her left served as a guide when dense tree growth blotted out the path. Loner prodded, forcing her to put one foot in front of the other and close the distance.

At last they broke through the heavy forest. Moonlight shone on a forbidding cluster of craggy, towering monoliths reaching for the stars. The sight of her sanctuary brought a choked cry of gladness from her. Home. She was safe. In the small hours of the morning, the last of her hideaways had never looked so good. She slipped between the granite pillars and collapsed, her legs twitching, unable to carry her another step.

Loner curled around her, sharing the warmth of his body.

The rocky floor felt like a feather bed; the wolf's coat provided more comfort than a down-filled quilt. Exhaustion throbbed in every bruise. Lorilie closed her eyes. She was safe. For now.

Dreams of happier times filled her sleep. Her optimistic nature seldom allowed sad memories or bad dreams to get a solid foothold.

The dreams of better times faded. Something in the real world called. Groggy, Lorilie roused from a healing sleep.

The noise registered slowly in her fuzzy state.

Loner.

She groped for the warmth of his fur in the darkness, but could not find it.

His keening howl sent shivers up her spine. She had never heard him cry this way.

The habit of years sought answers through the use of the gift feared by Outsiders. She opened her mind to the wolf and sought the reason for his abandonment.

Loner stood outside the monolith fortress. The tremendous fear she sensed in him eluded definition. Waves of confusion mingled with life-threatening fear and the instinct to flee.

His terror sparked fear in her. For the first time since discovering her gift with wild animals, she failed to comprehend the impressions she received.

Lorilie peered into the complete darkness of the outer chamber she occupied. Prickling awareness sent her heart racing.

Something Loner feared more than being cornered by Ketchums shared the chamber with her. Lorilie recoiled while opening her senses to the beast invading her fortress.

It felt strange, powerful. The aura of death permeated the darkness.

Chapter 3

THE BALEFUL TONE of Loner's howling outside
the sanctuary kept Lorilie motionless in the dark. Whatever had sent the wolf from her side was inside the cavern.

She remained still as the terror Loner emanated charged
him to flee. But he remained, entreating her to join him.
Unable to endure his distress, she broke the link.

His howling assumed a deeper, more urgent lament.

She peered into the blackness, willing the thing lurking
there to make a noise.

She feared nothing from the four-legged mountain denizens, only the two-legged ones. Her thoughts jumbled.
Of course, with the wolf present no man would venture
inside her fortress.

Loner continued howling.

A surge of irritation rippled through her battered body.
This was her refuge.

She pushed to her feet, making barely a sound. Whatever shared the sanctuary with her had to move on.
Arms outstretched, she felt the smooth walls and took her
bearings.

Two steps to the right at shoulder level she found the lantern Grandfather had insisted she keep fueled for emergencies. Knowing every crevice and corner of the stronghold had increased the temptation to ignore his warnings. Now she was glad she had heeded them.

She groped the ledge. Fatigue and hunger trembled in her hands. Smooth rock edges glided beneath her raw fingertips. The old tinderbox fell onto its side. She fumbled it open and withdrew a precious match.

Lorilie turned her head away, then struck the match. The flare of combustion lit the chamber. Black granite formed the high ceiling as smooth as the floor and walls. The area was nearly as large as the house her grandfather had fashioned out of stone for her grandmother many years ago.

Holding the match high above her head, she scoured the oval chamber.

Her heart quickened. Her stomach tightened along with the rest of her body ready to flee the strange mass huddled against the far wall.

While she stared, the match burned down to her fingertips. She dropped it.

She swallowed the lump in her throat and took as soothing a deep breath as Loner's incessant howling allowed. Maybe the wolf was right. She ought to run.

But there was nowhere to go.

She gathered her composure. This was her sanctuary. Whatever huddled against the far wall must be addressed.

She withdrew another match from the tin, then struck it. Without so much as a glance at the interloper, she lit the lantern. After a slight wick adjustment, she squared her shoulders and lifted the lantern from its perch.

The indiscernible mass remained unmoving. Maybe it had crawled in here to die.

Lorilie watched without blinking, unsure what had invaded her territory. Wary, curious, she inched closer.

Still, the object defied comprehension. Nothing in her

vast knowledge of the forest and its denizens came close to looking like . . . what? A giant mud ball?

Lorilie held the lantern ahead and leaned closer. In disbelief, her free hand rose to her mouth.

The mud pulsed slowly.

Impossible.

Drawn by the inexplicable, her heart thundering in her chest, she leaned forward for a better view. The lantern dangled just above her head.

The mass assumed a vaguely recognizable form. Curiosity won over caution, she edged closer and lowered the lantern. The pattern of the forest in dappled shadows peeked through the mud and dust coating the mass.

She watched for long minutes while Loner howled outside. When her heart steadied, her curiosity prodded her bravery. The tenuous calm she achieved allowed her to concentrate on the creature. The gift that made her different from the Ketchums slipped into the forefront of her consciousness. If the creature was a wild animal, she could control it, understand it, and perhaps help.

She opened herself, prepared to feel the creature's fear, his pain, even the unreasonable compulsion to kill caused by rabies.

And sensed nothing.

Amazed, she straightened a bit. Her aching legs cried for respite. Perhaps her physically depleted condition accounted for her dulled senses. Determined to discover the nature of the beast at her toes, she tried again. This time, she picked up a long, crooked twig with dead pine needles on the end and poked the breathing mass.

It moved. She dropped the stick.

Lorilie's hand shot to her mouth and stifled the scream welling up in her throat. She watched in paralyzed horror as the thing at her feet came alive. A head lifted. Two legs shot forward from a snarl of limbs. A heavy boot grazed her ankle. A second head seemed to grow out of the man's chest.

Not one man. Two men. Dear God! Men. In her sanctuary. Why hadn't they run from the wolf? How had they found the fortress?

Black, green, and gray streaks covered the stranger's mud-daubed face. Only the light glinting off his teeth through dry, cracked lips and the whites of his eyes bore resemblance to something human. Then she was staring into eyes the color of storm clouds in winter. The intensity of his gaze reached inside her nervous soul.

Waves of confusion rolled off him, flooding her senses to the point of dizziness. Her eyes proclaimed him human. Her gifted senses conveyed a tightly controlled beast capable of delivering death in the blink of an eye. She refused to blink.

As he straightened his spine, his gaze shot downward. Lorilie followed the direction.

A second man lay bunched in the cradle of the bigger man's legs, his bowed head supported by powerful arms coated in the same mottled black, green, and gray skin.

What sort of people were these?

Lorilie licked her dry lips. Swallowing hard to keep her traitorous heart from leaping out of her throat, she retreated a step. If the big man moved toward her, she would drop the lantern and dart outside before he extricated himself.

Sorrow so piercing she nearly cried out assaulted her senses. She tried to withdraw. She had never experienced a link with another human.

In a dark corner of her mind a voice screamed for her to run. He might look like a man, but all her instincts warned he was a predator more dangerous than anything roaming the mountains. She met his flickering gaze, and she could not move. The trembling coursing through her sent the lantern into a slow swing.

The longer she stared at the men, the stronger she sensed the agony of a wounded, trapped animal. Disregarding the inner voices screaming for her to escape, she sifted through her perceptions. Instinct classified him as an animal. Her vision proclaimed him a man. Gradually it came to her. The man staring back at her possessed no fear.

Perhaps he was both man and animal. The animal nature she detected gave her no cause for alarm. The man side of him heightened her fear.

When the Tomcats dropped their Blue-109s, Rafe had accepted death. While he had no idea what awaited him in the afterlife, or even if another realm existed, he sure as hell didn't expect this. The great white light summoning him through the tunnel of ethereal bliss was no brighter than a dim flashlight. Had his life added up to no more than a meager candlepower welcome by only one ragtag spirit?

What kind of afterlife guardian was covered in mud? Or was it sackcloth and ashes? Upon closer examination, he realized the attendant to the next world was female. Her gaping shirt revealed the swell of her breasts. Strange, even her chest was coated with mud and bits of grass. Pine needles and odd clumps of sticks and leaves protruded from tangled clusters of hair dangling around her shoulders.

He straightened, pulling his gaze from the gatekeeper with the lantern to assess the netherworld. The brass could take a lesson from Wal-Mart door greeters. But then, there probably weren't any Wal-Marts in hell, just red-light specials in front of the Eternal Flame. If the body count from all his missions appeared under his name in the St. Peter's records, he'd undoubtedly earned a front-row seat in hell.

Inwardly he winced against the agony besieging each cell in his body. What had happened to him? Six angry men with two-by-fours couldn't have punished him more.

The green eyes probing him lured his attention. For an uncertain, incredible instant, he recognized those eyes. As quickly as it came, the impression of familiarity vanished.

A thunderbolt of realization struck him dumb. The force sent him sagging against the rock behind him.

Maybe he wasn't dead.

The thought chilled him to the bone. He'd never wanted immortality, never believed in it, and had questioned the existence of such a thing after death.

The green-eyed gatekeeper held his gaze. A lifetime of training sent his instincts into battle mode. His hand slid along the ground, his fingers stretching, groping for his weapon. When he didn't find it, his gaze raked the area.

Nothing.

Both his and Craig's weapons were gone. She'd taken them.

He glared at her.

The smell of her fear strengthened him. If she feared him, she might not unleash the dark horrors in store for him too quickly. Better yet, she might hold the power to end this bleak limbo.

The longer he gazed into her expressive, mud-stained face, the more she changed.

Again, a sense of recognition flitted across his awareness, then disappeared.

A hint of compassion furrowed her brow as her head tilted slightly to the side.

Rafe straightened away from the wall.

She froze. Even the swing of the lantern diminished to a near-stationary position.

Slowly her hand rose in the universal gesture for him to remain still. He glanced at her upraised hand, noting the abrasions and cuts in her dirty fingers and palm. Long scratches scabbed with blood and mud ran up the inside of her arm, disappearing into her filthy sleeve.

He stared back at the woman slowly crouching beside Craig. "Who are you?"

Her fine eyebrows lifted in surprise, as though she hadn't thought him capable of speech. Then, perhaps she didn't understand English. What irony. Even hell had language barriers.

Crouched just out of his reach, she set the lantern down. "Who are *you*?"

"Captain Raford Stricter," he answered, trying to place her accent.

"Captain? You are with the cavalry?"

He repeated his name and rank.

"There is an army unit close by? Why? How could I not have known?"

The consternation drawing her fine eyebrows together peaked his suspicions. Did war games continue after death? Was that part of his eternal sentence? He couldn't imagine anything worse.

"Are you reconnaissance?" Likely. Why else would she expect to know about troop movements.

"Reconnaissance? I don't understand that word." She dismissed him by lowering her gaze to Craig. "Why does your friend remain sleeping if you are awake?"

Gazing at Craig, the last notion of immortality fled. He pressed his fingers to Craig's neck. A weak, thready pulse rendered the verdict of life. Unless Rafe found help for him soon, Craig would fade away—without him.

"Craig's wounded. We need a doctor. Look, I don't know what unit you're attached to, but I'd appreciate any help you give him." He pressed his lips together, contemplating what he could trade for Craig's life. "If it's surrender you want, I'll go peacefully, providing you get a doctor for him first."

"Surrender? You are surrendering to me?" Startlement brightened her dirty face. The first hint of a dangerous smile lifted the corners of her generous mouth.

Angry, resentful that he had no choice if he wanted to save Craig, he nodded once. Whatever happened had robbed him of his sanity. Part of him railed at surrendering to a frail female without a weapon. But whatever was happening—had happened—any price was worth a second chance for Craig.

He gazed into the darkness. Everything had changed. The cavern was nothing like the cramped niche he and Craig had taken shelter in. He held Craig with one hand and shifted for a better look at the walls around him.

"Please, we will both find more peace if you remain just as you are while I examine him." Something in the woman's calm voice rubbed a fine layer of angst from his soul. The necessity to explore the area ebbed into nothingness.

Before he comprehended how or why he failed to act on his instincts, she lifted the lantern and started examining Craig.

"He is badly hurt. I smell blood, but I cannot see the wound through the dirt. You are an imposition on my domain, but you may stay as long as you respect my ownership."

As quickly as the raging turmoil welled inside him, it ebbed. A glimmer of the peace he experienced while preparing to die returned as she spoke. The longer he stared into her eyes, the louder a distant voice in his head shouted for him to find answers.

"What happened to your friend?"

"A bullet tore through his side. I've stopped the bleeding. Craig needs a good trauma unit, a gifted surgeon, a few units of B-negative blood, and a gallon of strong antibiotics. Can you arrange that?"

Lorilie had no idea what he meant. Running her hand along the side of the man named Craig, she found the injury. The way her fingers dipped into the wound covered by a bandage led her to believe the injury was fatal. Blood soaked both men. What the man needed for any chance of survival was Marica's healing hands.

Lorilie quailed at the notion of involving Marica. For reasons that eluded her, Captain Stricter had surrendered.

Uncertain which part of him acquiesced to her superior-
ity—the man or the raging beast—she remained wary.
What if these men could not be trusted? What if they were
no better than the Ketchums, and once helped, turned on
them with a fear-filled vengeance for what they did not
understand?

Laying a hand along Craig's cheek, she felt the fever
in him battle with his determination to live. "All life is
sacred. Every living creature has a purpose, even if it is
to procreate and ultimately feed creatures above them in
the forest hierarchy. Such is the law of nature. We are all
bound together and dependent on those who share the
mountain with us."

She stood and fetched the lantern. "Are you strong
enough to carry your friend?"

"Yes." Rafe shifted, protecting Craig's injured side.
"Do you have a name?"

"I am Lorilie McCaully." She retreated several steps,
careful to remain out of reach.

He shouldered their packs and gathered the limp man
who stretched out to better than six feet. Lorilie's heart
caught in her throat when Rafe stood. She had never seen
a man of his towering height. His size and demeanor reminded her of a mother grizzly bear. As long as he remained more beast than man, she could control him.
However, if the man dominated the animal side of his
nature, all hope of keeping him subdued would place her
at his mercy. But the deep-seated credo of the Gifted
made only one decision possible.

"Ma'am?"

Lorilie glanced over her shoulder. The softly spoken,
formal address from the giant seemed incongruous. "Yes,
Captain Stricter?"

"Call me Rafe. I have the distinct feeling my rank
doesn't mean jack sh—anything to you."

What a strange man. Half the time she didn't understand what he said. "Is your friend too heavy?"

"No." His head tilted toward the cavernous ceiling. "Where are we?"

"You do not know?"

"I wouldn't ask otherwise."

"But you would remember where we are if you left, would you not?" The statement echoed her uncensored thoughts. The back of her shirt felt warm from his analytical stare. Like the cougar and the wolf, the beast in the man scoured his surroundings for traps, weaknesses, and escape routes. The predator detested cages.

When he did not answer, she started walking toward the passage leading to the heart of the fortress. She waited until he was close before side-stepping between a break in the smooth, polished wall. "This is my sanctuary. I will do what I can for your friend. All I ask is your silence about me and this place."

"How do you propose to help him? Are you a medic?"

"A medic?" She slowed, rolling the unfamiliar term over in her mind. The corridor narrowed and twisted to the left.

"Do you have any training in medicine?"

"No."

"Will you get a doctor?"

"We have no doctor." She angled left again, slowing for him to catch up. By design, the illusions of dead-ends were easy to miss.

"How the hell are you going to help him then?"

She turned. He stood like one of the granite monoliths forming the shelter entrance. His friend rested in his arms like an overgrown, sleeping child. "I make no promises," she crooned in a voice that tamed the most savage beast. "You must trust that I will do all within my power to help him. And you. It is against my nature to do less."

"People go against their nature all the time to gain an advantage."

"There is no greater advantage beyond the preservation

of human life.'' She identified with the expectation of betrayal. How long before he turned against her?

"You didn't answer my question."

"You and your friend need fear nothing in my sanctuary."

"Where the hell am I?" A booming echo bounced in the darkness and sent a cold shiver up Lorilie's spine.

"I told you. In my sanctuary."

"That doesn't tell me jack, lady. Where the hell are we?" His angry tone conveyed frustration.

"You are in the mountains. The nearest settlement beyond here is Sutter's Fort. Even that is not large. It has only been there six or seven years. It is possible to raft down the delta to Yerba Buena, but I have not done such a brave thing. Yet."

An invisible hand seemed to push at him. As quickly as it steadied him, he resumed his granite stance. "There's no delta within a hundred miles of here. Give me a reference point where more than a dozen people live."

"You are mistaken. The delta is at the base of the mountains, in the wide valley."

"There are hundreds of wide valleys in these mountains. Could you be a little more specific? Maybe tell me how far we are from a road leading out of here and where it goes?"

Confused, she stared at him. Anger blazed in his eyes. A shiver ran up her spine. The beast in him remained subdued. The man was taking over. "I know of no road in these mountains."

"How the hell do you get supplies? Air drop?"

Again, he made reference to something beyond her comprehension. Sensing the fragile balance between man and beast, she chose her words carefully. "We have seldom found it necessary to leave the mountain. When Grandfather was alive, he journeyed to Yerba Buena, San Jose, or Monterey for what we needed."

For a long moment, he stared back, his face implacable.

"Those places aren't even near one another. What the hell are you trying to pull?"

Mentally she crooned to his animal nature, hoping to quiet the human side of him. "They are the nearest settlements. I do not believe the Church wanted their missions in close proximity."

"I'm not looking for a church."

"But the towns grew up around the missions. I am afraid I cannot tell you what you wish to know." She stepped back, uncertain of his reaction.

"Can't or won't?"

"Few men know the mountains of Alta California. My grandfather—"

"What the hell does California have to do with the Andes? This is Bolivia, for crying out loud."

"Bolivia?" She tried to recall if she had heard of a place named Bolivia and was certain she had not. "Where is Bolivia?"

"You're standing on it." The deadly calm in his tone sent alarms through her. "What is this? Some sort of game?"

Lorilie swallowed hard. "I assure you, you are not someone I would contest against. And I also assure you, I am standing in my sanctuary. In Alta California, a territory of Spain."

Agitated confusion rolled off him and swamped her senses. Stars above, but he was powerful! Not even a wounded, dying cougar harbored such raw pain. One by one, barriers rose over her senses. Through the protective veils she sensed his wild agony stemmed from an imperceptible emotional source.

"Lady, much as I'd prefer being in California, this is friggin' Bolivia."

"If you wish to call it Bolivia, that is your prerogative. I have no wish to argue."

"Neither do I," Rafe muttered, nodding for them to get moving. "Next you'll tell me you're going to bring in the local witch doctor to lay hands on Craig and heal him.''

Lorilie let the lantern sag. The light swung beside her calf. Could he be one of the Gifted? Given the wild predator she found in him, it seemed impossible. But how else would he know about Marica's healing gift?

Chapter 4

LORILIE MCCAULLY HAD hugged one too many trees. No doubt fumes from the sap had loosened her grip on reality. He'd have to be very careful. He needed her help with Craig. However, placing any trust in a woman who insisted the Andes were in California was more than he could stomach.

He shifted Craig's limp body and glared at the mud-encrusted waif. The sight of her enigmatic expression prickled all his danger instincts.

One minute she made profound, logical sense; the next she sounded as though she'd just dropped in from another universe—without a map.

"Show me where I can find water."

"A spring flows into a basin near the back of the main chamber. Follow me." She resumed leading the way through the rocky maze. "The passage narrows beyond the next turn. If you require help with your friend, I can lend a hand."

Rafe shifted the two hundred six pounds he carried, then ducked beneath the low ceiling ahead, and followed the small patch of light Lorilie carried. Craig mumbled something unintelligible, but did not regain consciousness. The passage shrank. The ceiling slanted lower. Rafe twisted sideways and bent so low that his knees touched Craig's back.

"You can stand after you clear the overhang," Lorilie said.

His shoulders ached. The way his muscles hurt, he ought to be black-and-blue beneath his filthy fatigues. Sweating from the aches and effort, careful not to jostle Craig more than necessary, he threaded the stone needle by scooting forward on his knees.

After a final turn, the constriction opened on a large cavern.

Granite walls rose as high as a two-story building. Halfway up, they tapered toward a conical hole in the ceiling. Below the hole, an elongated, raised hearth lay cold and blackened from countless fires.

Symmetrical recesses lining the lower portions of the walls were used as shelves. The unnatural sharpness of the insets and level platforms gave the impression they'd been chiseled into the hard rock, then polished.

"What is this? The other side of the mountain?" Had the bomb blasts opened a passage to another cavern? Could the force of it have hurled them to safety?

In an alcove on the opposite side of the hearth from the entrance, a stone table grew from the floor. Granite block benches surrounded three sides.

"I have never considered it other than a part of the mountain," Lorilie said.

Someone spent a lot of time honing this shelter from the rock. Maybe someone hiding from the world. Or the authorities. Or from political persecution. Someone who didn't know the difference between California and Bolivia.

"Whose place is this?"

"I have told you, this is my sanctuary."

"Are you going to tell me you built this?" His gaze settled on a wooden trunk, battered and scarred by age and use. It sat against the wall at the juncture where the granite yielded to the alcove.

"My grandfather . . ." Her voice faded, denying further explanation.

To his right, a pallet heaped with multicolored quilts invited the burden he carried.

The faint roar of a distant river ebbed and flowed. From the darkness on his right, the melodic trickle of water falling on stone caught his attention. He glanced overhead. A star shone down through an opening in the ceiling.

"He must be very heavy," Lorilie said. "Lay him down over here and rest a moment."

He settled Craig on the thick pallet of pristine comforters reminiscent of the type his grandmother made by hand.

He gently rolled Craig onto his right side and braced him with the downy quilts. The shallow breaths were almost imperceptible. Rafe pressed his fingertips against the sergeant's feverish neck. The pulse was weak.

"Come. Before we start on him, we had best clean up."

He followed Lorilie toward the sound of the water trickling onto the rocks.

The top of Lorilie McCaully's head barely reached his collar bone. Even in the tattered clothing hanging from her shoulders and waist, a stiff breeze could topple her. She carried no visible weapons and had made damn sure he didn't, either.

He touched his right hip.

He still had his knife, but his utility belt had been stripped of his sidearm and holster. How the hell had she gotten it off him?

"Care to tell me what you did with our weapons?"

She faltered as she looked over her shoulder at him. "Weapons? You have guns?"

"I'm referring to the ones you took."

"I took no weapons. Had I seen them, I would have insisted you get rid of them." Conviction squared her shoulders. "I do not allow instruments of death in my home."

"So you got rid of them. Where?"

"You had none."

Glaring at her, he wondered what her game was. In time, he'd find out, and find their guns. "Right."

In the near darkness, Lorilie lit a second lantern, then set it on a rock shelf. Light spilled over a wide, shallow basin into a larger pool flowing beneath a rock wall.

She picked up a hunk of soap from the ledge and scrubbed her hands and face. When finished, she offered the soap to Rafe.

He started to take it from her hand.

She dropped it, avoiding contact with him. "Sorry," she murmured.

Rafe snorted.

Her expression promised she wasn't a fool.

"I won't hurt you." It would take more than words to remove the suspicion from her shadowed face.

He'd never raised a hand against a woman. And never would.

Sensitive to the smallest changes around him, he scrubbed his face and arms up to his elbows. The gritty soap stung the gash over his eyebrow. The cut opened and bled freely. With two fingers, he fished a bandanna from his back pocket, then rinsed it. A couple of twists rolled it into a headband. As he raised it to his head, Lorilie tensed. He stilled.

"I doubt that rag is very clean."

Without thought, he soaped the black bandanna. Doing her bidding without conscious thought angered him, even though she was right. Infection awaited an opportunity from the smallest skin lesion. The jungle-bred bacteria was capable of laying a man at death's door with an agonizing slowness that made a skilled torturer envious.

He dipped his left shoulder into the water and scrubbed the gash on his outer biceps with the bandanna and soap. The sharp sting of the lather guaranteed not a single germ survived.

He wrung out the bandanna and used it as a towel before tying it around his head with enough pressure to seal the gash.

Lorilie filled an earthen pot from the stream of fresh water cascading into the shallow basin. It was a start. They would need many more bowls of water before Craig was clean enough to examine.

"I'll bring Craig over here where we can clean him up before exposing his side. We've crawled through some nasty sh—dirty terrain." She didn't need a description of the animal droppings, insects, birds, and snakes they'd shared the jungle floor with, or that they'd slept and hidden in the detritus for days. Undoubtedly she could smell it.

Lorilie nodded without turning. "Your way is best. I prefer not to soak the quilts."

Rafe returned to the pallet. After removing his pack, he unlaced Craig's combat boots. For a long moment, he stared at his pack. Where the hell were their weapons and how did she get his sidearm? He distinctly remembered gripping his Viper when the mountain shuddered under the first onslaught of bombs.

Later, after he tended Craig, he'd search for it where the woman found them. Perhaps she'd hidden their weapons in the outer chamber. The absence of his sidearm left him naked in unknown territory.

Returning to the task at hand, he gingerly removed Craig's trousers. He'd contemplated leaving Craig the dignity of his skivvies, then changed his mind. The ruined shirt again fell victim to Rafe's knife. He sheathed the blade and gathered the shirt remnants they'd use to wash the jungle off Craig.

Several minutes of vigorous scrubbing with the lye

soap cleansed the torn pieces of Craig's shirt. He laid them aside and retrieved Craig.

Lorilie adjusted the lantern near the basin and turned up the wick. Light bathed the basin and glittered off the water. "If you hold him, I'll wash him." She ran a rag over Craig's hair, then rubbed her thumb and forefinger together. "He is very dirty."

Rafe stared in disbelief. "Isn't that the pot calling the kettle black?"

She dragged a snarl of hair over her shoulder, then shrugged. "I suppose if a pot and kettle could speak, the analogy would hold." When she lifted her head and met his gaze, she retreated immediately.

"What's wrong?" Instinctively, he glanced behind him, expecting to see someone standing in the chamber. They were alone.

"Your face." Her eyes widened in open disbelief.

"It's looked worse."

"Your skin." She leaned forward, but remained rooted a full arm's length away. "It is like mine."

In the clear lantern light, her face shone. A flash of distant recognition shot through his mind again, then evaporated. "I wouldn't say that."

Color blazed in her cheeks from a vigorous scrubbing with the harsh soap. Big, green eyes framed by thick brown eyelashes dominated her elfin features with high cheekbones and a pert nose. She reminded him of a dirty angel with a scrubbed face and tattered clothes. Without warning, the lips of her generous mouth pressed into a line of consternation and spoiled the image.

Damn, she was young, not much more than a kid. What was she doing out here? What kind of crazy sect did she belong to? "Are you going to help me clean him up or just stand there all night?"

She cocked her head and drew a piece of rag over Craig's forehead.

"It won't come off without lots of soap and water. If it did, we'd have sweat it off," he said.

With quick, efficient motions, she soaped the rag and began cleaning Craig, starting at his head.

"What is this in his hair?"

"It's a mixture of insect repellent and camouflage grease. It keeps the ticks and lice away."

Though she worked efficiently without pause, Craig grew heavy. The press of his feverish body against Rafe's arms and chest bolstered his strength. He'd hold Craig in any position for as long as necessary. Whoever and whatever Lorilie McCaully was, she did a thorough job of cleaning the putrid jungle from Craig. By the time Rafe returned him to the pallet, the only dry spot on Rafe lay between his shoulder blades.

He opened his pack. The grenades and ammo clips were gone. Because the pack had rested between him and the rock when Lorilie first approached, he doubted she removed them. But if not her, who? Who rifled their packs? How the hell did they get his sidearm and holster? Craig's weight had rested against his belt buckle, and it was fastened.

Silently cursing the countless things that didn't add up, he laid out the contents of the first-aid kit. "What do you have in the way of medical supplies? Any penicillin? Streptomycin?"

"I have bayberry. Wild cherry. Garlic. Goldenseal."

Exasperated, Rafe sat on his heels. "Tell me, Miss McCaully, what kind of help do you expect to give my buddy? You have no medicines. No doctor. Nothing. Lye soap and water aren't going to cut it."

Rafe hung his head and stared at the stained sealant bandage he'd slapped over Craig's wound. Without a medic and the right medicines, Craig didn't have a hope in hell.

"Perhaps it is different where you come from, but here, a healer uses the bounty of the land as medicines."

"I may as well have come from the moon." He lifted a corner of the bandage. "Damn, that's a big hole." The tightness in his tone betrayed his deep worry over Craig's survival, but he didn't care. He'd field dressed his share of injuries, even learned how to suture a wound. The mercenary's bullet had mushroomed on impact and caused a wide rent. The more the flesh swelled around the wound, the greater the difficulty of stitching it. He touched the angry, red skin. If he stitched it and the swelling continued, the sutures would pull out. "We need a doctor, lady. Somebody with a clue of how to help him. I'm getting the nasty feeling it isn't you."

Lorilie arranged an armful of jars and bottles beside Craig's hip. "Move away from him. Your insults will do him no good."

The soft command sent Rafe to his feet and away from Craig. When he realized he was standing several feet away, he began to fume. Why the hell had he done as she asked?

"Do you know how to build a fire?"

"Yes," he seethed, aching to lash out and vent the rage roiling through his veins.

"Then would you please do so?" She tipped her head in the direction of the cold hearth and a collection of dry wood. "Once it is going, you can get fresh water and boil the rags we used to wash him."

He hesitated, not wanting to blindly comply even though reason dictated it the wisest course.

"We both want the same thing," she said in a voice that reached inside him and stroked the sting from his ire with a velvet hand. "We want this man to live. His life is precious and unique in the universe. Help me help your friend."

The wild tumult evaporated, leaving him astonished as he complied. Good God! He was losing his mind.

*　　*　　*

Lorilie examined the assortment of remedies Marica insisted she keep in the fortress. Her hands trembled as she removed the strange bandage. The edges clung to the angry, red skin around the wound as though it grew there. Rafe was right. It was a big, ugly hole. As she suspected from the onset, their only chance of saving the man was Marica.

Which was the more responsible? Endangering her only friend and the last of the Gifted who shared the mountainside, or letting the man survive or perish under his own ability to recuperate?

She wrestled with the predicament. Obeying the code of the Gifted had led to the Ketchums hunting her and ultimately to her grandfather's death. Deliberate responsibility was a new mode of thinking, one she had resolved to make second nature when she climbed out of the river.

Thus far, she had controlled Rafe by focusing on his animalistic nature. Though he did not suspect her intervention, he sensed it, and hated it. The subtle manipulation of the angry beast consuming him left him confused. The greater, indefinable conflict tearing at him defied her comprehension. That she detected its existence surprised her.

Grandfather had said the world held men who were more animal than human. Until now, she considered such anomalies detectable on sight, though she had no idea how they might appear. Grandfather's warnings concerning the outside world had conjured a creature part man, part animal, and all dangerous. Captain Rafe Stricter was all that, and more. Never in her wildest adolescent dreams of living in the forest with a mate who would love her until the sun fell from the sky had she imagined a male as powerful and glorious as the one who had stumbled into her mountain hideaway.

She glanced up from the wound she was carefully removing bits of dirt from and took a deep breath. The life

force in the injured man remained strong. He fought val-
iantly, which gave her hope.

"Tell me about the village, Yerba Buena." The resignation in Rafe's voice baffled her.

She splashed a dollop of distilled blackberry into the
closest bowl of hot water, then swished a rag in it.
She hoped she was doing the right thing. Only once had
she encountered a wound this grave. Grandfather had died
before she could fetch Marica to help him.

Vacillating, searching for the responsible course of action, she latched onto Rafe's question. "It is on the ocean.
Grandfather spoke of the many hazards and places where
a wrong turn on the delta can cost hours, even days to
reach it. Yerba Buena is closer than Monterey, though
they are both seaports. I have never gone farther than
Sutter's Fort, so I cannot tell you much about either
place."

When he made no reply, she glanced up. A contempla-
tive expression drew the jet black arches of his eyebrows
close under the black headband. He seemed not to understand. "You are of the world, are you not? An Outsider?"

"I've seen a good portion of it." Caution danced in his
flinty gray eyes. "As for being an outsider—I guess that's
a pretty accurate assessment. I didn't know it showed."

"It is obvious you are not from this part of the mountain. Your clothing is unfamiliar."

"Ditto."

"Ditto?"

"It means the same."

"The same what?"

"It means I haven't seen your kind of clothing either."

"I see." Though she really did not. Her ignorance
added to her discomfort.

"You were going to make a point or ask a question,"
Rafe said, looking away. "At least I thought you were."

"Yes, I was." She hesitated, collecting her thoughts.

"In your travels surely you have seen cities, have you not?"

His blank expression hurried her words. "I thought, perhaps, you might tell me what I would see if I visited one."

"Hell, a city. Buildings. Roads. Traffic. People."

She did not understand. Rather than risk increasing the pique she heard in his voice, she retreated into silence. She would find out about cities when she and Marica left the mountain.

"Care to shed some light on what Sutter's Fort is like?" He seemed calm, too calm, his voice strained.

"It is a fort near the sawmill. They cut trees and turn them into lumber. I believe Sutter has a grant from the Spanish or Mexican dons who govern Alta California, but I do not know this to be so."

"Spanish or Mexican dons? You mean Italian or Sicilian dons, as in the Mafia?" He looked away, adding, "More like drug lords."

Perplexed, she shook her head. "I have also heard some refer to them as Spanish. But I've never heard of Mafia or Sicilian dons. Are there Italian land grants I do not know of?"

"I don't think we're talking about the same thing." Rafe turned toward the fire and stared into the flames.

A shiver crawled up Lorilie's spine. The breadth of his shoulders and towering height blocked the light. He stood as still and unyielding as the granite forming the mountainside.

She returned to Craig, and tried not to think about anything. The long silence stretched until she finished her ministrations.

"Rafe?"

"What?" He kept his back to her.

"I'm ready to bandage your friend's wound."

"Wait." He crossed the expanse and crouched beside Craig. He took a paper pouch from his kit and tore off the top. By tapping his finger on the side, he distributed a fine, white powder over the wound.

"What is that?"

"It's an emergency antiseptic and antibiotic for field use. Let's just hope it's potent enough to do him some good." The next packet he selected was much larger. He tore it open with his teeth, then carefully removed two shiny pieces of stiff paper from a large, square pad. He laid the flimsy piece over the wound.

"What is that?"

"A bandage."

Curious, she leaned closer. "It is so small and thin. What good can it do?"

"Plenty. It's treated with a slow-releasing antibiotic to fight infection." His hands lingered at the edges he tenderly smoothed over Craig's skin.

She drew the quilts over the injured man.

Rafe began pacing. His easy grace and coordination of movements defied even momentary vulnerability. The tempest he harbored stirred the rage of his harnessed beast. She ached to soothe his turmoil with a touch of her hand. While she could do little for the man, she possessed the ability to subdue the beast. She started toward him, then hesitated.

A feral snarl warned of another presence.

Lorilie turned and saw Loner at the entrance. The hackles along his neck stiffened. His snarl drew back his lips and exposed his fangs to the interloper beside the hearth.

In a blur, light glinted off the edge of a knife. A carnivore intent on protecting his newfound territory, Captain Rafe Stricter attacked.

Chapter 5

RAFE CLOSED THE distance to the wolf.

"No! Stand still!" Lorilie's command reverberated off the stark granite.

Poised with his left hand open to grab the gray fur at the scruff of the wolf's neck, Rafe froze. The razor edge of his knife stopped inches from the wolf's throat.

Coiled to attack, all that moved on Loner was the saliva dripping from his fangs. His ears lay flat against his head. A ferocious growl rumbled a warning.

Lorilie exhaled a shaky breath and willed both predators away from one another. Her rapid pulse thundered in her temples. A bolt of fear that the man would defy her turned her stomach into a cramping pocket of molten rock.

Restraining his deeply ingrained killing response plumbed depths of her gift she had never tapped. The strain, combined with the realization she could lose Loner, trembled through her limbs.

"Release him." The command forced him to open his hand. "There will be no killing in my home." Fine beads of perspiration formed over her body. She met Rafe's flat, gray gaze as the wolf retreated. Rafe was not of the same mind. He stood like a statue of a man ready to cut the wolf's throat, but his quarry had already slipped away. The hand suspended over the phantom scruff of Loner's neck trembled.

"You do not need to kill him. He is no threat to you or your friend." She forced her feet to carry her toward Rafe. "Your weapon isn't needed. Put it aside."

To her great relief, Rafe slowly straightened. His awesome height towered over her. Violence chiseled his stony features into an impersonal harshness reflected in his flinty eyes. He lowered the knife, but did not sheath it.

The impact of frustration and confusion howling inside of him set her swaying on her feet. She didn't dare lessen her concentration. If he slipped out of her control, none of them was safe. She extended a shaky hand. If he permitted her touch, she would give him a form of peace.

Thus far, the unexpected ability to sense and restrain the animalistic side of his nature perplexed her beyond reason. Had her gift extended to controlling the bestial tendencies of man, she would walk among the Ketchums with impunity.

Something about Captain Rafe Stricter was different. The nature of that difference intrigued her nearly as much as the odd physical reaction he evoked. For no apparent reason, intimate parts of her body stirred when she looked at him. An odd shortness of breath accompanied a light-headed sensation when he returned her gaze during a rare moment when he appeared almost vulnerable.

Now suspicion darkened his eyes. He glared at her outstretched hand, then retreated a step, avoiding her touch.

Resigned, Lorilie lowered her hand. "Be seated. Rest."

Although he did not move, something changed. The threat she perceived subsided. "You have nothing to fear from me or the wolf if you keep your distance from us."

"What the hell are you?" The flatness melted from his eyes. Anger narrowed his menacing gaze.

He slid further into the logic of man and away from her control. "Lorilie McCaully," she said.

"I don't give a damn what your name is. I want to know what you've done to me."

"I have done nothing to harm you or your friend. All I ask is for you to be able to say the same when you leave us."

"Where the hell am I? What sort of game are you playing?"

The last ribbon linking her with Rafe slipped away. Fear prickled in the wake of the vulnerability that swept through her. She recognized that his anger was the most dangerous thing on the mountain. Seeking distance, she retreated and motioned for Loner to follow. Crouched on one knee, she opened her arms to the wolf. He rushed into her welcoming embrace. Being with the wolf who had protected her more times than she could count was its own security. At first she had commanded him to do her bidding. In recent years, he had become attuned to her and lived to befriend his acknowledged superior.

"Some pet." Rafe turned away and sheathed his knife.

"Loner is not a pet. He is my friend, part of my family." The wolf licked her cheek with his rough tongue. She buried her face in his fur and hugged his neck. She sensed fear lingering in the wolf. It went beyond the sudden confrontation moments earlier. He had been afraid to join her in the sanctuary. Only the bond they shared overrode his natural aversion to flee.

She held the animal's head behind his ears and scratched. "There will be no fight, Loner. The man did not know you were my friend." She rubbed her forehead against Loner's. "He even has a friend. An old rogue like you knows that makes him special and very, very protective."

The wolf whined and danced in place.

The mention of Rafe's friend brought her full circle to the problem of Marica. The decision hung in the balance.

She left the wolf and returned to Craig, sat beside him and tucked the edge of the comforter around his shoulders.

Loner followed her, his attention never wavering from Rafe.

When she lifted her head, Rafe had crouched on the balls of his feet, his wrists dangling over his knees, and his back against the granite wall. He waited, for what, she did not know.

"Can I trust you not to betray me to my enemies?" Lorilie asked softly.

"Depends on who your enemies are. For all I know, they're my allies and you're my enemy."

Grandfather was right. Dealing with men from the outside world was a difficult thing at best. "Who are your allies?"

"Other than Craig, I'm not prepared to say. Who are your enemies, Lorilie McCaully?"

Admitting she had enemies made her heart ache. She wanted nothing more than to live in peace. Since the arrival of the Ketchums several years earlier, that was impossible. They knew nothing about peace. "The Ketchums. They live in the next valley."

"What did you do to make them an enemy?"

She could recite a litany of the Ketchums's offenses, starting with the death of her grandfather. "Nothing. I did nothing but help them when they were in danger. That's all."

"Lady, your idea of help, while well intentioned, leaves a lot to be desired. You said you'd help Craig. If you know of something else we can do for him, speak up. In case you haven't noticed, the man is dying."

"I know." She laid a hand on Craig's feverish cheek. "I know." Then she knew what she had to do. This burden of making responsible decisions Grandfather had thrust on her was most troublesome. At times like these, weighing the code of the Gifted against the danger posed by Outsiders seemed an impossible task.

She pushed to her feet, fatigue weighting her legs. Loner followed her across the cavern to the wooden trunk. The hinges creaked as she raised the lid. After finding her mother's amulet, she secured it around Loner's neck.

"I must go out for a while. If I ask you to stay here, can I trust you will do so?"

"Craig's here. I'm not going anywhere."

Nodding, she left him alone with the crackling of the fire, the water trickling across the rocks, and Craig's shallow breathing. He noted she'd taken a lantern but didn't light it. Perhaps she didn't need to.

Rafe leaned the back of his head against the rock. Of all the things that could go wrong with a mission, this bizarre situation had never entered the realm of possibility.

Something he couldn't fathom was happening to him. Something insidious enough to rob his ability to act upon his instincts for self-preservation. Had he been drugged? The chances of a chemical controlling agent dimmed with the realization he had neither eaten nor drunk anything. It had to be something else, but what?

Watching Craig sleep, part of him wished for such a complete escape. Damn, but he ached all over. Why?

Rafe got to his feet and checked on Craig. As he did so, he glanced at his left wrist. A band of pale skin circled his arm. The man who did damn near everything by the clock hadn't noticed the absence of his watch—until now.

"Shit, I am a moron." Insanity was treatable; stupidity went all the way to the bone marrow.

Needing to do something positive, he retrieved the lantern by the basin. Lorilie McCaully might not need light to navigate the maze, but he did. He entered the narrow passage with relative ease. He made his way along the corridor, memorizing the twists and turns. Next time, he wouldn't need the lantern.

Craig's jacket marked the spot where Lorilie had awakened him in the outer chamber. Raising the lantern high, he quickly scanned the floor and smooth walls. Their utility belts and side arms weren't there.

He hesitated at the break in the walls leading to the place where the wolf had howled like a hell hound. The need for rudimentary reconnaissance tore at his urge to return to Craig, but at the moment, he couldn't do anything to help his partner.

The air seeping through the rock opening smelled of damp pine.

There were no pine trees in the jungle.

Rafe swore under his breath. He set the lantern on a rocky shelf beside the cold lantern Lorilie had carried out earlier, then drew his knife.

When the passage leading outside twisted and left him in darkness, he slid his left hand along the wall and felt for the drop of the ceiling. After a final, sharp turn, his hand slid into air.

Night sounds leaked through a wall of giant trees spiked against the stars. Tilting his head, he stared into the sky.

His hand tightened on his knife. What he was seeing couldn't be real.

He lowered his head and rubbed his eyes with his thumb and forefinger, then looked again. With a sextant and an ephemeris, he could come within a couple of miles of his location. But he needed neither to tell him the constellations were wrong. All wrong. This wasn't the same sky he and Craig had crawled beneath in Bolivia. This sky was too familiar, too close to home.

The longer he stared at the stars, the tighter the fist of dread twisted his gut.

"What the hell happened to us?" The question caught in the night breeze. An owl hooted in the trees, but no answer emerged.

Shaken, Rafe sheathed his knife and stumbled into the passageway. How the hell had they wound up thousands of miles from the air strike?

Death he understood.

Displacement . . . It was beyond comprehension. Beyond possibility.

Dazed, he returned to the main cavern and checked on Craig. He hadn't moved. His breathing and pulse remained steady.

"What the hell is going on?" His elbows propped on his knees, he folded his arms and rested his forehead. "This isn't possible."

If he hadn't seen the stars, he wouldn't have believed it. The freshness of Craig's wound underscored that little time had passed between the air strike and awakening in the outer cavern.

"How?" he breathed. The niggling suspicion that there might have been more in the underground lab than he knew clawed through his confusion. He grabbed at the possibility. Weapons were explainable. They had measured effects.

But no one had such a weapon.

He swore softly, then straightened and emptied his pockets on the ground beside Craig. Studying the paltry array, it dawned on him that all weapon-related items had vanished except their knives. A quick check of both packs showed the same. Ironically, even the meals-ready-to-eat they toted through the jungle had disappeared. Whoever or whatever engineered this impossible displacement had a sick sense of humor.

"Whatever we've fallen into here stinks." And so did he.

Unable to sit still, he removed his boots. After checking Craig again and finding no change, he went to the basin, stripped off his clothing, and bathed.

His knife remained within easy reach while he scoured off layers of sweat, camouflage paint, and jungle filth. The tepid water kept him alert and sent the aches deeper into his muscles. If whatever brought them this far north was responsible for his battered condition, he hated to imagine the toll it had taken on Craig. Perhaps that accounted for his comalike sleep.

He wrung out his clothes and put them back on. Chilled to the bone, he walked barefoot to the hearth, fueled the fire, then hung the rest of the clothes to dry on rocks jutting from the hearth.

He'd seen the stars, the outline of the trees, and inhaled the unmistakable scent of high-altitude pine. Something had transported him and Craig from the Southern Hemisphere to the Northern Hemisphere.

With no way to find out who or what, logic turned toward Lorilie. She was the key, the one with the answers he needed to make sense out of chaos.

Prying the secrets from her might be easier said than done. How had she kept him from killing the wolf? It was her. He was sure of it. He'd have never backed down on his own. It left him angry, frustrated, and confused. It was a hell of a lot easier to remain angry at her than acknowledge the stirring of long-dormant feelings he neither wanted nor could afford. At times her big, green eyes reminded him of the innocent spectators in a war. The same kind of vulnerability shone beyond the dirt covering her hair and clothing. She epitomized the innocence he had once sworn to protect. Perhaps that was why she had seemed familiar. Because he sure as hell had never laid eyes on Lorilie McCaully before this nightmare started.

Yet she was more than the epitome of innocence. Another side coexisted within her. He had no name for what he experienced when she spoke in a certain tone. Power was the only way to describe it. It didn't hurt. In fact, he didn't actually feel anything. Something she did with her voice reached inside him and flipped a switch. That had to stop.

"You better figure this out quickly, Stricter," he murmured. She made him uncomfortable in her presence, yet he was uncomfortable with her gone.

Head back, he looked up. A faint wisp of smoke drifted

through the opening in the ceiling. It must get colder than hell during the winter. Upon closer examination, the giant slabs of rock tilted like a giant teepee and the inset shelves appeared manmade. There was no way this could be a man-made structure, but it had all the earmarks of solid engineering right down to the smooth floor and walls. Life imitated art all the time, he decided. Why couldn't nature imitate engineering?

He found a coffeepot and a grinder someone must have rescued from an antique store. The coffee beans were of a more recent vintage. While the coffee boiled, he watched Craig and the entrance and listened. When she returned, he needed some answers, even if they weren't what he wanted to hear.

The aroma of coffee met Lorilie in the passageway. If Rafe had settled in a bit, he might be calmer. Although she had slept through an entire day and part of the night, fatigue lingered from her ordeal in the river. All things considered, the opportunity for more sleep was a long way off.

Lorilie entered the cavern and saw him sitting on the floor, his ankles crossed, his hands resting palms up on his bent knees. "Dinner," she said, raising two rabbits.

"They look a little chewed."

"Loner delivers a quick kill, if not a pretty one." She headed for the stone slab beside the fire.

"The wolf hunts for you?" He swung his legs around and stood. His strangely colored trousers appeared cleaner and damp along the seams.

"Yes. It is difficult to explain to an Outsider."

"I am that."

She detected nothing of the beast lurking in him. Without it, she had no way of gauging his mood. "How is your friend?"

"The same. He's running a fever." He unsheathed his knife.

Lorilie retreated instantly, her heart leaping with the thrum of fear.

"Where is the wolf now?" He gutted the first rabbit effortlessly.

"On an errand." She detested the thinness of her voice.

He paused, then cocked his head. "Are you afraid of me?"

"Even though you surrendered to me, you have given me no reason why I should not regard you as a threat."

"You're right." He set the knife down and stood back. A simple hand gesture offered her the privilege of finishing the task.

The knife was as long as her forearm. Wielding such a weapon would require more strength than she had at the moment.

"Do you want to finish skinning these, or shall I?"

"You can." Self-conscious, she found a second cup in the wooden crate near the fire. "I am glad you made coffee. This is a good night for it." Carrying the steaming coffee cup, she approached the sleeping man. Blond whiskers looked almost brown against his ashen pallor. She touched the back of her hand to his cheek. Rafe was right, the fever had caught him. Without Marica, he had no chance of mending.

She set aside her coffee and refreshed the damp cloth heating on Craig's forehead.

Rafe made short work of the dinner preparation while she drank the coffee. "We're going to need more wood."

A glance at the wood stack confirmed his assessment. "The firewood has run quite low the past few weeks. I'll gather more after we eat."

He faced her. "Why don't I do the wood while you clean up?"

"We can go together." She pointed beside the hearth. "I have a spit for the rabbits. Let's get them started. It has been a while since I last ate."

"How long is a while?"

Why did he care? "A day and a half or so."

"No wonder your clothes hang on you. Regular meals prevent that sort of fashion faux pas."

"A what?" Sometimes he spoke a completely different language.

"You are a babe in the woods, aren't you?"

"Since you almost smiled, maybe that is not as terrible as it sounds." Firelight glistened in his black hair. She doubted it was more than an inch long at the top of his head. The closely shorn sides and neck matched the whisker stubble on his face. "Are you as fearsome as you try to look?"

Then he did smile, only it wasn't a pretty sight. "Meaner." The smile lost some of its darkness when it reached his eyes. "But you have nothing to fear from me as long as you don't cross me."

"How is it we speak the same language, but half the time I have no comprehension of your meaning?"

"Must be the age difference. Hell, you ought to be in school."

"There is no schooling here. Not anymore. Besides, I've read all the books we have. I'm twenty-two and a grown woman." His assessment of her bordered on the offensive. A flickering glance at her clothing confirmed she did not look her best. Her scalp itched from the pine needles trapped in muddy snarls of hair. Her defenses rose, putting her on edge. What did it matter if he thought her a child? Too bad the Ketchums did not regard her the same.

"Besides, age has nothing to do with anything. My grandfather was decades older than I and we understood one another perfectly."

He arranged the fire, then put the rabbits on the spit. "I'll put my boots on and we'll go find some firewood after I check on Craig." He retrieved a pair of socks from his pack.

"There is little we can do for him at the moment,"

Lorilie said, swishing the head cloth in the medicated water. "I doubt he will awaken while we gather wood."

Lorilie watched in amazement as Rafe's big hands performed deft zigzags, setting the laces securely under their prongs. The boots were strange, nothing like those she wore or any she had seen in the catalogues Grandfather brought from Yerba Buena, San Jose, or Monterey.

Distracted, she let him head for the passageway without her. When she caught up with him, she realized neither of them required a lantern. "How did you learn the passages so quickly?"

"In my line of work, you memorize details about your surroundings or you don't live very long."

"What is your occupation?"

"Right now, wood gatherer and open-pit cook."

"You are an army wood gatherer and cook?" Knowing she caught him with his own words made her laugh. She had the feeling that if she understood him, she might discover he had a sense of humor.

He took so long before answering she wished she could see his face. "Not anymore." He followed her outside, then added, "And maybe not any less."

"You speak in riddles."

"Lately I think in them, too."

In the dim light of a wispy clouded moon, she watched him. The animal in him stirred. He assessed his surroundings the way a cougar studied his territory. He gazed at the stars with an intensity that gave her pause.

"What do you see up there?"

"Stars." He turned, his face still tilted toward the sky. "Northern Hemisphere stars."

"Do they look so very different elsewhere?"

"Yes. Very different, but if you know what to look for, you can navigate in either hemisphere."

It seemed inconceivable the stars would ever appear different from what she knew. However, she did not doubt his assertion.

"Goddamn."

Instinctively her mind scanned the trees for an impression of danger. The forest creatures remained undisturbed. "What is it?"

"We're in the damn Sierras."

The whisper of tortured disbelief came so softly, she looked at him. "Where did you come from?"

He shook his head and turned away. "Hell."

A shiver of foreboding traveled her spine. Rafe was entitled to his secrets. People seldom asked questions about the past. Grandfather had warned her that most men came West to escape something in the East. Perhaps Rafe wished to escape, too, and had run so far that he'd lost his way.

"There is an old deadfall through these trees." Generally she gathered wood from farther away, preferring to leave the forest near her sanctuary unaltered. The Ketchums had all the advantage she would afford them.

It seemed he read her fears about detection. He gathered pieces from several places, leaving the forest unchanged. She worked beside him, marveling at his silent economy of movement. Together they made quick work of wood gathering. The amount he carried would have required three trips for her.

"Lorilie?"

His soft call caught her off guard. She adjusted her load and turned.

"How long have you lived here?"

"I was born a few miles from here, in my grandfather's house."

"You know these mountains."

"Yes." She shifted her burden of firewood and started toward the entrance.

"Then you know where the towns and hospitals are."

The warning note in his voice raised the small hairs at the nape of her neck. "There is no hospital or doctor at John Sutter's settlement."

The whisper of a soul-jarring oath forced her to look over her shoulder. He stood like one of the magnificent monoliths guarding her fortress. The night hid his expression, but not the glint of wildness in his eyes. The man in him, the part she could not fathom, was in torment.

"I am sorry I cannot fetch a doctor for your friend. John Sutter was unable to entice one."

"Where, exactly, is John Sutter's place?"

His unnatural stillness made her heart beat faster. Something was wrong. For the life of her, she did not know what. She swallowed, then answered. "Two mighty rivers run out of the mountains and flow into the delta. About eight years ago, Mr. Sutter chose the place near the confluence of those rivers to built his fort."

"Eight years ago?"

She nodded in the darkness. "Are you lost, Rafe?"

"Lost?"

The load of firewood grew heavy in her arms. She had no idea of what to say. For reasons she could not define, the beast in him cowered behind the shield of the man. She expected it to spring into action with each pounding heartbeat throbbing in her temples.

"Do you know where Sacramento is?" he finally asked.

Relief swept through her. "It is a river, one of the big ones near John Sutter's fort." She turned toward the entrance. "We should tend your friend. Perhaps we can get him to drink something."

He followed her so silently she had to listen hard to make sure he was there. In the narrowest part of passage, where the ceiling dipped, he set down the firewood.

"Lorilie?"

She added hers to the pile and prepared to scoot into the main chamber. "Yes?"

"When did John Sutter build his fort?"

"In 1839, I think, though it might have been 1840."

"In 1839," he repeated under his breath. "One more

question. Did you see me and Craig . . . arrive?''

''No,'' she answered, wondering again how they had managed to find the sanctuary. ''But I suspect that Loner did.''

When he began passing the firewood through the opening, she avoided his gaze. The silver fire burning in his eyes roused the beast in him. Regardless of what disturbed the man so profoundly, she was grateful she could control the beast. She suspected Rafe Stricter—the man—was the worst enemy she could ever have.

Chapter 6

T HE MOTION OF stacking wood kept Rafe's agitation from exploding. He didn't want to believe Lorilie. Without batting an eyelash, she implied a time shift as incredible as his displacement from Bolivia to Sierra Nevada. If she had shown one drop of insincerity, he could have discounted everything she'd said.

Even if she was lying—and a damned good liar—he couldn't dismiss the truth he saw in the stars. Logically, if he accepted what he knew about where he was, then *when* became just as possible.

He sat beside Craig and ate without tasting anything. The jolts to his reality seemed to shut down his senses.

Craig stirred, then moaned.

Rafe set aside the remnants of his meal and threw a mental bar over the maelstrom of their circumstances. "Hey, Craig, you going to join us? You going to open your eyes or just lie there?"

"Is this hell?" The raspy tone barely escaped his lips. He started to clear his throat and wound up groaning.

"Lorilie, would you get him some water?"

She was already moving.

"It's not hell, but you probably hurt like it is. The fever is dehydrating you." He took the cloth draped over Craig's forehead and wet it in the bowl of water Lorilie left for that purpose. After replacing the damp cloth, his hand lingered on Craig's dark blond hair.

"You gotta pull through this, buddy."

"Medic," Craig groaned softly.

A sinking sensation turned the meal in his stomach into a hard ball. "Sorry, buddy, no medic here."

"Make him drink slowly." Lorilie offered a cup of water.

"I'm going to shift you so you can drink. Ready?"

A weak nod accompanied the opening of Craig's glassy brown eyes.

Rafe moved him as gently as possible. A flood of perspiration washed over Craig's strained, pale face. A sharp hiss of air through his gritted teeth bespoke the effects of each movement.

"Rest a minute." Rafe gauged the labored rise and fall of Craig's breathing.

He met Lorilie's worried gaze. The sense of helplessness returned in a rush. Having no options, no way of obtaining the resources available in another time subdued him.

"The tea steeping on the hearth will ease the bite of his fever."

A flicker of hope took root. "Okay."

"Mud people?" Craig asked, squinting to focus on Lorilie as she left his side.

Funny, he'd stopped noticing the dried mud in the snarls of Lorilie's hair. "No, not exactly," Rafe answered. "I haven't quite figured out what she is, but she's different." He lifted the cup. "Ready?"

A faint nod was Craig's only response. Rafe lifted Craig's head and brought the cup to his parched lips.

"Whoa, slowly. Give yourself time." He drew the cup

away. Agony rimmed Craig's eyes. Sip by sip, he helped Craig drink two cups of water.

"He needs to eat something," Rafe told Lorilie.

"No. He shouldn't have anything to eat now. The tea is steeping. If he keeps it down, then maybe we will feed him later."

Irritation flashed through Rafe. They'd eaten little enough during the jungle mission. Both men had lost weight. What he wouldn't give for a handful of vitamin supplements for Craig.

"Where are we?" Craig's voice was a raspy whisper.

Rafe met the confusion adding to the strain in Craig's face. "We're safe enough."

"Where?"

Rafe looked away. Lorilie knelt on the other side of the pallet. She offered a cup of dark, pungent liquid. "I've cooled it with water so it won't burn his mouth."

He took the cup and lifted Craig's head. But Craig wasn't interested in drinking; he stared at Lorilie.

"Drink this. It smells terrible, so it must be good for you."

Lorilie touched Craig's damp cheek. "Help is on the way."

Hope and despair warred in Rafe. He'd know soon enough if she offered empty promises or a lifeline.

Marica Thorne and the wolf stood in the trees, listening. When satisfied neither she nor the wolf detected anything more than normal night sounds, she slipped silently between the monolithic guards of Lorilie's fortress. She had no idea what awaited within the cavern walls Joseph Ramey had coaxed out of the earth. The amulet around the wolf's neck had belonged to Bernice, Lorilie's mother. The message conveyed by its presence bespoke danger and need. Lorilie would not have sent her most precious possession otherwise.

She adjusted the heavy pack weighting her shoulders with a shrug. "Show me the way, Loner."

The wolf rubbed his head against her thigh. She reached down and groped for the canvas sacks slung over the animal's back. Bent toward her guide, she accompanied him through the narrow passageways leading to the heart of the sanctuary.

The scent of cooked meat assured her that Lorilie was eating. At least her injuries did not prevent her from preparing the bounty Loner had brought earlier.

Marica entered the lighted cavern and stopped short at the sight of a man, an Outsider. She set down her medicine satchel. Lorilie appeared unhurt. Mentally, Marica breathed relief. It was not her friend who needed her skills. Someone needed her though, she felt it.

The man staring over his shoulder at her had the haunted look of a wounded animal in his gray eyes. A shirt stained with half a dozen blotches of color clung to his large frame. Even seated, he was big and powerful. All her danger signals prickled in awareness.

"Marica, I had no choice but to send for you." Lorilie rose from the opposite side of the pallet where a still figure lay beneath the quilts.

"Who are these people?"

Lorilie hurried toward her. Marica opened her arms and gave her a comforting hug and kept her gaze fixed on the man.

"Outsiders. One is hurt very badly." Lorilie kissed her cheek.

Marica examined Lorilie. "What happened to you?"

"The Ketchums." She glanced at the big man. "We will speak of it later. The important thing is that I got away. They may even believe me dead."

"I hope so." Marica tipped her head toward Loner, then shrugged out of her weighty pack. "I brought supplies for our journey," she whispered. "Hal Ketchum came to see me last week. After he finished playing the

Grand Inquisitor concerning where you were, he left some supplies. Apparently old man Ketchum thought they owed me something for saving Bobby last December. They hunt you, but they are certain I won't run.''

"We will, though.''

Marica hugged her tightly. "Yes. Soon. We've the supplies we need. The snow melt is dwindling in the rivers. Very soon we'll be able to cross safely.''

"Who are you?'' the stranger demanded.

Marica handed the pack to Lorilie and picked up her satchel. She crossed the expanse and stopped beside the pallet. A young man gazed up at her with red-rimmed, pain-filled brown eyes. "Marica Thorne. Tell me what happened to him.''

The Outsider glared back in silence.

"Rafe,'' Lorilie called from near the hearth. "Marica is Craig's only chance. There is no one else.''

The Outsider grimaced as he glared at Lorilie. Abruptly, his entire body relaxed. "He caught a bullet. Are you a doctor?''

His subdued response surprised her. A glance at Lorilie's expression of intense concentration confirmed that there was far more going on here than appeared. Her curiosity begged the satisfaction of a long talk with Lorilie. Then she gazed down into agonized brown eyes and put her concerns aside. A ripple of awareness coursed through her. She knelt on one knee beside the injured man and touched his face. Impressions of death swamped her senses. Immediately, she withdrew.

"I have no formal training as a doctor.'' Shaken, she met Rafe's gaze. "I am a healer. With my intervention, he may survive.'' Drawn to the wounded man, she continued, "He has a strong will and a remarkable endurance.''

"She's an angel, Capt'n,'' Craig whispered, his eyes holding hers.

Marica stood and removed her cape. She rolled up her

sleeves as she approached the basin. "Your name is Rafe?"

"Rafe Stricter. My friend here is Craig Blackstone."

Marica scrubbed her hands, wondering if she had imagined what she had sensed by touching Craig. Pain and illness often stripped away the layers protecting the secrets held close to the heart. Something was amiss. She had healed Outsiders before. None had possessed the serene ability to control that much pain. The terrible wound in his side was only partially responsible for the onslaught she experienced. His entire body throbbed. Why?

"How did he get shot?" She shook the excess water from her hands and returned to Craig.

An occasional crackling log in the hearth and the muffled clank of Marica rifling her satchel punctuated the silence. After a moment, she met the flinty stare from across the pallet. "Are you wanted by the law?"

"No. Where we come from, we are the law."

"What kind of law?"

A fevered hand closed on her wrist. Surprised, her gaze darted to Craig. "He can't . . ." Craig swallowed. "Mother Hen's harmless to you."

The truth burned up her arm. Incredibly, the injured man sought to protect his healthy friend in a manner that defied Marica's comprehension. No stranger to the outside world, she understood whatever bonded these men ran deep. "Are you his brother?" she asked, folding her free hand gently around Craig's fingers.

"His right arm." A faint smile strained his lips as he stole a glance at Rafe.

"You are that, Craig," Rafe said with a casualness belying the storm of his dark scowl.

Marica caught Lorilie staring at the big Outsider with a rapt expression that boded trouble. Whether he knew it or not, the Outsider had accomplished something people had tried to do for years—he had captured Lorilie's complete attention.

"Lorilie, these men and I are going to be busy for a while. This might be a good opportunity to get rid of some of the mountainside you're carrying and put on clean clothes."

"It does itch." Lorilie went to the trunk for clean clothing.

Marica unwound Craig's fingers from her wrist, but did not release them. "This will not be easy for either one of us," she warned, wishing she knew how to interpret the strange impressions radiating from him. She concentrated on easing the sharpest edges of his pain by taking it into her body. Instantly, her left side felt as if she'd been stabbed with a hot poker. Perspiration beaded her upper lip as the pain passed through her with the force of a firestorm.

"I've heard it said, falling in love is the easiest thing in the world."

"Is that what you think is happening?" She managed a smile, liking his sense of humor. Only one man had fallen in love with her, and she did not expect to know love again. Craig's brown eyes twinkled, holding her gaze when she would have preferred to look away.

"I know exactly what's happening here," he whispered, then licked his lips.

"Do you?" She lowered her protective barriers and touched his pain, feeling him gain strength and herself weaken.

"Ahhh, God! You are an angel."

Marica continued staring into brown eyes that looked into her soul. There seemed no bottom to the abyss of his agony. If careless, he might draw her into the fiery depth, and they would both be lost. "Not an angel, a healer," she whispered. Sweat dampened her hair and ran in small rivulets between her breasts.

"Are you going to hold his hand all night or do something that helps him?" Rafe ran his fingers through his short hair.

"Ignore him," Craig whispered.

"You must let go of me for a moment, Craig. Let me examine your wound." With her free hand, she drew back the comforter. A mat of dark blond hair covered his chest. Not an ounce of fat showed in the lean muscle and sinew sculpted over his long bones. The only similarity between this glorious specimen of masculinity and the myriad of men she had healed in the past was the basic placement of his limbs.

"Your friend is going to help roll you onto your good side." She shot a commanding look at Rafe who immediately positioned himself to oblige.

"Whatever you say, Angel."

Rafe eased Craig onto his right side and braced him with comforters. Marica sat back on her heels. Eyes closed, she meditated, neutralizing as much of the pain she absorbed as possible, then prepared for the greater onslaught. Clearly, this would be a long, slow process that taxed every fiber of her being.

"Now what?" Rafe asked.

Marica opened her eyes, ready for the next step. "Now you go over there and fix something for me to eat when I have finished here. I will be famished." The reluctance of his demeanor bordered on defiance. How did Lorilie calm him so easily? If he were a wild animal, she'd understand. But a man?

"Lady, I don't intend to leave his side while you're here."

"Please, Capt'n, do it," Craig panted as though he'd just run ten miles. "Trust me, whatever she's doing, it helps."

Reluctantly, Rafe stood. "I'll be close by."

Marica shut her eyes again and tuned out everything except Craig. "Relax as much as you can. Think only of your next breath. Nothing else." She listened as his breathing slowed, amazed by his mastery over his body. After a few minutes, they breathed in synchronous rhythm. "When I touch you, it will be different from the last time," she whispered. "Give me a moment to learn the extent of your injury."

She leaned forward and placed her hands squarely atop his wound. Pictures shot through her mind's eye with lightning speed. A cumbersome rifle pointed at Craig as he brought his own around. A flash, then the impact of the bullet tore through Craig. And there was another death, one she saw in her mind's eye but did not feel. The man who fired the rifle lay dying under Rafe's knife. The swiftness startled her as much as the pain burning through her side when Rafe hoisted Craig over his shoulder and began running through a world so alien, she wondered if it existed at all.

"Think only of your next breath," she managed through gritted teeth. "Nothing else! Keep your past to yourself. I don't want it! I cannot withstand your conscience *and* your pain."

The images faded, allowing her accelerated breathing to slow until it fell in tune with his again. As her concentration returned, she probed the damage beneath her palms. She focused on stanching the steady seepage of blood. One by one, she shut down the fine capillaries.

The hardest task lay ahead.

Panting, she withdrew her hands and covered her face. Fatigue swept through her, making her tremble.

"Angel," Craig whispered.

"We have more to do," she rasped. "I just need a moment of rest."

"No more. I don't know how you're doing this, but I feel it. I see what it's costing you. I won't do this at your expense," he rasped.

She opened her eyes and saw the torment she heard in his voice. "It is what I do, what I am. I cannot walk away knowing I can do more."

"You and Rafe gonna save the whole damn world?" Agitated color rose in his neck and cheeks.

"I know nothing about saving the world, but I intend to do my best to save you. The pain relief is temporary. I may not be strong enough to . . . to . . ." *Save your life.*

"Do what you have to, but don't jeopardize yourself."

She could not promise anything. "You can make it easier for me if you think only of breathing."

Rafe took his time sorting the provisions stashed in Marica's packs. He found rice and dried peas. A wooden box beside the trunk held battered pots and lids. Keeping an eye on Craig and the woman as they spoke in hushed tones, he prepared the meal.

Meanwhile, he studied the woman as she placed her hands on Craig's wound. Whatever hocus-pocus she did, Craig believed it helped. Belief was half the battle.

Gazing at Marica's upturned face, he guessed her age close to his own, maybe a few years more. Like Lorilie, she possessed the height and grace of a willow. She had hazel eyes under finely arched eyebrows. Her even, generous features hinted of classic, enduring beauty few men appreciated during their youth. Straight auburn hair parted at the middle of her crown and gathered in a coil at the nape of her neck. Little blue-and-white flowers patterned her full green skirt that ended well above her ankles. She wore a long-sleeved yellow-and-blue striped blouse with a crocheted ruffle around the high collar. Strange clothing, he decided. Old-fashioned.

Regardless of what angle he scrutinized Marica Thorn from, he failed to detect the slightest hint of angelic quality.

He checked the rice, then added more water. After a glance at Craig and Marica, he boned the rest of the rabbit and cut up the pieces. In a few minutes, he'd toss the meat in with the rice. It wasn't gourmet food, but it would fill an empty stomach.

"Rafe."

He turned at the sound of his name, stunned by Marica's sudden ashen pallor and shivering blue lips. He bolted toward her, worried she might collapse. "What happened?"

"All is as it should be. Cover him up. He sleeps soundly. His fever will begin climbing in a while." Taking long, deep breaths, Marica hung her head.

Rafe drew the quilt over Craig. To his amazement, Craig felt cool to the touch, his fever gone. "Are you sure about the fever?"

She nodded without lifting her head. "I need food."

Every bleak thought he harbored about the woman fled. Hell, she didn't need food, she needed a week of bed rest and a dozen IVs. He crouched beside her. "Put your arms around my neck. You're cold as ice. Let's get you to the fire."

"I am cold." Her trembling arms slid around his neck.

He lifted her. "What did you do?"

"Later," Lorilie said as she joined them. She picked up Marica's cloak. "She needs time to recuperate."

Rafe's mind spun with questions. He set Marica at the stone table. "Wrap her cloak around her and stay beside her in case she faints."

What could lay a healthy woman so low so quickly? The answer floated from the back of his mind. The same thing that drained the fever from Craig. Biting his tongue, he stirred the meat and rice, then found a clean plate and fork.

"Coffee?" he asked.

"Pour some of the tea I brewed. It is better for her," Lorilie answered.

He filled a cup and handed it to Lorilie. The two women had a serenity about them that baffled him. Rather than dwell on it, he dished up a plateful of food. Seeing Marica's shaking hands, he hesitated.

"She's famished," Lorilie said.

He set the steaming plate on the table.

Marica grabbed the fork and started eating. Damn, not

even the recruits downed chow that fast. She didn't slow
until the plate was empty.

"There's more." He emptied the remaining peas onto
the plate, then scraped the last grain of rice from the pot.

Marica plowed through the second serving at a slightly
slower pace. Her hands were steadier. A hint of color
returned to her face.

"What is Craig's life worth to you, Rafe?"

The question staggered him. Immediately suspicious, he
glanced at Craig. They had worked together for four years
and in the process, they'd become closer than brothers.
"He's my friend."

He found a wary understanding in Marica's clear, hazel
eyes. "I'll be damned if I know what's happening here."

"At this point, all I am giving him is time, and the
strength to keep his condition from worsening. I need him
at my home where I can treat him." Marica shoved another heaping forkful of food into her mouth.

"What did you do to him?"

Marica stopped chewing. She and Lorilie stared back
at him as though he'd committed a heinous crime.

"Does it really matter as long as she saves his life?"
Lorilie rose and refilled Marica's cup.

"It matters, but if the trade-off is silence and helping
him, or answers and no help, I'll hold off—for now."
Compared to what he already did not know, what were a
few hundred more questions?

"You have yet to answer my question," Marica reminded him.

Rafe regarded the women for a long time. With the mud
scrubbed from her white-blond hair, Lorilie was quite attractive. She'd tamed the wild mane into a long braid that
hung down her back. Both women radiated a quiet
strength. They reminded him of lovely orchids forged of
titanium. With fresh insight, he realized he had no right
to question them. For reasons he might never understand,
he and Craig were here. Although cautious, both women

had offered help, and might possibly save Craig's life.

"You save Craig, and there is *nothing* I won't do for you."

"I will claim your debt when the time is right," Marica said slowly. "Meanwhile, I would have your word you will not raise a hand to Lorilie or myself."

Angry indignation rose from his gut and heated his neck and face. "Why in hell would you think I'd hurt either one of you?"

The two women exchanged dubious glances. "Why indeed?" Marica asked, shrugging.

Rafe picked up the dirty dishes. "You have my word I won't raise a hand to either of you. I hope it makes you sleep better, which is what I intend to do after I wash these up." He headed for the water basin. "Maybe, if I'm lucky, I'll wake up at home."

Chapter 7

DAWN BRIGHTENED THE sky. Low, early-morning clouds grazed the treetops and dampened everything they touched. Moisture coaxed a tangy aroma from the pines. Loner took the lead through the forest. Lorilie followed Marica and Rafe, who carried Craig in a blanket sling across his chest. She caught Marica's over-the-shoulder glance and read her concern weighing heavily on both their minds. Dealing with Outsiders was risky. If these two proved no more honorable than the Ketchums, she and Marica might never escape the mountain.

As they negotiated hidden trails, Lorilie again questioned the wisdom of revealing the location of Marica's cabin. The line between acting responsibly to ensure their safety and the inherent duty thrust upon a Gifted person blurred into gray confusion.

What Lorilie did not question was Rafe's devotion to his friend. He carried Craig with the tenderness a mother cat would lavish on a newborn kitten. She watched him closely along the winding mountain trails. Circumstances dictated a tenuous trust. Though she believed Rafe prized his honor highly enough to disallow casual betrayal, she worried over the meanings of the strange words and terms he used. At times, he spoke of things in a near-alien language, as though he expected anyone over the age of twelve to understand.

Watching his shoulder muscles bunch beneath his thin, mottled shirt, she admired his physical prowess. The unreasonable urge to touch the flesh straining under the load he carried made her fingers tingle. He was so unlike any man she had encountered here or at Sutter's Fort.

Seeking to clear her mind of the growing anomalies surrounding Rafe, Lorilie doubled back along their route and carefully erased all signs of their passing. Allowing evidence of her presence on the land nullified any edge she had gained by jumping into the river.

In retrospect, she was unsure whether the leap was a foolish action or a wise tactic. When a clear analysis seemed impossible, she reexamined the situation. Jumping from the cliff had saved her from old man Ketchum's inquisition and becoming Bobby Ketchum's whore. A shiver raced up the inside of her belly at the thought of Bobby Ketchum touching her. The price of escape was well worth the bruises and momentary terror of confronting death. Exhaling hard, she decided she had not only acted responsibly but with a sage wisdom Grandfather would have applauded.

"There is a small clearing ahead. Would you like to rest for a moment?" Lorilie asked Rafe.

"No. The sooner we get there, the better for Craig. His fever is climbing." Rafe adjusted his burden and bent into the rising slope.

"It isn't far." Marica held aside a low branch for Rafe.

Lorilie noted the tenderness of Marica's hand on Craig's cheek when Rafe passed and the uncharacteristic worry pinching her features. For an instant she questioned whether these two Outsiders possessed a mystical power that allowed them to reach inside a Gifted person and touch the special place reserved for a life mate.

Lorilie slowed. If they did possess such a power, she and Marica were in greater danger than either had imagined.

She caught the branch before it snapped back into place. Agitated, she surged forward. "I will circle your cabin, Marica. If the Ketchums are near, we need to know."

"We'll wait by the thicket," Marica said, nodding approval.

Lorilie slipped into the brush. With the whisper of a summer breeze, she zigzagged across the rocky terrain around Marica's cabin.

Like a hummingbird darting away from a flower, the wood nymph disappeared from Rafe's sight. Within seconds she became part of the forest, betraying no hint of her presence to his keen senses. He kept moving. His admiration for Lorilie's reconnaissance skills was tempered by questions concerning the enemies she guarded against.

When he reached the thicket, Rafe settled on a boulder and adjusted Craig in the blanket sling biting into his shoulder and back. Marica patted Craig's sweat-beaded brow with a clean rag.

"Why are the Ketchums her enemy?"

Marica stroked Craig's cheek, causing his eyelids to flutter and the hard edges of stress to fade around his mouth. The sleeping potion she'd fed him eased the trauma of the journey. "The Ketchums fear Lorilie."

"People often hate what they fear," Rafe mused. Still, it made no sense for grown men to fear a small woman who used a pet wolf to survive in the forest. "Do they fear you, too?"

"Yes. But they fear my absence even more." Cool hazel eyes met his. "I'm a healer."

The set of her jaw implied the explanation was complete. Hell, he'd interrogated zealots, hardened killers, and fanatic soldiers in several of God's armies. None frustrated him more than these two women. Every answer they gave spawned a half dozen more questions.

"Would you mind telling me how you acquired the skills to do what you did for Craig?"

"Yes, I would."

Her response startled him, though it shouldn't have. He'd tried the straight-on approach before and wound up with nothing but a headache from beating his forehead against the rock wall of their reticence. While he loved women, he sure as hell didn't understand them. What he needed was a new tactic, one that snuck past their mistrust.

"Suppose I go talk with the Ketchums. Tell them what a nice lady Lorilie is. Maybe teach them a few manners," he suggested. A good fight might be just the thing needed to siphon off some of the edginess riding his loins. It was always like this after a mission. The best way to assuage the demons heating his blood was between a skilled woman's willing thighs, or a good barroom fight.

His gut knotted. He wanted Lorilie. When the breeze blew her baggy shirt against her body, she exhibited all the attributes of being a curvaceous, if somewhat thin, woman but she was just what he needed to restrain himself with. Skilled? All his instincts promised she was a virgin, or damn close to it.

Mentally he shrugged. Last night he'd decided the circumstances of his presence here had made him crazy. And stupid. Why deny it when even his body supported that conclusion.

"Teach them manners? Are you out of your mind?" Marica stared at him with open incredulity.

"Very possibly, I am."

"How do you think the Ketchums are going to greet you, Captain Stricter? With open arms?" Marica turned away, then glared over her shoulder at him. "More likely with loaded guns. If you get yourself shot, it will take me much longer to heal both you and Craig. If they don't kill you outright.''

She stomped into the thicket. "Teach Ketchums manners. Pshaw! It'd be easier to teach Loner to fly like an eagle.''

Well, that approach didn't work. He'd think of another before talking with Lorilie again.

Inside the cabin, Lorilie built a fire in the hearth. By the time she had water on to boil, Marica had Craig settled and joined her.

"Do you have meat or shall I send Loner hunting?'' she asked Marica.

"Enough for now. In a day or two, I may need more.'' Marica gathered jars and bottles from her medicine shelf. "I want you to eat before you go. Why don't you fix some mush and leave the biscuit making to me?''

Lorilie started to protest. Marica had enough to do without feeding her. "I can make the biscuits.''

Marica shrugged. "I have a feeling your friend requires large portions.''

"Whether or not he is my friend remains a question.'' She washed her hands and reached for the towel hanging on a peg beside the dry sink.

"Let's hope he proves to be just that, Lorilie.'' Marica placed the bowls she brought from the shelf on the table. "What are we going to do with him?''

"He can go with me. He certainly cannot remain here. The Ketchums believe me dead. They no longer have a reason to search for me. Most likely, one of them will pay a call to deliver the news.'' She dipped a bowl into the flour barrel.

"Lorilie, this man could be very dangerous.'' Marica's soft warning accompanied a glance at the bedroom door. "Trading one threat for another more imminent one is hardly a good solution.''

"There is no choice now. The die is cast. Besides, I

doubt he will harm me. He gave his word. I believe he means to keep it.''

Disbelief furrowed Marica's brow.

Lorilie set the bowl of flour on the dry sink. Watching the bedroom door, she spoke in hushed tones. "Something about him is different, Marica. It is almost as though he is part animal, though that cannot be, of course. At times, I sense him. I can touch the animal nature in him.''

"Impossible.'' Marica gripped Lorilie's shoulder, her fingers hard.

Lorilie shrugged. "It has never happened before, but it is happening now. I have no explanation. He knows something is different when the situation calls for me to soothe the savage side of him. He does not like it, but he submits.''

"Does he realize you influence him?''

Lorilie nodded and glanced at the door. "He suspects, but not how or why it is possible for me to do so.'' She met the worry in Marica's wide eyes. "I have no understanding how I do it.''

"I wonder if your gift is growing. You've changed since Joseph's death. . . .''

Lorilie shook her head sadly. The raw wound of Grandfather's death ached anew. "I considered the possibility. If that was the explanation, why couldn't I thwart the Ketchums when they cornered me? Why did I not sense their approach? At the least, I should have felt the old man and Hal.''

A long sigh escaped Marica as she glanced toward the bedroom. "Who are these two men? Where did they come from? I cannot believe the Ketchums are unaware of their presence.''

"I wouldn't recognize a Ketchum if I ran over him with my pickup truck,'' Rafe said from the bedroom door. "Care to enlighten me on these sterling members of society?''

Lorilie's heart jumped to her throat. How much had he heard? "Wh-what is a pickup truck?"

"Never mind. I'm done playing cat-and-mouse games, unless one of you wants to take a turn as the mouse for a while. Otherwise, if you want to know something, ask me. You're both a damn sight better at asking questions than you are at answering them."

Marica walked to the table. "How is your friend?"

"Restless. He's waking up and in a lot of pain."

"I need him fully awake before I work with him again."

Lorilie mixed the biscuits while mentally reaching across the room into Rafe. The agitation of the caged animal in him gave way to sudden stillness.

Lorilie froze. In the ensuing silence, only the fire snapped a comment.

"I'm waiting."

The expectation in his stance made her question just what he waited for.

"All right, which one of you wants to start the interrogation?"

"Would you like a cup of tea?" Lorilie placed balls of dough into the biscuit pan, unable to meet the piercing heat of Rafe's irritation. She had no intention of playing games either. The Gifted had not survived by exposing themselves to skeptics or those who sought to exploit their talents.

"What I want can't be found in a freaking teacup."

"Right now, tea and a meal is what we are offering," Marica said firmly.

Lorilie continued ignoring him while she fixed the meal. She and Marica often worked in prolonged silence.

Rafe leaned against the bedroom doorjamb and folded his arms across his chest.

With unprecedented, hard-won discipline, Lorilie confined her gaze to preparing the food. Not once did she respond to the heat emanating from Rafe. She did not trust herself or the odd sensations he evoked with a simple look.

When the meal was ready, they ate in tense silence.

The calculated manner in which Rafe arranged his empty bowl and eating utensils charged the expectation in the warm cabin air. When he straightened in his chair and folded his big hands on the edge of the table, Lorilie finally lifted her gaze. The sudden thump of her heart heralded a warmth racing through her veins. Even the heavy growth of black whiskers failed to dim his chiseled beauty.

"Ladies," he began in a mellow baritone, but did not continue until Marica gave him her full attention. "Let's clear the air. Under the present circumstances, I am indebted to you both. For as long as my partner and I are in these mountains, I am at your service.

"You," he said to Marica, "have his life in your hands. He tells me you are an angel."

Lorilie exchanged wary glances with Marica.

"Maybe you are. Maybe you aren't. What's important is he thinks so, and whatever you do for him, well, it seems to help. He's still alive."

"Marica is a Gifted healer, Rafe, not an angel or a mystic," Lorilie chided. Though his left eyebrow twitched, she sensed nothing but the impenetrable wall of man.

"So the lady has said. After what I saw last night . . . Well, let's let that be.

"What I'm trying to get at is, I'm the last person in these mountains you need to fear. Obviously, you've jerked somebody's chain pretty hard and wound up with the Ketchums as enemies. In this sort of circumstance, I know of only one way to deal with an enemy on the offensive. You made it pretty clear last night you didn't want them eliminated. I can't say I agree, but I'll respect your wishes as long as neither of you are endangered by them."

"No killing," Lorilie said, suspecting the man was far more cunning than the beast. "And we have no chains. If we did, why would anyone want to pull them?"

"Forget the chains. What I meant was, for reasons you don't care to reveal, you've got enemies who aren't as benign in their beliefs as you two are."

"True. The Ketchums do not hold life sacred." Lorilie stacked the empty dishes in front of her as she spoke. This facet of Rafe Stricter added to her unease. He seemed to grasp too much about them. How fast would he turn against them once he discovered the truth of their individual skills? Like the Ketchums, he would probably shuttle his wrath away from Marica the Healer and focus on her. As long as she held her invisible edge, she need not fear for her safety, unless the man was as much a killer as the beast inside him.

Lorilie slumped in her chair.

Should that be the case, once again she would be running. Only this time, her adversary possessed more skill and possibly even less conscience than the Ketchums. They had not killed her because they wanted something from her. Rafe wanted nothing from her. If he turned against her, all she had was the unexpected, fragile influence over a facet of him he now hid.

"Lorilie."

The soft summons brought her suspicious gaze to his. For an instant, she saw compassion in his eyes and something deeper, something far deeper.

"I am not like the Ketchums."

"Not yet."

"Do you expect me to become like them?"

Again, silence became her defense.

"Do you mistrust me because I don't have the same reverence for saving my enemy's life that you and Marica do?"

Heart beating faster, no answer formed.

"What I do have is a code of honor I've lived by and

will continue to do so until I draw my last breath. That code says I will lay down my life to protect those to whom I give my loyalty.

"I don't pretend to understand everything that's happened. But I do know an ally when I see one. I recognize we have a delicate détente—"

"A what?" she managed, needing to understand the whole of what he was trying so hard for her to comprehend.

"A truce of sorts. Peace between us. At least, that's what I'm striving for."

"I have no quarrel with you."

"You have no trust in me, either."

"I can think of no reason to trust you. I cannot even say I know you or anything about you."

Frustration narrowed his gaze. "And you're trying very hard not to learn, too."

Before Lorilie could reply, Marica laid a hand on her forearm. "Let him finish before you argue."

After a pause, she nodded. The magnetic pull of Rafe's gaze drew her.

"Other than Craig, now there is no one to whom I owe my loyalty. Everything, and everyone else, is gone. I'm a soldier without an army. The only cause I have is keeping Craig alive. You and Marica are my best hope for that. Consequently, I give you my loyalty, Lorilie."

"What, exactly, does that mean?"

"As long as I'm around, anything or anyone who wants to harm you has to go through me."

"Other than Loner, who keeps me safe from you, Rafe?"

Anger flared, then faded in the quick working of his jaw. "You've been burned in the past, haven't you?"

"No." Mystified, she examined her arms. "These scrapes and scabs are from climbing a cliff, not a fire."

"Yes, we have known betrayal," Marica chimed in. "The time when we trust an Outsider merely because he says he is trustworthy belongs to the past.''

Rafe held his silence for a moment. "Fair enough. Because of your assistance with Craig, you have earned both my trust and my loyalty. What that means, Lorilie, is you have nothing to fear from me. Your disbelief does not make it any less true.''

Sensing he had just given her something he considered valuable, she stared at him. The pledge came from the man side of him. His sincerity lay bare in his open expression.

"Then I guess I will have an opportunity to discover this truth. You and I are leaving as soon as we clean up. It is too dangerous for Marica if we linger. The Ketchums believe me dead. I want to keep it that way until your friend is well.''

"What will you do then?''

She caught Marica's nod. "We are leaving the mountain.''

"Because of the Ketchums?''

Lorilie nodded.

"And in the meantime you expect me to leave Craig here?''

"There is no choice,'' Marica said. "I must have him here to help him.''

"If the Ketchums are as bad as you say, what's to prevent them from walking in here and shooting him where he lays?''

"Ignorance,'' Lorilie answered. "And fear. They think they hold Marica here because she has no one. As long as they believe me dead, they will also believe she is stuck.''

"Not good enough,'' Rafe said through gritted teeth. "I'm not leaving Craig in danger from anyone.''

"You would rather carry him out of here and let him die?'' Marica's tilted head revealed her incredulity.

Rafe glared at her without answering.

"Marica knows the ways of the Ketchums,'' Lorilie

said. "Hal visited her a short while ago. He will stay away now. The Ketchums prefer to watch her from a distance. They need her, but they dislike her almost as much as they dislike me. As long as she does nothing to rouse their suspicions, they will not suspect Craig's presence."

"Then I'll stay, too."

"You may visit." Marica's iron will showed in the set of her shoulders. "At night. Late. The Ketchums seldom venture out then." She leaned closer to Rafe. "I will not allow you to do anything to jeopardize me or Craig. You either take him and go right now, or do this our way."

Chapter 8

THE DEVOTION RAFE showed for his friend touched Lorilie. By the time she convinced him to leave Craig in Marica's care, the late morning clouds had melted. Puffy remnants clung to the snow-capped mountain peaks.

As she pondered the morning's discussion, his pledge of loyalty assumed a muddled meaning. Loyalty she understood in the deepest place in her heart. Grandfather had been loyal. But he had loved her. She doubted the hole in her heart created by his loss would ever mend. Love and loyalty walked hand in hand. She and Marica shared the same bond for the same reasons.

It was inconceivable for anyone to pledge his loyalty to strangers. Yet Rafe had done so with unquestionable sincerity.

Sliding a glance at him, she wondered if there were different levels of loyalty.

"What?" Rafe asked, ducking under a pine branch glistening with dew.

"I was thinking." She pointed in the direction she wanted to take.

"About me?" A mischievous glint danced in his eyes.

"Yes."

"Now what?"

"You are so very different from anyone here or in Sutter's Fort." After a brief hesitation, she decided on truth. "I tend to be inquisitive. It has inhibited my prudence on occasion."

Soft laughter rumbled in his chest and slowed her step. She dared not look at him now. Already the odd tingling sensations rode her body like a phantom. She suspected no tonic or potion would cure them. The cause and the remedy walked beside her.

"I am different, more different than you can imagine."

"Why is that?" Lorilie asked.

"I don't know. I can't explain it. I just . . . am."

"Is your difference the reason you watch the land with an eagle's eye?"

He glanced at her and she looked away. "Do I do that?"

"Yes. I have seen rabbits less attentive than you, even when they scented a predator nearby."

"Habit," he murmured, glancing behind them.

"Is someone hunting for you?"

"No. Care to tell my why the Ketchums hunt for you?"

Lorilie shook her head. "They are small-minded men given to brutality. I did them no harm."

"Do they think you have?"

"They do not think at all." Disliking the turn of his questions, she crooked her finger at him. "Follow me." She dashed uphill through the brush, ducking and weaving to avoid fallen branches and stubby boulders peeking through clumps of decaying leaves from last autumn's surrender to winter. She halted at the crest of the ridge and drew an invigorating breath deep into her lungs. The forest smelled clean and alive.

"Is this not the most magnificent country in the whole world?" Below, a late spring lingered in a hundred shades of green splattered across the rugged landscape. Alpine meadows splashed with new grasses and a profusion of wildflowers covered the scars of old avalanches.

Gray granite thrusts reached from amid the vegetation and basked triumphantly in the sunlight. Wave after wave of tree-softened rises yielded to snow-covered arêtes wearing cloud haloes.

How she loved the land and the creatures who made it their home. "Spring is a glorious time of year. Life starts fresh with the cubs struggling to open their eyes, anxious to explore the adventures awaiting them."

She spied a familiar nest in the highest tree on the connecting ridge. "Look," she ordered, pointing at the winged predator bringing a meal to her young. "She is strong and attentive. Her offspring will roam the sky with her by the end of summer."

His silence tempered the natural exuberance that flooded her when she visited this special vantage point. Curious, she glanced up at Rafe. "What do you see when you look across the mountains?"

"A place frozen in time," he answered slowly. "Terrain where an enemy can hide so well, finding him could take days."

The unexpected response drew her attention to the panorama at her feet. How could he see only danger in the majesty beyond?

"Without the right equipment, a man would have nothing except his training and his senses. A man without a weapon is at the mercy of his enemies."

"The land is not your enemy, Rafe. It is beautiful unto itself. Can you not feel the harmony it vibrates?" Pity dampened her mood. What sort of life robbed the ability to appreciate the splendor arrayed before them?

When she gazed into his face, resignation slackened his jaw and something akin to yearning filled his eyes.

"I stopped looking at the world the way you do a long time ago. My job was to make it a safer place for people like you." He turned his head and faced the vista.

"Explain that, please."

"One day, these mountains will look very different, Lorilie. They will be filled with modest hideaways and opulent homes."

"Oh, that cannot be, Rafe. Almost no one knows we are here. These mountains offer nothing the settlers coming west want. Grandfather said the new people seek the farming land in the flat valleys near the rivers." The indulgence in his sad half smile disturbed her.

"Don't worry. It won't happen in your lifetime," he assured her.

"Then how do you know it will happen at all?" To her astonishment, his expression turned hard and his gaze narrowed in confusion.

"I know," he said with a finality that closed the subject.

She turned away. "I doubt I can come here again without envisioning it populated by cabins, and the animals slaughtered. Thank you for your depressing enlightenment."

"Lorilie," he called, following her.

"Keep your prophesies for someone who might appreciate them."

"I'm . . ."

When he faltered, she spun on her heel and faced him. "You are what?"

"Sorry." The word seemed to leave his lips by sheer force of will. "You're right. Unless I traveled through time and saw this place say, a hundred fifty or sixty years from now, how would I know? I didn't mean to rain on your parade."

"Parade?" Did he think she was leading a parade through these mountains? He spoke in as many riddles as her body posed when he stood too close.

A flash of frustration dissolved into a low exhale. "It wasn't my intention to change the way you see that." His thumb jabbed over his shoulder toward the top of the ridge. "Do you understand?"

"Yes, I understand your words." Confused, not wanting to be taken in, she resolved to keep a distance. Heavens, it seemed almost impossible to suppress her impulsive side and act only after weighing the ramifications. Detouring to the ridge was a mistake. He lacked the ability to open his eyes to the splendor she cherished. It certainly had not lightened his mood, or hers, for long. "You are a strange man, even for an Outsider."

"That's why they call people like me *strangers*." A sudden grin banished the storm from his eyes.

Lorilie shook her head; a reluctant smile formed as the tension ebbed. "I suppose so." A fresh thought dimmed her smile. "Do I seem so strange to you?"

"Would you be offended if I said yes?"

"Perhaps. Perhaps not." For inexplicable reasons, she did not want to be as strange to him as she was to the Ketchums, or he to her.

"Why don't you ask again in, say, a week?"

Willing to delay his answer, she nodded.

They walked in companionable silence for over an hour before Rafe spoke again. "Where are we going?"

"Home."

"Home is that way." He jerked his head in the direction of the monolith spires.

"Not the refuge. My old home. If you would agree to carrying a few things, we can get what I need in one trip instead of three."

"Sure. Is it another cave?"

"It is the place my grandfather built for my grandmother many years ago when the Indians lived here. They have long since abandoned this valley and the ones around us. If the Indians had remained, I doubt the Ketchums would have chosen to settle here."

"Sounds to me like the Ketchums are in hiding, or they'd be living in Sacramento."

"Sacramento? Where is that?"

"I meant Sutter's Fort."

"Why did you call it Sacramento?"

Visibly uncomfortable, Rafe studied the surroundings as though memorizing the placement of each pine needle. "How much farther?"

"Over the next rise." Obviously, he had no intention of explaining. Her pace slowed. Although eager to return for whatever she might salvage, she dreaded seeing the place again.

A stone weight formed in Lorilie's chest at the first sight of the devastated homestead. The stock pens yawned open. Some of the animals had fallen prey to wild predators. Such was the natural order of things. Still, it saddened her to witness the aftereffects of the slaughter.

Distance and harsh terrain had added to the difficulty of acquiring farm animals. The small settlement of Yerba Buena prized their treasures brought by sea from distant places. Grandfather had brought a pregnant sow from Yerba Buena less than a year before their dreams went to ruin.

The Ketchums had absconded with the mule, the chickens, and the yearling pigs.

"What the hell happened here?"

Lorilie bristled at the anger in Rafe's voice. She shook her head, unable to give the horror of the ruin more power by making the explanation he demanded.

"You don't know, or you're not saying?"

She pushed aside the broken boards of the garden gate.

Her earliest memories were of Grandfather in the garden. The profusion of plants gave up their luscious fruits and seeds. In the far corner, the herb garden fought for survival. The expanse at her feet had once shimmered with vibrant green plants of every hue.

Lorilie closed her eyes, wishing with all her might that when she opened them, the rows of potatoes, squashes, corn, beans, beets, and peas still grew in the garden.

A hitch in her chest stuttered her breathing when she opened her eyes again. All the wishing in the world would not bring back the dream she and Grandfather had worked so hard to achieve. A few volunteer plants struggled among the weeds. Like ghostly reminders from the past, rotting stalks lay where they had crumpled beneath the now-melted winter snow.

"Will you answer me? What the hell happened here?"

"Does it matter?" she snapped, hating the compassion in his voice, hating that it made her want to curl into a ball and weep for a thousand years, and hating that he saw her vulnerability.

"Hell, yes, it matters."

"Why? Telling you cannot redeem my losses." She crouched beside a seedling struggling for space amid invasive clusters of weeds. With painstaking tugs, she gave the little potato plant room to grow. At least something remembered Grandfather's tender care and sought to flourish for another generation.

She gazed across the neglected garden, at the broken fences, and the posts scattered like discarded twigs. The signature of destruction lay etched in each piece of wood. Gazing at the wreckage, she saw the homestead with a clarity that forced her heart to accept the totality of the change thrust upon her.

Suddenly, Rafe hunkered in front of her. The width of his shoulders blotted out the ruins.

"What happened here, Lorilie?"

Tears stung her eyes, blurring Rafe and the wreckage around them. A familiar swelling thickened around her vocal cords, denying speech.

The only response she managed was a head shake. She wanted to run from the sympathy carved into his features and the anger in his eyes.

What did his compassion matter? Nothing could change what was.

Abruptly, she stood.

"Lorilie?"

Shaking her head, she waved him away. She swiped at her eyes with the back of her hand and broke into a run. She kept running until she reached the graveyard. The ultimate desecration of Grandfather's toppled marker broke the barrier of control. She dropped to her knees beside the crude marker and sobbed aloud. With loving hands, she caressed the stone as though it were made of beloved flesh.

The floodgates of loss burst.

Grandfather, I miss you every minute of the day. It is so hard to be strong without you. I try to be like you, wise and insightful. How did you know so much? I need you. God, how I need you now.

Haunting, grief-stricken cries of empathy filtered from the distant slopes. Wolves lifted their heads and howled in agonized commiseration. Cougars unsheathed their deadly claws and screamed their outrage. Bears stood on their hind legs and roared their fury. Deer and moose bellowed in commiseration. Overhead, hawks and eagles screeched in cacophonous anger.

Moments of black grief descended on her without warning. Caught in a downward spiraling vortex of loss, the pain alone should have crushed the heart aching in her chest and left her lifeless flesh nothing more than carrion.

Plummeting into the abyss of sorrow, she succumbed to the soul-searing misery until she reached the bottom of the emotional chasm.

The sobs wracking her body ebbed. The sheets of tears she cried dampened her shirt and the stone marker. The draining aftermath offered little peace, though the uncontrollable onslaughts of bereavement scrubbed away denial. Grandfather was gone. She would go on.

Void of energy, Lorilie lowered her forehead to the cool, tear-soaked stone. The distant cries of outrage and empathy from the forest denizens diminished into an un-natural silence.

She had not intended to share her pain. She loathed her weakness for allowing it to overwhelm her.

When she raised her head, Rafe sat across the grave from her. He clutched his chest in a clawlike hand, as though trying to carve out his own heart. The healthy tan on his face and arms had changed to an ashen pallor.

"I'm sorry," she whispered, tempted to reach out to him, afraid she was not strong enough at the moment for what she might encounter.

"I think I'm having a friggin' heart attack," he rasped.

She was too tired for this. "You think your heart is attacking you? Why?"

"Lady, I think I'm dying and I'm lookin' forward to getting it over with."

"You are not dying." With growing confusion, she wondered if her sorrow had touched the wild part of his nature. She started toward him, then hesitated when she sensed nothing of the beast in him. The catharsis of tears left her vulnerable. Heaven only knew what sort of fires would ride her blood if she tried to soothe him.

"Rafe, tell me what is wrong." Caught in the residue of emotional release, she struggled to comprehend his distress. He appeared in great pain, yet she saw no reason for it.

"Shit." He straightened slightly, his flat palm massaging his chest in growing circles. "What the hell is happening to me?"

"You will be fine." She drew a guilty breath and brushed loose debris from Grandfather's headstone. "The other, the sorrow, will fade soon." As her thoughts cleared, she marveled that Rafe felt anything at all. Perhaps his strangeness embodied the heart of a predator more powerful than his very human, stilted soul.

She pushed to her feet. "I will return shortly."

At the well, she drew a bucket of water. She stared at

the dented dipper still waiting on the hook for the next thirsty user. Resigned to do what she came to do, she lowered the bucket and fetched water.

"Drink this. It will help."

He reached for the dipper, then hesitated. "What's in it?"

"Water. Just water."

He drained the dipper twice before dropping it into the bucket. "What the hell just happened? Damn, if I didn't know better, I think I got zapped with a taser at the San Diego Zoo. Damn animals howling and screeching."

So much about Rafe defied her comprehension, she had no choice but to ignore it. She was in no mood for exploring a new language. The one she had was fine. "The animals were expressing their grief." She lifted the dipper to her lips. The cool water slid down her raw throat like a balm.

"For what? Why? How do you know?" Rafe stood and stretched without raising his arms. The sheer size of him forced her to turn away.

"Are you going to answer me, Lorilie?"

She shrugged. Prudence dictated silence. A partial explanation was insufficient. Rafe would never let go once he sank his teeth into any portion of her truth.

"Damn it, Lorilie. What's going on here?"

She continued walking to the well. The small hairs at the nape of her neck rose when she sensed his desire to pounce. Her grip tightened on the bucket. She tested the man side of him with every step she took.

He kept his distance. She hung the dipper and inverted the bucket on the well sill. When she ventured a glance toward the graveyard, Rafe was gone. Just as quickly, all impressions of him evaporated.

A jay squawked from the roof of the house, bidding her to get about her tasks.

Her stomach churned when she entered her old home.

The Ketchums had returned since her last visit. What had survived their initial demolition, they had taken. Only broken relics of the life she cherished between these walls remained. The chairs Grandfather had lovingly carved and Grandma Blanch had upholstered were gone. The spinning wheel lay shattered against the wall. Precious books collected over generations littered the dusty floor stripped now of the braided rugs she had made.

The sturdy worktable used for meals and countless other tasks over the years was gone, too. Broken ladder chairs leaned against the wall. The shelves in the cooking area had been ransacked, her reserves stolen.

"What were they looking for?"

Startled, she spun, then gripped the doorjamb. Rafe had entered so silently, she had not heard him, nor had she sensed his presence.

"Me," she answered without thinking.

Rafe picked up several books and examined them closely. "Maybe. From the looks of this place, they were looking for something else too." He studied the room. "I wonder if they found it."

Calmer, Lorilie shook her head. "They took everything usable."

Wanting to leave quickly, she headed for the two bedrooms at the rear of the house. In Grandfather's room, the ticking of his straw mattress gaped open. Clumps of old straw and grasses were strewn across the bare floor. The bed frame remained, the rope mattress support slashed. The patina of age rimmed the places where Grandfather's trunk and the armoire Grandma Blanch had once prized stood. Heaps of clothing too small for any of the Ketchums littered the room.

"Hate is a poison," Lorilie recited. An unknown concept just a few years earlier, she now comprehended the full impact of the emotion.

"Sometimes it can keep you alive," Rafe murmured. He retrieved several articles of clothing and shook away the straw. Dust particles and tiny bits of debris swirled in the sunbeams streaming through the paned window.

Lorilie shook her head and left the room. "No. It benefits no one for me to become what they are. Nor will I give them part of my soul by hating them."

"You're human. Hate 'em. Be angry. Hell, you've got the right. It's probably even healthy for you, unless you aspire to sainthood."

Other than a few books and an old blouse, nothing remained in her room. Teeth gritted, she growled deep in her throat. "They took it all! Even my clothes."

Rafe joined her, his arms full of books and clothing. "Why?"

She knew why. They intended for her to share her possessions. The vile thought made her shiver. "Bobby and the rest of the Ketchums can have my bed, my clothes, and everything else."

"But they can't have you, right?"

"No," she whispered. "I would resort to something drastic and very, very wrong if it came to that."

"Look at me, Lorilie."

Unable to stare into the empty room for another painful second, she obeyed. No trace of his agitation lingered.

"No Ketchum will force you to do anything as long as I'm here. Do you understand what I'm saying?"

She nodded, awed by his sincerity. "Why?"

"You really don't understand, do you? It's what I do—protect, in ways you would never comprehend. Or approve. Nonetheless, you are now my mission." A soft smile lifted the corners of his mouth. "I've never failed a mission."

For reasons her exhausted state refused to analyze, she believed him. "Are you a Guardian?"

"I suppose I am, in a way."

"Are you my Guardian?"

"Yes, for as long as I'm here."

"Did Grandfather send you?"

His shaking head lent to the puzzlement lowering his eyebrows. "I haven't a clue." Clearly uncomfortable by the subject, he turned away. "Get what you want and let's leave."

She did not know what to say to the broad-chested giant who acted as though his sole purpose in life was ensuring her safety. The enigma of his tenderness and commitment lay at odds with the predator who took life without a second thought.

"Very little remains for me to take," she said at last.

Rafe examined the ceiling and walls. "Your grandfather did amazing stonework. I've only seen rock cut to fit without mortar in a place in South America." He turned away. "Some people actually thought extraterrestrials built it. If they saw this house, they'd have to reevaluate."

Just when she had a glimmer of insight, he spoke in that foreign tongue she almost understood, but not quite. Steeled for the task ahead, she set about gathering the residue of a life now over.

By late afternoon, she led Rafe away from the home of her childhood. No backward glances this time. The violent rape and destruction of the homestead precluded returning other than to visit the small graveyard.

"You're very silent." Rafe adjusted the makeshift packs of books and clothing.

"I am very tired . . . of so many things." The weariness settled into her bone marrow. The emotional purge at the graveyard had served as a reminder of how alone she was.

"Why don't you give me your bundle?"

"You already carry more than a horse would over this terrain. Besides, home is close." Without warning, she felt the predator in Rafe come alive with one intent.

Kill.

Chapter 9

RAFE DROPPED THE packs he toted. Danger. He sensed it, smelled it, tried to identify it.

"Rafe?"

His gaze flicked over the green eyes regarding him with mounting anxiety.

She still did not understand that he would protect her. Safeguarding her gave him purpose; it sculpted reason out of chaos.

Without further deliberation, he donned the emotion-dissolving cloak of predatory instinct. The hilt of his knife rested securely in his right hand.

The bushes rustled on both sides of the deer trail they followed.

Unexpectedly, wolves broke the thick cover. Four sets of bared, deadly fangs glistened through the snarls.

"Climb a tree, Lorilie."

"Do not!"

"Do it now!" The order hissed through his teeth with the bite of an asp.

Instead of racing for a tree, she bolted toward the closest wolf. Her arms spread wide, as though embracing the death the gray beast would deliver with a snap of his fangs into her soft throat.

Rafe bellowed the raging protest welling up from his gut. The wolves could not have her. Bent on saving Lorilie from self-destruction, he charged.

And all his killing instincts, even the will to defend Lorilie, vanished. His limbs refused to move.

Stunned, he swayed in the invisible net holding him in place.

Disbelief sank to a deeper level as he watched the wolves close around Lorilie. Instinct battered the passiveness sapping his will, stealing his ability to act. He strained, trying to pick up his feet, but his boots did not budge an inch. Determined, he fought immobility. The exertion set up a relentless throbbing in his temples.

Horror raced through him as the four beasts swarmed Lorilie, bringing her to her knees. Teeth and paws in a frenzy of gray and white fur obscured her.

Still, he could not move. He'd promised to protect her but could do nothing. Any second, their fierce muzzles would turn red with Lorilie's blood. The beasts would tear her fragile body to bits.

His outrage vented in a long roar that sent the nesting birds into flight.

The wolves turned in unison.

Lorilie rose from behind the gray-white wall of fur and fangs, her hair tangled with pine needles and leaves, her green eyes bright.

"Be calm, Rafe. There is no danger here." The quality of her voice reached past all logic and soothed him with the softness of a lover's caress.

The presence of the wolves belied her claim. Terror for her wrapped an icy fist around his reason.

He had not frozen out of fear. Something inexplicable had reached inside of him, just as it had at the graveyard, and flipped a switch. A violation so complete, so effective that it rendered him helpless and challenged more than his sanity. It threatened his spirit. Worse, it bent his will in a manner that forever changed him. He was not in command of his basest, most essential responses. And he did not understand how or why he'd abdicated.

A subtle shift inside him freed him from immobility. He became aware of his pulse pounding in his extremities. Though a vision of the wolves tearing Lorilie apart lingered, he sensed no danger. The knife that was as much a part of his anatomy as a finger grew unreasonably heavy.

Vaguely, he realized whatever happened earlier wasn't over. *Same song, different verse.* In defiance, he lifted the knife, straining every muscle in his arm, shoulder, and back in the process.

The thing trying to control him wouldn't win. He'd find the source, then eliminate it. Nothing would control him. Nothing.

"You are among friends. Please, Rafe, put your weapon away. You do not need it."

Another layer of his resolve crumbled. He struggled, wanting to hold on to the knife, and wanting to sheath it simultaneously.

Flanked by the gray carnivores, Lorilie approached. Sorrow pinched her brow as she watched his knife shake in his straining hand. Inexplicable shame washed through him. In a final act of submission, he sheathed the knife.

"I am sorry, Rafe. So very sorry. The wolves are my friends."

Somehow he had missed a signal, looked past a sign, or misread the situation. Yet even as the thoughts formed, he denied them.

The melee in his head raged, decrying that no sane man would consider four wolves in the wild as benign, let alone friendly.

When she met his gaze, he knew with the certainty of

drawing his next breath that Lorilie controlled the situation—and him.

Last night, she had kept him from killing Loner. Today . . . Damn, today she'd paralyzed him without so much as a glance. Had she also incapacitated him in the graveyard? Why? And how did a wisp of a woman reach inside of him and flip the switch of his emotions, his physical responses, even his free will? How did she disable him more effectively than a bullet?

"How?"

"Rafe, I am very sorry. I should have told you about the wolves." She ruffled the head of the closest one. "We grew up together. As a child, I played with their parents and grandparents. They are curious about you. They will not attack you." A second wolf nudged the closest one aside for some head scratching. "And they are happy to see me. I've had little time to play with them since . . . I started living in the sanctuary."

"How, Lorilie?" he demanded through gritted teeth. His anger moved him forward a step. The wolves turned their big heads toward him, their fangs bared.

"It does not matter how bloodshed is avoided, only that it is," she said sympathetically. A flick of her hand silenced the snarl from the largest wolf.

"It damn well matters to me. What the hell did you do?"

"What are you accusing me of doing, Rafe?"

If she'd come after his body, he'd have helped her get their clothes off. But his mind . . . For the first time, he understood the total horror of rape. Damn, she'd coldly, callously stripped him bare without so much as a kiss or even a smile. "You know damn well what you did to me." His fingers tightened on the hilt of his knife. "I want to know how you did it."

She glared at him with an intensity reflected in the predatory eyes flanking her. "Grandfather said it is good to want things. Even so, we seldom get what we want in life.''

''Don't play freaking word games with me, Lorilie.''

''What are you going to do? Badger me like the Ketchums? Threaten me? Destroy the last place I can call home?''

''If you did this to any one of them, it's a wonder you aren't dead.''

''I did nothing to them,'' she shouted. ''Nothing!''

''You call rendering a man helpless, breaking his instincts, and paralyzing him *nothing*?''

Surprise widened her eyes. ''Are you going to kill me, Rafe?''

His instincts for self-preservation demanded that he do so. No enemy had gotten to him the way she did, and he didn't even understand her weapon. ''I gave you my word I'd protect you. I keep my word.''

''Good. Shall we go?'' She ruffled the head of the closest wolf.

He didn't want to go anywhere with her. ''As soon as you tell me what you did and how, I'm ready.''

She turned her back. ''I have said all I am going to say. Stay or go, it makes no difference to me.''

The ghost of the soft caress he'd experienced earlier swept away the red roil of his anger. ''Don't,'' he ordered through clenched teeth.

The impression disappeared. He made a final grasp for the familiar blood-lust inspired by a brush with danger. It, too, slipped away as his rage retreated further and finally cowered in a dark, quiet corner of his mind. Defeat so crushing it made him tremble plunged through his heart.

The longer he stood in the rising sea of despair, the greater became his sense of powerlessness. When he finally moved, he sought purpose for continuing in this strange place where little fit into the rational tenets he took for granted.

He retrieved the packs and started walking. ''This isn't over.''

He dared not look at her. In the span of a day that seemed a year long, the absolutes of his world took a left turn into anarchy. The gut-level certainty of it strengthened with each step.

Rafe had fought for his life hand-to-hand, jumped out of airplanes and helicopters in the dead of night, survived blistering heat and sweltering humidity, and he'd plodded through thin, frigid elevations of mountains covered in ice.

He'd broken several bones, suffered infected insect bites, and endured more than his share of stitches. He'd faced death and adversity without upsetting his adrenal glands.

Looking at Lorilie McCaully he realized he'd led a sheltered life.

During his forays into places mapped only by satellites, he'd discovered mysteries that defied scientific explanation. While he did not believe in the supernatural, extraterrestrials, or paranormal abilities, he didn't disbelieve their possibility.

A grain of logic emerged through his despair as she and the wolves ran ahead of him.

Whatever Lorilie did to him, she had also done to the wolves. Still, it didn't explain what she had done to him. He was no animal seeking acceptance or anything else on the warm and fuzzy emotional spectrum.

Lorilie darted through the forest. The wolves loped after her.

Watching the twists and turns of her agile form, not even the havoc seizing his mind blunted his physical reaction to her.

The chaos in his mind recoiled at the odd impressions. Any minute, one bizarre event too many would short-circuit his brain.

His body didn't care about esoteric thought processes.

It reacted with the mindless morality of a rabbit to the stimulus prancing with the wolves.

He wondered if her hair felt as soft as it looked. He'd love to find out by finger combing it over her naked back and the full swells of her breasts.

Irritated that part of his mind had followed the dictates of his body into a flight of fantasy, he shunned the ridiculous speculation. He ought to be fantasizing ways of getting answers out of her. She was dangerous, maybe the most dangerous person he'd ever encountered.

When they reached the monolith fortress, he paused. "Are you ready to tell me what happened back there?"

Cool green eyes regarded him for a long moment. "I have nothing to say."

Inside the shelter, he dropped the meager booty saved from the stone cabin. The invasion of his psyche left him feeling violated, unclean.

After bathing in the basin, he lathered his face to shave. In the yellow light of the lantern, the face of the stranger Lorilie claimed he was stared back from his signal mirror. The edge of his knife glided over the meager soap suds. The realization that he might never see a can of shaving cream tempted him to grow a beard. He hated having a beard.

Deliberately, he tried to think of nothing. When that failed, he recited codes long memorized and still used by the Rangers. He stuck to the safe, familiar mundanities of complex cryptographs with clear-cut meanings.

Dusk colored the sky in long streaks of lavender when he left the sanctuary.

"I'm going hunting," he told Lorilie.

"It is not necessary." She set down an armful of wood on the pile near the entrance. Without a backward glance, the wolves melted into the long forest shadows.

"Sure it is, if we plan to eat on a semiregular basis."

"The wolves will bring dinner in a little while." She bent at the waist and ran her fingers through the heavy tresses of her corn-silk hair. Bits of leaves fell to the ground.

"Maybe I'd like to find my own dinner." Rafe looked away. The familiar tightening in his groin followed a sudden image of having her naked with those pale tresses flowing over even paler skin.

"Maybe you just want to hunt and kill something. Will you be happier if you do?"

"Don't know," he answered tersely. "Probably." Hell, nothing would make him feel better other than a good lay with a hot woman in his own time where things made sense and he was in control.

The weak flames of the embers cast a meager glow. Shadows danced along the walls. They jumped in retreat when the coals of the dying fire reignited a branch and burst into life. Curled on her pallet, Lorilie stroked Loner's head. Rafe's presence in the sanctuary filled the near darkness with anxiety.

Her thoughts flitted from one uncertainty to another; all involved Rafe. The vision of him when she had stopped his attack on the wolves appeared each time she drifted toward sleep. His wild, almost inhuman gray eyes had pierced her with condemnation, and a violent rage that knew only one solution—death.

How she wished Grandfather were here. He would share his wisdom. He would tell her if what she was doing was right. On one hand, subduing Rafe as she did a feral creature was an unconscionable violation of his privacy. On the other hand, it was the only way of preventing needless death.

The defeat she had sensed in him earlier had seemed unnatural and new. The self-loathing for his powerlessness hurled a shard of guilt through her. This could not continue. Too well she knew the consequences reaped by the erosion of self-doubt. He did not deserve that.

Wrestling with the dilemma for which she had neither

guidelines nor mentors, she wondered how long Craig's injury required to heal and when the two men would leave the mountains. After their departure, she and Marica faced a journey of their own. They had laid the groundwork with great care so as not to alert the Ketchums.

A faint sound penetrated the mire of her disquiet. She listened, her heart slowly accelerating, her muscles coiling.

Rafe slipped so quietly from the chamber, she would never have heard him if her bothersome conscience had allowed sleep.

Where was he going? To meet the Ketchums? Though part of her denied a betrayal, her fear refused to be silenced. Once again, trust fell casualty to harsh experience.

She waited several minutes before leaving Loner curled against her pallet. With an ear toward the narrow passageway, she listened for Rafe.

Familiar silence permeated the darkness.

Cautious, she debated fetching a lantern. If he lurked in the dark . . .

Disgusted by her petty fears, she ducked into the black passage.

If Rafe intended harm, which she was becoming more convinced by each discussion that he did not, waiting for an opportunity in a dark corridor was unnecessary. Given his lightning movements when confronting her furry friends this afternoon, if Rafe caught her unaware, he could kill her before she subdued the beast in him.

Outside, the crisp night air bit through her grandfather's baggy flannel shirt. She hugged her arms to preserve warmth. A quick sweep of the land yielded no sign of Rafe.

Wide-eyed, she wandered through the trees. It mattered little where he went, as long as he stayed away from the Ketchums. Again, she questioned his readiness to kill men he did not know. It seemed incongruous for one man to be so eager to take another's life with no more discrimination than a bear slaughtering fish during spawning time.

Just as the cold air enticed her to return to the shelter, she saw Rafe leaning against a tree, watching her.

"Are you a creature of the night?" she asked, squaring her shoulders to ease her shivers.

"When I need to be." He shifted against the tree and lifted his face to the splash of stars crossing the sky. "Are you?"

"When I need to be," she answered, more comfortable with tossing his answer back than making an explanation that led to more questions.

"I didn't think I had awakened you."

"I was awake." She stood on the lee side of the tree.

"So you decided to follow and see what I was up to?"

Caught, she nodded even though he could hardly see her in the dark. "I am unaccustomed to having anyone in the sanctuary."

"You're waiting for the other shoe to drop, is that it?"

She glanced down. He wore both shoes. "This is one of those times when I understand your words but not their meaning."

Rafe pushed away from the tree and walked several feet to a cluster of boulders thrust from the forest floor. Before sitting, he removed his jacket and tossed it at her.

Lorilie caught it, not quite sure what to do with it.

"Put it on. I can hear your teeth chattering from here."

The residual warmth and masculine scent of his body clung to the coat. The strange fabric sliding beneath her fingers had the texture of a smooth, light mackintosh. The garment engulfed her and hung midway down her thighs. She folded the lapels over and held the sleeve cuffs in her fists to confine the heat.

"Your wall of silence is very effective, Lorilie. I've myself to blame for letting you maintain it. I know a dozen ways of coercing information from someone who doesn't want to divulge it. However, I can't use any of them because I gave my word to protect you from harm.

"I can't decide whether you're cunning enough to have figured me out as soon as you saw me, or too sheltered and naive to understand what you're doing." The slight sag of his shoulders reminded her of the overwhelming defeat he had experienced earlier.

Holding the coat tightly against her body, she approached, not daring to sit on the adjacent rock. "I am unsure of your meaning. If you think me cautious, please understand caution has kept me alive and free. Even before . . . before Grandfather died, I spent many nights in refuges scattered across the mountain."

"Why did you stay if you were being hunted?"

It was a question that had gnawed at her since Grandfather's death. "Even though this is our home, we had planned to leave during the heart of winter, when the Ketchums would least expect it. Once they discovered us gone, a multitude of animal tracks over ours would have hidden our trail."

"But you didn't leave then. What happened?"

The catharsis at the graveyard had eased the shackles of pain fastened on her heart whenever she thought of their plans. "Grandfather died five months ago. Without him, we would have perished."

"We? You and Marica?"

"Yes." Her answers carried as much honesty as she could afford. Revealing Grandfather's special talents with the land begged explanations she could not, would not, provide.

They sat in silence. In the distance, a wolf howled. Overhead, an owl hooted.

"Tell me about the sheep in wolves' clothing we encountered today." His eyes glistened with a silent plea. "Your four-legged friends."

The precarious direction of their conversation made her wary. Though they skirted what he ached for her to explain, she owed him a response. She had no stomach for torture, which was exactly what she realized she had done to him this afternoon. If the situation were reversed, she admitted she might see it the same way.

"It is much as I said. I started playing on the mountainside with the wolves when I learned to walk." She gazed into the night. "I have known most of the wild animals in these mountains for generations. They do not fear me, rather they befriend me."

"You mean they would protect and defend you."

Grimacing, she continued staring into the shadows. "The Ketchums shoot them at every opportunity. I would not want any of them to jeopardize their lives for me. The wild creatures are my friends, my family and companions." She turned her head and searched his face in the light of the rising moon. "Would you jeopardize Craig's life for your own safety?"

"That's not the same. We're trained to minimize the risks we take."

"Is he not your friend?"

"Yes," he admitted.

"If you wish answers to your questions, which I have been providing," she warned, "answer mine, Rafe."

For a while, silence reigned. When he spoke, the emotion in his voice surprised her. "I think my willingness to ensure your safety, as well as Marica's and Craig's, as much as you allow, speaks for itself. Giving my loyalty is akin to giving you my soul, Lorilie.

"That aside, in answer to your question, I'd fight to the death to save a buddy, a friend, but no, I would not risk anything for an animal. I'm not much on the religion bit, but I happen to agree with the preachers who say God put the animals on Earth to serve man. Not the other way around."

"Even if they are, as you say, less, do they not deserve my protection?"

"Damn, you sound like a Green Peace poster girl," he murmured. "Why not? This is 1847. Maybe you started the movement. Makes as much sense as anything else that's happened.''

Apprehension rippled along her neck. "I fail to understand.''

His direct stare sent gooseflesh over her arms.

"I don't understand you, either, Lorilie. After what I saw at your home, the calculated destruction and outright theft, and the graveyard—'' His ire slipped into a savage realm. "They desecrated your family's graves. Hell, even the lowest dregs of humanity have a certain fear of the dead, if not respect for graveyards. Don't you want retribution? Justice?''

"And what is your concept of those things, Rafe? I should destroy their graveyard? They have none. I should pillage their homestead as they have done mine? Even if I could, even if I wanted to do these things, what would it accomplish?''

He leaned forward, his elbows braced on his knees. "Justice. An eye for an eye. A life for a life. You don't need to do it, I can extract reparations from the Ketchums.''

The beast in him prowled and strained against invisible tethers. "How? By killing? By destroying? It is not our way.''

"It's *their* way. It's what they understand, and nothing else will get their attention.''

"It is *your* way. What drives you to want to kill men you do not know?''

"Looking at you. Seeing a thin waif running through the forest. Knowing you're being hunted by predators more vicious than we both know the wolves are.

"They've dispossessed you of everything, including your grandfather and your home. They're nothing but frigging bullies with guns. I hate bullies, Lorilie. I hate people who prey on the weak. Where I come from, drug lords—'' Abruptly, he hung his head and became silent.

"I suspect you seek a so-called justice on my behalf

for your own gratification. I do not understand this need of yours for retribution. Is it possible you do not value their lives because you do not revere your own?''

Rafe stood and thrust his hands into his trouser pockets. ''Make no mistake there, Lorilie. I place a high premium on my life. I'm not bothered by second thoughts in a crisis. It's me and mine first, everybody else can eat a bullet. I've seen what man does to his fellow man. Death is not the worst option.''

The harsh words dripped with conviction. Seeking to quell the agitated beast of his nature, she touched his chest.

The thrum of his heart quickened under her fingertips. The agitation she sought to relieve evolved into a powerful, vaguely familiar entity. The tingling aches she experienced since Rafe's arrival bloomed in her body.

Desire.

Startled by the realization, she started to withdraw her hand. Rafe's fingers curled around her wrist and held it in place.

''You've been very careful not to physically touch me, until now. Whatever you do to my mind is unacceptable, Lorilie. And whatever you've found by touching me now is scaring the hell out of you. I see it in your eyes, on your face.''

Her hand took on a life of its own and pressed hard against the solid wall of his chest. She understood the mating ritual and had seen the animals procreate since she was old enough to roam the forest. But this, this raw, beautiful, sense-heightening desire racing through her frightened her as much as it awed her. The passion emanating from him went beyond the undeniable drive and instinct to secure the next generation. It implied an all-consuming pleasure.

''What are you doing to me?'' Torment laced his raspy demand. He pulled her hand away from his pounding heart, then released her.

Lorilie swayed on her feet. Gazing into his shadowed eyes, she marveled at the urgent ecstasy he craved. Until now, she had thought the beast side of him strong enough to govern the man.

She was wrong.

"Impossible," she whispered. She should not have sensed the man. Her gift affected only untamed animals. Rafe was not an animal. An animal did not project passion. Animals could not delve into a well of reason and restrain a primary instinct that raged through them with the force of a wildfire.

"What isn't possible?"

Head shaking, jaw working, she had no explanation for the impossible. "You."

"As I stand here living and breathing, I know I'm possible, just not why. You're not going to help me understand any of this, are you?"

She wanted to tell him all he desperately needed to know. Doing so opened her to unknown dangers while Marica tended his friend. What if she revealed their secrets and he reacted like the Ketchums? She had nowhere else to hide, so she chose silence.

"No more interference like this afternoon, Lorilie. I'm beginning to understand what you do, and you're not doing it to me again."

He caught her hand and placed it on his chest.

"Explain why a woman who can do what you've done to me can have enemies you fear. Explain why they'd look for you when you can reach inside them and paralyze their minds."

"I cannot."

"You can't . . . what?"

"Stop them." If only she could, so much of the life she'd grown up cherishing might have survived the last few years.

"But you can reach inside me," he spat. "Interfere. Control. Break me without lifting a finger."

Guilty, she said nothing.

"No more, Lorilie. I know my mind and the power of discipline. I won't let you in again. I'm ready for you."

Not so much as a ripple of what she experienced moments earlier lingered. Astounded, she tried to sense the animal aspect of his nature. Again, she found nothing.

The brush of his warm, firm lips against hers ignited a blaze that surged through her body. A small sound escaped the back of her throat as she leaned closer. He rewarded her with a slower brush of their lips. The electrifying contact wasn't enough to quell the sudden hardening of her nipples or the inexplicable ache growing inside her.

He turned away, and swore under his breath.

Stunned, she stared at the storm carved into Rafe's clean-shaven face. For a brief moment, he had done all the things he accused her of doing earlier. She had stood helpless while he robbed her ability to move, to think, to heed the instincts that kept her safe.

When she could move, she removed the coat and laid it on the rock. The outpouring of raw desire surging through her innermost being continued as she headed toward the shelter.

She faltered, too overwhelmed for the impact of his promise to generate fear. From the shadows, she looked over her shoulder.

Rafe stood in a patch of moonlight, watching her.

Despite the ramifications clamoring in her mind, all she could think about was coupling with an Outsider she had not chosen as a life mate.

Chapter 10

"MAKE IT PAST 'em. Leave me. I'll hold 'em off."

Marica stroked Craig's brow. She had reached the limit of her gift. For now, all she could do was treat the symptoms of the exotic infection rampaging through him. She used the fever as an ally and controlled it by using tried-and-true concoctions.

When he rambled as he did now, his body jerked with pain-inducing emphasis. She moved from the rocking chair beside the bed to the edge of the mattress. With a gentleness wrought by her compassion for the tenacious Outsider, she cradled his head against her shoulder. The sheen of perspiration coating his face and hair mingled with the cool dampness of the cloth she draped over his forehead. When he quieted, she dribbled sage tea across his lips.

He drank, though his eyes remained closed.

"Sleep, Craig. Let your body heal." Marica's gentle crooning quieted him. He downed half the tea before agitation overcame him.

"I'm afraid, Capt'n." His raspy admission accentuated the dark half moons below his eyes.

His rambling rendered her attempts with the remaining sage tea futile. She set it aside and rocked him like a baby. ''Shhhh. There's nothing to fear.''

His lashes fluttered and his body tensed into unnatural stillness. When his eyelids lifted, he stared at her without recognition. ''Capt'n? Why aren't we dead? How'd you save us?''

Alarm prickled Marica's scalp.

Undoubtedly Craig anticipated his own death. The hole in his side should have killed him outright. The true miracle was that he'd survived.

''You're safe, Craig. Nothing can harm you here,'' she lied, gazing into his fever-bright eyes. If the Ketchums knew she harbored an ailing Outsider, no one would be safe, not even her.

''Where are the bombs?'' A fine trembling rode his frame. ''I feel 'em. Capt'n . . .''

''They cannot touch you, Craig. You're safe. Sleep.'' She stroked his cheek, wishing she possessed the ability to ease the demons robbing his peace of mind. The fever gave them strength to roam and destroy the calm necessary to conquer the infection ravaging within him.

His eyes closed and the trembling stopped. Except for the quick, rhythmic rise and fall of his breathing, he was limp in her arms, his sweat-soaked head resting against her breasts.

The alarms returned with vigor. Intuition warned her that the ramblings held important meanings. Craig's phenomenal control kept some part of him focused on a mystery he alluded to only because he envisioned her as Rafe.

Rafe Stricter had some explaining to do when he returned. And return he would. Soon. She was sure of it.

When next Craig began rambling, she let him talk.

Before dawn, Marica left the bedroom with tears streaming down her cheeks. While she did not understand much of what he said, she knew the depth of grief Craig suffered over the loss of his sister and father. His mother's eventual withdrawal into something that sounded like a religious order left him alone in the world. He had remained apart until he met Rafe.

If even a small portion of Craig's ramblings held merit, he and Rafe were warriors unlike any in legends of yore. Dangerous and devoted to whatever cause they embraced, they would lay down their lives for one another and "the mission." From the bits and pieces she gleaned out of his ranting, Craig believed the captain he idolized had done just that.

In his delirium, Craig could not make the connection with the reality of Rafe Stricter being alive. Her repeated assurances met unexpected resistance.

Rafe died because he stayed with Craig instead of flying away.

Flying away. If only she and Lorilie could fly away. . . .

Eyes stinging, Marica sat at her table and lowered her head onto folded arms. It took a while for the crux of her emotional upheaval to surface. Heavens, but she was tired. If she weren't, she wouldn't be jealous of Rafe Stricter.

A brittle laugh escaped her.

Although she had never felt so deeply or in such a personal way for any man in her care, she did so now. Otherwise she would not be teetering at the brink of her endurance. Caring from that part of the heart led only one place. Disaster. Craig was close to a decade younger than she. And an Outsider.

"Disaster," she whispered, then closed her eyes.

"Hey, buddy, wake up and talk to me." Rafe tucked the rocking chair beside the bed under him and sat. "You look like the morning after a three-day binge."

Craig opened his eyes and stared at the ceiling for a moment.

"Are you in there?" Rafe leaned forward.

"Hey, Capt'n.'' The weakness in his voice heightened Rafe's anxiety.

"Hey, Craig.'' Rafe grinned, despite the worry augmented by the dark circles under Craig's eyes. Three days, and Craig wasn't any stronger. But he wasn't dead, either. "Have you decided whether you're going to live or die yet?''

"Guess I'll live. We already tried dying and it didn't work . . . or did it?''

Rafe shook his head. After a quick glance toward the doorway, he lowered his voice. "We're a long way from home. And a long way from being dead.'' *I hope.*

As though the confirmation absolved all his sins of the past, Craig smiled. "Going home is the last thing I want, sir.''

"Quit calling me sir. I'm still trying to figure out the situation. As near as I can tell, we've been deactivated. Discharged without ceremony.''

"Honorably, I hope.''

Undoubtedly, the brass thought them dead in the bowels of the Andes. Col. Livingston probably slipped a couple of citations and matching medal certifications into their service records before burying their records deep in the Pentagon's storage facilities. "Yeah. There goes the retirement benefits.''

"Are you sure we're not dead?'' Craig's gaze drifted toward the open doorway. "Sometimes I think I'm in hell. Then Marica sits beside me and I know there aren't any angels in hell, so maybe I'm in heaven. But there's not supposed to be pain in heaven, so where am I?''

The truth burned the tip of Rafe's tongue. Still feverish, Craig wasn't strong enough for the paradox of their situation. Arcane methods aside, he marveled at Marica's healing skills that defied understanding. The whole mountainside was straight out of a Stephen King novel.

"You're in a comfortable bed with only one objective:

to get well," Rafe said, glancing at Lorilie as she entered the room with a tray.

"Marica fixed a meal for you. It smells delicious," she told Craig.

"I'll help you sit up. You don't want to make a bad impression by dribbling your soup all over Marica's sheets." He leaned forward and grasped Craig by the shoulders.

"When she and I mess up the sheets, it won't be with soup," Craig mumbled into Rafe's ear.

"You're healthier than I thought." They worked together until Craig rested against the pillow-padded headboard

Lorilie adjusted the tray, hesitated, then left. Rafe forced himself not to watch her go.

Craig tired before finishing the meal. Rafe removed the tray and made him comfortable. "I'll check on you before I go."

"Go where?"

He brushed the back of his fingers over Craig's forehead. "Not far. I'll be back." The fever burned, but not destructively. He took the tray into the main area of the cabin, and closed the door.

"You've done a helluva job with Craig," he told Marica. "He thinks you walk on water. Maybe you do." He set the tray down and glanced at Lorilie seated at the table.

"Here." Marica handed him a steaming cup of tea. "I have a few questions."

He studied each of the women in turn. Both met his scrutiny without flinching. "Why do I get the impression the grand inquisitor Tomás de Torquemada is about to enter with torture devices in tow?"

"Perhaps you have a guilty conscience," Marica quipped, settling at the table.

"One must have a conscience in order to suffer from guilt." He lifted his cup to hers, ready for the challenge.

Instead of occupying the chair across the table from the two women, he remained standing.

"Every man has a conscience." Lorilie's relentless stare disconcerted him. If he wasn't careful, he'd get lost in the depths of her green eyes.

"If so, then every woman thinks she can twist it for her own gain." A sharp turn of his head broke the connection with Lorilie.

"This isn't about gain." Marica's voice dropped solemnly. "This is about learning what we've gotten ourselves into. You saw the destruction at Joseph and Lorilie's home. If you are as astute as I suspect, you realize the kind of danger we, particularly Lorilie, live with."

The destroyed homestead haunted him.

"You and Craig are warriors." Marica's flat assertion allowed no room for argument.

People living in 1847 might consider them warriors. "We're soldiers."

"In whose army?" Lorilie's pointed question belied her earlier assumption of the U.S. Cavalry.

Rafe hesitated, buying time by testing the tea. Revealing details defied his training even though they had become insignificant the moment he awakened in Lorilie's shelter.

"We have a problem here, ladies." He placed the cup on the table with deliberate slowness. "It's called a catch-twenty-two."

"Please, Rafe, we need an explanation we understand." Lorilie leaned onto the edge of the table.

During their three days together, Lorilie had grown increasingly outspoken. The spirit and intelligence emerging from her, despite her waifish appearance and baggy clothing, shone brighter by the hour.

Rafe chose his words carefully. "We want information from each other with the intent of determining whether or not the other can be trusted. Without that information, neither side is willing to divulge too much. Follow?''

A study in similarities and contrasts, their solemn eyes
regarded him without expression.

Satisfied, Rafe began pacing. ''You expect answers.
What are you willing to give in return?''

''You wish to negotiate?'' Lorilie asked.

His pacing detoured to the window. ''Serious negotia-
tion implies the very thing we're holding in question, Lorilie. Trust.''

Silence stretched on a thin wire until Marica spoke.
''You have entrusted Craig into my care. By your own
words, that justifies your trust.''

''Is information your price for helping Craig?'' He
abandoned the window and resumed pacing in front of the
table.

''No,'' came her slow answer.

Rafe caught the wary glances exchanged by the two
women. ''By the same token, you've trusted me with Lorilie's life.''

''You cannot hurt me.'' Lorilie's quick answer halted
him in front of the table.

''Ahh. Now we're getting somewhere. You think I *cannot* when the truth is, I *will* not.''

''We are nowhere.'' Lorilie straightened in her chair.

''I'm not one of your wolves.'' Palms down, he leaned
on the table. ''I'll shut you out at the first flicker of
doubt.''

''You—you cannot.'' The pale lantern light sapped the
color from her cheeks. ''Can you?''

''What is he talking about?'' Marica turned on her
friend, her hazel eyes widening in unabashed dread.

''Yeah, why don't you explain it, Lorilie?''

''I owe no one an explanation.'' Lorilie squared her
shoulders and dared a glance at Marica.

''Neither one of you is willing to explain anything.''
He leaned farther across the table. ''Blind trust is not in

my nature. In short, you're asking a helluva lot without expecting the door to swing both ways."

"We are at an impasse?" Lorilie folded her arms across her abdomen.

The distraction of her shapely breasts defined by the pull of the worn fabric evoked a spontaneous reaction. Rafe straightened and turned away. "You learn quickly."

Marica stood slowly. "Lorilie? You . . . did something to him?"

He saw Lorilie tilt her head and stare up at Marica. She was no more forthcoming with her friend than she was with him. For reasons he couldn't define, her silence was a source of satisfaction.

When Marica approached, he stared out the window. "Craig has spoken of many things while in the grip of the fever."

"Delirium has a tendency to neutralize discipline." He hadn't considered the possibility of Craig telling everything he knew.

"He spoke of his father and sister, about bombs putting holes in birds and dropping them out of the sky, his mother entering a religious order and disowning him as her son. He said many things I did not understand. Your home seems very different from our simple life."

Although Craig considered the subject of his family off limits, Rafe knew the gritty details from the comprehensive battery of psychological tests and background checks each of his men endured. Craig had mentioned his mother moments before the bombs fell in Bolivia.

"The difference is far greater than cultural." Greater than miles. Greater than the fifteen decades. "Much greater."

"Is the purpose of a warrior, a soldier, one of honor and chivalry?"

Rafe snorted. "We're not exactly Knights of the Round Table, but we operate by a similar code."

"I see."

Her long silence forced him to look at her. "Just what do you see?"

She released a long breath before lifting her face. "You are a Guardian."

Instinctively, he recoiled. Lorilie had asked him if he was a Guardian.

"When you gave us your loyalty, we became your—your mission." Marica's smile smoothed careworn years from her face. "I did not understand before, but perhaps I do now. If you are half the man your friend believes you are, your word is your life."

Give this lady the grand prize. "That's the way it is."

"It is enough for me."

"Enough for what?"

"My peace of mind when Lorilie is not with me. If the Ketchums did not watch me from a distance, I would insist she stay here."

"But not enough for explanations."

She lowered her head and gazed out the window. "Win Lorilie's trust. She has the most to lose. I would suggest you proceed slowly."

At least Marica had assumed a fence-sitting position. He doubted he'd learn anything concerning his and Craig's leap through time until both women spoke freely. He'd take Marica's advice. Maybe if he quit trying so hard to avoid Lorilie, she'd loosen up. Though being close to her without the insulation of emotional distance played havoc with his lusty nature.

"Slowly," he agreed, warning himself against the danger she posed.

Marica drew a breath, then released it. "The price I asked for Craig's life is Lorilie's safety. Protect her. Be her Guardian until we are safely off the mountainside."

"Sounds fair enough. Your friend for mine."

Marica turned away. Before she reached the table, he called over his shoulder. "I would not mention his family once the fever passes."

A curt nod acknowledged the conspiracy forming a fragile friendship between them.

Lorilie joined him at the window. "We should go soon."

Without a word, he crossed the room wanting to see Craig again before they left.

"If he awakens, get him to drink as much of this as you can." Marica poured cool water into the hot concoction.

Rafe entered the bedroom and closed the door. "Titanium orchids," he murmured.

He listened at the door when the two women spoke. Though fluent in five languages, he had no idea what they said.

"Craig, old buddy, I think we've stepped in deep this time."

The aroma of food coaxed Lorilie awake the next day. She reached beside her pallet for Loner and found only hard rock.

"Better rise and shine or your four-legged friend will eat your share of breakfast." Rafe's cheerful warning drowned the rumble in her empty stomach.

Lorilie groaned and crawled out from the quilts. Since Rafe's arrival, she'd slept in her clothing. Running her fingers through the tangles in her wild hair, she stepped into her boots.

After washing her face and taming her hair into a long braid, she felt almost energetic. "Mush never smelled so good. What did you do to it?"

Rafe dished up a steaming bowl and handed it to her. "I added a little sugar and a handful of dried fruit I found in your provisions box."

A glance at Loner bespoke the wolf's approval. She frowned. "I have never offered Loner mush. He forages for his meals."

"Really? The woman who puts animals on a par with

humans does not feed them?'' He picked up his bowl and settled on the edge of the table. ''Seems pretty one-way since he hunts for you.''

She fished a spoon from the utensil box. ''Perhaps, but if he became dependent on me for food, he might not want to hunt. If something happened to me, he might starve.''

''How does a wolf hunt for mush if not in your kitchen?''

Lorilie laughed. ''I can't imagine Loner stalking mush.''

''You should have gotten up sooner and you'd have seen him beg for his own bowl.'' He indicated the teapot. ''I had to give him tea, too.''

''Why?''

''He asked for some.''

''Loner does not drink tea.'' As if to prove her wrong, Loner lapped the dark liquid from the bottom of a bowl. ''Unbelievable. You offered him mush and tea? And he accepted?''

''Begged for it.''

Every time she turned around Rafe handed her a surprise. ''What's next? Apple pie?''

''Got any apples? I'm a modern man, self-sufficient and hell on wheels with a microwave.'' No sooner did the words leave his mouth then he lowered his head and concentrated on shoveling mush between his lips.

''A what?''

''Nothing,'' he mumbled. ''Just a figure of speech.''

His unexpected withdrawal unnerved her. While eating, she studied him. ''You have more mood swings than a breeding woman.''

Startlement banished his pensiveness. The sudden widening of his eyes and sag of his jaw at the comparison made her laugh.

''Breeding? A pregnant woman? Please. You refer to a situation I've avoided even watching.'' Head shaking, he scraped the last of the mush from the bowl. ''Come here, wolf.'' He placed the bowl on the floor. ''Wash dishes.''

Obediently, Loner licked the bowl clean.

Dumbfounded, Lorilie watched. ''I can see I've not taken full advantage of your talents, Loner.''

At the mention of his name, the wolf curled up at her feet and eyed the bowl in her hand. A long, pink tongue reamed his chops in anticipation.

Chuckling, Lorilie finished eating. ''I suppose you want to lick it clean.'' Crouched in front of him, she set the bowl on the floor. ''This will not be a regular practice.''

The wolf whined and licked her hand.

''What have you started, Rafe?''

''A friendship, I hope.'' He tilted the pot toward her. ''There's a spoonful left. Want it?''

''No.'' She reached for the teapot.

''Here, wolf. Job security as a kitchen slave.'' He set the pot beside the bowl braced between the wolf's paws.

''I don't think Marica would approve. She is very specific about keeping animal and human domains separate.'' Try as she might, she could not recall the reason.

''Do you do everything Marica advises?''

Lorilie collected the bowls Loner had licked clean. ''Yes.'' She laughed softly. ''No.''

''In other words, whatever suits you.''

''No. Marica is very wise. It would be imprudent of me to heed her only when it is convenient.'' She waited until Loner finished licking the pot. ''She is not afraid of you, either.''

''I never thought she was.''

''I think you are accustomed to being feared.'' She stacked everything in the pot and headed for the water basin.

''Why?''

Hearing him on her heels, she dropped the dishes into the water, then rolled up her sleeves. ''You are a predator. As such, it is your nature.''

"A predator," he mused, leaning against the basin and watching her.

Suspicious, she glanced at him out of the corner of her eye. He was different this morning, friendlier, more talkative. Lorilie was unsettled, wondering what had brought on this sudden change.

"You like the company of predators." He rubbed a scab on his jaw from his morning shave.

"Most of them, yes." She finished washing the dishes. "What are you about, Rafe?"

"Me?" Eyes wide, his eyebrows rose as he stepped back and pointed to the center of his broad chest. The feigned innocence he managed with amazing finesse made her laugh.

"I take that back. You seem far too animated to be an emotionless killer."

"Maybe I'm both."

He stood so close she felt the warmth of his breath on her face and caught his unique, masculine scent. His nearness incited the familiar tingling with a relentless plea for exploration and appeasement. "I have no doubt you are, Rafe." She met his smoky gray eyes. Perspiration beaded at the back of her trembling knees. The longer she stared into his eyes, the sharper the ache to close the scant distance between them became.

"There are many kinds of predators, Lorilie." His head lowered a fraction, and his gaze dropped to her mouth. "Not all of them kill."

What would it feel like to press her lips to his? Heat radiated through the mottle-colored shirt stretched over his muscle-sculpted chest. Without sound or motion, it called her. "I think you may be the most dangerous of them all."

"Not to you."

To her, he was the most magnificent creature ever to tread the mountainside. With a life of its own, her hand rose to his chest. Fingers splayed, she rested it over his heart. A rapid thrum as harsh and steady as a drumbeat pulsed against her palm.

She stared at his slightly parted lips and her mouth went dry. A sudden acceleration of his heartbeat followed her slow exploration of his chest. "I suspect you are, especially to me."

With supreme resolve, she withdrew her hand. Her fingers and palm prickled with disappointment and a desire for more contact with the pleasure-giving wall of heat. "I have never encountered anyone like you."

"And you're curious."

She licked her dry lips and fought the urge to rise onto her tiptoes and test the texture of his inviting mouth. "Curiosity is a vice I work hard at ridding myself of. It leads to trouble."

His hand closed over hers. "In that case, I'll help you," he breathed against her mouth just before unleashing a lightning bolt of desire through her with a soft kiss.

All her senses ignited with a hunger reflected in the slow, sinuous movement of his hand guiding hers over the sculpted planes of his chest. The tantalizing, light kisses he trailed along her cheek and up to her temple stole her breath.

Beneath her sensitive fingers, his heartbeat quickened. She leaned against him, awed by the unwavering strength of his thigh and his unyielding hips. Her pulse sent a liquid heat through every part of her body. The slow exploration of his chest and shoulders drove her wild. When he released her hand, she reached around his neck and lifted her face. She ached for his kiss. In that moment where rational thought ceased, all her instincts cried out to rid them of their clothing and make him her life mate.

As quickly as he had taken possession of her body, mind, and senses, he retreated without giving her the kiss every fiber in her being cried out for. Lorilie held fast to the wad of shirt clutched in her hand. The incredible daze

swirling through her disappointed body left her light-
headed.

"Still curious?"

She closed her mouth, then swallowed before answering. "Curiosity is dangerous."

"You got that right." Drawing a deep breath, he
straightened, leaving a shock of disappointment racing
through her. "Let's go exploring."

Wasn't that what she had been doing? Exploring very
dangerous, exciting territory? Gathering her fragmented
thoughts, she retreated a step. "Yes. The bears are out of
their dens with the cubs by now."

She watched Rafe gather the dishes and turn toward the
hearth. Only then did she realize she had not felt anything
from the predator side of him. Not even the wild desire
that had shocked her the other night. He was completely
closed.

A single candle of fear ignited in the great void of her
uncertainty.

Chapter 11

RAFE CROUCHED ON one knee and scratched Loner's head. He and the wolf had a great deal in common at the moment: neither liked being this close to the bears. The territorial nature of wolves, bears, and men made them all enemies. With only his knife for defense, he could quickly find himself on the losing end if the grizzly decided she didn't want him around.

Lorilie cavorted with the two cubs tumbling over her and their mother. The undiluted joy in her bursts of laughter touched a tender spot in him. Her play denied danger. The mother grizzly, with claws capable of slicing Lorilie in half, stretched on the ground, then rolled on her side. The cubs scampered in circles before finally taking advantage of their mother's offering of nourishment. When they started feeding, Lorilie stood and dusted herself off.

Beaming with satisfaction, Lorilie approached Rafe. The sunlight caught wild strands of her blond hair. The halo enhanced the glow of her smile. A fresh sparkle danced in eyes.

Rafe's breath caught in his throat. Her alluring beauty

shone from an intangible source deep inside of her. The profound impact of his unreasonable urge to protect her assaulted him anew. Her uninhibited innocence and generosity of spirit knew no pretense. It nestled uncomfortably close to his heart.

If he lived to be a hundred, he'd never comprehend her way with animals. Clearly, she loved the wild creatures and understood the perversity of nature's laws. And if he hadn't known they were incapable of human emotion, he'd have sworn the bears returned the affection.

The big grizzly laid her head down, her black eyes focused on Rafe in mutual distrust.

The hair at the back of his neck tickled.

"We're leaving, I hope." He patted Loner's head, then stood.

"Yes." Lorilie grinned mischievously. "You could have played with the cubs, you know."

Incredulous, Rafe frowned at her. "I don't think so. This was close enough. The mother doesn't consider you a threat, but she and I don't share your benevolence."

Rafe followed her through the thickets. The grace of her movements in the forest left it undisturbed. She coexisted with the creatures who called the mountains home. Their camaraderie defied logic.

"Is it like that in the outside world?"

"Like what? Bears allowing people so close? No."

"Ah, Rafe, I do not anticipate living among people who regard me with constant suspicion. I will have to be very careful and work at curbing my impulses." She caught a frail white flower between the edges of her palms. "They will regard me as a threat if I visit the bears or play with the wolves. Perhaps they will burn me at the stake. It has happened to our kind before."

"Just what is *your kind*?"

"People who are easily misunderstood." Curiosity shone in the slight turn of her mouth. "Have you never been misunderstood?"

The direction of her fears crystallized. His protective instincts crashed in on him with a startling skip of his heartbeat. He had no idea how people beyond the mountains might regard her affinity with animals. He hadn't even considered how they'd regard him and Craig.

"I do know what it's like to be misunderstood by people you're helping."

Lorilie lowered her face and inhaled the faint, sweet scent of the flower. "I suspect Outsiders seldom tolerate those who fall short of conventions."

Staring at the delicate white petals in her hand, he chose his words carefully. "When you leave these mountains many things will change."

"I will most likely shrivel and die in a city filled with people who see nothing of the beauty surrounding them."

"People like me?" He scrutinized their surroundings through years of training that jaded his outlook. Somewhere along the line, he'd quit seeing the world as anything except a place fraught with danger. He could no longer appreciate the simple things, like the flower Lorilie held in her hands.

"People similar to you, but not like you." She released the flower. "You have faith in your ability to control events around you. And a strange power to make it so."

Probing green eyes regarded him with open admiration. How he wished her assessment was true. He controlled nothing. During the short time he'd spent with Lorilie, he'd experienced emotions he thought long dead and buried. Worse, he'd neglected planning his next escape or preparing for confrontation with the enemy.

The enemy.

Who was the enemy now? The Ketchums? The city dwellers? He no longer knew.

"We are very different, you and I." He cupped the side of her face and relished the softness of her fair, smooth skin against the calluses lining his palm. The hunger in her gaze fixed on his mouth promised that she was thinking of the brief kiss they'd shared. "But we do have one thing in common. Neither of us has any idea what awaits beyond your mountains."

The silken arches of her pale eyebrows drew closer. "Surely you must have some idea of society's attitudes concerning those of us . . . who are different."

He ached for an answer to ease the worry from her bottomless green eyes. "As long as no one interfered with my way of life, I never cared about society's feelings."

"I suspect few challenged you." Her cheek moved in the cradle of his hand as though she found comfort in his touch.

"No, no one did." The admission settled like a stone. Away from his men and job, he had no existence.

"How did you become such a . . . hardened man?"

"When you make your living by hunting people who want to kill you, a soft man doesn't last long."

"You're also quite intimidating." Her chin glided over the heel of his hand.

"I didn't intimidate you. Not even when I shut you out."

She stilled. Her eyes widened when she met his gaze.

"There are more levels inside the mind than we understand. Sometimes, when all we think about is survival, we lose track of them. And our humanity."

He lowered his forehead to rest against hers. "Once, I was trapped in a jungle. Men hunted me in ways you can't understand. I found a hole, climbed inside, then covered myself. If I moved a muscle, they'd find me. I used my mind to control my body. I lowered my heart rate, my body temperature. The longer I remained in that state, the deeper I explored myself. Something inside me changed because of it. As a result, I can shut you out, Lorilie. Sometimes I think I can shut out the entire world.

"And I don't know why the hell I just told you that."

"How long did you stay in the hole and the places you found inside yourself?"

"Thirty-seven hours, twelve minutes. When I came out of it, a damn snake was tasting my nose." He straightened and released her cheek.

"It is possible you are a Gifted man." The awe lighting her expressive features embarrassed him.

"The only gift I have is for the tactical elimination of the enemy." The sum of his life's efforts sounded impoverished. "And staying alive."

The feather touch of her fingers on his forearm halted him. "Surely, Rafe, you have a talent to preserve life."

The warmth of her touch reflected the goodness in her heart. It sought the same in him, then shamed him when he fell short. "Sometimes the only way to preserve lives is to take others."

"What do you think when you meet your enemy?"

"Nothing. One of us is going to die. My job is making sure it isn't me or my men."

"And will it be the same when you leave the mountains?"

Rafe gazed around them. The close-growing trees provided cover for snipers. The rocky, dappled terrain offered a thousand places for hiding explosives and detection devices. He peered deeper into the forest, seeking the source of Lorilie's delight each time they entered a new section or crossed a ridge. The beauty of the place eluded him.

Her hand slipped into his, then tugged.

Sorrow filled her eyes, but a brave smile lit her face. "You are distressed. The day is too beautiful for dark thoughts. Come, let's go fishing for dinner."

He nodded, amazed she used words instead of attempting whatever she'd done to him before. He would have known if she tried to violate the sanctuary of his mind. To her credit, she had not.

"I'm glad we went fishing this evening. Marica enjoyed the trout." Lorilie glanced over her shoulder into the darkness. The faint glow from Marica's cabin winked out behind the trees.

"Where's your wolf?"

"Loner? He's not *my* wolf; he is his own and he's hunting for dinner."

They walked in silence for a while. Night sounds mingled with the breeze whispering secrets in the pines. Lorilie contemplated the changes in Rafe and herself since last night. While no less intractable, he was more generous with his revelations. She still knew little about him, but he could say the same about her. In a flash, she realized she wanted the barriers between them torn down.

"Where are we going?"

"Not far out of our way. Do you mind?"

"No. Lead on."

How easily he agreed. Could it be he had found a grain of trust with her name on it?

Lorilie smiled into the darkness.

Near the river, she held up a hand. "Be careful here. It's a long way down and the water is very cold."

"Sounds like you're speaking from experience." He peered over the side of the cliff at the swift running, silent river. "It doesn't seem possible you'd survive the fall, but you have a knack for doing the unexpected."

She led the way along a ledge traversing the cliff above the river. The moon rose high, softly lighting the path ahead. The shortcut offered by the jagged cliff shaved an hour from the trek she planned.

"Why are we doing this at night?" Rafe changed handholds as though he scaled hazardous obstacles every day.

"Because the Ketchums usually stay home at night. They avoid nocturnal predators." Lorilie leaped across a gap in the path.

"You've come this way before."

His dry assessment made her smile. "Many times. However, these days, I seldom have a reason for crossing the cliff."

"Tonight you do. Why?" In one easy stride, he breached the gap of the missing ledge.

"You will see when we get there."

"How far?"

"Oh, just a mile or two."

The glances she stole at him as they made their way along the deer trails fostered doubt. Comfortable in the darkness, his gaze scanned the new territory as though memorizing each branch and rock. Occasionally, his gaze settled on a place in the blackest shadows as though expecting a rival predator. No amount of assurance would convince him they had no enemies in the night.

"We're here." She held aside a cluster of willows. A moose stood shoulder deep in a moonlit lake. He dipped his head below the surface and pulled up a clump of long, reedy grasses. His chewing paused while he regarded them. After a moment, he continued eating.

"Ahhh. Tomorrow's dinner awaits." Rafe's hand found the knife hilt.

Lorilie touched his wrist. "Not dinner."

"Why? Is he a friend of yours, too?"

"You cannot kill him, Rafe." The instant rigidity of his stance warned that she had chosen her words poorly.

His left eyebrow rose menacingly in the moonlight. " 'I cannot?' "

"Perhaps you can, if he does not sense your intent and flee. Please do not. I will not stop . . . try to stop you if you choose to take his life."

"Why not?" His grip relaxed, but his hand lingered on the knife hilt.

"Because the laws of the forest decree that a predator may choose his prey. If you are swifter and stronger than the moose, and you have chosen him as your next meal, it is your right to go after him." This was not going the way she planned. "Bringing you here was a mistake. I apologize for wasting your time." She turned away. "Do what you wish."

In the blinking of an eye, he caught her wrist. "You brought me here for a reason that had nothing to do with laws of the forest or the moose. What is this place?"

The searing contact of his hand around her wrist warmed her. Drawing on a composure steadily eroded by doubt, she gazed across the water and decided to press forward. "You wanted to know about us. It began here. Long ago, an Indian tribe lived on the far side of the lake. My ancestors were the first light-skinned people they encountered. For a generation or two, they remained beside the lake."

"What happened to them? Disease? War?"

Lorilie shook her head. "No one knows. One day, they packed up and left, and never returned."

Rafe released her wrist. For the first time all night, he ceased watching the forest with the intensity of a predator. She followed him along the lake shore.

He scooped up a handful of pebbles, then halted beside a bleached log stretching into the midnight water. "This is 1847, right?"

"Yes." She settled beside him wondering why he attached such great significance to the date.

"Lorilie, what are we talking about? Maybe 1800 when your ancestors came here?"

"Oh, before then. The family Bible shows Angus Ramey was born here in 1784. He was my great-grandfather."

"That isn't possible. No one lived in these mountains until just about now."

Irritation flashed through her. "You said you wanted our trust. Now I tell you something about our history, you accuse me of lying. You are a very strange man, Rafe."

She picked up a pebble and threw it into the lake. "How would you know when my family came here? Have you the gift of clairvoyance?"

"No, I sure as hell wouldn't claim that." He tossed a

pebble into the brush and flushed out a field mouse. "And I'm not accusing you of lying."

He settled on the log. Telling him anything seemed pointless.

"Cut me a little slack, will you? All I'm trying to do is piece this together."

She had laid the first plank for building the bridge they needed. Before laying a second, she studied him in the moonlight. Through his haunted hunger for understanding, she found sincerity.

"Allow me to start at the beginning, in Scotland. There was trouble in my ancestors' village. Some of the villagers decided to leave. They pooled their resources and found a willing sea captain in Edinburgh. He brought them to Monterey.

"The Spanish dons made life difficult. A few years after arriving, the leader—his name was Liam—moved from Monterey, bringing most of my ancestors with him. The People of the Mountains, Indians, lived beside this lake then. One of their women helped bring Angus Ramey into the world.

"After Liam died, no new leader was chosen. Each family claimed a portion of the valley and went about their business, just as they had done in Scotland. They called upon one another, lent a hand, and formed alliances through marriage.

"About three years before I was born, several families banded together and left for a new place. My father was among them. He and my mother were life mates, so he had no choice but to return and seek her out. Once they sealed their bond . . ."

"Where are they now?"

"They died."

"Sorry."

"I grew up among people I love and who loved one another. There was music and dancing. And laughter. So much laughter."

She paused, remembering. "Sometimes there were tears and angry words, but not often."

"Sounds like a fairy-tale world." Rafe skipped a pebble across the water.

"I was twelve when my parents decided to visit my father's people. I remained with my grandparents. That was the last I saw of my mother and father."

"Why did they stay away?"

"After a year, Grandfather went out in search of them. When he came home, he placed two markers in the graveyard. I knew they were never coming back."

"I'm sorry." Genuine sorrow creased the frown lines around his eyes.

"Why? What is there for you be sorry for? You did not rob and kill them, did you?"

Instantly, his regret turned to outrage. His broad shoulders squared in protest. "No."

Puzzled by his abrupt mood shifts, she sought the serenity of the lake. The moose waded closer. His lazy ruminations contrasted sharply with the riddle beside her.

"Where are the rest of the people who stayed here? Surely you and Marica aren't all that's left."

"We are."

She met his over-the-shoulder glare, then skipped a pebble across the lake and watched the ripples dance. Perhaps revealing the history of the Gifted had consequences much like the intersecting, blossoming circles shimmering on the moonlight dappled water. She had said far more than she'd intended.

"What happened?"

"Over the years, they left. An altercation between the Ketchums and my grandfather last spring sent the last two families away. By then, it was clear the Ketchums would never be peaceful neighbors."

"But you and Marica stayed. Why?"

"Grandfather wanted Marica and me to leave him behind and go with the last group of families led by Nicholas Graham. Of course, we would not leave. He was an old man confined to his bed at the time. It took most of the summer for his leg to heal.''

''What was wrong with it?''

''The bones here''—she touched Rafe's left thigh,''and here''—she tapped his shin, ''were badly broken. Marica set them and started the mending process, but she could not weave the torn ligaments. There is a limit to her gift. Because of his age, he mended slowly.'' Recalling the painful injury, she hung her head. ''He could not travel. That's why we decided on a winter departure. However, by the time we were ready, it was too late.''

''Why not go now?''

''Marica must tend to your friend. She will not abandon him. When he is well, she and I will leave here. We have no choice.''

''How did your grandfather break his leg?''

She stood, uncomfortable with the bleak memories relating to Grandfather's suffering. ''Hal Ketchum found him in a shelter he made for me. Hal and Grandfather argued. Hal hit him with a board. He might have killed him if not for Loner frightening Hal's horse. The horse's cries brought Hal running.''

She clamped her jaw shut. She had revealed enough. He did not need to know how the wolves had rallied against Hal Ketchum. Their loyalty had cost two of them their lives.

Rafe dropped the rest of his pebbles and stood. With a crooked finger, he lifted her chin until she looked at him.

''Who are you, Lorilie?''

''At times, I am certain I am a lost soul seeking impossible peace. I have no way of knowing if my father's people fared any better than we have in recent years. My peace may not be out there, either.''

''We'll find out together. I'll take you and Marica when Craig can travel.'' He stared at her for a long moment, his expression unfathomable. ''Are you still curious?''

"Yes," she whispered, her heart skipped a beat in anticipation.

"So am I." His head lowered. The soft whisper of his lips brushing against hers banished every dour thought.

Her senses spun. His mouth was firm, but gentle, teasing something that lived deep inside of her into a frightening, delicious recklessness.

With eager abandon, she embraced his neck, wanting to experience the fullness of his mouth against hers. The warmth of his arms enfolding her sent her heart racing.

"You're so young. So fresh."

The glide of his lips against hers vibrated down to her toes when he spoke. Lured by a craving for more of the heady sensations he coaxed with the softness of a hummingbird sipping nectar from a flower, she rose on tiptoes. Her lips parted, matching his.

"Lorilie . . ."

He cradled the back of her head, then tilted it slightly. Her arms tightened around his neck. Slowly, deliberately he traced her lips with the tip of his tongue, leaving her breathless. Finally, his mouth settled on hers in sweet reward for her patience.

Lorilie held on to him as the world around her melted into vapor. He was solid and strong. He was the source and cure for the sweet hunger consuming her senses. She swayed, overwhelmed by the waves of needy desire coursing through her.

Unexpectedly, he broke the kiss. He held the back of her head away, as though denying them the folly of more temptation.

Shock brought Lorilie into reality with a shattering jolt. He regarded her with dark eyes glittering from the reflection of moon glow off the lake. Even in the dim light, she saw regret etched into the stony planes of his features.

"I'm sorry," she murmured, unable to look away and hating the necessity of removing her arms from around his neck.

"*You're* sorry? Damn, you're so young—"

"I have been a grown woman for a long time, Rafe. I'm twenty-two. You're not the first man to kiss me."

"I haven't even begun to kiss you yet."

Without thought of proving him right or wrong, she leaned against him and locked her fingers behind his neck, then pulled his head down. "Then show me how it is done."

Her lips parted in invitation. She was ready this time.

The power of his hands molding her to him robbed the air from her lungs. The erection pulsing against her abdomen set her aflame inside her skin. He was what she wanted, what she burned for.

A formidable, relentless jolt of desire inundated her senses. It took several rapid heartbeats for her to realize she felt his desire. It lived and breathed in her body, in her heart, and in her consciousness. The astonishing excitement fed her own. The intensity of his need sapped the strength from her bones. A cry escaped as the potency of mingling passion rode roughshod over her senses.

Rafe gripped her shoulders and set her on her heels. She teetered, her fingers groping across his tight-fitting shirt for a hold. She caught the lapel of his jacket, then swayed. Her knees buckled under the onslaught of combined emotion.

"Stay outta my head." His teeth remained clenched as he growled at her.

Dumbfounded, she shook her head in denial. "I did not do . . . I could not . . ." At a loss, she closed her mouth and let the wild pulse of her heart hammer. Quaking against him, she saw the predator in his eyes, but did not sense him.

Truth emerged through the chaos. "You," she whispered. It had to be him; it was not her. Even if she dared break his barriers, she lacked the ability to do so now. She craved the promise of his lips on hers foretelling a pleasure beyond expectation.

"You, Rafe, you did that." Both her voice and conviction were stronger this time. So was the anger glinting in his dark eyes and the clench of his jaw.

She unwound her fingers from his jacket and turned on shaky legs. The only possible explanation hammered at her. He was Gifted. The link of passion existed only with another Gifted chosen as a life mate. It was neither possible nor deniable.

With a sinking heart, she stumbled toward the forest. If he was Gifted, he was also a rogue. A gift for killing defied everything their code of life revered.

"You are not my choice, Rafe!"

Small wonder she was powerless in the spell of shared desire. He was Gifted. Yet he did not know it. Nor did he know he was her life mate.

Lorilie started running and would not stop until she found the edge of the earth. Though she desired Rafe Stricter beyond reason, she could not, would not be bound to him for the rest of her life.

Chapter 12

R AFE RAN AFTER Lorilie. She practically flew through the darkness, leaping obstacles with the grace and surety of a gazelle sprinting across familiar turf. The abrupt presence of the wolf pack made it clear his company was not welcome.

He slowed and let her disappear into the night.

Anger returned with the force of a steamroller.

"You couldn't let it be, could you, Lorilie," he seethed. More than her willful violation ate at him. He'd forgotten what she could do . . . forgotten and left himself open. And she had surged through him with a fire of desire that damn near incinerated him.

Controlling himself with an inexperienced, curious wood nymph who heated him in ways beyond his comprehension was difficult at best. Her sweet, eager lips learned so quickly it damn near broke him in half to give them up.

"What are you, Lorilie? Who the hell are you?" The anguish of his bellowed plea rocked the night.

He glared at the stars and wished he knew the answer.

"Why?" he shouted, venting the furious frustration roiling through his veins. "Why?"

The night wind whispered secrets in the trees. He listened, aching for a glimmer of comprehension. He received none.

Resigned that he wouldn't find reasons for the inexplicable ache in his heart over what he considered betrayal, he started walking.

She epitomized the mystery embroiling him in a realm that defied logic and shifted time. Grappling with a reality he couldn't deny and Lorilie's predilection for invading his most private thoughts and emotions scared him. Being afraid angered him. It was a stupid reaction, but one he couldn't ignore.

Why did you lie to me, Lorilie?

Hell, he didn't have to trust her to sleep with her. She was available and willing. Lord, she was willing. The way his body was screaming for hers, all he needed was to get her out of his head. It was as simple as that.

At least, that's what he told himself as he returned to the granite fortress. When Lorilie showed up, he'd demand an explanation.

"I'm losing my damn mind. Somebody ought to shoot me and put me out of my misery."

"I'm confused, Grandfather. How can this be? We have not chosen one another as life mates. How can he share his desire and not know it?" She rested her forehead on Joseph Ramey's cold, damp headstone. The early morning sun cast long shadows over the ruins of the Ramey homestead.

Echoes of Rafe's potent desire continued trembling in her limbs. The mating instinct that drove male animals into battle over a female possessed the same blinding urgency Rafe had projected. Had he not pushed her away, they would have joined together as their natures demanded.

"Who is he, Grandfather? Is he the Guardian you said I should seek? He is certainly big and strong enough. Oh, but his heart sees no beauty. His head thinks only of danger."

Caressing the stone, she sought the elusive peace of happier memories from days long past.

The first time she'd made biscuits.

Reading James Fenimore Cooper's *The Last of the Mohicans* aloud.

The monthly gatherings of the Gifted where they drank ale and fine Scots whisky, laughed, traded, danced, and courted.

The sun climbed the peaks and long morning shadows began their march across the land. Before departing the graveyard, she carefully removed any sign of her presence.

Flanked by the wolves, she started back to the sanctuary and Rafe. As they neared the top of the rise, a flock of birds took to the sky with a noisy protest. Instinctively, Lorilie ducked into a thick copse of trees.

Someone was coming. Not Rafe. He moved with the forest and seldom startled the birds.

Ketchums.

Her heartbeat quickened. Not wanting to draw attention, she dispatched the wolves. They would be safer away from the Ketchums's guns.

The sound of shod horses on the hard earth, the creak of saddle leather and the occasional jangle of the harnesses sounded loud in the quiet morning.

"Don't know. What're *you* gonna do when we find the gold?" She recognized Abner's voice. Though he bore a striking resemblance to his brother, he lacked old man Ketchum's mean streak.

"I think I'll set up a store, maybe in Monterey. Live like normal folks. Maybe find a wife," Clyde answered.

Lorilie held her breath as the horses shied from the copse of trees hiding her.

"Whoa. Easy, boy," Clyde crooned to his mount. "I don't like this place either."

"Don't know why the hell Gaylord keeps sending us back here. Hal says the girl's dead."

"Pa doesn't believe anything he can't see. We're going to have to bring him a corpse." Clyde urged his mount toward the ridge. "Let's get this over with and be about the business of panning for gold. If Joseph Ramey found it, we can, too."

"Be easier if we jest found his stash," grumbled Abner.

She waited until they were well over the rise before emerging from her hiding place. Warned that they hadn't totally given up on either Grandfather's gold or the possibility that she was alive, she took extra precautions on the way home.

By the time she reached the sanctuary and bid the wolves good-bye, she had decided on a course. Rafe blamed her for what had happened between them. Though she knew differently, convincing him seemed unlikely. She would act responsibly. She would tell him the truth. Up to a point.

She stood inside the first chamber, her eyes adjusting to the darkness.

"I was on my way to look for you." Rafe moved behind her from the spot in the shadowy passageway where he had been waiting for her to return.

Startled, Lorilie flinched. Her heart responded with sudden thunder. "Why? I know where I live."

"You could have fallen down a ravine, tripped on some scrub, or a hundred different things. It's daylight. Isn't this when the Ketchums hunt you?"

She gathered her wits and prepared for the confrontation ahead. "As long as Hal believes me dead, they won't search enthusiastically."

The press of his fingertips at the small of her back prodded her forward. ''Then giving them an incentive isn't the wisest tactic, is it?''

Lorilie strode through the darkness. ''You are not my father, my grandfather, or my life mate. I choose what I do, where I go, and when. I have no obligation to consider your admonitions.''

''Even if they make sense?''

The heat from his body warmed her back. If he walked any closer, he would walk right over her. ''Must you follow at my heels?''

''Apparently. Someone ought to look out for you.''

Where were all her plans of civility? She ducked through the low arch and into the main chamber. Her plans, like her good intentions, had remained outside melting in the sunlight.

Lorilie turned and stared at Rafe. Arms crossed over his massive chest, feet apart, he was a smoldering mountain of temptation. The scowl darkening his face reached into his gray eyes glaring at her like pieces of shiny flint.

''I can take care of myself. You are not needed, Rafe, nor is your anger, or your closed-minded, narrow perceptions.'' She might not need him, but she certainly wanted him. One look at him in the lighted cavern reignited the flood of desire.

''Damn right my mind is closed, so stay out of it,'' he said through gritted teeth.

Fists clenched, she faced him. ''Let me clarify my position. I did nothing to you. *You* did it.''

A mock salute accompanied a forced, brittle smile. ''An outraged offense is usually a good defense. You get points for trying, but I'm not buying.''

''Once again you resort to words that mean nothing to me. Is that how you disguise your feelings and circumvent the truth?''

The slight flicker of his left eyebrow and the return of his bleak scowl gave her confidence. Inadvertently, she had struck a nerve. A moment earlier, she had considered his defenses impenetrable.

"The average person knows what I'm saying." His growl rumbled from his forbidding, clenched jaw.

Lorilie's chin lifted in sharp rejection of his intended intimidation. "I am an average person, and I say you speak in meaningless riddles. You don't want me to understand. That way, everything can be my fault and you remain blameless."

Rafe's left hand arced through the air. "Average? There's nothing average about living in a cavern with running water and a fireplace. No, Lorilie, this is not average. It isn't close. Neither are you." His hand dropped.

She bit back the sting of having her differences dragged into the light. "For an Outsider, you show a remarkably narrow tolerance of the culture you have inflicted yourself upon. You make hasty judgments about how I should live, what I should do. I have no obligation to change my ways to fit your perceptions. It is you who needs to adapt. This is my domain."

She returned his glare with defiance, not regretting a single word of her diatribe. Silence descended on the cavern. Neither moved, nor retreated.

"I'm trying to understand what I'm expected to adapt to," Rafe said slowly.

"You think I have no need for the same understanding? Am I supposed to accept things as they are and make the best of it? Are you saying you have less sense and fortitude than I?"

"Now you're the one speaking in riddles. Knock off the comparison crap. It won't get us anywhere."

"You wish me to do things your way and abandon mine?"

"You're the one with the proclivity for acceptance and fortitude. How about a demonstration?"

She thought quickly around the trap she sensed. "Such as?"

"Tell me how you do what you do to me."

She turned away, head shaking, and settled on a stone bench. "Gladly, Rafe, just as soon as you tell me how and why you did what you did to me at the lake."

"All I did was kiss you. You—"

"Did nothing!" The outrage echoed in the cavern. When it died, she crossed her arms and focused on him. "I did nothing other than kiss you."

"We both felt it." Smugness tilted his head and turned his scowl into a faint smile. "Got a little more than you bargained for, did you? What scared you into running away, Lorilie? What you felt from me, or my anger because you'd crossed the line?"

"You should not have been able to do that to me."

"Only one-way, huh?"

"No. It should not be like that, either way, not unless . . ." She pressed her lips together, effectively silencing herself. She had avoided his trap only to step into one of her own making.

"Unless, what, Lorilie?"

"Unless we are life mates." Her heart quickened with the admission.

"Life mates? Married?"

Suddenly he saw too much. The mesmerizing power of his gaze held hers. "Life mates, like the wolves and the hawks. They have one mate until death."

"And you think I'm your life mate?" He broke the rigid stance holding him in place and approached her.

"For a man intent on hearing every pine needle drop in the forest, you listen poorly. I said it should not have happened."

"I heard that part. Now I'm asking what you think. Do you think I'm your life mate?" He crouched in front of her and rested his forearms on her thighs. Instinctively, she drew back. Cradled in the vulnerable vee of her legs, he was much too big, too close, and too dangerous.

"I cannot imagine a more unlikely match. You are the

antithesis of my hopes for a life mate. Undoubtedly you find me equally unsatisfactory.''

"How can I possibly draw that conclusion? I don't know enough about you. Enlighten me, Lorilie. I want to understand you even more than I want all the fiery, sweet passion I felt in you.'' He ran the tip of his finger along her jaw. Her chin lifted in response, leaving her open for his exploration. Heaven help her, she had never wanted anything in her life the way she wanted Rafe Stricter. "Which, as you know, is considerable.''

The fine muscles around the corners of her mouth flexed under the tenderness of his touch. She wanted honesty, but not particularly on this subject. But if fate sent him as her Guardian and life mate, no power could change their course. They would be bound for the rest of their lives.

"I would rather live without a life mate than shackle my soul to a man who cannot see beauty in the world, and kills without conscience.''

"But I do see beauty, Lorilie. I see it in you. You have a purity of spirit that scares the hell out of me, yet leaves me in awe. Most men would walk on their knees for ten years in exchange for an hour of the love I've seen you give your friends and the uninhibited passion I felt from you.''

"But not you, Rafe. You are not like most men, are you?''

His hand dropped from her face and settled on her knee. The jolt of fire that rode up her thigh made her flinch. "No. I tried the love and relationship route. It ended in disaster.''

The admission surprised her. Picturing Rafe as a Gifted man capable of leaving his chosen life mate was beyond her imagination. However, he also did not acknowledge his gift any more than she accepted that his talent was for killing. "Did you love her?''

"Yes, but not well. I didn't put her first when it was

important. She left and found someone who would.''

"What did she want, Rafe?"

"Marriage. Children."

"How could you not give her children? You have such a strong mating drive. . . .'' Her words trailed when she realized she had spoken them aloud. Embarrassment crept up her neck and colored her cheeks.

"Where I come from, we have many ways of preventing the conception of children without forgoing the pleasures."

Though she did not understand, pressing for an explanation seemed unwise. The growing hunger in his eyes consumed his anger. Her lips tingled with the memory of his kiss. "We cannot always have what we want here, Rafe."

"How well I know. Give me one answer."

Wary, she nodded curtly. "If I can."

He rocked off his toes onto his knees in a smooth motion that moved him deeper into the vee of her legs. The heat of his hips against her inner thighs rippled up and down her body before settling in the juncture so close to him.

Instinctively, Lorilie retreated. "What are you about?"

"I'm about to kiss you and find out exactly what happens." He cradled her face and ran his thumb across the corner of her mouth, his lips only an inch from hers. "I don't think I've ever wanted to kiss anyone as badly as I want to kiss you right now."

She braced a hand against his shoulder. "I cannot mate with you. You must know that."

"Cannot? Or will not?"

"It matters not. Mating . . . solidifies the bond between life mates. Nothing thwarts or dissolves the bond once it forms. I could not bear a lifetime with a man who regarded me with disdain and refused the blessings of children."

She searched his implacable expression when her proclamation gave him pause.

"You believe making love, mating, will create a metaphysical dependence we couldn't break?"

"I have witnessed the changes in two people who become life mates. I do not understand why it is this way with my people, but I am not foolish. Because you choose disbelief does not negate reality."

Her fingertips danced over the shadow of whiskers on his cheek. "Eventually, you would leave me for the life you lived before you came. Perhaps I would want you gone, but we would never be free of each other."

"That frightens you."

She nodded, not trusting her voice. The fever burning in her veins weakened her resolve. As he drew her closer, all she thought about was kissing him.

"We won't make love, okay?"

Again, she nodded and watched his dilated eyes search her face.

"You'll stay out of my head."

She met his gaze and whispered, "Yes, I promise."

"We'll see," he murmured, then brushed his mouth against hers.

Her arms wound around his neck. The butterflies in her stomach fluttered their wings.

His hands molded around her hips and half slid, half lifted her to the edge of the stone bench. By drawing her closer, her thighs spread wider. She had no time to think. The delicious press of her breasts against his chest mingled her rapid heartbeat with his.

He lowered his head and slid his lips against the side of her throat. She gasped at the flash of heat replacing the butterflies in her belly. The fiery sensation of his sensuous mouth against her neck sent her head arching, allowing him free access, inviting more of the heated pleasure building with every flick of his tongue and grate of his teeth.

Suddenly daring, she explored the breadth of his shoulders. Once she started, the hunger ravaging her senses abhorred the thin cloth barrier between her hands and his flesh.

"You taste like heaven," he murmured, then nibbled on her earlobe.

"I cannot taste anything." A flick of her tongue moistened her dry lips.

"Do you want to?" he breathed into her ear.

"Rafe . . ."

He stroked the long braid at the nape of her neck. Heat suffused her when his mouth found hers. He was right. This *was* heaven. She arched against him, twining her arms around his neck.

A low rumble vibrated his chest and sent an odd thrill along her limbs. The restraint of his tender kiss promising more of the dizzying urgency emboldened her. Tentatively, she explored the seam of their lips with the tip of her tongue.

Without warning, he pulled her hips forward. The cradle of her femininity pressed against his growing desire. She inhaled sharply, astonished by the depth of intimate need the contact created. A strong hand held her in place as the raw sensation quickly became hunger. Only the barriers of their clothing kept them apart.

The untamed kiss became ravenous. His tongue delved into her mouth in urgent exploration. The inside of her thighs clenched in response to the sinuous motion of his hips. Lost in the sweet sea of sensation, nothing had ever felt so right, so incredible. In that instant, every fiber of her being ached to claim him as her life mate.

The force of his desire rocked her. The waves of hungry need assaulting her senses overwhelmed her. It was too much. She could not survive the primal lust burning inside him. He would tear her apart in a rapacious frenzy.

The instinct to flee shouted the waves of desire pulsing

through her veins into screaming submission. She pushed against him, struggling for freedom.

Rafe broke the kiss. The awesome desire inundating her senses retreated. She became still, unsure that escape of any kind existed. The wild passion in him was surely lethal for one of them, probably her.

He buried his face in the crook of her neck and shoulder, then held her in a crushing embrace. Fine tremors wracked him.

She rested her head against his.

Rafe was her life mate.

The certainty burned with an exhilarating brilliance that rivaled the despair subduing her. The aches of a broken promise of passion throbbed in her breasts and loins with a life of their own. While his desire no longer inundated her, his need remained alive between her legs.

"Lorilie . . ."

"I did nothing," she whispered. "It must be you."

As though it pained him, he released her. He stood slowly in the breech of her knees, then gazed down at her.

When she met his eyes, fear shot through her. Though he appeared controlled and outwardly calm, his gray eyes possessed the haunted, untamed quality of a feral animal. She leaned back and braced her hands against the rock.

After a long moment, he turned away and she breathed a sigh of frustrated relief. She watched him duck into the passageway. The totality of the ensuing silence settled into the marrow of her quaking bones.

Without a doubt, Rafe Stricter was her life mate.

Chapter 13

TENSION INCREASED DAILY the week following the catastrophic experiment. Although Lorilie made it easy for Rafe to keep a physical distance, he considered his hard-disciplined restraint no more effective than plugging a leaky dam with his fingers. Sooner or later he'd run out of fingers and the structure would crack and drown him.

Nightly sojourns over the ridges eased Rafe's concerns for Craig. Marica tended her patient with the unquestioned authority of a benign dictator. Her methods worked. Craig was out of bed for several hours at a stretch. Soon, he'd walk without holding his side like an arthritic old man on a rainy day.

"I have a request." Marica stood on the planked porch of her cabin as they prepared to take their leave.

Loner sprinted from the shadows and nestled against Lorilie's leg.

"Sure," Rafe said, dragging his gaze from the rhythmic glide of her fingers through the wolf's pelt.

Marica withdrew a paper from her apron pocket. "Bring me these."

Rafe took the list and scanned it. He recognized only two items. "Plants?"

"They are herbs I need for concocting medicines. Normally, I harvest them, but I worry about leaving Craig alone. I keep expecting a visit from the Ketchums with news of Lorilie's demise. I fear they will come as soon as I leave for an hour or two. They have no qualms about entering when I'm not here."

Rafe disliked the Ketchums more every day. "Can you recognize these?" He handed Lorilie the list.

"I know where to find them. We can gather everything you need and bring it tomorrow night." She folded the paper into her pocket, then resumed scratching Loner behind his ears.

"Thank you." Marica entered the cabin and closed the door.

The sliver of moon riding low on the horizon furnished scant light. During the frequent trips over the ridge, Rafe had memorized each hazard. Led by the wolf, he and Lorilie walked in silence. Thoughts neither dared share consumed them.

He lingered outside the sanctuary after Lorilie and Loner went inside.

She was right. He was the one who needed to adapt. Heaven knew, he was trying. His long-term survival might well depend on his ability to blend into the world beyond the mountains. Thus far, he'd found no clue of how he and Craig wound up here.

Could an explosion of momentous proportions have hurled them through a fragile veil of time? He recalled the legions of men missing during the wars he'd studied. How many of them had met similar fates?

A month ago, he would have laughed at the notion. Today the hypothesis held potential. However, it had a serious drawback—there was no way of returning. The capability for detonating an explosive force the magnitude of the one unleashed in the Bolivian Andes was decades in the future.

Try as he might, he found no common trigger other than the massive bomb explosion to account for the time shift. A one-way ticket was unacceptable. He clung to the hope of finding a way back. If he stayed around Lorilie much longer, he wouldn't want to leave. And he wouldn't stay where he wasn't wanted. She had stated her opinion clearly about being saddled with a man who made his living by delivering death.

He didn't like her censure, but he admired her.

Once again, his thoughts had spun in a full circle and focused on Lorilie.

He headed for the sanctuary. Tonight he'd meditate and seek escape in the quiet recesses of his mind.

A light drizzle filtered through the fog shrouding the mountainside. Fat drops of water collected on the ends of pine needles and leaves, then splattered on the forest floor.

"We have an early start on a fine day for herb gathering." Lorilie pulled her mackintosh closed at the throat.

Rafe studied the heavy mist. "Yeah, looks like we beat the rush."

The forbearance in her tight smile reminded him how vast the gulf of difference yawned between them.

"The rain softens the ground and makes our task easier. Several of the herbs Marica needs require the root."

Rafe zipped his jacket against the chilly rain. Loner remained on the ridge when they began traversing a steep slope nestling above a creek. The drizzle coating the ground made for a slippery, slow descent.

Halfway down the ravine, Lorilie paused, then crouched beside a tree.

"Are you okay?" Rafe dropped down and searched her face for signs of strain. He saw only delight.

She brushed away decaying leaves and pine needles at

the base of a gnarled oak clutching the hillside. ''These seldom grow this high.''

He stayed her hand when she reached for the brightly colored mushroom cluster. ''It's poisonous, Lorilie.''

''Most plants are, if used indiscriminately. The more potent they are in the wild, the stronger their healing properties when properly extracted.'' Eyes as green as the freshly washed forest regarded him inquisitively. ''I wonder if people are like that.''

''Experimentation though trial and error is dangerous.'' One more encounter with her passion, and he wouldn't care about consequences. He believed her assertion that she had done nothing when they kissed. On the other hand, *he* had not caused the phenomenon. Once again, he straddled an invisible fence in a limbo of gray uncertainty. Acceptance, he discovered, was a humbling journey.

She focused on the mushrooms. ''I know. Some things are best left alone.'' As though confirming that they weren't discussing plants, she plucked the mushrooms, then wrapped them in a cloth tucked into her gathering basket.

At the bottom of the ravine, an energetic creek scoured a ribbon of moss-covered stones. Tall trees formed a thick canopy over the rocky creek bed. Delicate ferns grew in the shelter of gray boulders protruding from the humus along the higher banks.

Rafe scanned the slopes. The sharp rises formed two sides of a box.

Deliberately, he trained his gaze on the rushing water. He felt like one of the jagged stones with Lorilie as the relentless water softening his outlook. He noticed little white flowers growing from the moss on the bank. As delicate as Lorilie, they held their place in the face of the elements. The flowers epitomized her inner strength.

The insight amazed him. In the past, flowers were either poisonous or nonpoisonous, big or little, and categorized by color. Staring at the delicate, tiny petals reaching for elusive sunlight on filament stems, he saw beauty.

In the wake of his awe, irritation swept through him.

He'd worked damn hard at honing his survival instincts. Spending even a moment admiring flowers could get him killed during a mission.

A knot formed in his gut. He had no mission, other than Lorilie. Unless he found a way back, he'd never have another.

"I can show you the plants Marica needs." She pointed upstream.

Grateful for the distraction from his grim thoughts, he followed her along the creek, noting the plants she indicated and which ones required the root.

"We will get the others on the way back," she announced. "If you start here, I can go upstream a little ways and gather watercress. Though she did not indicate it, surely she needs some. Besides, it is good to eat."

He unsheathed his knife and bent onto one knee. "I was wondering what I'd do when my next craving for a watercress sandwich struck."

"I was unaware you are fond of it. I will gather a good quantity."

Her unabashed delight at discovering something she thought he favored knocked the starch from his irritation. He'd cut out his tongue before admitting he'd never wanted to eat a watercress sandwich in his life. "How far upstream are you going?"

"Not far, just around the bend." She turned on her heel and started off.

"Around the bend. Yep, that's me," he murmured, and set the collecting basket beside his first victim.

When the basket was half full of freshly dug stream-washed roots and plants, Rafe straightened. He headed upstream. By now, Lorilie must have plucked the creek clean of watercress.

Ahead, half a dozen birds took flight into the drizzling fog.

Rafe froze in his tracks.

Battle senses commandeered his reflexes. He listened. Nothing out of the ordinary penetrated the insulating fog. The shimmering veils of gray drifted among the trees. He removed his jacket, then tucked it and the basket beneath a heavy cluster of ferns.

He chose an approach screened by thick tree trunks well above the creek. While he traversed the slope paralleling the water, he studied the land, smelled the air for the scent of his enemy, and listened for the small sound that betrayed a threat. He navigated the steep terrain in swift silence.

A hundred yards beyond the bend, the creek spilled from a deep, still pool. Fog collected on the surface and thickened as he made his way upstream.

Where was she?.

A strange panic welled from his heart. Emotion hampered his killing instinct. He squashed it with the force of a hammer on an anvil.

Racing across the foggy landscape, he searched for Lorilie. The gray billows teased him with glimpses of the pool below, then closed.

He heard the threat before he saw it. He darted around a rocky thrust and began his descent.

''Have you taken leave of your senses?''

Lorilie. Her voice never sounded so sweet.

''Put the damn rope around your waist. If I hafta do it, you ain't gonna like it.''

A thinner patch of fog drifted through the trees. A big man on horseback jiggled a rope snaking toward Lorilie ten feet away at the water's edge. ''You expect me to neatly tie myself up and go with you? You have taken leave of your senses. Go, before I scream.''

''Scream all you want. There's just you and me, Lorilie. I'm takin' you to Pa.''

Rafe used the momentum of his downhill speed and lunged at the man. He caught him below the shoulders and held on. The impact of his two hundred twenty pounds hurtling through the air knocked the man cleanly from the saddle.

Rafe held on and rolled. They stopped short of a towering lodgepole pine. In a flash, he stood and dragged the intruder up, then pinned him against the tree with his knife blade poised at the soft flesh of the man's throat.

Dazed, the man gaped at him, his dark eyes struggling to focus.

Rafe yanked the buckle open on the gun belt riding low on the man's hips. It fell with a thud. He smelled the fear darting in the man's eyes. "Who are you?"

"H-Hal. Hal Ketchum. Who the hell are you?"

"I'm your worst nightmare," Rafe seethed. "My name is Death and I'm here for you." He pressed the knife harder against Hal's whiskered neck. A red pearl of blood beaded on the edge.

Fear drained the color from Hal's ruddy face. "Don't kill me." His frantic eyes continued pleading.

"Why do you hunt her?"

"She's a witch. A damn witch. She sends her wolves after our stock." His right hand fluttered helplessly in protest. "Ain't you seen her with 'em? Only a witch can walk the mountain with them wolves in the dead of night."

Rafe afforded a quick glance at Lorilie beside the pond. Her eyes were damn near as wide as Hal's. "You ignorant moron. What the hell do you think those wolves would do if you captured her? They'd tear you apart. If there was anything left, the bears and cougars would shred the rest." Utter disgust roared through him. "You're too stupid to live."

"Oh, God, don't kill me. I won't chase her no more. Bobby can find hisself some other female. Just don't kill me. I'll do whatever you say."

"Don't lie to me. Right now, you'd promise me your soul and sell your mother into hell to save your hide. It isn't salvageable. See, I want you to die. I'm going to enjoy killing you. I'm not a pacifist. Nor am I a helpless old man who can't fight back. Got that, Hal?''

Movement at the water's edge caught his attention, but he didn't look away from Hal. ''Stay out of this, Lorilie,'' he warned. ''This is between me and Hal.''

Fear paralyzed Hal. His gaze froze on Rafe's face.

''Where did you come from, Hal? Why did you settle here? It's awful far away from the nightlife, isn't it?''

''P-Pa found out about this place a long time ago.''

''How?''

Hal took a slow, shuddering breath then tore his gaze from Rafe.

''Answer me, or I swear, you're not going to like what I do.''

''My Pa would cut my tongue out iffen I told you.''

''He isn't here. I am,'' Rafe said calmly, then grinned. Hal's eyes widened in terror.

''And I'm asking nicely. This time.''

''Me and Pa were up in these mountains about ten years ago. We come across a man and woman and traveled with 'em some ways. Ya know, there ain't many women in these parts. Pa wanted the man to share his woman. He wouldn't do it. Neither would she, so he killed 'em, and we went back to the coast.''

''He killed my parents?''

While intent on extracting information, he'd not taken into account Lorilie's reaction. Damn, she'd heard it all. He cussed himself as six kinds of a fool for not protecting her grieving heart.

''He killed my parents?'' Anguish dripped from each word.

''You son of a bitch.'' Up to this point, the rhetorical threats were designed for terror. Now he genuinely wanted to watch Hal take his last breath.

''I—I didn't know Pa was gonna kill 'em.''

''Shut up!'' Rafe caught a glimpse of Lorilie, but kept

his focus on Hal. One weak second, and Hal just might commit suicide in the guise of bravado.

Lorilie was the picture of dejection; her head hanging, her shoulders slumped. She sagged beside the water and stared into the fog.

"Why'd you come back?"

"We—we seen Joe Ramey in Yerba Buena. We seen his pouch of gold. Pa said where there's one pouch, there's two, maybe more.

"We followed Joe Ramey when he left Yerba Buena. We lost him, but after a time, we figured out where he's going. We come up here lookin' for gold."

"You mean looking for a way to *steal* his gold."

"Okay, we was gonna take it. Only . . . he died without tellin' where it was."

"You mean you killed him."

Beads of perspiration ran from Hal's forehead and his thin eyebrows. He blinked once, giving his answer.

"You killed Joseph Ramey for his gold and his grand-daughter. Hell, you're real TV talk show material." Rafe glared at Hal.

"I told ya what ya asked. The truth, too. Please, mister, ya gotta let me go," Hal begged.

"I don't 'gotta' do anything." Rafe drew a heavy breath and searched for a reason not to kill Hal Ketchum. When none surfaced, he shrugged. "But I'm going to be kind today, Hal."

"Oh, God bless you." Air gushed from his lungs with relief.

"I'm sure He has, in His own special way. He sent me to you, Hal. How do you want to meet Him? You want me to cut your throat or hang you?"

Hal wet his pants and didn't notice.

"For a mighty hunter of defenseless women, you don't have much backbone."

"Let him go, Rafe." Lorilie sat beside the water with her back to them.

"Do what?" Surely he hadn't heard correctly.

"Let him go. Please."

She wasn't serious. The man admitted being a party to her parents' murders. He'd killed her grandfather.

"Lorilie—"

"Let him go. It is not our way to take a life."

"Well, hell, Lorilie, he doesn't care—"

"I care, mister. I really care," Hal said quickly.

"I'm not talking to you." He glowered at Lorilie. Why hesitate? He ought to kill Hal and be done with it. "Retribution is his way. You think he won't hunt you if I let him live? He and that bunch of Neanderthals will look for us until they die of old age."

"Then they'll die a natural death, won't they?" The distance in her softly spoken conjecture hinted of despair.

"I won't tell nobody she's alive. I swear, I won't say a word about you." Hal crossed his heart.

"Lying offends me."

"I ain't lying. Swear to God, I ain't lying."

Rafe leaned forward until his nose was barely an inch from Hal's. "You'll change your tune as soon as I let you go. You're like a pet scorpion. You'll bite the hand that feeds you every time." The pulse in Hal's throat vibrated the knife. A push. A tiny push. That's all it would take to rid the world of another heartless killer.

The gentle touch of Lorilie's hands on his raised arm quelled the tirade gathering steam for full assault. He felt the sorrow weighting her blithe spirit. On one hand, she'd endured enough for today. On the other, if he didn't take care of Hal Ketchum, they'd both regret it tomorrow.

"Please, I implore you to let him go. If you kill him, you are no different than he is."

"In whose book?" If he did as she asked, the Ketchums would comb every blade of grass in the Sierras for them.

"In mine, Rafe. You are better than they are. Killing him is unnecessary."

"The hell it isn't. Even if you aren't concerned they'll hunt you again, I am." Inwardly, he railed that Hal Ketchum deserved to die. "Have you no wish for justice?"

"I have no wish for the loss of more life. Hal's death cannot return my family. Killing him only deepens the differences between us." Her fingers moved up his arm and pleaded in a language of their own. "But the choice is yours."

She deserved justice, but she didn't want justice. He wanted justice, but he wanted her content with the manner in which he dealt with her family's killer. "Doing what you're asking goes against everything I believe in, which is to never leave an enemy behind."

"He has done nothing to you. He is not your enemy."

"He's yours, and you're my responsibility."

"I am not."

"You are my mission, and as such, my responsibility. He's a threat to you. That makes him my enemy." He pushed Hal harder into the tree. A strangled sound vibrated against Rafe's knuckles at his quarry's throat.

She knelt beside him and rested her forehead against his thigh. "I beg you for his life."

"Jeezus, Lorilie! Get off your knees!" A gut punch from a six-hundred-pound gorilla wouldn't have staggered him more than the sight of Lorilie on her knees begging for Hal's life. "I may kill this SOB out of sheer frustration with you." Humiliating herself and groveling for a killer's life shamed him.

Unable to look at her, he glared at Hal. "There's your witch, idiot, begging for your life, not setting the wolves on you. Get up, Lorilie. Go get your basket."

Without another word, she obeyed.

"You owe her your life, Hal Ketchum. She's had enough grief. I won't add to it. Today." Glaring into Hal's frightened eyes, Rafe spoke through gritted teeth. "But get this clear, Hal, if you ever come near her again, you won't walk away. Your ass is mine, and I'll hang it from the highest tree. No amount of begging from anyone will change my mind. Got that?''

''Yes,'' Hal rasped. The movement of his Adam's apple sent another red bead across the flat of the knife blade.

Abruptly, Rafe stepped back. ''Leave.''

With a hand at his throat, Hal bent to retrieve his gun belt.

''Touch it, and I'll break your neck.''

Hal scurried toward his nervous horse. He fumbled with the reins and tried three times before getting his foot into the stirrup. Once mounted, he urged the horse into a gallop and never looked back.

Rafe wrapped the gun belt around the holster.

Lorilie walked into his arms. ''Thank you.'' She rested her forehead on his chest.

He tucked her against his side. ''He'll be back—with his friends.''

''Maybe not.''

''No maybe about it, Lorilie. I frightened him. When he gets over it, he'll be angry and want revenge. He'll come looking for us like gangbusters. Besides, they haven't gotten what they really want, have they?''

''What? Me?'' Sorrow glistened in her green eyes trying hard not to cry.

''You. And your grandfather's gold. They wouldn't have risked killing him if they didn't think you knew where it is.''

She regarded him with fresh sorrow. ''Do you want the gold too?''

Rafe shook his head. He wanted something very different. ''If I need gold, I know where to find it.'' In a couple of years, so would the whole world. He took her basket and started them downstream where his jacket and basket waited beneath the ferns.

A form of shock settled over him. He'd violated his own survival code and let Hal Ketchum go because Lorilie had gotten on her knees and pleaded. Fourteen years of training and all his instincts had died with just one look from her green eyes.

Shit. He was losing it badly.

"Rafe?"

Troubled, he watched the trail and the steep slopes of the ravine and remained silent.

"You are not a killer. Life takes more heart and courage than death."

He halted, then turned on her. "Get this straight, Lorilie. I am what I am, and I'm proud of it. Letting Hal Ketchum go went against everything I believe in concerning treatment of the enemy. And he is the enemy. Don't ask me to do it again.

"And for God's sake, don't ever get on your knees and beg again. That works only once. The next man who so much as raises your pulse gets no mercy. Understand?"

"Why did you let him go if it offended you so?"

"I didn't want you looking at me the way you looked at him when you found out about your parents." The explanation spilled from his mouth without thought. "And I'm losing my damn mind, Lorilie."

"Or perhaps you are discovering your true path."

He doubted it. No man ignored his code of survival to please a woman unless he'd slipped over the edge.

Chapter 14

"PLEASE REST, CRAIG. If you push yourself any harder, you'll have a setback." Marica arranged the drying racks for the herbs she expected from Rafe and Lorilie.

Craig had the constitution of a bull and a stubborn streak as tenacious. Though her healing gift and medicinal skills were considerable, his recovery exceeded her most optimistic hopes.

Chair legs grated against the wooden floor. Craig settled slowly, favoring his left side. "Yeah, I'll give it a rest for a while."

He picked up the ball of yarn from the center of the table and began squeezing it with his left hand.

"Why do you do that with the yarn?" She untied a knot in a waxed drying string, then laid it with the others stretched on her medicine table.

"It works the muscles around the wound, not much, but enough for now."

She set aside the preparations and joined him at the table. The myriad of questions burning the tip of her tongue begged freedom. She took a deep breath and folded her hands.

"What is Mother Hen?"

Startlement broke his concentration. The ball of yarn stilled. "I talked, huh?"

Nodding, she removed the yarn from his hand and tucked in the loose end. "About many things. People often ramble when delirium grips them. Your survival is a miracle."

He took the ball of yarn into his left hand and resumed squeezing. "You're my angel and my miracle."

She smiled and averted her gaze. When his face lit in unabashed adoration as it did now, her common sense fled. Old, familiar sensations awakened, reminding her of the joy a woman could find with a man.

"Why do you live out here alone? In this day and age, you could have your pick of men."

"You accept this is indeed 1847? You must have roamed the mountains a long time, or perhaps the fever made you lose track of the year." Recalling his shock when she told him several days earlier banished the remnants of her smile.

"Let's say I've been out of touch for a while. Why are you alone?"

"I have not always lived alone. Twenty years ago, I left the mountains for a time with my family. We crossed the great valley and more mountains and settled in Monterey. My mother was an Outsider here. In some ways, we were Outsiders in her world. I was young and adaptable. Eventually, I married an Outsider." She gazed at her hands, amazed by her detachment from the brief history.

"Where is he?"

"He died in a knife fight several months after our wedding. No one came for me until he was dead. I have no idea if I might have saved him or eased his passing. Sometimes that is the best I can do." She drew a breath, then forced a smile and met his empathetic brown eyes. "The following year, I came back here where people abhor the senseless taking of a life.''

''And things were fine until the Ketchums arrived.''

''Well enough for me.'' A slow smile turned the corners of her mouth. ''You are very good, Craig.''

His golden eyebrows rose. ''At what?''

''Diverting the subject. You were going to tell me about Mother Hen.''

''Did I say that?''

Marica laughed. Through their constant togetherness and the unwanted insights garnered when she called upon her healing Gift, he had become transparent. ''I'm sure you would have if you had given yourself the opportunity.'' With a curt nod, she added, ''Mother Hen?''

''Rafe.'' His hand relaxed around the yarn ball as he gingerly stretched his left side.

''What about Rafe?''

''He's Mother Hen.''

The image of the hulking giant as a mother hen herding chicks though the yard struck her as incongruous. She chuckled, holding back her laughter. ''He is so large. So fierce. Why would anyone call him that?''

'' 'Cause that's how he was. Checking, double-checking, taking care of his men. Cleaning up their messes. Protecting them from all kinds of dangers. And tossing them out on their butts if they didn't measure up rather than risk them getting killed.'' He rolled the yarn ball across the table.

She opened her hands and caught it.

''Don't ask me about Rafe. All you need to know about him is that he's closer to me than a brother. There is little''—he leaned closer—''damn little I wouldn't do for him.''

The seriousness schooling his features quelled her laughter. ''Would you kill for him?''

''In a heartbeat. And have, Marica. We weren't Boy Scouts on a camping trip when we undertook a mission.

We were the good guys doing our jobs and staying alive at all cost. You need to understand how it is. Or was.''

Bits of the unwelcome impressions he'd inflicted on her the first time she laid hands on him flashed into her memory. The sobering reminder reeked of death without malice. It still made no sense.

''When you leave us, you will resume your . . . job,'' she mused, bracing for the inevitable.

''Have I ever mentioned leaving you, Marica?''

She gazed into the soft brown eyes of a man ten years her junior and felt his hold on her heart tighten.

Contentment eased the last strains of tension from Craig's face. ''You're stuck with me until the day you look me in the eye and tell me to go.'' A faint smile lit his eyes. ''And I'll know if you don't mean it, Angel.''

Hope collided with reality. ''I am not an angel, Craig. What you feel is gratitude—''

''I know what gratitude is, Angel, and this isn't it.'' He rose from the chair and made his way into the bedroom.

Stunned, Marica stared at the yarn ball. At thirty-six, her prospects of having a lover or a family had dimmed. Common sense decried what her heart longed for with Craig. If she foolishly indulged the fantasy of a life with Craig, heartache would follow.

He was Adonis, a decade younger than she. He would want children. What if she could not give them to him? In another ten years, he would still be an attractive man, and she would be wrinkling and gray. What would he feel, if not regret, when he gazed upon her then?

She weighed the potential for heartbreaking disaster nearly an hour before she rose from the table and walked into the bedroom.

Light from the main room of the cabin slanted through the bedroom door and spilled across the floor. In the near darkness, she studied Craig. While unsure of his feelings, she knew her heart. She had not wanted love, had not thought it possible love would come twice in her life.

But it had.

She bent down, and placed a tender kiss on his warm lips, her heart clutching at impossible dreams.

A shaft of light reflected in Craig's eyes as his heavy lids rose. "I think I've died and gone to heaven."

"Get well, Craig."

Giddy, afraid, but determined to seize her heart's desire, she smiled, then left the room and closed the door.

She was thirty-six and had nothing to lose except a heart she had already given away.

"Did I leave anything out?" Lorilie asked Rafe.

Head shaking, he remained silent.

Watching the kaleidoscope of Craig's reaction while she related the day's encounter underscored the enormity of Rafe's concession. His actions had cost him in ways and for reasons she could not fathom.

"You let him walk away." The flat accusation hung between Rafe and Craig.

Rafe sat with his arms folded over his chest and stared at Craig.

"The man who taught me never let an enemy on the hunt walk away. I don't believe this." Craig winced and eased his grip on the yarn ball.

"Believe it," Rafe whispered, as though struggling for the same acceptance.

"You're angry with him because he chose life over death?" Marica asked Craig.

"Not angry, just trying like hell to understand what's going on. What happened in the jungle—"

Rafe's head snapped up. "Don't go there, Craig. Not now."

Lorilie saw a silent communication pass between the men. The way Craig locked his jaw ended his inquiry.

"Now that they know you are alive and have a Guardian, they will search for you again." Marica's warning heightened the tension gathering in the cabin.

A Guardian? Rafe had acted as one today. "They will not find us." Three sets of eyes turned on Lorilie in disbelief.

"Use the animals. They can at least warn you of danger," Marica urged.

"And be in danger themselves." Recalling the friends lost to Hal Ketchum's guns, she shook her head.

"Why don't you tell us how you could use the animals as a warning?" Rafe uncrossed his arms and turned in his chair until he faced her. "What happened today ties us together until Craig can travel and we take you someplace safe. You don't want me to hurt the Ketchums, and from the sound of things, you don't want to help protect us from being killed by them."

"Rafe—"

"How far behind my back do you want my hands tied, Lorilie? Look at me. I'm one man. I've got one gun and a couple dozen rounds, taken from Hal Ketchum today, which I'm leaving with Craig for self-defense. How many Ketchums are there? How many guns and bullets?"

The maniacal gleam in his eyes frightened her. Everything he said smacked of truth. "I wish no one harmed, Rafe. Not you. Not my friends." Defeat crushed her with reality. "You are right. They will look for us. They may even use Marica to force me out. I cannot allow that. Changing what happened is impossible, but I can put a stop to the danger my actions placed you three in."

"How? By putting yourself in their hands?" The hushed quality of his voice carried a deceptive calm.

He was ahead of her. Avoiding the anger seething from him, she turned her head away. "Yes."

"You think that will end it?"

"Yes." She breathed the admission with a finality settling in her soul.

"You think I'd let you do that?"

"The choice is mine. Not yours."

"Choices have consequences."

"I am prepared to accept them."

"You don't know what they are."

"I do, Rafe. I know exactly what they want from me." She swallowed hard. She would probably choke on her own vomit the first time Bobby Ketchum breathed his foul breath into her face and touched her skin.

"And you accept them?"

Not trusting her voice, she nodded. Heaven help her, she saw no alternative. Risking Rafe's life for hers was unacceptable.

"Then it won't bother you when I kill every one of them."

Her head snapped around and her stomach dropped. "What do you mean?"

"Consequences, sweetheart. It's real simple. They get you. I kill them. I take you back. You hate me forever. We go our separate ways."

"No! There are eight of them. All you could do is get yourself killed. I am trying to avoid bloodshed. Would you make it all for nothing?"

"First of all, I wouldn't take them on all at once. The most effective tactic is one at a time. They won't see me until I allow it."

"Impossible. You cannot think of it!" The idea of him lying in wait for the Ketchums one at a time was inconceivable. But when she met his hardened gaze, she knew that was exactly what he would do.

"I can, and will."

Frantic for denial, she sought Craig. He regarded her with stoic indulgence, then nodded. Frightened, she pounded her fist on the table. "You will not!"

A casual shrug lifted Rafe's shoulders. "If I move fast, they won't get the chance to rape you, Lorilie."

"All right. I will not surrender to them," she shouted. If he meant to terrify her, he succeeded in grand fashion. Trembling, she glared into the gray ice of his eyes. "What happens if they find us?"

The chair creaked as Rafe settled back. "They'll take you over my dead body."

She gazed at the ceiling and tried not to scream. "That is unacceptable. If they find us, you will not interfere. No killing. Not you. Not them."

"They won't take you, and we will survive." He crossed his arms again. "If you want to do it without violence, then help me."

"What? What do you want?"

"Tell me about the animals, how you get them to do what you want."

A glance at Marica's open amazement warned she was on her own. "I fail to see how that helps you."

"They're a resource, maybe the best one available. I need to know how it works, what it can do, and the reliability factor."

Heated anger colored her cheeks a bright pink. "You were bluffing me with frightening stories in order to manipulate me into telling you something that is none of your business? Of all the underhanded—"

"The Capt'n never bluffs," Craig said on a quiet voice. "If anything, he toned it down for you, Lorilie."

Her hands covered her face. Her elbows rested on the table. "You are trying to manipulate me now, Rafe."

"Yeah, but not very hard. If we do this your way, I need help, and I need to know who and what I can rely on." The chair creaked when his weight shifted.

The gentle curl of his fingers around her quaking wrists summoned stinging tears. Not wanting him to see, she resisted his light tug and shook her head. When he released her, she let her head sag into her hands.

"You win, Rafe, I will tell you what you want to know." She swallowed hard. "I have a Gift. Few Outsiders understand it is a talent I was born with, like pale hair or skinny legs."

She sniffed and brushed the tears away with the heels of her palms. "My Gift is with wild animals. We communicate in our heads. It is very difficult to explain something for which I have no words. In many ways, the animals regard me as an unchallengeable leader, not as a threat.''

She scrubbed the tears from her cheeks. ''When I met the Ketchums, I found out how Outsiders regard me. To them, I am an abomination who controls the forest animals. That is only part of it, Rafe.

''Sometimes I quell their killing tendencies. Remember the grizzly and her cubs? One day several years ago, Clyde and Hal Ketchum thought teasing her cubs would be fun. The mama grizzly took offense. Hal was almost mauled to death before I intervened. Marica healed him, and because of that, they have left her alone. They are afraid of incurring her ire.''

As she lowered her hands, her watery gaze rested on her dearest friend. Although Marica nodded encouragement, emptiness settled inside her being. ''As you have noticed, Marica is a miracle worker.''

''She is,'' Rafe agreed. ''In your own way, so are you.''

She shook her head in denial. ''What I do only works with the forest animals, Rafe. Never with men.''

''Is it possible this Gift of yours has grown?'' The coarse rasping of his callused fingers against his whisker stubble took on a rhythm.

''I would know if it did.'' No explanation existed for the link she found with Rafe. Not even life mates could interfere with one another the way she had with him. In the wake of recent events, she suspected the answers lay with him, and he did not want to know the power or frailty of his true nature.

''Not all those born of Gifted parents possess an apparent Gift,'' Marica interjected. ''For those who do, the degree, or strength, varies. Lorilie's parents were both Gifted, though only her mother had an apparent Gift with plants and vegetation. Her father had none.

"My mother was an Outsider," Marica continued. "My father was Gifted, but his abilities did not extend beyond domesticated animals. There is no way of knowing what kind of talents are passed to the next generation." She lowered her gaze. "Or if there will be another generation now that we are scattered like dandelion seeds in the wind."

Rafe caught Lorilie's hand on the tabletop. Her fingers curled into a fist. "Look at me."

When she refused, he leaned closer and curled a finger under her chin. "I want you to do something with your Gift."

She shuddered, dreading his request. Slowly, she raised her lashes and met his gaze. Compassion had melted the ice in his eyes. "What do you want, Rafe?"

"Use your telepathy and ask my fellow predators out there if they will keep a watch on the Ketchums. Just ask. They don't have to approach them or put themselves in harm's way, but just watch, and tell you. Is this possible?"

He made it sound so reasonable, she felt foolish for resisting earlier. "It is possible." She was not done being angry, frightened, and frustrated. "You are the most unnerving person I have ever encountered."

The smile softening his chiseled features crumbled her ire. "I'll take that as a compliment."

"You would." She lifted her chin from his finger and straightened. "I will do it." Squaring her shoulders, she asserted her position. "Not because of your manipulations, Rafe. And certainly not because of your threats. I will do it because it is the responsible, logical course." She dared his gaze. "And because you are not looking for firewood to burn me at the stake."

The predator in him shone in his unblinking eyes and hungry expression. Gooseflesh rippled up her arms and down her body before settling in her breasts and lower abdomen. He did want to burn her at the stake, not with wood and matches, but with passion.

"I do not understand," she whispered, turning her hand over and opening her fingers against his.

"Neither do I, and maybe that's okay, for now."

"Let me see the gun you brought," Craig said, breaking the spell.

Reluctantly, he released her hand and rose. "It's in good shape. He kept it clean. The trigger has been honed."

Craig took the gun belt from Rafe and unrolled it. He opened the revolver cylinder, then examined the bore. "I'd say the Ketchums know a little something about weapons."

He closed the empty cylinder, pointed the gun at the floor, then tested the trigger without letting the hammer slam. "Let's hope they stay away from Marica and the cabin." Apologetic, he met Lorilie's puzzled gaze. "I may not be Quick Draw McGraw, but I shoot faster than I run."

Lorilie understood he would defend Marica and himself by any means necessary. The sooner they left the mountains, the greater the chance of avoiding confrontation. "How soon can you travel, Craig?"

"A week."

"At least two." Marica cast a disapproving look at Craig. "Even three is tempting a setback."

"You underestimate me," Craig grumbled.

"I don't." Rafe turned the chair around and straddled it, resting his chin across his hands at the top of the ladder back. "I'll give you two weeks. Then you and Marica will join us. We'll have to be prepared to go when you two leave the cabin."

"Where?" Craig asked.

Lorilie stared at Rafe. He comprehended the necessity of a quick departure, but neither wanted Craig's recovery jeopardized. "To a place I know of," Lorilie answered.

"McCaully Valley?"

She nodded at Marica. "Unless you have a better place in mind."

"There may not be anyone living there."

"Then we'll find another place," Rafe assured her. "Some place where Lorilie can find peace."

Chapter 15

LORILIE DREW HER knees up on her pallet and stared into the dark cavern. Before tonight's confrontation her litany of shortcomings had not included closed-minded stubbornness. Rafe had forced her into the admission with a strange kind of logic and a gruesome picture of the consequences. It seemed the harder she resisted, the more he taunted the final secret from her.

The revelation of her Gift stripped her cupboard of secrets bare.

A strange freedom settled over her.

The magnitude of Rafe's loyalty amazed her. She had not fully comprehended his unswerving pledge before tonight. His motivation for bestowing the great treasure eluded her.

She tucked the quilt under her chin.

Dealing with Outsiders was more difficult than she had imagined. Their actions encompassed layers of convoluted motives.

The wiles of the animal world embodied simpler, direct inducements. Among her wild friends, eating, mating, and playing were paramount. The wolf pack often worked in concert during a hunt. Their objective was always the same: food, survival.

In retrospect, she discovered an insight that eluded her earlier. By piecing together fragments gleaned from him and Craig, she realized Rafe had once hunted in a pack, only he had hunted men. He also hunted with Craig as his sole ally. Recalling his chilling demeanor in Marica's cabin, she realized his stalking preference.

Alone.

Though their philosophies concerning the preservation of life were diametrically opposed, their preferences for sharing adverse consequences were similar.

Her chin glided over the edge of the blanket in a soothing rhythm.

Contemplating Rafe lying in wait for the Ketchums boggled her mind.

She recalled the way he had ensnared Hal by the pond. The silence of his approach had escaped detection. Nothing had moved on the slope. Then he was there, flying through the air and taking Hal off his horse. He had moved faster than a cougar, with a knife instead of claws and fangs, and more terrifying than the cat who delivered swift death.

She shivered and covered her chin.

What tempted a man's soul into embracing such graceful, calculated violence?

She rolled over, intent on watching him sleep or sit in his strange cross-legged position with his eyes closed and the back of his hands resting on his knees.

He was gone.

She threw back the quilts and pulled on her boots. As she bolted for the passage, she snagged her jacket.

She found him in the trees, beside the flat boulder cluster.

"Going somewhere?" he asked.

"I—I was looking for you." Panting with anxiety, she slowed.

"Why? Did you think I'd sneak over to the Ketchums and kill them in their sleep?"

"No. I . . ." In truth, she did not know why she ran after him.

"You've had a rotten day. Go to bed."

She settled on a boulder angled toward him. "I cannot sleep."

"You should be exhausted."

She pressed her hands between her thighs to keep her fingers warm. "So should you."

"I learned how to get by on a few hours a long time ago."

"Why?"

He snorted. "You're vulnerable when you sleep."

The night concealed his face, but not the impression of his scowl. "You detest being vulnerable."

The ensuing silence allowed her to collect herself.

"I misjudged you, Rafe. I thought you were like other Outsiders."

"Like the Ketchums?"

"You are not like them."

"Other than the Ketchums, how many Outsiders have you met?"

Was there no end to the ways he discomfited her? "A few, besides the ones who lived in the valley as life mates of the Gifted. And I've been to Sutter's Fort."

"I see."

That was the trouble, he saw right through her feeble attempt at an apology. "You are angry at me."

"No more so than usual."

"What did I do now?"

"Nothing. Not a damn thing." He shifted in the darkness. "You're not even angry, Lorilie, are you?"

"No. Should I be?"

"Yes. You should be raging, screaming, breaking

things, and ranting against what the Ketchums have done to you.''

Lorilie straightened in disbelief. ''Why? Anger is so useless.''

''It also serves as a doorway and a vent for grief.''

''What are you grieving for, Rafe, that makes you so angry?''

''I'm not grieving for anything. Maybe I'm angry because you're not. Hal Ketchum and his family killed your grandfather. Your parents. Somebody ought to be pissed.''

''It will not bring them back.'' She shifted on the boulder. The underlying violence of his tone revealed the tumultuous state of his spirit.

''For a woman who passionately abhors violence and death, you take the slaughter of your family without much emotion. I don't understand your attitude, and that's what angers me, Lorilie.''

''Why must you understand? So you can try to change me?''

''Hell, I don't want to change you. I'm looking for a way to make sense of this.''

His anger exceeded her refusal for the justice he wanted to deliver in her name. ''You wish to be their judge, jury, and executioner. I do not. There is the difference between us.''

''It's a helluva lot more than that, Lorilie.''

''When you pinned Hal against the tree today, you were frightening, and in complete control. The only time you were genuinely angry was when I pleaded for his life. You were angry with me. But you let him go.''

''Yeah, I let the son of a bitch go,'' he spat through clenched teeth.

''You did not know my family. Do not use them or me as an excuse for venting your fury.'' She suspected the Ketchums were a small part of his rage.

She stood, wishing she had not followed him outside.

"Anger is useless. Set it aside and take a look at the source. It isn't the Ketchums. Even I can see that, Rafe, and it required no special Gift."

Certain of his retreat into silence, she left him in the darkness. On shaky legs, she returned to her pallet and stared at the shadows.

The first glimmers of dawn lit the hole at the apex of the cavern before she closed her eyes. Rafe had not returned.

Late in the afternoon, she visited with a tawny cougar scarred by territorial victories. The cougar would watch her enemies.

After a romp with the accommodating grizzly and her cubs, she and Rafe fished for dinner in a trout-laden creek.

"How does your telepathy work?" Rafe laid the dinner fire with wood he'd collected on their return.

"Telepathy? What a strange word." She continued their dinner preparations. The routine they developed simplified their efforts. "Animals relate to images and the sound of my voice. A few understand when I speak aloud. Mostly, they respond to tones combined with an image I project. If they are fearful, I absorb the brunt of their fear and soothe them with reassuring images."

"Does the transference of their fear make you afraid?"

"It passes though me like a breeze goes through the trees." She set her knife aside and looked at him. "Does that make sense?" Laughter trickled out of her throat. "Possibly not. Words are inadequate for describing what goes on in my head."

"Actually, what you say does make sense."

"What a relief." She resumed preparing the trout for the skillet.

"I tried what you asked of me, Rafe. Turning a cougar or a bear into a watchdog may take some time. They are like you." She tucked her chin and spoke an octave lower.

"See the threat. Flee or fight. Fight with a killing intent until the threat is gone."

"Hmmm. Very sound logic. What about the wolves?" He laid the final log on the smokeless blaze.

"Loner is easy. He has accompanied me for a long time. He knows and anticipates my habits. The other wolves might be useful in warning when the Ketchums enter their territory. However, they, too, will take some cultivation."

"We may not have time for training." The way he studied her made her uncomfortable.

"I will do my best." She set the skillet aside, then crossed her arms and faced him. "Are you still angry with me?"

A half smile lifted the left side of his mouth. "You know, for someone who hasn't had a wide acquaintance with Outsiders, you're very astute."

"I'll take that as a compliment."

"It is. Tell me, the . . . gifts you were born with, can they bend time and fold space?"

Just when she thought she understood his odd phrasing, he confounded her. "Time is invisible."

"So is the breeze that passes through your mind and removes the fear you take from the animals."

"But that has nothing to do with time. The exercise of a talent demands a toll. Tonight, I am very hungry because I spent so much time communing with the animals. Remember Marica when she first laid hands on Craig? How ravenously she ate?"

"Yes." He nodded thoughtfully.

"Ours are tangible Gifts. Controlling the wind is exhausting." Her hand followed her assessment of the fine sanctuary Grandfather fashioned. "Molding rock like this takes months and prodigious concentration and energy. Grandfather ate like a bear during the salmon run when he made this shelter."

He eyed the cavern with a mix of satisfaction and admiration. "I wondered about that."

"An intrinsic element of the universe, such as time, is unfathomable. How would you hold back a second or move forward a minute?" Mulling over the concept, she carried the frying pan to the hearth. "Minutes, hours, days. Those are names we give portions of time, just as we call a wolf, a wolf. Believe me, the wolf does not call himself a wolf. Another creature is either his kind, food, or a threat."

She set the skillet on the grate over the fire. "I digress. The man born with the Gift of molding time would have to be very strong physically and mentally, and the Gift extremely powerful." She took the spatula he offered and arranged the fish. "How would he even know he had it?"

"You're sure it would have to be a man?"

"I believe so because of the physical toll such a Gift would demand. Of course, we are speaking hypothetically. I cannot be certain." Head cocked, she studied Rafe. "Why would you ask such a strange question?"

"Let's say I'm looking for a quick way to travel." He arranged their cups on the hearth and made a show of pouring the strong tea she brewed.

"If you found it, where do you want to go, Rafe?"

"Home."

When he met her gaze, the yearning in his eyes sent waves of gooseflesh down her body. "Where is home?"

"A long, long way from here."

For the span of several heartbeats, she sensed an overwhelming sorrow from the predator within him. It flowed through her mind in gale-force winds.

"I can make the pain go away," she whispered in a shaky voice. "For now."

"How, Lorilie? By stealing bits of my black soul a piece at a time and polishing the stains? Why can you read me so easily?" Anguish tinged his words. Sorrow chiseled his features.

"I don't know. Could it be you have become as much a predator as you are a man?" The daring conjecture escaped in a whisper.

"Very possible." The soft answer sent a chill along her spine.

"When I . . . Before . . . When I stayed your hand from the wolves . . . I meant no harm, but I hurt you, didn't I?"

"You damn near broke me into a million pieces, Lorilie. You robbed me of my will. You paralyzed my body. You neutralized my instincts, but you left my conscience, and I had promised to protect you. When the wolves knocked you off your feet and I couldn't move . . ." He swallowed hard, his eyes narrowing in remembered anguish. "I understood the true meaning of defeat."

Tears stung her eyes. The predator in him remained quiet. "I never meant to hurt you."

"But you would do it again, given the same circumstances."

"No," she cried, longing for understanding. "I would never do that to you again. I swear to you, I will not. Have you no idea how dear you are to me? I would go to the Ketchums rather than put you at risk."

With the speed of a lightning strike, he closed the distance between them and gripped her shoulders. "Never, never ever think that again. Understand?"

The anger storming his furrowed brow was a relief from his pain, though she saw it was only a mask. "The last several days, I make you angry or I make you sad, and I am at a loss why," she said.

He gathered her against his chest. The scent of him, of pine and fresh air, filled her nostrils. Her arms rose to circle his waist. Embracing him was like caressing sun-heated stone. The press of his cheek on the crown of her head provided a sense of security. The steady thud of his heart sounded like music in her ear.

"What a mess this is," he breathed, his whiskered jaw gliding across her hair with a grating sound.

"I suppose it is." She stroked the corded muscle along his backbone. "Can we fix it?"

"We have to. I'll work on it." He kissed her forehead, then released her. "Right now, we're going fishing."

Lorilie let her fingers trail over his ribs, reluctant to abandon the peace she found in his embrace. And she wanted so much more. "Our dinner—"

"Is ashes." He wrapped a rag around the skillet handle and lifted it from the grate. "If we soak the pan for three days, it might come clean."

"It might rust into nothingness." She retrieved her jacket.

Dusk colored the western sky. Fortunately, the fish were hungry, too. In a short time, they returned to the sanctuary and carefully watched their dinner.

The next nightly visit with Craig and Marica passed quickly. Curiosity sharpened Lorilie's hearing as she listened closely to the conversations between Craig and Rafe, but gathered no further insight. At times, they seemed to say more with their silences.

Patience, she reminded herself when they left the cabin. Rafe possessed the nature of a predator: he might be led, but never pushed. In a time of his choosing, he would tell her about his home and the ones waiting for him.

"Will you do something for me?" he asked.

"If I can." She smoothed the quilts on her pallet.

"Don't argue with me."

Perplexed, Lorilie looked over her shoulder in disbelief. "What is it you think I will argue with you about?"

"You going back to Marica's and staying put for a couple of days."

"Why would I go Marica's?"

"So Craig can watch out for you." He spoke with a parental note of authority.

"Are you going somewhere?"

"We need reconnaissance. I'll be back in a couple of days."

Lorilie plopped cross-legged onto her quilts. "Why? Where?"

He pulled on his extra shirt, the one with the mottled blotches. "Around twenty-four centuries ago, a Chinese general named Sun Tzu laid down the principles of adversarial engagement in what became a book called *The Art of War*. The most important criteria is knowing your enemy, learning his strengths and weaknesses, how he thinks, what he's likely to do in a crisis."

At a loss, she watched him tie a black cloth around his forehead.

"I won't engage them. They won't even know I'm there."

"Where?"

"Watching them. Do the Ketchums have dogs?"

"Not that I have seen or sensed. Rafe, how are you going to watch them without them seeing you?"

"By becoming part of the forest." He ran his fingers through the ashes, then smeared the gray-black residue across his face. "This is a piece of cake, Lorilie. They're arrogant and therefore aren't likely to have laid perimeter defenses.

"When I return, we'll set a few annoying diversions of our own. A man"—when he grinned, his teeth flashed a gleaming white in his sooty face—"or a woman, can't be too cautious."

He pulled on his jacket. "Meanwhile, I want you safe. With Craig."

Incredible. He planned to watch the Ketchums and worried about her safety.

Something about him was different. Whether urgency or anticipation, she did not know which. "Doing this excites you."

Rafe crouched in front of her. The whites of his eyes

shone in his blackened face. "For the first time since I got here, I know what I'm doing."

"You have watched your enemy before?"

"Many times."

"They did not see you?" Intrigued, she assessed him. Dressed in clothing that melded into the forest foliage, an unsuspecting passerby would not notice him in the scrub. The predatorial aspects of his nature would govern him. Like a cougar, he would stalk the threat he could not eliminate outright.

A sudden grin sent a slash of white across the blackened vista of his face. "If they'd seen me, I wouldn't be here. The Ketchums are pikers by comparison."

"Pikers?" Exasperated by yet another indication of their differences, her shoulders bunched. "Do you make up words to confuse me?"

Rafe shook his head. "A piker is the equivalent of a tiny fish in a small pond. Understand?"

Lorilie nodded.

"I'm accustomed to shark hunting in the ocean. The only worry I have is you. I can't watch all eight of them and keep an eye on you at the same time."

She stood, prepared for another battle. "Go do whatever you must. I will do the same."

"Good. Get your jacket."

"The reason I do not live with Marica is for her safety. Besides, I am much quicker and more adept at hiding in the mountains than in a tiny cabin."

"Damn it, Lorilie. I need to find out what we're up against. How the hell am I going to do that and keep an eye on you?"

Gazing into the blaze of his eyes, she almost smiled. "I've taken care of myself for a long time, Rafe. Truly, it is unwise for me to go to Marica's. I will compromise with you, though. I'll remain here during the day."

The dangerous glint in his eyes shone brightly in his sooty face. "That's supposed to be assurance?"

"You want assurance instead of compromise?"

A formidable scowl twisted his face. "I want you at Marica's where Craig can protect you."

"You want." She folded her arms. "I want you to stay here. The thought of you prowling the Ketchums fills me with terror. But I did not tell you what to do or not do. Don't presume you have the right to dictate to me."

"You're a stubborn woman."

"A practical woman who can take care of herself," she insisted, lifting her chin in defiance. She refused to blink while he tried to stare her down.

"You'll stay here during the day?" he asked in a soft, lethal tone.

"Yes."

"When you visit Marica, will you go with the wolf pack?"

"Yes, I will travel with the wolves." Perhaps some solitude would do them both good. "Go."

Rafe hesitated as though weighing words locked behind lips she very much wanted to kiss. His features softened as he turned to leave. At the low passageway, he paused, then ducked through.

After the silence settled, she wondered what he might have said if he had allowed himself.

Chapter 16

A NEW MOON turned a blind eye on Rafe's stealthy exit from the ramshackle barn he had entered before dawn. The time spent buried in a stack of moldering grasses used as animal fodder had proven worth the discomfort. Several of the Ketchums had worked in and around the building for most of the day. By dinner, he understood their desperation for finding Joseph Ramey's gold. Not one of them liked the isolation of the Sierra Nevada. Daily survival was a full-time occupation demanding effort the Ketchums preferred expending in saloons. Here, they had little whiskey and only each other as combatants.

Old man Ketchum ruled his brother and six sons with an iron hand. When they lamented the need for a woman, he promised they'd have all the women they could handle once they found the source of Joseph Ramey's gold.

Rafe sifted the information gleaned from the unsuspecting Ketchums in the past two days. The remoteness of the mountains fostered an arrogant carelessness in his quarry that Rafe relished.

Most important, he would not underestimate the Ketchums. Men adept at outwitting pursuers were equally good at stalking and laying traps for unwary victims.

Watching the men, Rafe judged Clyde, the third of old man Ketchum's six sons, the most intelligent and the only one with a thimbleful of common sense. At least he could read. On the bottom end of the scale, Bobby didn't have the brains to pour piss out of a boot with directions on the heel. The cruel streak Hal and old man Ketchum displayed posed an unpredictable danger. Hank, Cyrus, and Bart were followers, like their Uncle Abner. None crossed Hal or the old man.

Earlier in the afternoon, Hal's tale of his encounter with Lorilie's protector nearly made Rafe laugh out loud. The story unfolded with all the dramatic accuracy of a supermarket tabloid. When the exaggerated tale ended, six of the other seven men expressed reluctance for searching the forest for Lorilie and her fearsome guardian.

Old man Ketchum had scoffed. There were eight of them. What man would confront them or stand in their way? Lorilie was the key to everything, even the ruin of her new defender.

Rafe climbed the hill behind the Ketchum place.

Old man Ketchum was right. To a point. Lorilie was his weakness. Somewhere along the line, she had captured his heart. Hell, until recently he'd forgotten he had one.

He had intentionally forgotten a lot of things.

At the crest of the hill, he climbed a tree and watched the homestead until well after the last light disappeared from the windows.

He made his way slowly through the dark forest, listening for predators sharing the cloak of night. He paused at a stream and drank his fill. In the faint starlight, he dug up an Indian soap-plant. Content with his solitude, he stripped, then washed. Working up even a small lather in the cold water kept him warm.

Invigorated, dripping, he donned his shirt and jacket.

What he wouldn't give for a hot shower and clean clothing. Assuming they'd be there when he returned, the lack of amenities had never bothered him while on a mission.

Here, laundry had gone the way of canned shaving cream, never to return—unless he found his way back.

Reluctantly, he admitted nothing would be the same in his own time. Though he fought it, he was changing. Lorilie had awakened a part of his shadowy soul and dragged it into the light.

God knew, he wanted her with an unreasonable, dangerous passion extending beyond the physical. Dismissing the craving of holding her against his heart as merely the lust of a man too long without a woman no longer worked. In matters of survival, he did not deceive himself. And that was the trouble. He'd begun linking his survival with hers.

Initially, making her his mission gave him purpose in a time of chaos. It still did. But that purpose had grown and taken hold of something inside him.

Old man Ketchum was right about one thing. Lorilie held the key. She knew the location of others who possessed psychic gifts. Though the notions of paranormal abilities didn't sit comfortably with him, not once did he doubt their existence.

When Lorilie led him into the valley of her father's people, perhaps one of them could return him and Craig to where they belonged.

It was a long shot, but significantly more palatable than the theory of blowing up the mountain in an attempt to punch a hole into his own time.

The thought of leaving Lorilie behind slowed his pace. Who would watch out for her? Who would protect her the next time Hal Ketchum or someone of his ilk cornered her? And there would be a next time. Given her Pollyanna outlook, he was as sure of it as of the sun rising in the morning.

Stark terror ripped through him at the thought of the

consequences she'd endure at the hands of the Ketchums or anyone like them. The residue of the fleeting emotion firmed his resolve. Starting tomorrow, he'd teach her protective and defensive measures.

Loner stood on a boulder beside an old pine. Beyond him, the wolf pack prowled the brush.

Rafe grinned at the wolf, then put away the knife he'd drawn. It still unsettled him when the big wolf acted like an overgrown, friendly puppy.

"Waiting up for me, huh?" He scratched the wolf behind the ears as he'd seen Lorilie do countless times. The fickle beast didn't seem to care whose fingers gave him pleasure. Loner panted, tongue hanging between his lethal fangs, and closed his eyes.

"You're a hedonist." Using both hands, he gave the wolf a head scratching that shook every hair in the beast's pelt.

"What is a hedonist?"

Surprised, Rafe glanced up and saw Lorilie standing before him. Then again, where the wolf pack was, she couldn't be far behind. "It's a creature who prizes pleasure for its own sake."

"All animals are hedonists, then."

Rafe inhaled deeply as she neared. She smelled of wildflowers tonight. The aroma conjured sweet, soft, seductive carnality. His body responded with a force typical after any kind of mission or reconnaissance. The rush stilled his hands in the wolf's pelt.

Though he could barely make her out in the shadows, the habits of her body language were clear. The slight angle of her shoulders indicated she stood with her weight on her right leg and her arms loosely folded beneath her tantalizing breasts. The acceleration of his heart followed the mental image of her breasts bared to his view, his touch.

"I missed you." Her soft admission heightened the fever racing through his veins. Her candor threw him off stride.

He cleared the sudden tightening in his throat. "It was only a couple of days." In her presence, it seemed more like weeks.

"I know. Perhaps I have become accustomed to your scowl," she said lightly. "Did you think about me?"

The flippant retort he typically made to barroom temptresses shriveled on the tip of his tongue. Although Lorilie was undoubtedly the most tempting, she didn't know it. Once she learned the seduction game, heaven help the man she chose as a life mate.

"When I'm on reconnaissance I try not to think about anything except what I'm doing." He patted the wolf, then started toward Lorilie. "However, you have a way of wiggling inside my head whether I want you there or not. Yes, I thought about you." More than was wise and far more than was safe.

Horrified, she retreated a step. "I did not do anything—"

He reached for her, intent on easing her fears. "I know. I know. It was just a figure of speech."

She relaxed into his embrace with an audible sigh.

Holding her brightened the shadows inside him. She radiated a light his dark essence recognized and a lure that vibrated a siren's song in his loins.

Her cheek moved against his chest as she tucked her arms beneath his jacket. The moist heat of her breath electrified his skin. He reveled in the subtle pressure of her hands on his back.

"Lorilie, this isn't a good idea."

"Will you please kiss me?"

"No," he said, then lowered his mouth to hers, stopping short of kissing her.

Lorilie rose on tiptoes until her lips touched his. Rafe became rigid with anticipation of what she would do next. Her mouth was satin heat and more tempting with her innocent daring. Though she barely seemed to breathe, her lips were vibrantly alive against his.

His callused hand slid to the thunderous pulse in her throat. In response, her spine curved, thrusting her breasts against his chest. Desire shot through him at the speed of light. Physical needs were one thing, but Lorilie's honest, vulnerable response aroused him beyond belief.

She deepened the kiss. The intrusion of her tongue accompanied the press of her hips against him, igniting a passion that thundered through both of them. His palm skimmed her shoulder and traveled lower for the treasure pressed to his chest.

His hand wormed beneath her coat, then closed on her breast, torturing them a moment longer, aching for the next level of excitement and mutual possession.

Hot, sharp desire raced through him like a heady narcotic. He struggled to think, but it was far easier to give in to the mounting, surging demands of desire.

Commanding the last threads of willpower, he broke the kiss.

Breathless, he realized that a moment longer would have been one too many.

"I think I am melting," Lorilie whispered, her unwavering gaze caught on his.

Rafe cleared his throat. The ghosts of shared desire faded softly into the night. A modicum of reason flickered. "You're not melting. It's starting to rain."

"Rain? Oh."

The cold drops had less of a sobering effect than he needed, but enough to restore his senses. "We'd better get moving. The next couple of miles are going to be wet and slow going."

"I have another shelter close by." She released him, but held his hand. "This way."

Flanked by the wolves, they turned south, away from the sanctuary they called home.

* * *

She had thought about kissing him the past two nights. In fact, she thought about little else. Last night her dreams sang with intoxicating speculation. She had awakened perspiring and out of breath. She recognized the delicious craving seizing her entire being as the mating urge. The longer Rafe was gone, the stronger the urge grew.

"Did you see Marica and Craig while I was gone?"

"Yes. They act strangely at times, Rafe. Oh, they are well enough. Craig has taken to walking outside at sunrise and sunset. Marica is . . . skittish, though she laughs easily. Perhaps she is happy Craig is an accommodating patient. It amazes me."

"What does?"

She reached behind her and touched him in the darkness. He moved quietly along the base of a scree. "Craig drinks the potions Marica concocts with an eagerness that astounds me. I know from experience, some are truly foul tasting, but he drinks them like honey water. I have never seen anyone work so hard at recovery."

The noise Rafe made sounded like a combination of a snort and laughter. "Maybe he's on a personal incentive plan."

"I doubt Marica knows about that. But perhaps he told her of it," she mused. "For whatever reasons, I did not think they wished my company tonight, so I did not stay long."

She followed Loner along a trail where the forest edge met the crumbled rock-strewn slope. She had excellent night vision and perfect memory of the terrain, but trusted the wolf's keen sight more in the almost total absence of light.

Soon the path twisted and doubled back. "You will have to crawl inside the shelter and follow the wall around the turn, then you can stand." She caught his hand and guided him along the flat boulder hiding the low entrance. "I left wood the last time I was here."

Loner sought the shelter of his own accord, but Rafe

remained stationary. "Rafe? Are you coming?"

"No," he answered after a moment. "You go in. I'll wait out the rain here."

"Why?" She turned, feeling her way across the expanse of his chest, her pulse accelerating with the contact. The next thing she knew the wall of his warm body was pressed hard against her. With unerring accuracy, his mouth found hers. Eagerly, her lips parted, hungry for the dizzying rush accompanying his exploring tongue.

Her arms wrapped around him, and not a heartbeat too soon. The flood of desire mingling in their shared passion besieged her senses. He craved the mating act even more than she. It hardly seemed possible.

Writhing, needing a closeness denied by the chilled night and the barrier of clothing, a second heart-stopping, breath-stealing sensation assaulted her. The predator in him wanted to devour her.

A cry sounded in her throat. Her fingers clutched at his shirt and jacket with no intention of taming the predatory desire focused on her.

Unexpectedly, he pushed her away, breaking the delicious kiss and the link of desire inundating her senses.

"That's why," he growled. "Jeezus, Lorilie. You ought to be quaking in your boots."

"I am," she answered, gasping for a semblance of normal breathing. "But not with fear, as I think you mean."

"If I go in there with you, we'd probably wind up making love."

"You mean, we will mate." Gazing into his face obscured by the night, she fervently hoped so. For two days and three nights her curiosity had built upon itself. It no longer mattered whether exploring the sweet desire they shared was prudent, or even responsible. Each time they kissed, the potency grew with a life of its own.

"I suspect with you, making love will be far more than sex or mating, as you call it." His forehead rested on hers, protecting her from the rain. "The first time . . ." His voice faded and he cleared his throat.

Lorilie smiled, pleased by his concern. "Marica explained the physical changes a woman encounters during the first mating." Obeying an unquenchable impulse, she stroked his cheek. Four days growth of whiskers were already becoming a soft beard. "I want this, Rafe. I want you. When we are together like this, an excitement seizes every part of me and makes me gloriously alive in ways I never dreamed possible."

He groaned softly and rocked his forehead against hers. "I'm trying like hell to do the right thing here, Lorilie. What you feel is desire, pure and simple. The worst of it will pass."

"But it does not go away."

"No, it doesn't."

"It grows stronger each time I'm near you."

"I know," he whispered. "God, I know."

"It is like the clouds above. The burden of their rain becomes too much and they spill over. It is inevitable."

"Inevitable," he murmured. His fingers tightened on her shoulders. "I'm the antithesis of everything you believe in, the way you live. . . . A stranger you know nothing about. I'll leave you, Lorilie, and never come back. Is that the sort of man you want to give yourself to?"

"Some things happen because they are destined." Cradling his face in both hands, she lifted his head. The drizzling night hid his face. "You may go away, but you will never leave me. You are already in my heart." She kissed the corners of his mouth, then outlined the contrast of whiskered skin and smooth, firm lips with the tip of her tongue. "We will slake the longing between us. If not tonight, then tomorrow or the next day."

The deep tremors of his body pressed against hers felt like an endless earthquake.

"Get out of the rain, Lorilie."

"Only if you accompany me."

Rafe straightened and drew his face from the crib of her hands. She sensed resignation in the long release of breath and the sudden relaxation of his body.

"Heaven help you, woman. You've made an offer difficult to refuse."

Triumphant, she led the way through a winding tunnel on her hands and knees. The darkness inundated them until she reached the larger interior and lit a lantern.

Lorilie took his hand. Big, callused fingers laced through hers as she led him around a stone trunk covered by an aging wooden plank lid.

Loner curled beside the hearth and watching the dark tunnel. "Lift the lid." She gestured at the weathered planks. When he complied, she retrieved a pallet and quilt. The need pulsing through her veins prodded her to hurry. She set the lantern beside him. Her heart in her throat, she coaxed this morning's decision into the light. "I choose you, Rafe."

He tossed a match into the flame growing beneath the firewood laid in the hearth. He turned without touching her. "What do you mean, you choose me?"

"I choose you as my mate."

"I'm no wolf or hawk when it comes to making the kind of lasting choice you're talking about." He turned away, heading for the dark passage into the rainy night.

"You are like the cougar or the bear. You follow your instincts because your nature disallows denial." A stone formed in her stomach. "Yet you are more than they. You are a man, and I suspect a complex one."

When he neither moved, nor answered, she reached for the pack slung over his left shoulder. "Do I frighten you?" The strap slipped effortlessly over the sleeve of his coat. She set it on the floor, then pulled on his shoulder until he faced her.

"Why do you hesitate?" she asked

"I smell a trap I have no intention of walking into

because I wasn't thinking with the head on my shoulders.''

''A trap? How can I trap sunlight? When I stand near you, I feel the heat burning inside you. When I seek the complexities shaping you, you are as elusive as the sunset with your answers. Though I know as little about you as I do the sun, I cannot deny the beauty you share or the excitement I experience in either presence.''

She studied him. Whenever he assumed a statue stillness, it seemed he retreated further from her reach than the distant ocean. Tonight, she would not allow it.

Chapter 17

RAFE WAS NEITHER a saint nor a fool. He had ached for possession of Lorilie's delectable body from the beginning. Now she offered herself, practically seduced him by cajoling him with absolutions of the "inevitable." Avoiding the trap he sensed meant walking away, or in this case, crawling into the rain.

But nothing dissolved the willpower of a man as disciplined and jaded as he like honesty and innocence. He wanted a hot, carnal one-nighter rife with libidinous indulgence.

His entire body tightened in readiness. If the testosterone storming his system was whiskey, he'd pass out drunk.

"I want to touch you," she whispered. The glide of her hand along his arm to his shoulder sent his heart rate into double time. "Without your clothes."

Beyond the expansion of his chest as he breathed deeply to steady the rampage of desire he barely kept in check, he remained motionless when her hands slipped beneath the plackets of his jacket. "Let's get something clear, Lorilie. The light you think you see in me isn't the sun. It's the fires of hell incinerating my black soul.''

The growing fire in the hearth illuminated her small, knowing smile.

In a lightning motion, he reached for her and crushed her mouth with his. The jacket she had started removing from his shoulders caught on his upper arms. Tasting, exploring her mouth, he shrugged it into place. The compulsion to touch her all over splayed his fingers across her shoulders and narrow waist. The flare of passion was instant, and seized his senses without mercy.

After a moment, he broke the kiss, knowing he'd lost the first skirmish in a war he couldn't afford to lose. Defeat would cast him into a personal hell. She was the angel leading him into the brightly burning, enticing pit. With brutal openness and incredible innocence, she acted as torturer while promising the salvation of her passion. All he had to do was walk through the fire of his own conscience and take what she offered.

''Kiss me again.'' Her nimble fingers worked beneath his jacket, tugging, pulling his shirt from the waistband of his fatigues.

''When the time comes for me to leave, I'll go,'' he warned, then tasted her lips with the tip of his tongue.

''I am not asking you to stay.'' Her hands slipped beneath his shirt. The heated passion of her fingertips on his flesh became branding irons.

The ravenous predator in him roared for the release found in hot, fast, wild sex. The man in him pulled the reins tight with a slow, thorough kiss that revealed every secret her mouth possessed. Sweet secrets. Eager for his discovery. Hungry to learn their counterparts.

''You're right. We have too many clothes on,'' he said, lifting his head.

He followed her gaze to the pallet and quilt, then released her. The hunger gnawing at his soul forced him to watch her lithe movements as she straightened the pallet.

Propping one foot, then the other, on the edge of the hearth, he unlaced his boots.

Lorilie settled in the middle of the pallet, removed her boots, then tucked her feet in a cross-legged position. Damn, she was so artless, so guileless, she had no idea of how she made him burn.

Staring into the bottomless green of her trusting eyes, Rafe knelt beside her. The fire in the hearth flickered behind her and cast nervous shadows on the dark, smooth walls.

He slid her tattered coat down her arms, then became statue still while she removed his. The slow trailing of her fingers on his shoulders and arms had an unreasonably soothing yet exciting effect.

"I won't make love with you, Lorilie." He heard the words flow from his mouth even as he unbuttoned her shirt and lowered her head.

"I did not ask for love." With the lightness of a butterfly, her fingers skimmed the nape of his neck.

"Don't expect—" Her mouth rose to his, cutting off the litany he recited to stave off the wondrous, heady effects of the desire they shared.

The flood of her passion blending with his gripped his senses. He had to have her, be inside her. He needed her with every fiber of his being.

He laid her down, holding the kiss as though the lifeline linking him to her soul was the only reason for his existence. Incredibly, she felt fragile yet strong as she straightened her body against him. And so right. So damn perfect.

Her breast fit his hand as though made just for him. The soft moans and whimpers of surprise she unleashed from the back of her throat danced in the connection between them.

The kiss wasn't enough.

He eased away and let her pull his T-shirt over his head.

"I want to feel your skin on mine," she said in a husky voice as short of breath as he felt.

He lowered his mouth to the tantalizing breast protruding from her open shirt. A ripple of satisfaction scorched his veins when he drew the nipple between his teeth. The reflexive arching of her body set up a pulse in his loins and a familiar ache of release too long denied.

Her hands moved over his skin, stoking the heat racing like a wildfire through his blood. Feather light one instant, then hard and greedy the next, he experienced the wonderment of her explorations, and tempered his need. Everything he did to her, all the sensations he introduced, were new for her.

The jackhammer trip of his heart against his chest warned him that he wouldn't live long enough to make good on his vow not to make love with her.

He fumbled with her belt, then the buttons. The trousers slid down as he cupped her buttocks and drew her against the throbbing erection stretching his fatigues. Rocking them together in the rhythm battering his raging body, he kissed her with all the desire hammering him. Damn, if she wasn't heaven in his arms, it didn't exist.

He coaxed her thigh up until her knee rested on the far side of the valley of his hipbone. The pressure of her breasts on his chest increased with each rapid breath she drew.

She slid her mouth from his. "This is burning me up, Rafe." The breathy rasp allowed her a handful of rapid heartbeats before his mouth slanted over hers in a series of brief, rapacious kisses.

The nourishment of her uninhibited response taunted his hunger. Sweet and soft, naive and devastating, her unchecked desire tore at the layers of his self-control.

In the moist recess between her legs, he found the jewel of her femininity. The sudden cry she unleashed broke their kiss. Her breasts heaved against his chest as she regarded him wide-eyed.

"Just feel," he rasped, inhaling the intoxicating scent of her desire and staring at the beauty of surprise on her upturned face. He stroked the moist valley gently, letting her grow accustomed to his presence.

The sensations surging across their shared desire and binding them reached into his loins. He had only to open his fatigues and she was his. Now and for all time.

Lorilie groped at his waistband.

"Not this time," he ground out, feeling the first promises of her climax. "Just ride it with me."

Whatever protest she intended died when he slipped a finger inside her.

She clung to him, her fingers digging into his shoulder to keep them both anchored.

"That's it," he whispered, feeling the tiny contractions against his encouraging fingers. She was radiant in her need, her innocent passion without barriers.

Her sudden climax shot through him like a bullet. The release was so powerful, the swirls of desire and satiation so complete, it was a moment before he realized he might have won the war, but he'd lost another skirmish.

Lorilie snuggled against him. The fragrance of their sex lingered. He drew the blanket around her, kissed her temple, her cheek, and stopped short of her mouth. All the while, he stroked her back, and ran his fingers through her long, silky hair that tumbled around her shoulders.

"We did not mate," she murmured.

"Close to it," Rafe breathed. Mercifully, the link between them was fading.

"Why did you give me so much and deny yourself our mating?"

He drew a breath and stroked the halo of wild blond tresses encircling her head. "It would bother me if we made love and you regretted it."

She pushed against the restraining hand he slipped onto her shoulder. "There is no reason for regrets."

"What I'd take from you, you can only give once."

"My body is mine to give, is it not?"

"It is," he agreed softly. "What you offer is precious.

If it weren't, we wouldn't be talking now. The only thing stopping me is knowing I'll leave you, Lorilie. You want . . . you need something I can't give.''

''So you have said.''

He tucked her head beneath his chin and held her to his heart. He cared too damn much about her. Somewhere along the line, she'd wormed her way in to his heart. ''Go to sleep.''

When she slept soundly, Rafe left the pallet. He sat cross-legged with his back against the hearth. With great effort, he focused on breathing. He couldn't sleep, but he could meditate in a place where not even the simmering carnal fires of his body held influence. He struggled to find his safe inner harbor again. Once there, he might discover the reason for his benevolent masochism.

Lorilie's eyes flew open. The cobwebs of restless sleep vanished.

Four men on horses approached the shelter along the edge of the scree. Silently she thanked Loner, then bid him to stay out of sight.

''Rafe.'' Her whisper cut the near darkness lit by the glow of embers dying in the hearth.

On hands and knees, she crawled around the stone. ''Rafe!''

He barely breathed.

She found his thigh and shook.

He bolted, grabbing her, then pinned her to the floor. In wide-eyed terror, she pushed at him, then stilled in submission to his physical power. ''Ketchums are coming,'' she whispered in a shaky voice, the flash of terror fading as rapidly as it had shot through her.

''Ketchums?''

''Yes. Loner is out there. He saw them along the rock fall.''

Relief flowed through her when he rolled onto his side and collected his boots.

She hurriedly dressed, keeping her eyes on Rafe.

"Do they know about this place?"

"Yes." She tugged on his arm, eager for escape.

"Damn it." The boot laces flew as he fastened them.

"Can you swim?"

"Yeah. I hear water. Is it deep enough to hide us if they come inside?"

"You will have to hold your breath a long time." She pulled on her jacket, then handed his over.

"You've done it before?" he asked, punching his left arm into a sleeve.

"Yes."

"Then go. I'll be right behind you."

Recalling the twists and turns through the mountain ending at the base of a waterfall, she grappled at Rafe in the near darkness. Measuring the breadth of his arms and shoulders, her optimism plummeted. "You are too big. At the end, the water splits into smaller channels. You cannot fit through any of them. I shall stay with you."

"Nope. You're going. Now. Summon the wolf pack and go home. I'll meet you there."

Everything in her railed against leaving him. Before a protest reached her lips, he picked her up and set her in the water. The shocking chill made her gasp.

"Take another deep breath. You're leaving."

Clearly, he had won the test of strength. She drew a series of deep breaths, then crossed her arms over her breasts.

For the next minute, she thought about nothing beyond surviving the harrowing ride through the mountain. The twists and turns taxed her effort to hold her breath. A cascading waterfall masked her splash into a gathering pool.

Cautiously she searched the banks through the curtain of water. When nothing moved, she swam into an alcove and climbed the slippery rocks. If Rafe Stricter thought she would blindly obey his dictates, he was wrong. She was not abandoning him.

She scrambled up the cliff face, scraping her elbows and knees on the jagged rock. Lingering clouds from last night's storm bumped against the mountain peaks.

At the top of the waterfall, she darted into the tree line. Loner joined her with two companions.

Flanked by the wolves, Lorilie darted across the rough terrain. The burning in her legs when she sprinted up a rugged slope barely registered. If she reached the rock fall before the Ketchums entered the sanctuary, she might distract them long enough for Rafe's escape.

Panting, she hunkered behind an outcrop. Through a thin curtain of pine and scrub, she saw the bottom of the scree. Old man Ketchum and Hal remained mounted. They held the reins of two saddled horses an easy fifteen feet downhill from the sanctuary entrance.

Lorilie's heart plunged. She was too late. Like ravenous foxes raiding a chicken coop, whatever lay inside became easy prey.

They could not have entered the shelter more than a few minutes before her arrival. No gunshots had split the air. Rafe had a knife against four men with guns and a taste for senseless death. Hal Ketchum would show him no mercy.

Using shadows and scrawny clusters of manzanita as cover, she crept lower. Inspiration born of desperation halted her. The mountain denizens might be able to do what she could not. Loving the idea, she hunkered against a tree and concentrated.

She lost track of time.

"What the hell're they doin' in there?"

Old man Ketchum's growl rocked her into awareness.

"Check on 'em, Hal."

She projected an urgent need for speed to her furry minions.

Hal swung his leg over the back of his horse, then

froze. "I ain't goin' in there with them, Pa."

A half dozen skunks trotted single file along the edge of the rock fall. Without hesitation, they skittered around the flat boulder hiding the entrance to the shelter, and disappearing one at a time.

Lorilie exhaled a quiet sigh. Her impromptu plan might work after all.

Hal swung back into his saddle. His horse shied, threatening to bolt. "I say we back off, Pa. If they rile those skunks . . ."

Muffled shouts grew louder. First Abner, then Bobby scrambled outside. Both men scurried toward their horses.

A lone skunk peeked around the boulder, chattered, then turned and lifted his tail with imperial authority and unmistakable threat.

"Ain't no one in there." Abner tossed Rafe's pack at old man Ketchum. "He was there, though. Left that."

Old man Ketchum caught the pack and eyed his brother. "Back off slowly, boys. We don't want skunk stench on us." He reined his horse away. "She's gotta be round somewhere."

"She ain't in there no more." The volume of Bobby's voice betrayed his distaste for the skunk he watched over his shoulder. "She's been there and left a bed. There was still coals in the fire, so she ain't been gone real long."

"How long, Abner?" Old man Ketchum studied the rain-softened ground as his horse retreated from the scree.

"Can't say. The bed was cool, but not cold. She can't be more than a few minutes away. She's not living there. No food. No sign of anything cooked in the fire, either. I took the time ta check the ashes."

Lorilie shrank into the shadowy, gnarled manzanita. Where was Rafe? He could not have left the sanctuary without the Ketchums seeing him.

At a safe distance from the skunks and out of hearing range from Lorilie, the Ketchums talked at length. Not daring movement, Lorilie watched. Surely Rafe had not tried the watery escape. If so . . .

Yet she could think of no other way he might have avoided Bobby and Abner. The longer she waited, the heavier became the morose pall settling on her shoulders.

When the Ketchums finally headed away from the rock fall, she remained fixed amid the manzanita. The wolves crept away. Using their impressions as her guide, she steeled against the urgency prodding her down the slope. If Rafe did try the water escape, nothing would bring him back.

Without a sound, she navigated the slope. Satisfied the Ketchums would not return while she investigated the shelter, she entered. The skunks scurried outside.

She fumbled for the lantern. Her fingers stumbled over the matches.

The flare of the match lingered as a fireball in her vision. She found the lantern and lit it. Holding it high, she was unsure what she expected to see. Of course, the pallet was rumpled, but they had not destroyed it. Had Hal or the old man done the searching, they would have burned it. She kicked the quilts aside and headed for the water.

"Rafe," she sobbed, sure she had lost him forever.

"Up here."

The sound of Rafe's voice startled her so badly, she nearly dropped the lantern. Swallowing the lump in her throat, she held the light up and to the side, then looked toward the sound of his voice.

Wedged in the jagged ceiling above the water, Rafe clung to the rocks in the shadows. In total disbelief, she watched as he extricated himself from the rock, then swung over the water and landed at her feet.

"How did you get up there?".

"With great difficulty."

"They didn't see you."

"They didn't expect to see me on the ceiling. Let's get out of here."

She doused the lantern and let her eyes adjust in the dark passageway. They scrambled into the bright daylight.

"By the way, Lorilie, nice defensive touch with the skunks."

"You knew I sent them?"

"I knew they'd been invited here by their leader. You don't obey me worth a damn, you know that?"

He was safe and as dictatorial as ever. Her heart sang with joy. Yet the notion that he wanted everything on his terms stung with the memory of his refusal to mate with her last night.

"I am not your wife or your daughter. I am not even your lover. I do what I please, where I please, and when I please. You made it very clear you want nothing to do with me."

She started up the slope and headed home.

Rafe watched her assault the slope with Loner. Several days ago, he'd thought a little time apart would help the situation.

Wrong again. He'd thought 1847 was supposed to be "the good old days" where life was uncomplicated. The same couldn't be said for the women or his own unexpected . . . what? Chivalry? Figuring out last night eluded him.

"Hell, there must be something in the water that's making me crazy," he muttered. He almost laughed aloud at his paranoia. It wasn't the water. It was the woman.

He turned his attentions on matters he understood— stalking his enemy.

Based on his reconnaissance, the other four Ketchums were at the river panning for gold or slaving over the upkeep of their crude homestead and the stolen animals.

Satisfied that Lorilie had the good sense to go home and remain with the wolves, he followed the Ketchums. The lure of watching his adversaries' hunting tactics firsthand fit comfortably in his agitated thoughts.

"Know your enemy," Sun Tzu said. *"There's no time like the present."* Besides, old man Ketchum had his pack and he wanted it back.

He found the opportunity when the Ketchums tied their horses and traversed a steep bank to a creek where they ate a meal they'd brought. For Rafe, it was easy pickings. Almost too easy. The temptation to create a little mayhem proved overwhelming. He loosened the cinch on Hal's saddle.

By late afternoon, old man Ketchum noticed he'd lost the odd pack Abner had found in Lorilie's small shelter. They backtracked in search of it.

Rafe watched from a tree. The thrill of personal triumph damn near made him laugh out loud when Hal reined his horse too sharply. The loosened cinch did its job. The saddle slid sideways and dumped Hal onto the ground.

Any one of a dozen times while he'd shadowed the Ketchums, he could have disabled them one at a time. Though the idea appealed, particularly in the case of old man Ketchum and Hal, he refrained. Undoubtedly, their kin would haul them to Marica and open another can of worms.

He followed until they turned for home in the long shadows of late afternoon. He wished he could manage a creditable wolf howl. How sweet it would be to hasten them on their way.

He started for the monoliths and Lorilie. God, he hoped she was there. After watching and listening to the ugliness of the Ketchums, he craved her goodness and inner beauty. And he would probably crave her body six months after he died, too.

Chapter 18

MARICA WATCHED THE cabin door anxiously. She heaved a sigh of relief when it opened. "You were gone longer than expected. I was starting to worry."

"We've had company." Craig adjusted the curtains on the window near the door. The early morning sun streamed over the far ridge and cast long shadows across the trees on the ridge. "Two horses, maybe late yesterday. Let's hope Lorilie is right about the Ketchums not venturing too far away from their place at night."

"I've expected one of them to drop by for a while now. They like to remind me I live here undisturbed at their whim. The only good thing about a Ketchum visit is the time between them. You must stay out of sight. They know about Rafe, but not about you." She poured a strong herbal tea and set it on the table. "Let's keep it that way as long as we can."

Craig craned his neck, then grinned at the tea. "What? No yummie green stuff?"

Suppressing a smile, Marica reached for the cup. "If you prefer—"

"*Au contraire,* fair damsel." Craig caught her hand and brought it to his lips.

Marica's mouth became dry. No one had ever kissed her hand. Intrigued, self-conscious, her hazel eyes widened. Amazement ebbed into a slow stirring in places once awakened, then abandoned, years ago. Craig coaxed them to life again by simply kissing her fingers. His sparkling eyes met hers as he turned her hand over and placed an intimate kiss in her palm. He caressed the pulse point in her wrist, then lifted his sultry, knowing gaze when her pulse quickened. The glide of his teeth over the sensitive spot promised an end to the dormancy of her sexuality.

Slowly, Craig relinquished her hand. "Thank you for the tea."

"If you hold the tea in such high esteem, I can hardly wait until you taste breakfast."

"I had something other than food in mind for breaking a fast much too long for both of us."

Marica stared at him, unsure of his meaning. "Food is what you need."

"You're calling the shots—for now." Health glowed in his teasing smile. A week ago, she doubted such a swift recovery possible.

"I will get your breakfast." A bit light-headed from the delicious honey sweetening her pulse, she ladled up a bowl of forest stew fortified with pheasant.

Craig settled at the table with relative ease. "Marica, there are three kinds of information in the world. What we know. What we don't know. And what we don't want to know."

Sensing an importance in his slowly spoken statement, she brought the bowls to the table and sat down.

"I want to tell you something in the second category, something you don't know."

"About you?"

Mentally, she held her breath. She wanted to know everything about him.

Nodding, he swallowed a mouthful of stew.

She followed his lead. The reward of her quiet patience lay at hand. The bite of stew hit her fluttering stomach like a stone.

"You were an Outsider in Monterey, right?"

"Yes," she answered uncertain how her past related to him. "I was very careful about revealing my Gift for healing. Disbelief can be very cruel."

"What seems impossible is often frightening. People have a tendency to regard the unknown as dangerous."

"I accept that I am different from Outsiders," she said simply.

"So am I, Marica, only not the way you and Lorilie are." He left his spoon in the bowl and stared at it a moment before studying her.

"Just tell me."

A curt nod replaced his lighthearted expression with solemnity. "Rafe and I should be dead. God only knows how we ended up here instead of becoming part of the Bolivian landscape. We were ready to die, as ready as any man can be. One minute we're sitting in a cramped cave, the next we're in Lorilie's shelter."

"Wait. I can understand why you thought you might die. You nearly did. But Rafe? Why?"

A nervous smile twitched the corners of his mouth. "That sorta falls under part B. We're still on A."

"All right. For the moment, I accept you both expected to die . . . and instead, you ended up . . . here."

"Kind of hard to swallow, isn't it?"

She sipped her tea, her appetite gone. "It may become clearer once you explain part B."

"Part B is, Rafe and I were in Bolivia over a hundred and fifty years from now, Marica. It was June tenth, 1998. The reason we expected to die is because we'd called in an air strike. Bombs."

Marica's eyes grew wide. "When did you say?"

"Shhh. Let me finish, then you can ask anything you like."

She had questions. Lots of them, but she nodded for him to continue.

"These bombs contained explosives powerful enough to level the mountain we're sitting on now. There isn't anything like it in 1847 I can use for an analogy to help you comprehend the destructive power I'm talking about. In short, Rafe and I knew the score. We were dead men. The bombs dropped. We felt the first ones. Then . . . nothing.

"Instead, here we are." A soft chuckle escaped him. "We went from being bombed in Bolivia to being clueless in California. Where's Bill Nye the Science Guy when you need an explanation?"

"Who?"

"Forget him, he's irrelevant. Let's get to what's important."

"There's more?" Oh, dear God! These two men had traveled through time? Unlikely. Improbable. But not impossible. No, considering Craig's feverish ranting, maybe not even improbable.

"Not exactly. I thought you ought to know about Bolivia before I asked you to think about marrying me."

"M-marrying you?"

"I love you, Marica."

"You love me?"

"Yes, Angel, from the first time you touched me and looked into my eyes. Hell, I had to pull through. I've looked for you all my life. I know what I want, and I'll go after it hard. You may as well say yes. You haven't got a chance of getting away from me."

"I, ah . . . Craig . . ."

"Sort of swept you off your feet, huh?"

"It is good I was seated." She folded her arms on the table and peered at him. "Craig, 1998?"

"Yes. Trust me, it's a very different world."

"From 1998? That means you are more than a century and a half younger than I." She had worried over the difference of a decade almost as much as being able to give him children.

"Do you have something against younger men?"

Marica laughed nervously. "This is incredible."

"Sure as hell is. I'm finally a whiz at history, only most of it hasn't happened yet."

"How did this . . ." The enormity of his assertion silenced her.

"That's the miracle of it, Angel. It's like the sun in the sky. The creation of the universe. It just happened and made me the luckiest man to ever draw a breath. I found you."

The sound of horses startled them.

"Into the bedroom." She rose. "Here. Take your tea and food."

Juggling his stew and cup, Craig ducked into the bedroom.

"I think you left out a few things I need to know. Later."

Marica remained at the table, her mind spinning.

"I love you."

His words echoed through her head. She loved him, too. In a flash of clarity, she cared not where he came from or whether he was one or sixteen decades younger. Whatever miracle had sent him to her would be cherished with open arms and a glad heart.

A banging on her door firmed her resolve. She had a second chance at love and no one, not even the Ketchums, was taking it away. Shoulders squared, she answered the door.

"Marica." Hal Ketchum tipped his hat. "We're looking for Lorilie."

"Haven't you grown tired of looking for her? Why not leave the poor girl alone?"

"You gonna invite us in?"

"Now, why would I want to do that?"

"It's the neighborly thing to do."

"What would you know about being neighborly, Hal? You've frightened off all the good neighbors we had."

Hal pushed on the door and Marica stepped aside, resisting a worried glance at the bedroom door. A prayer of thanks they had not come while Craig was feverish silently left her thoughts.

"You're not thinking of doing something stupid and runnin' off are you, Marica?"

"I have nowhere to go and no means of getting there if I did." A quick scan of the room let her breathe a bit easier. There was no sign of Craig's presence.

"Hullo, Marica."

Bobby stood in the doorway, his hat crushed between his dirty hands.

"Bobby." She acknowledged him with a nod, then diverted her attention. "Did you need something, Hal? Or is this merely an annoyance visit?"

"You have a sharp tongue, Marica. Better watch it." He picked up her cup and sniffed, then scowled. "Mind if I take a look around?"

"Lorilie knows there is no safety for her here."

"Tell me about the man she's got."

"Lorilie has a man with her?"

"Don't make like she didn't tell you."

"She has a Guardian, hmm? How interesting. Small wonder I seldom see her in the forest anymore. Who is he and how did you find out about him, Hal?"

"None of yer damn business. You don't fool me none, Marica."

"Why would I try to fool you? It appears you know more about Lorilie's business than I. Perhaps he took her away, maybe to Monterey or San Jose." She leaned against the table.

"He didn't take her nowhere. We found where she's been sleepin'. She ain't livin' there, just sleepin' there.

No more, though.'' Hal stomped into the bedroom and looked around.

Marica followed, content nothing was out of place in the crowded room. ''As you can see, I am very much alone.''

''That ain't natural for a woman.''

''As you've pointed out before, I am not a very natural woman. My herbs content me, and I have the ghosts of the those who died in my care as company.''

''Miss Marica, I ain't gonna haunt you iffen I die,'' Bobby said from the porch. ''You done healed me and Hal. I won't never forget it.''

''Thank you, Bobby. I was glad to help you when you needed it. You have never hurt me. As you know, I have no obligation to help those who do me harm.'' With a bit of satisfaction, she noticed Hal's shoulders tense.

''Yes, ma'am. I ain't never gonna harm ya.'' He poked his head into the cabin and looked around. ''Ya need me ta hunt some game for you?''

''Thank you, Bobby, but I prefer taking care of myself. I just want to be left alone unless someone needs my healing and my medicines.''

''I'll do like ya said,'' Bobby replied, then turned away from the door.

Hal checked under the bed.

''You think Lorilie is hiding there?'' Crouched on his hands and knees, he looked absurd. The most he would find were a few dust devils.

''Lorilie's a crafty piece of work. It'd be like her to hide there.'' He stood and wiped his hands on the quilt covering the bed. ''Her friend wouldn't fit.''

''Hmmmm. Big fellow?''

''A goddamn giant.'' The rage twisting Hal's grizzled features stifled the scathing comment on the tip of her tongue.

''Hmmmm.''

''What the hell are you hmmmming about?''

"Nothing, nothing at all. I'm listening."

"And I ain't tellin' you nothin' you don't know, am I, Marica?"

"Why, yes you are, Hal. Personally, I find great delight in you being afraid of any ally Lorilie finds."

"Never said I was afraid of him."

"Pardon me. It sounded as though you were. My mistake."

He backed her against the doorjamb. "You're a real smart-mouthed bitch, Marica, but you don't say nothin' I wanna hear. I ought to teach you a lesson."

Summoning courage, she glared at him. "That may be, but you are intelligent enough not to hurt the only person who can really help you if something happens to you. These are wild lands, Hal. Sooner or later, everyone runs into trouble."

"I want Lorilie any way I can get her. Got that? I shoulda seen you were the way to get her. She'd trade herself for you."

"That would hurt me gravely. You don't want to do that."

"Maybe I'll take my chances."

Bobby shuffled his feet at the front door. "Pa don't want nothin' happening ta Miss Marica, Hal."

"Shut up and go check her outbuildings. This is between her and me."

"No, it is not," Marica retorted. "What you do affects all of you. You do not understand us. You never did. Never will. Lorilie would not trade herself for me. The way we live denies the notion of frivolous life swapping.

"Tell me, Hal, even if you convinced your pa that he might get Lorilie by taking me, what happens the next time one of you needs my help? What happens the next time you need an herbal remedy? Am I going to help you? Or make it worse? Maybe prolong the suffering? And how would you know?"

"We're gonna find Lorilie. She's gonna give us what

we want and be Bobby's woman. Then we're gonna get the hell out of this miserable place. But before we do, I'm gonna kill you, Marica.''

''I know,'' she whispered, believing him without reservation.

A satisfied smirk confirmed his victory. ''Slowly.''

She believed that, too.

Hal stormed across the cabin. At the door, he sneered over his shoulder. ''We'll be keepin' an eye on you, bitch. You ain't as alone as you think you are.''

Braced against the bedroom doorjamb, she watched him mount his horse.

''Find anything, Bobby?''

''Nah.''

''Let's go hunt your woman.'' Hal reined his horse away.

Bobby scurried around the corner of the cabin and swung into the saddle. ''You sure Lorilie'll come ta like me? She don't seem none too eager.''

''She's a woman. She'll get used to you.''

''Not in a hundred years,'' Marica breathed. When she could move, her wobbly legs carried her to the front door where she watched until they rode out of sight.

She closed the door, then settled at the table. Absently, she lifted the cold tea to her lips and wetted her parched mouth.

Several minutes later, the door opened again. Craig set the revolver on the table, then drew her from the chair and into a warm, comforting embrace.

''You are one cool customer. I could smell the fear and hatred rolling off him like sweat.''

''Fearful men are dangerous enemies.'' Her arms slipped around his ribs. Warm and solid, he instilled hope in her dreams.

''The bastard threatened you, didn't he?''

''It was more of a promise.''

''He won't get the chance to carry it out.''

"I am safe enough as long as Lorilie is. Our fates were tied together a long time ago. When the Ketchums killed Joseph, they were sealed. Then you came. Now it seems everything has changed, yet it is still the same." She lifted her face and found his compassionate brown eyes warming her heart. "Are you a Guardian or my life mate?"

"I'm whatever you need, Angel." The gentle kiss melted the remnants of fear. "I'm the man who loves you."

"How can you be so sure?"

A ready smile broke the planes of his serious expression. "You remember the three kinds of information?"

Not trusting her voice, she nodded.

"Loving you falls into the first category: things I know in every cell of my body. I've been in lust a lot of times. But with you, it's love. I never wanted marriage before you, now I do."

"What if I am too old to give you children?" She had to ask and feared the answer.

"Then we'll have a great time trying, and adopt." His lips grazed her forehead. "Making a baby doesn't make you a mother or father. Loving the kid does."

"You have a strange perception of things."

"It's very different where I come from."

"Will you return there?"

"Not without you. Never without you. I'm holding everything I want, here or there."

"I love you, Cr—" His mouth covered hers with a restrained urgency. The stirrings she experienced earlier bolted into a screaming desire to express the joy in the most intimate way possible.

"I want to make love with you," he breathed into her ear. "I want to feast my eyes on you, touch you, love you, and feel your heart beat next to mine." He caught her earlobe in his teeth.

The cascade of her hair falling from the neat chignon at the nape of her neck added a giddy freedom to the desire blossoming in her. "It is too soon for you."

"Trust me. It isn't."

The pressure of his hand slid down her backbone, then rested below her waist and drew her closer. It might be too soon for his wound, but not for the desire growing steadily inside him.

Marica groaned wanting more. "I will be on top."

Craig laid a fiery trail of kisses along her neck. "Okay," he murmured.

Marica arched her neck, giving him free access and total surrender. "And you must not move."

Craig lifted his head. A slow grin crept across his lips. Excitement danced in his brown eyes. "This is going to be interesting."

Before her knees melted, Marica took his hand and led him to the bedroom. "I promise you, it will be much more than interesting."

A low chuckle rumbled in his chest. "Yes, it will. Sit down, Angel, and I'll take off your shoes. I believe it's my turn to play doctor." He knelt in front of her and unlaced her shoes. "I'll have to run some tests, check your responses and reflexes."

His sense of play delighted her beyond measure. "Have you a concoction for rust?" she asked.

The sudden grin and rise of his brows made her laugh, and she said, "Don't you dare answer that. I can hear your mind working."

"Well, then, you know Dr. Blackstone is also a handyman with a tool for everything."

Giggling like a schoolgirl, Marica had no idea what a handyman was, nor did she care. She reveled in the fun he created. She had always considered sex a serious matter. Craig's antics cast aside her old perceptions.

"Your role as the patient is helping me research what feels good. And what feels better." Long fingers slid across the outside of her calves, followed her knees and splayed across her thighs until stopping just short of the juncture aching for his exploration.

"Do I get a turn at this with you?" Arching her back, she ran her fingers through her hair. God, he made her feel feminine. Beautiful. Desirable.

"I'm counting on it."

"In that case, I'm in your hands."

Craig parted her knees, straightened in the breech and started unbuttoning her blouse. "Yes, Angel, you are," he agreed, cupping a breast.

Chapter 19

LORILIE ADDED THE last greens into the pot bubbling on the hearth.

"Yes, Loner, I hear him." Relief swept through her. She had worried since he left to stalk the Ketchums this morning.

Loner rested his head on his paws.

The sight of Rafe smeared with mud startled Lorilie almost as much as the tree branches protruding from his clothing and tied onto his torso and limbs with vines.

Laughter tickled her throat. He looked as if he had lost a battle with the forest.

The branches on his chest expanded when he breathed in the aroma of the venison cooking in the heavy metal pot. A low stomach growl betrayed his hunger.

The image proved too much. Laughter broke the dam of her restraint and there was no holding it back. She looked away from him, tears running down her cheeks. The notion that anyone as large as Rafe Stricter could hide among branches tied to his limbs was hilarious.

When she dared another glimpse, he shifted his weight

onto his left leg and watched her impassively. Fighting for control of her laughter, Lorilie turned away. As long as she didn't look at his face, she might be able to gather her wits.

"Let me guess," she managed after a moment. "The animals and humans are untouched, but you killed a tree today."

"Nope, didn't kill one, but I've climbed plenty of them the last few days."

"Please allow me a second guess. You experienced a profound change of heart and have decided to become a roost for the birds and provide shelter to the squirrels."

"I did get up close and personal with a couple of obnoxious jays." He unsheathed his knife and offered it, hilt first. "How about cutting these vines?"

The knife was amazingly light for its size, and well balanced. "Truly, you surprise me by trusting me with your knife. What if I slip and cut you?"

"It crossed my mind. I figure you're probably entitled to a pound of flesh."

Not a scratch marred the flat, gray-black blade. The edge gleamed in the firelight. "Is it as sharp as it looks?"

"Sharper." He pulled sprigs of pine from his pack, then tossed it against the wall.

The knife in her hand forgotten, she stared at the pack, then at him. "How did you get it back?"

"I took it when they weren't looking. Stealth is the name of that game." A playful wink accompanied his grin. "Maybe they thought I was a walking tree. Then again, maybe they had no idea I was within ten miles of them."

Considering his foliage, the former seemed most probable, until she recalled him clinging to the ceiling at the small shelter. Neither of the Ketchums had suspected his presence. "Do you have any idea what they would do if they caught you?"

All traces of levity vanished. "Probably a better one

than you do, Lorilie. Men like the Ketchums live in every era and in every country. The more advanced the culture, the greater their depravity and the misery they spread.''

''You followed them the last couple of days?'' Her fingers tightened on the knife. The man possessed a death wish.

''Yeah. They're an easy day job since they go home at dusk and huddle around their fire. Do us all a favor and keep the wolves serenading them at night I don't want them to rest easy.'' He pulled branches out of the vines looping his thighs and calves. The fire flared, fueled by the branches and twigs he tossed on the flames.

''I understand, somewhat, why you sat on the hill and watched them for two days. From a safe distance, you had room for escape if they saw you. What do you gain by following them?''

He paused. ''Think about it, Lorilie. A cougar stalks his prey. He learns its habits, which way it will run when attacked, where it will hide, and what sort of defensive measures it will take. He calculates when it will turn and fight and how hard. I'm just getting to know the neighbors.''

''Rafe, this is dangerous. Very dangerous.''

''Cut these off me or give me back the knife.''

''You are the most stubborn, contrary, overbearing, dictatorial person I have ever met.'' She reached for the vine around his chest. ''Exhale.'' She pulled hard, then cut it. The vine whipped through the air, then writhed on the ground like a dying snake.

''On second thought, maybe I'd better do this myself.''

''Too late.'' She wiggled her fingers under the loop at his waist. When he exhaled and sucked his stomach into concavity, she sliced through the bond.

''We may have trouble.'' He took the knife from her and worked on the fastenings around his legs.

''Do they suspect the sanctuary is here?''

''I don't think so. Hal and Bobby paid Marica a visit.

I found Craig climbing out her bedroom window. I hung around until they left, then followed them. They don't know Craig's staying there, but it sounded like Hal has a bone-deep hatred of Marica.''

''Hal Ketchum hates anything he's afraid of, especially Marica and me. He pesters her every now and then, but he will not harm her.'' She returned to the hearth and stirred the greens. ''After you wash up, we can eat.''

Eyeing the mud flaking from his arms and face, she released a sigh. ''You are very dirty. I suppose I could show you the hot spring.''

Disbelief blanked Rafe's features. ''What hot spring?''

She mimicked his expression. ''You certainly did not think I bathed in tepid water, did you?''

''Hell, yes. I did. You've been holding out on me?''

''Do you honestly think Grandfather would spend the time carving this place from the stone and not provide hot water?''

''When it comes to that, I live in ignorance of what's possible. But while you're at it, why don't you show me the back door. After seeing the last shelter, I'm sure there is more than one way out of here.''

''There is.'' Lighting a lantern as she crossed the cavern, she led him around the water basin. At what appeared to be a granite phalanx, she angled through an opening.

''I am impressed,'' Rafe said from behind her. ''It's an optical illusion. I stood in front of this wall and didn't see the passage. Your grandfather knew his stuff.''

''He was an amazing man. Kind. Gentle. At peace with himself and those around him.''

''Until the Ketchums.''

''Until the Ketchums,'' she agreed, hoping a calm tone would soften the flare of injustice she perceived in his mood.

Inside the hot spring's chamber, she set the lantern down. The mica-lined walls and ceiling reflected the golden lantern glow in a million gleaming facets. Lazy steam curled across the pool surface.

"It is not scalding hot, just comfortable. I believe it has cooled a little since Grandfather died, which is to be expected. Molding nature into human concepts requires a constant diligence. Without it, nature reverts back to her old ways."

"It looks like a hot tub built in stone." Rafe knelt and tested the water.

"I just told you that is what it is." The chamber grew warm at the thought of him naked in the water.

"Uh, yeah. You did." He pulled a root from his pocket, crushed it, and lathered the sap over his hands and face. "Damn, I can shave with hot water."

"It is easier with hot water?" If she had shown him the chamber earlier, he might not have cut himself every time he scraped his whiskers.

"Much." He splashed water over his arms and face, then rose. "Where are the exits?"

She retrieved the lantern and led him through a mica-plated passage as artfully disguised as the one leading into the hot spring. The sound of the raging river grew louder with each step. She doused the light before taking the final two turns. "Put your hand on my shoulder. I'll lead you out."

She stopped on the narrow ledge. Below, the river raced to the sea. Overhead, stars cut a swath across the black night. The heat of Rafe's hand on her shoulder made her overly warm. She shrugged it away. The ghostly impression turned icy cold.

"The twists in the passage thwart the wind. The escape route is along the cliff face. You must walk sideways on the ledge outside for a little ways. Where it ends, if you look closely, you can detect handholds and steps. From the far side of the river, they appear a part of the rock."

"Does the other escape route end here, too?"

"There are two others. One comes out left of where

we're standing now. The other is a tunnel. . . . It's questionable whether you could fit through. The passage emerges about a quarter mile from the entrance we use, on the downslope of the ravine among the mossy boulders. Right now, several badgers are living beside it.''

''Thanks for the warning.''

''Let's go back. I'm hungry. I'll show you the others after we eat.''

''Will you go to Marica's with me tonight?''

She glanced over her shoulder. The dampness from his freshly washed trousers seeped into the clean shirt he wore. ''I thought you might want to go alone. They have not seen you for a while.''

''I'd like you to come. I missed you today.'' A strained tightness laced his admission. He sat on the floor and pulled on dry socks. They had kept a silent distance since the Ketchums found them in the small shelter.

Lorilie resumed fastening the clusters of herbs on the drying rack. ''I will go.'' The hand of a fool who had missed him, too, reached for her coat.

''Wait, Lorilie.''

She pushed her arm into her coat sleeve. ''What for?''

''Do you want to talk about what . . . didn't happen last night?''

Horrified at the prospect, she backed away. Caught in his grasp, her coat sleeve peeled down her arm. She clung to the cuff. ''What on earth makes you think I wish to put my humiliation into words? Especially with a man who found me unworthy of mating with?''

He motioned toward their usual seats. ''Women seem to want to talk about how they feel when they're angry or hurt.''

''Apparently you know a lot more about women than I do. Since you are more knowledgeable, you talk and let me listen.'' She relinquished her coat, then assumed her favorite perch on the trunk.

Her gaze gravitated to his clean-shaven face. Showing him the hot spring was a mistake. As a mud-caked tree, his allure was less potent. Avoiding the steady scrutiny, she wedged her hands between her thighs and swallowed the lump in her throat. If she kept her mouth closed, she would not make a bigger fool of herself.

"I've made difficult decisions before and lived with the results. Sometimes men died because of my decisions. Men I'd trained, lived and laughed with. Good men." The rigidity of his shoulders and the precision of his words revealed his difficulty in sharing such private thoughts.

Lorilie paid close attention, wondering why he allowed the glimpse into his secret self.

"Our adversaries had no mercy. Neither did we. We were part of a quiet conflict. Those adversaries were far more depraved than the Ketchums, and a lot smarter. They had resources you can't begin to imagine, Lorilie." He tented his fingers and rested his elbows on his knees. "The men on both sides knew what they were doing. They knew the consequences.

"Last night, you knew what you were doing too, but you didn't know the consequences." His eyes softened in a silent plea for understanding. "I don't want you hurt. I don't want to see your big green eyes weeping when I lie down to sleep ten years from now, knowing I was the reason you were hurt and filled with regret.

"After I'm gone . . . you wouldn't hate me. You wouldn't even want revenge. But you'd never forget, and neither would I."

Lorilie studied him. "What kind of place do you come from where you take life with impunity, but deny the marvelous mating our bodies pleaded for? The sensations you awaken in me are part of life, not death. Death cannot be so exciting, so wondrous." Her fingers curled into fists and resisted touching him.

"You deserve more than a quick affair and a hasty

departure. You need someone who will stay around—''

''Rafe, you have repeatedly assured me you are not such a man. Look at me. Really see me as I am, not a frail damsel like those in the books I've read. I roam the forests with the wolves. My companions have fangs and claws. I've faced death, including my own. My great fear is dying without knowing completion with my life mate. If by innocent you mean I have not mated, then yes, I am.''

''Lorilie—''

She waved off his objections, and continued. ''Innocence does not mean ignorance. Animals and people have similarities. Some choose a life mate. Some mate for a season. Some mate with as many as they can, then move on. Is that what you mean, Rafe? You will leave after our season and go your way?''

''Yes,'' he answered, his face unreadable. ''I'd only last the season. You want more. You deserve more. I want a clean break when the time comes.''

''If you left today, my heart would ache and I would forever wonder why you refused me. Finally, I wonder who put you in charge of making a decision for me when you will leave as quickly as a male grizzly once he is certain his seed is sown.''

The tips of his tented finger supported his chin. ''I don't want it that way.''

''You made your intentions clear from the beginning. I expect nothing from you.''

''Maybe not. But I do. When I'm around you, I end up doing things I wouldn't normally do. It goes against my nature.''

''Letting Hal live?''

''For one. I can tolerate it. Just barely.'' His shaking head lowered until his forehead rested on his spiked fingertips. ''You. This place. This time. It's changing me. Damn it! I don't want to change. I need the calluses.''

''A callused man would not care for anything beyond

the mating urge. Why did you come here if it is dangerous for you?''

''Damned if I know.''

''Rafe, this is a long way from any settlement. No one ventures here by accident. I cannot believe you have no idea why you climbed into these mountains.''

His head shot up. Agony blazed in his piercing gray eyes. ''You tell me how I got here.''

Struck by his barely harnessed fury, she recoiled. ''How would I know?''

''Somebody knows. You're the most likely one here.''

''I have no idea where you came from, let alone why you came here.'' The fine hairs at the nape of her neck rippled in warning.

''Not why. Hell, I haven't gotten to why,'' he growled. ''How! *How* I got here.''

Loner trotted up beside her. Reflexively, she stroked his head, soothing them both. ''It appeared you walked.''

''Carrying Craig while he bled to death?'' He bolted off the stool, shoved his hands into his pockets and looked around the cavern as though it was a cage.

A flick of her tongue wetted her dry lips. ''When Craig was shot . . . Where were you? Where is the man who shot him?''

''He's dead. I killed him.'' Cold eyes found her and sent a chill along her spine. ''Before I knew he'd shot Craig. It was a long way from here, Lorilie. A very long way.''

Prudence cautioned her on the side of silence, but something stronger than curiosity prodded a whisper. ''How far away?''

''Far. Let's go. It's getting late.''

It was too much. ''I think not.'' Anger rose and brought her to her feet. ''You enter my fortress uninvited. You tell me where and when I can go. You impose your ideas of what is good for me. You ask for my dearest secrets, and get them. And what do you give in return? Nothing except edicts and orders.''

''You're right. I'm a class-A bastard. End of discussion.'' He grabbed his jacket and rammed his arms through the sleeves.

''I care nothing about your parents' marital situation. This discussion is not over. You may refuse participation, but that does not end it, Rafe. It changes nothing.''

''Don't accuse me of not making concessions, Lorilie. Every breath any Ketchum takes is a concession from me. The sooner you're away from here, the better. All I ask is directions into the valley where the rest of the Gifted are.''

''Then you will leave?''

He picked up her coat. ''As soon as I find the man who brought us here, we're gone.''

She tucked away his small revelation. Pressing for answers netted only his anger. At the moment, they had indulged it far more than was wise. She took her coat and shoved her arms into the sleeves. ''I am going to Marica's. Are you coming?''

He snatched his jacket from his pack and doused the light. ''How much fuel do you have for the lanterns?''

He could change the subject and clamp down his ire in the blink of an eye. Lorilie could not. ''Enough for now.''

''But not enough for later, whenever later is,'' he grumbled.

''What does it matter?''

''Just figuring out if I need one barrel or two.''

She scurried through the passage, then waited for him in the outer chamber. ''The big general store is over a hundred miles west of us. If you leave before dawn, you might make it in a week.''

''No need. The Ketchums have plenty. Let's call it a trade for the pigs they're fattening up.''

''Of course they will give it to you when you knock

on the door and ask.'' She slipped into the chilly night and checked the cloudless sky.

''We'll see.''

Several wolves from the pack joined them. Tonight they took a longer route.

Savoring the freedom and simplicity of the wolves, Lorilie ran ahead with them. When Rafe seemed in no particular hurry, she scrambled up a sharp rise. Flanked by old friends, she surveyed the land rising into the starlight. The absence of moonlight turned the vista below into a sheet of darkness. In her mind's eye, she saw the contrasts and angles shaping the hidden panorama.

The wolves howled lonesome calls across the distance. The return howls carried a forlornness she felt whenever she thought of Rafe leaving.

When she caught him on the trail, she walked beside him.

''Are you done being mad at me?'' he asked

''For now. Are you done being mad at you?'' She tilted her head just enough to catch his sudden grin.

''Probably not.''

''Is it possible you have things backwards? Maybe men need to talk when angry or hurt. I see no need of it for myself.''

He tugged the braid running down her back and chuckled sadly. ''Lovely Lorilie, I've told you more about myself than I've ever told anyone else. Men like me, we're trained to be tight-lipped. When we do talk amongst ourselves, most of us swap lies, but nobody calls them on it.''

''Lies? About what?'' Why would men who liked one another lie?

''Sex. Women. Drinking. Sports. You name it. We don't discuss anything that points out our differences, like religion or politics.''

"Your secrets are safe with me." The soft glow of Marica's cabin winked through the trees. "Wolves do not speak and the rest of the night creatures don't care."

"I care," he said, and kept walking.

Chapter 20

CRAIG RADIATED THE thoroughly satisfied contentment of a man who'd spent the day in bed. And judging by the tender glances and constant touches he and Marica exchanged, the healing hands she laid on him had little to do with medicinal intent.

Rafe didn't know whether to congratulate Craig or box his ears. If Lorilie noticed the change, she gave no sign.

"How light can you travel, Marica?" Rafe took stock of the shelves laden with containers bearing cryptic inscriptions.

The shine in her hazel eyes dimmed as her gaze flitted from one item to the next in the homey cabin. "I can leave everything but the essential medicines. I need seeds for my next herb garden. And my journals. The rocking chair . . ."

"Stays," Rafe said softly. "I'm sorry."

"Stays," Marica agreed, her eyes lingering on the heirloom barely visible in a shaft of light probing the darkness of the bedroom.

"I'll make another." Craig took her hand. "We'll put it in the house I'll build for you."

Furniture and houses? "Excuse us." Rafe opened the cabin door and Craig followed without a word.

"What did I say to anger Rafe?" asked Marica.

"Nothing, Marica," he heard Lorilie say as Craig pulled the door closed. "They are going to talk about women, sex, sports, and something else they lie about."

"What?" Craig asked, heading back toward the door.

Rafe caught him. "Leave it alone. Trust me, you'll be a happier man if you don't ask her any questions. They multiply in Lorilie's head like cloned rabbits with a missing link in their DNA."

"Thanks for the hand this morning. I would have hated like hell for Hal to have caught me climbing out Marica's window. Another week, and I'll be able to do that without damn near killing myself."

"Good. I want us out of here in less than two weeks. The Ketchums are spending more and more time looking for Lorilie." Rafe walked away from the porch and well out of earshot from the cabin.

"I'll be ready. Meanwhile, what the hell is eating you?"

"What are you doing promising Marica furniture and a house?"

"Making her happy, I hope. She's consented to marry me."

The proclamation rolled around Rafe's head like a ball bearing on a warped roulette wheel. Once it settled into a niche, the wheel continued turning. He braced himself against a tree. "Did you say . . . marry?"

"Yep. If I had a cigar and a bottle of Jack Daniels, we'd celebrate right. I'm a happy man."

"You told her." The words came out flat.

"Why not? Thank God she didn't think the fever burned up my last brain cell. She's an amazing woman, Rafe. I couldn't ask her to marry me without telling her where I came from."

"Technically, we're missing. We got here one of two

ways. Either the explosion of bombs split some sort of time veil and hurled us back here, or one of the Gifted summoned us. If someone brought us here, they can send us back.''

''To what? I didn't leave anything in Bolivia. Choosing between staying here and going back is a no-brainer. I'm sure as hell not dying in Bolivia when I can live here with the woman I love.''

''It may not have to be to the same place.''

''You're guessing. You don't know that.''

''Right. But I intend to find out when we get the ladies to the village.''

''You're forgetting something. There may not be anyone there.''

He hadn't forgotten. The possibility nagged at him constantly. ''I'd kill for some air recon on her father's village.''

Craig chuckled. ''I grew up in Nevada City and fished every lake within a hundred miles. Once I can walk a few miles without wishing for a bottle of aspirin, I might get an idea of where we are.''

''You're lucky you're breathing.''

''Damn straight, and I owe you.''

''You don't owe me jack.''

''Yeah, I do. But you should know, I'm not going back if you do find a way. I've got a second chance. I'm staying and grabbing it. With Marica.''

The finality in Craig's stance settled hard. In the Bolivian Andes, he'd begged God to give Craig a second chance, and He had mercifully answered. However, Rafe's duty to return to his unit remained steadfast. He had an obligation to bring his men home. Not once had a man refused. ''I can't condone going AWOL.''

''From what?'' Craig threw his hands into the air. ''This is 1847.''

''We have a duty.''

"The army is a hundred and fifty years from now. And it's not my army anymore."

"My hitch isn't up. Neither is yours." Rafe slapped the tree he leaned against. He had a better chance of making the pine listen.

"Yeah, it is. The only thing I'm AWOL from is death. I gave the Rangers full measure, a hundred and ten percent. So did you."

"That doesn't end our obligation."

"It ends mine. I've got a no-deposit, no-return miracle. I'm staying."

"If there's a way back, I'm going."

"You do that. Colonel Livingston will send you out again and again, until you come back in a body bag. But that's what you want, isn't it? You're a helluva lot more comfortable with death than you are with life."

"Cut the bullshit, Sergeant." Rafe straightened, his body tense.

"I'm not a sergeant, not here. I'm a civilian."

"You're a Ranger." Training as deep as Craig's didn't go away with a change of scenery. He'd come to his senses. Remember his duty. When the chips were down, he could count on Sgt. Craig Blackstone.

"No, Capt'n. You're the lone Ranger here."

"Appears that way, doesn't it?"

"Damn straight. Look around you, sir. These are the freaking Sierras the way they were meant to be. Nobody from our time ever saw this—they only dreamed of it. There's a helluva difference between a change of scenery and a change in life. I got both. You can't see either."

"You look around, Sergeant. It's a freaking mountain where we're outmanned, outgunned, and I'm barely keeping track of them with one hand tied behind my back and an anchor on my foot."

"You know, maybe you ought to go back. You'll never see the beauty around you, Capt'n."

"Give me a GPS satellite and modern weaponry any

day. Those are the tools of our trade, Sergeant.''

''Not mine. Not anymore.'' Craig turned away.

''Coming so close to dying changed you, Craig. You're getting soft, loosing your edge.''

''I think I'm just finding it. Death is easy. It's living that takes courage. Don't misunderstand, sir. I never figured you for having less than a lion's share.''

''I think you'd better go inside.'' Tense, angry, Rafe glared at Craig. He waited until Craig reached the porch, then added, ''Tell Lorilie I'm waiting for her.''

He turned his back to the cabin and leaned against the tree.

The changes in him put him at war with all he knew, all that was safe and certain. He envied Craig's tenacity for grasping what he wanted and not wavering. Then again, Craig was one of the Changed Men. He'd felt the scythe of the grim reaper. The escape had left him believing in angels and miracles.

Considering the shape Craig was in when they woke up in Lorilie's fortress, it *was* a damn miracle Craig survived. Marica had saved his life.

Rafe shook his head—he wasn't sure what he believed anymore. Concrete facts and schooled tactics formed the bedrock of his thinking. But now the concrete had shattered and reason meant little in this world that he and Craig had been hurtled into. Stability was elusive, always just out of his reach.

When he heard the cabin door open, he headed into the night. Lorilie followed, and said nothing.

He wasn't sure where he was going, then found the trail they'd taken earlier. He climbed the rise where Lorilie had stood with the howling wolves. The angst boiling in his gut ached for release. He considered howling, then decided against it. The wolves were Lorilie's allies; he would not distract them from guarding her.

The black landscape at his feet became a chasm of fickle serenity. It was not the benign emptiness it seemed on a moonless night. Beneath the shroud lay danger. And beauty. The admission seeped into his awareness.

Lorilie settled beside Rafe and watched the stars slide across the horizon. He had changed. The furtive glances over his shoulder had diminished. At times, he walked the forest with an air of belonging and was neither the hunted nor the hunter.

The most startling change was his argument with his friend.

"You should summon the wolf pack and let them accompany you home," he said softly.

"Home is where I find harmony, not a rock fortress. I am home."

"If that's the criterion, I have no home and never will."

"I know you are unhappy. It hurts my heart to see you grieve so, Rafe. Go. Seek whatever will give you peace. When Craig is well enough, we will leave the mountain. He and Marica have chosen each other, so they will remain together for the rest of their lives. You are free." Only the bond of being her life mate could make him stay. He did not want it, or her.

"I don't know where to go. You'll have to show me."

"How? I cannot know what brings tranquillity to another's spirit. If I did, I would." With a heavy heart, she knew she would give him anything he asked.

"I'm not looking for tranquillity. I need you to show me the way into the valley of your father's people. The Gifted. I need the man who can bend time."

"I see."

"No, I don't think you do."

"Of course, I can take you. Will he give you the peace you seek, Rafe?"

"With a little luck, he'll send me home."

For once, curiosity surrendered to the wisdom of silence. Bits and pieces swirled through her memory without coalescing.

"Aren't you going to ask where home is?"

"You already told me it was far, far from here. If you wish me to know more, you will tell me."

Rafe stretched against the tree at his back. "That's part of the problem. I shouldn't want to tell you."

"That is a dilemma." *Tell me,* she pleaded silently. *Help me understand how to help you shed what is tearing you apart.*

"I figure if your time bender can reach forward, he can send us . . . me, close to where he grabbed us. Is that possible?"

"I have no idea of what is possible. The Gift of time mutation is strange to me." A sinking sensation accompanied the realization that his departure would be forever. One thing was clear, he truly meant to leave.

"Everything I've worked for, the code I've lived by, dictates rejoining my unit. They think I'm dead, not missing." A snort conveyed his frustration. "Something is missing all right. Direction. Guidelines."

She ached to touch him, to ease the bleak pall surrounding him by holding him close to her heart.

"The world I spoke about earlier, that's 1998, Lorilie. I didn't walk, ride, or fly here. Craig and I . . . As near as I can tell, we materialized in your fortress."

Just when she desperately needed to understand, he lost her in a jumble of gibberish. "In 1998—"

"Hard to comprehend, isn't it? You probably think I'm certifiable."

Lorilie drew a long breath, the released it slowly. "You came here from 1998?"

"Yeah. One minute we were in a tiny cave in Bolivia, the next, we were here. Right now, the best explanation I can find is that we were brought here by one of the Gifted."

"I know nothing concerning time bending or how a Gifted might employ it for another's benefits." She grappled with the notion of Rafe traversing such a great span of time. "It hardly seems possible."

"I know. It takes some getting used to, just like finding words that haven't changed their meaning over the decades does." He met her steady gaze for a moment. "You've called me on that a number of times."

"Called?" Once again, understanding danced out of reach.

"You're doing it now. Means the same as questioned in this case. Understand?"

She nodded slowly. "What I fail to comprehend is what you said about being certified."

The ensuing silence quaked with the low rumble of a laugh erupting into the night.

Lorilie eased away several inches. "You can still laugh, regardless of the reason."

"You haven't said I'm a brick short of a full load by professing to come from 1998." He chuckled softly. "That means crazy. Nuts."

"Your explanation of mutated time makes far more sense, considering your actions, your speech, and your clothing, than saying you came from Monterey. There are more things possible in the world than impossible, Rafe. Part of the joy in living is discovering the next marvel or witnessing a mystery no one else can experience. How fortunate you and Craig are to share an adventure of such magnitude. I am awed by its magnificence, and honored you are here to tell me of it."

"Only you would be, Lorilie."

"While I know nothing about where you come from, I understand your wish to return. Being whisked away from all that is familiar and losing those you love is the source of great heartache."

"You know the pain of being dispossessed, Lorilie. I don't. No one mourns me."

"Surely you are mistaken. You are a good man, Rafe. Someone loves and misses you."

"Once it might have been true. Jennifer and I loved each other when we lived together. She said I loved the Rangers more, then left me. Turned out she was right. I loved her, but not enough. I didn't put her first, and should have."

"Do you still love her?" As soon as she asked, she wished she had kept her curiosity in her pocket.

He exhaled audibly and relaxed against the tree. "No. She's happy with her kids and husband. I'm glad she found the right man. It wasn't me."

"Ahhhh."

"What the hell does that mean?"

"She needed someone who would stay with her, not love her and leave," Lorilie said slowly. "That is what you also say to me. It seems you measure all women by the same yardstick without regard to their fabric."

"The ones who matter, yes."

"There are women who do not matter?"

"Let's not go there."

"Those you mated with, then left?"

She returned to his sadly intriguing assertion that he had left no one who loved him in his own time. "Surely those you work with will be glad to see you return."

He bent a knee and dangled his wrist over it, then stared across the black abyss at their feet. "I was thinking about them after we left Marica's. When I show up, they'll have a few million questions I can't answer, and just as many tests they'll want me to take, too. The army's funny that way. If they treat me like a lab rat, I'll be sorry I went back."

"A lab rat?"

"A test subject. I'd represent an anomaly they'd want solved. They'd put me in the equivalent of a cage and poke needles into me, then analyze the results. They'll ask the same questions I'm asking now. I wouldn't want to tell them about you, Marica, and Craig, but I might not have a choice. We manufacture some amazing drugs in the 1990s.''

A deep panic churned inside of her. "You cannot allow it, Rafe. It would injure your spirit. The predator in you could not tolerate confinement. You would rebel.''

"I could take it. For a while.'' He chuckled softly. "The good news is, you won't be there. You're better at opening me up than drugs.''

"No, I won't be there.'' She would be in her own time with the wolves. The image of him in a cage with needles puncturing his flesh saddened her to the brink of tears. "But you will be here.'' She touched her breast. "In my heart. As long as I draw a breath, wherever you are, your heart will know someone misses you. Someone loves you enough to help you find a way home.''

She rose, brushed the dust off her trousers, and headed for the fortress. Why did loving hurt so much?

"Lorilie . . .''

The wolf pack crept out of the bushes. She started running.

Too unsettled for sleep, Rafe was on the hillside overlooking the Ketchums at dawn. They'd taken a new tactic. Traps. Some were crude and homemade, others were simple and store-bought. All were designed to maim or kill the wolves.

Nothing would lure Lorilie within reach like an injured wolf.

Rafe systematically sprang and disabled each trap he found. The Ketchums had just upped the ante. Every instinct he possessed warned him to get Lorilie off the mountain. But Craig wasn't healed enough to travel. Even the week Craig projected probably wasn't enough. It would have to do.

Meanwhile, the only course left was watching. It would be so satisfying to take the Ketchums out one at a time. Their arrogance made them easy targets.

He retreated from the hillside. Mending the saddle cinches he cut before daybreak would keep the Ketchums busy for a couple of days. Meanwhile, the mountain would be a safer place.

It was past time he made a few weapons of his own. Sooner or later, he was going to tangle with the Ketchums.

"May I help?" Lorilie asked Rafe later. She examined the bundle of thin branches piled against his pallet. Following his lead, she stripped the leaves and let them drop onto his open jacket. "What are we saving? The leaves or the branches?"

"The branches. I'll take care of the leaves later." The razor edge of the knife shaved off a long strip of bark.

"Are you going to Marica's with me tonight?"

"Summon the wolves and go with them. I'll meet you over there." His gaze lingered on the scarred trunk against the wall. "Unfortunately, you'll have to leave most of this behind when we leave the mountain. If we could take your trunk and Marica's rocking chair, we would."

"I know." The trunk had been her grandmother's, handed down from generations dating back to a time in Edinburgh, Scotland. For that reason alone, leaving it sparked regret. If it could talk, the stories it told would pass an entire winter without repetition. Grandfather had brought the trunk into the fortress when the Ketchums became aggressive. He had laughed about Lorilie passing it down to her daughter. He had anticipated dandling her child on his knee.

Because the man she'd chosen as a life mate would not lie with her, the trunk had reached the end of the line. The fortress was a fitting tomb for heirlooms and impossible dreams.

She continued stripping the branches while Rafe checked on dinner. The way he assumed the mundane chores of daily life provided a welcome break from doing everything alone. Of particular delight was his cooking dinner every other night. His sense of fairness in shouldering the most distasteful tasks further endeared him to her.

"Keep an eye on Craig until I get there. He's pushing himself too hard."

"Marica is concerned, too. She threatened him with the green medicine. It tastes horrible. Personally, I prefer lying in bed and staring at the ceiling for a week."

"Craig is a man in love. He'd carry her rocking chair on his back all the way to the coast if she asked."

"She would never ask such an unnecessary thing."

"How much do you need to take from the trunk?"

"The family Bible. I have practically memorized the rest of the books. They can stay. Craig can buy me new ones when he is strong enough to venture into a town."

"Lorilie, Craig doesn't have any money. Pick out your favorites and I'll carry them."

"It is unnecessary. I can give Craig gold. Marica will go with him when the time comes. She knows what I like."

"Will she buy clothing for you, too?"

Lorilie grinned back at him. "I do not need much, maybe a pair of boots. Books are preferable."

"Smart woman. I'll take books over clothes and furniture any day." He approached the trunk. "May I?"

"Of course. You carried most of the books here. Leaving them for the field mice or to rot was unthinkable. I don't think I thanked you for bringing them."

"You have. Every day I spend here."

Their gazes locked. Desire simmered under pressure.

Rafe lifted the trunk lid, then straightened. She noticed the movement of his throat as though he swallowed a lump similar to hers that kept her from speaking. She would remember him this way, hungry for her, tense with denial, and loyal to his commitment until he drew his last breath.

In her dreams, she stood first in his heart. In her dreams,

she slept in his intoxicating embrace at night and he moved mountains by day. If she came first, together they would strip away the calluses layered upon his tender heart. Together they would explore the fiery passion searching for the tiny fracture in their weary defenses and ready to overwhelm them. In her dreams, she professed her love freely and heard him whisper that he loved her, too.

In her dreams.

With wrenching deliberateness, she lowered her gaze. A long, straight branch filled her hand.

"What are you making with these?"

"Weapons."

Their fundamental differences registered with the force of a slap. She tossed the branch onto the pile like another broken dream.

Chapter 21

LORILIE PREFERRED BITING her tongue until it bled to asking how Rafe got lantern oil. Whenever she thought of him entering the Ketchum's homestead and risking capture, her knees buckled and her vision blurred.

In the light of the lanterns blazing beside the river, she slid an ax blade along a tree trunk, smoothing the surface. The night sounds changed. Thuds, bumps, and swishes marked Rafe's strenuous progress as he hauled another tree trunk through the brush.

Building the raft for the first leg of their trek through the mountains was crucial for their departure plans. The two of them had worked from dusk through dawn the last three nights. Potential discovery added an unspoken urgency. Eventually, one of the Ketchums would stumble across the cut tree stumps in the daylight. The prospect of them finding the raft before it was completed added incentive to finish quickly, then leave.

Satisfied the branch stubs along the log were smooth enough, she glanced at the sky before starting on the next. "It will be dawn soon."

"This is the last log we need." Rafe bullied the heavy tree trunk into place, then untied the hauling rope. After coiling it, he unfastened the rope and hide harness fashioned around his chest and shoulders. With brute strength, he had prodded and dragged each log to the riverbank.

Lorilie rocked the final log with her foot. Most of the branch nubs were already hacked clean. "I can do my own chores, Rafe."

Crouched at the river's edge, he doused cold water over his sweat-soaked face and arms. Lorilie listened to the splatter and splashes between bites of her ax into the wood. How she would love to wipe away each bead of perspiration coating his marvelous body.

"The hard part is done. All we have to do now is lash the logs together and build a rudder. We ought to finish tomorrow night," he said.

"Then leave the next morning?"

Rafe wiped his face with the hem of his shirt, affording her a glimpse of his sculptured abdomen.

"If our luck holds and the Ketchums keep their distance, we'll rest. We'll load and leave the next morning." He rinsed his black bandanna and retied it around his forehead. "You must be near collapse. I've seen few men, and never a woman, work as hard as you do."

When he reached for the ax, she stayed his hand. "You work hard enough for three men. This is my task."

"Pull the branches over the logs and we'll go home. It'll be safe enough tonight."

"Why? What have you done, Rafe?"

"Nothing much."

She straightened, the ax dangling in her hand. "What?"

"Kept them occupied for a while." The twitch of his left eyebrow promised he had enjoyed whatever mischief he made for the Ketchums.

"Doing what?" At times, he was as infuriating as he was alluring. "Specifically."

"They're undisciplined and don't keep good watch.

While Abner was sleeping, I dropped their harnesses and bridles into their well." The corners of his mouth twitched. "After I dropped a bag a salt into it."

"They will be so angry." She glared at him, her knees quivering at the consequences if they had caught him.

"I've got to slow 'em down, or they'll find the raft. Frankly, killing them would be a lot easier and more satisfying."

"But you will not," she whispered, knowing he would if she allowed it.

"Not if they leave me a choice." He wiped his hands on the front of his mottled shirt. "Let's finish up. It's almost sunup."

"You go. Loner watches the Ketchums. For the moment, all is quiet. It is safe."

He hesitated while looking at the scarred cougar keeping watch in the tree. "No. We go together." He picked up a branch and began concealing the felled logs.

She stretched the ache in her lower back. "It's your turn first in the hot spring. You had better be quick, because I am not waiting long before I get in."

"Tired as we are, it probably wouldn't matter." The way his gaze slowly skimmed her body betrayed his desire.

For an instant, she caught his eye. Memories of the glorious things he had done to her in the small shelter set her body afire. She craved his touch and ached for the mating he refused.

She resumed hacking away the stubs while he spread branches over the felled logs. Regardless of how tired she was, falling asleep with him watching her grew more difficult every night. The frisson increased in the near darkness of the chamber. Yet he never spoke of it or made the slightest move toward her. Although they avoided anything hinting of intimacy, the desire they shared blossomed, making the mere drawing of breath a seductive caress.

* * *

The darkness of the fortress's outer chamber promised sleep. In the heart of the shelter, Craig and Marica cuddled like fitted spoons on her pallet. Knowing the Ketchums watched Marica, they had waited until now to leave her cabin. The evidence of their night-long labors lay in tidy bundles and neat stacks near the hearth.

Rafe went ahead to the bathing pool.

Lorilie removed her boots and gathered clean clothing. She took her time straightening Rafe's pallet, then looked around for a place to sleep.

Light peeked from beyond the water basin. Eager to soak in the warm water, Lorilie started forward. The sight of Marica's rocking chair made her smile. The healer could not take it, but she would not leave it for the Ketchums either.

She met Rafe at the basin. In the gloaming light, he was as provocative as her dangerous dreams. Tiny beads of water clung to the lush mat of hair on his chest. The swath of cloth around his hips left the hard planes of his body bare and failed to disguise his growing arousal in her presence.

Lorilie's mouth turned dry. Her heart wanted to leap from her breast, embrace him as her life mate, and know the joyful pleasure found only in a complete sharing of their bodies.

She drew a shaky breath and averted her gaze.

"It's all yours," he said in a low, terse voice, then moved on.

The hot spring soothed her aching muscles, but did nothing for the ache spawned by need.

She rolled her head back and forth and watched the lantern light glisten on the mica facets like captured stars. While leaving her beloved mountain was inevitable, only now did the enormity of the impact take shape. Once the raft carried them downriver, the places of her childhood and the home Grandfather had lovingly fashioned from stone were gone forever.

Loss tightened her chest. In over one hundred years, long before Rafe's birth, the mountain would reclaim all signs of their presence. She wondered if he would search for the remnants of the fortress when he returned to his own time. Would he miss her as she would him until she drew her final breath? Would he regret leaving?

With a sigh, she climbed out of the water.

The only regrets concerning Rafe were hers for him. Though she hated admitting it, he was probably right. If they shared the intimacy of mating, her heart would crumble when he left. But her heart was breaking anyway.

She wrung out her clothes and carried them into the zigzag passage leading to the ledge over the river. The sight of Rafe's clothing drying in the slight breeze leaking through the cut made her smile. She hung her shirt and trousers beside his, then dressed in clean, dry clothing.

In the cluttered main chamber, the light peeking through the vent at the apex grew stronger. Watching the rhythmic rise and fall of Rafe's shoulder, she approached, her heart racing, then slowing with resolve. He might be angry when he woke and found her sharing his pallet, but it was worth the risk if she could lie beside him for even a few hours.

Careful not to disturb him, she slid beneath his quilt. Other than the brief drawers clinging to his hips and barely containing his sex, he was naked. Avoiding temptation, she put her back against his chest and tucked her left arm beneath her head. The moist warmth of his breathing fluttered beside her ear.

Too late, she considered removing her clothing. How delicious it would feel to have his flesh pressed against hers. She would settle for his unknowing closeness.

His arm arced around her, drawing her possessively against his body. His face grazed her hair as his hand closed around her breast. He exhaled heavily, as if an invisible weight the size of the mountain lifted from the core of his soul. "Ahhhh, Lorilie," he murmured. Gradually, the tension coiled in his muscles eased and his breathing assumed a serenity she had not heard during the long nights she listened in the near darkness.

She felt his love for her in the sound of her name and the rightness of being held against his heart. Whether he knew it or not, he loved her. He was her life mate.

She squeezed her eyes shut against the threatening tears. The big hand cupping her breast relaxed. The fires of desire yielded to the bittersweet joy of his warmth intimately curled around her. The weight of his arm over hers almost promised he would never allow her away from his side.

She opened her stinging eyes.

In the muted light, her blurry gaze met Craig's across the expanse of open floor. Sorrow lurked in his frown.

The first tear leaked from the corner of her eye. She blinked it away, then closed her eyes in defeat. The tears spilled without restraint.

For a little while, she could pretend all was right with the world. The arms holding her were there forever.

The weapons Rafe crafted made Lorilie uneasy. The sturdy bow represented death and violence. While he polished arrow shafts until they gleamed, Craig reworked the disassembled pieces of Marica's rocking chair and her old trunk onto a wheeled base.

With discerning neutrality, she and Marica sorted their possessions, then sorted again. The meagerness of what they could take must be balanced against the provisions they needed. Unsure of what awaited in the valley of her father's people, Lorilie insisted on bringing as many of Marica's medicines and prepared herbs as possible. Beyond her family Bible and a few tokens of the past, she required little more than essential clothing and a quilt.

"How much gold?" she asked the two men working beside the hearth.

"How much do you have?" Craig asked without looking up from the wood he chiseled.

"Six sacks."

"Take them all." Rafe wetted his fingertips and ran them along the feathered ridge of an arrow. "In a couple of years you're going to experience a harsh economics lesson called inflation. Everything you have to buy will cost a fortune. If Craig is right about where we are, this area will be swarming with gold miners from all over the world about then."

"I'm right." Craig fitted a brace into the base of Lorilie's trunk. "We're leaving the neighborhood before urban sprawl strikes. Depending on the location of your valley, Lorilie, we might not stay there either."

"If the valley is not safe, where would we go?" She caught Marica's eye and shrugged.

"I was thinking of the mountains south of the mission in Santa Cruz and north of Monterey. Or we could try south of Monterey in the Big Sur country," Craig said. "You two can decide which location you like best. There won't be gold miners there and the country is wild."

Since she could not remain on her mountain, one place seemed as good as another as long as she could roam with her friends. Lorilie hoisted a sack of gold onto the hearth ledge. "Your cart had better be very strong, Craig, if we are taking all of this."

Rafe bolted to his feet. Arrows clattered along the stone floor. "Damn it woman. You're going to hurt yourself. Take the sacks out of the bag." He caught the heavy bag as it tipped. Nuggets spilled and tumbled over the floor.

Stunned by his abruptness, she clutched at the gold. "This is the sack. There are five more over there." She pointed at the recess exposed by rolling aside the cover stone.

"Good grief," Craig whispered, scooping up several nuggets. "It's the mother lode."

Rafe's eyes widened as astonishment paled his tanned face. "We can't take all of it." He righted the sack and tied it off, his gaze darting back to the recess. "Jeez, Lorilie. No wonder the Ketchums are hell-bent to find this."

"They have no idea Grandfather collected this much. Even if I gave it to them, they would still hunt me. Gold cannot buy away a man's prejudice or fear." Revulsion left a bitter taste in her mouth. "Let them keep looking for their precious gold."

Rafe tossed a nugget into the air, then caught it. "If this area becomes part of the gold rush, I wonder why the Ketchums haven't found gold on their own."

"Grandfather had a gift with the rock," she explained patiently.

"And?"

She shrugged. "For him it was a simple matter of letting the gold in this part of the mountain sink. Eventually, water and nature will take its course. When his influence fades, the Ketchums will find what has been there all the while." Wistfully, she drank in the magnificence of the fortress.

Rafe lined up the gold sacks. "He meant for you to have this. Your future is secure. You'll never want for anything with this much gold at your fingertips. If wealth equated to love, your grandfather loved you immensely, Lorilie."

"I never needed gold to know how much he loved me. However, I understand its importance in the outside world."

"If we break the bags down into small pouches, it will pack easier. We'll load as much as we can, then unload it if it's too heavy for the trek."

Lorilie sighed. The gold was nothing but trouble. "It will buy what we need to start over since there is no time for planting a garden. Craig will have to purchase our winter provisions. Perhaps Grandfather foresaw such a need.''

Rafe caught her hand and led her to the back of the chamber and well out of Craig and Marica's earshot. He curled a finger under her chin. Her face lifted in surprise at his touch.

''Yes, it does have benefit. Think of it as new books, comfortable boots, a warm coat, a good roof over your head, and enough food to feed an army of your friends forever, okay?''

Gazing into his eyes, she forgot the gold and slipped into a fantasy world where he whispered her name and caressed her breast. The memory turned her legs into pliant candle wax. When his lips parted, her heart leaped with hope. Reflexively, her lips responded, eager for the rapacious pleasure of his mouth on hers. A tingling heat crept through her limbs and settled in her lower abdomen and breasts. The longer he gazed at her, the hotter it burned.

''It isn't so hard for you to touch me, is it?'' she whispered, desperately trying to understand his restraint.

''I like touching you too much. You're a fire in my blood,'' he whispered.

''But you refuse me. Which do you fear most, what you might lose or what you might find worth keeping?'' Her voice quavered at her own daring.

He closed his eyes and pressed a kiss on her forehead. ''Both.'' He removed his finger from beneath her chin.

Her pulse thundered in her temples. Through the sharp disappointment for the loss of his touch, she realized something had changed between them.

''Let's go build a raft, sweet Lorilie.''

She nodded more to herself than him. The change she perceived made her heart sing. The anger he used like a shield against soft emotions had vanished.

*   *   *

Assembling the raft took the four of them most of the night. When finished, Lorilie proclaimed it strong enough to float Marica's entire cabin over the rapids. After ferrying it into a safe niche downriver, Rafe sent Marica and Craig to the fortress. Though Craig denied it, the heavy work extracted a debilitating toll.

An owl hooted, then spread his great wings, flapped once, and took flight into the starry sky. The scarred cougar bounded up a tree and made himself comfortable.

Rafe eyed the cat. Lorilie's friends acted with more noble honesty than most two-legged predators he'd known.

"He takes orders well." Rafe spread the branches they had brought for camouflage over the raft.

"I didn't ask him to watch here." Lorilie tucked a pine bough beside the tiller arm. "I have you."

The casual words struck him with the force of a divine revelation. All the secret nooks and crannies that had yawned open when he woke with Lorilie in his arms flooded with the very understanding he tried to avoid. She did have him—heart, soul, and mind. Whether here or in his own time, she'd always be part of him.

Before laying eyes on her, he'd thought he knew the joys and anguish of love won and lost. Now, stealing a glance at Lorilie, he admitted he'd never scratched the surface of love.

"That should hide it well enough." Lorilie brushed her hands together.

Rafe settled atop a cluster of soft pine boughs in the middle of the raft. "You can't hide from it, can you?" he murmured, resting his wrists on his bent knees.

"Why would I want to hide from the raft?" Lorilie asked with a laugh, then came to kneel in front of him.

He gazed at her. In the light of the lantern burning onshore, the disheveled strands of golden hair escaping her braid took on an aura of divinity. The shadows dimmed her features, but not the glowing countenance of her inner beauty.

"I wasn't referring to the raft." He tucked an errant lock of hair behind her ear.

Lorilie's brow pinched in confusion. "Oh."

He gathered her into his arms. "Sweet Lorilie, you're the most beautiful woman I've ever known. I didn't know such goodness existed anywhere, in any time." Feeling her relax sent a thrill though him. It melted into a low, familiar pulsing of his ravenous desire. He drew her into the vee of his legs and against his heart.

"I don't know if I've lost or won." Rocking them slowly, he kissed the top of her head.

"I have no idea what you mean, Rafe." She lifted her head.

"All the time we've spent together, and the times I . . . ran . . . it wasn't you I was fighting. It was me." The soft flesh of her throat felt like satin under his fingertips. The dark pools of her eyes searched in confusion.

"You're like your mountain, ever changing, resilient, and enduring." He tucked her head under his chin and held her tight. "You remind me of a story I read as a child." Unable to stop touching her, he stroked her hair and shoulders.

"Tell me the story."

"The wind and the sun saw a man walking along a road. They made a wager over who could get the man to remove his coat.

"I'm like the wind," he chuckled. "He blew hard. When that didn't work, he blew cold and summoned the thunder clouds and blotted out the sun. When that didn't work, he became a gale, seeking to rip the man's coat away with sleet and lightning. But the man turned his back on the wind and cursed while continuing into the teeth of the blow. He clung to his tattered coat. It was his only defense against the harsh elements whose whims he did not understand.

"Then the patient sun took his turn. Like you, he merely smiled on the man and allowed him to bask in the light. He warmed him with the kindness of his presence and eased the cruelty inflicted by the wind. Of his own accord, the man removed his coat."

"What happened to the man?" Lorilie asked.

"I suppose he kept walking, unaware of the battle over his coat. If he had known, he might have told the wind how futile it was to rail against a man's nature. Given a choice, he might have opted to walk with the sunshine for the rest of his life."

"Would the wind allow him such a choice?"

"I don't know." He captured her fingers tentatively exploring his chest like miniature flames and kissed them one at a time. "All I do know is the wind stopped blowing inside me when I woke up with you in my arms this afternoon. You were like the sun shining on the ravages of a storm."

He rubbed his chin over the crown of her head. "I'm not good with words or baring my soul." The press of her lips against his chest became a circle of heat expanding along his flesh. The frisson of denied passion charged through his veins. "God, I love holding you, touching you. I never want to let you go."

"Then listen to your heart," she whispered. "At least, for a little while."

Chapter 22

IN THE BLINK of an eye, Lorilie found herself lying on soft evergreen boughs and staring up at Rafe. The war usually raging in his enigmatic gray eyes quieted in a temporary truce. Now she saw the pure, raw desire of the man. His body pressed against hers, teasing delicious tingles along her spine. She stroked his face. The shadow of his whiskers appeared darker in the lantern light.

"I love you, Rafe. I always will." He was vulnerable and did nothing to protect his emotional nakedness from the profound effect of her declaration.

His throat worked for a moment before he murmured, "I know," then lowered his mouth.

In the next heartbeat, she felt his surrender. He loved her, but could not say the words.

The kiss imparted a reverence so tender and deep, tears stung her lids and wet her lashes. Tendrils of desire unraveled in a chaos mirroring the river rushing along the outer edge of the raft.

"I will not ask you to stay if you must go tomorrow," she breathed. She wanted him without deception or thought of any fate beyond the moment.

A small furrow creased his forehead as his eyebrows drew together with an unfathomable emotion. "I know," he whispered so softly, she barely heard him over the river.

Her fingertips stroked his short hair. "I want all of you, Rafe, your desire, your—"

"I know," he breathed so close to her lips that she felt the promise of forever in her soul.

His mouth claimed hers. The anticipation of sharing the delicious sensations sweeping her senses built. The flood of commingled desire left her dizzy. She rode the crest of their pent-up need. The hunger for his kiss, his touch, his body joined with hers, burned like a dry summer wildfire. Desperate for the feel of his flesh, her fingers coiled in the close-fitting fabric of his shirt.

She drew in his scent, his heat, and the press of his manhood against her thigh. The rise and fall of their rapid breathing built with unspoken promise. The heady kiss made her anxious, reckless. She tugged at his shirt, then stilled when his kiss blended with the ravaging need of a predator too long denied. Wild, raging, and wonderful, his raw sexuality swamped her senses.

Without warning, he slid his mouth from hers, then gathered her in an embrace so intimate and close, she could barely catch her breath.

"Slowly," he rasped. "We need to go slowly." His forehead rested against hers. "You're so sweet, so soft, so much love. I don't want you hurt."

"How—how do we go slowly?" Given the desire they shared, halting the river beside them seemed more likely.

Rafe ducked his head and kissed her shoulder. "I go slowly, sweet Lorilie. You hold on and tell me if I do something you don't like. Just let me make love to you."

When he straightened, straddling her thighs, he pulled off his shirt. Lorilie's mouth became a desert one moment, an oasis for her parched lips the next. Black whirls of hair glistened across his upper chest, then tapered at his abdomen into a thin line disappearing into his trousers. Anxious to explore the destination, she reached for the belt fastening his trousers.

"Why don't you let me get rid of my boots first?" Rocking his weight onto his heels, he worked the laces with both hands. With a deft motion, he unfastened his belt and whipped it through the loops. A ripping sound released the band securing the end of the knife scabbard to his thigh.

When she started unbuttoning her shirt, he caught her hand. "I've dreamed of undressing you."

The gentleness in his thick voice stilled her eager, trembling fingers.

A smile touched Lorilie's mouth. "I wear few clothes. It must have been a short dream."

"Not necessarily." A wicked lasciviousness lit his eyes. He scooted down her legs and removed her boots. "And not if I do it the way I've dreamed of, a little bit at a time."

As if to demonstrate, he straightened her oversized shirt by running his hands along her hips, his thumbs pressing softly on her lower abdomen. They came to rest at the apex of her pubic bone.

The flash fire riding through her reflexively parted her thighs. They bumped against the iron vee of his knees.

"My God, you were meant for me."

Unsure whether he understood the truth he'd spoken, she watched him open the bottom button on her shirt, then leave the placket neatly in place. He released each button without so much as grazing her skin. Her breath grew short at the sight of his hands between her breasts. "Touch me," she exhaled. "Let me touch you."

With deliberate precision, he lifted the bottom hem of her shirt, then unfastened her trousers with the same painstaking intensity. His head bowed in homage.

The hot moist sensation of his mouth at her belly button wrestled a cry of bewildered delight from her. Flames of desire ignited along the path of his mouth. The flick of his tongue alternated with deep kisses savoring a widening circle of her tender flesh. The shirt gradually parted below her breasts. The trouser fly gaped open above her pubis in the wake of his heated sampling of her skin.

The skim of his chin through her hair evoked a gasp for his daring and the excitement of a strange, new hunger he created. Her nightly dreams of touching and being touched lacked the breadth of possibilities he revealed with each foray across her body.

He lifted her hips as though she were a feather and slid her trousers to her knees. The maddeningly erotic exploration of his mouth continued with his roving fingertips paving the way, then titillating a delicious investigation ranging down her thighs and hips.

"What are you doing to me, Rafe?" Her breath came in pants. The delicious ache he created flourished to an almost painful level.

"Should I stop?" he asked with a slow smile as seductive as his touch.

"Oh, no. I had no idea there was so much . . . ritual."

"Ritual comes in many flavors." He resumed his exciting exploration high on her ribs. He grazed the bottom of her breast, then lifted his head. Taking the shirt plackets in each hand, he folded them back exposing the valley and rise of her breasts, then nuzzled deeply. Never idle, his hands stroked her breasts through the fabric of her shirt.

Lorilie caught her breath. How could anything be more exciting, more arousing than the lightning he created with a caress? Her nipples peaked as he gently pinched and rolled them between his thumbs and forefingers.

The heady waves of excitement swept through every pore of her skin. Amazement mingled with a hunger far deeper than she thought possible.

The completeness of surrender, his and hers, settled in her heart. This was what her instincts had awaited. Only her life mate could send the core of her life force into such glory.

He, too, understood the specialness, the rightness of being her life mate. Their shared desire intensified until she thought she'd burst into flames. In the heart of the heat, she felt love—hot, patient, and ravenous.

As if reading her mind, he swept aside the shirt and caught her bare breasts in his hands.

"God, you are beautiful," he murmured. "So beautiful." His mouth closed on her nipple.

A delicious moan escaped her. All she could do was abandon herself in the wild conflagration of his hunger. The sinuous rhythm of desire pulsed between them as he suckled and nipped until she thought she'd go mad. She whispered his name in a plea for more.

He toyed leisurely with her other breast before lavishing it with the worship driving her to ecstatic agony.

They were breathing hard and fast when the chain of fiery kisses searing her skin to cinders broke at her ear. At last he was close enough for her greedy exploration. She took full advantage of her freedom. A sheen of perspiration coated his shoulders and back. His body had the texture of sun-baked granite, but alive and rippling with each motion.

His kiss consumed her. She wanted to cry out for him to join with her. The intoxicating plunder of his tongue drove her hips hard against him. She tugged at his trousers, but they remained steadfast.

Arching her back pressed her breasts against the unyielding wall of his chest.

He ended the kiss with painful tenderness. She gazed up into eyes crazed with need and chiseled features schooled in control. He rolled onto his side. "Unfasten my pants." He kissed the sides of her mouth, then ran the tip of his tongue along her lower lip, back and forth, delving farther inside each time.

Lorilie's trembling fingers fumbled his trousers open.

To her dismay, the brief drawers he wore still confined the erection pulsing against her hands. She slid her fingers beneath the edge and worried them down.

Breathing hard, Rafe lowered his forehead beside her ear.

"No holding back this time."

Lorilie's arms tightened around him. There was no hiding, no masks when life mates gave themselves to one another. "Suddenly, I feel small compared to . . ." The words faded, unneeded because he understood her concern.

"We'll fit together fine," he promised. "Unless you want to change your mind, Lorilie."

No, she did not. He was her life mate. She would deny neither him nor herself anything. "I ache for you, Rafe. It is as if I will explode in a million stars with our next kiss."

He stroked her body. Instead of soothing, his touch fired all her nerves in greater anticipation. She reached for his manhood, wanting to hold him and the life throbbing within.

"It would be best if you didn't touch me, sweet Lorilie. It's been a long time. I need every ounce of control I can muster." His head dipped toward her breast, effectively putting the prize she ached to stroke out of reach. "Next time. Next time, anything you want. Any way you want it." He drew her nipple between his teeth, and catapulted her senses into red desire.

Any disappointment she might have experienced vanished when his fingers raked the hair at the juncture of her legs. The stroking parted her legs. As his hands and mouth tantalized her, his knee slipped between her thighs and widened the wedge.

Her hungry fingers roamed the contours of his chest and the ripples of his abdomen. While she did not understand the restraint he considered essential, all thought of it vanished once his hand slipped between her legs. He worked magic in the moist valley of her desire. Coaxing. Teasing. The outrageous manipulations made her gasp for air. She clutched his arms in mindless desperation for an elusive intimacy rising within her reach.

"Yes, sweet Lorilie. Feel it build," he encouraged, carrying her higher and higher as he moved between her legs. "You're so ready."

Whatever she was ready for needed to come right now! The invasion of his finger brought a separate life to her hips. She wanted more of the sensations building one on the next until nothing mattered except him and the glimmer of pure ecstasy he sent her surging toward.

"Pleasure first," he whispered, then broadened the incursion.

Without warning, ecstasy burst inside her. She cried out as it swept through her in waves.

"Live in it. Hold on to it."

A blend of his pleasure and restraint leaked into her awareness. It felt like love strong enough to last a lifetime, resilient at the roots and capable of weathering the storms of life.

Vaguely, she felt Rafe grip her shoulders and position himself on top of her. He entered her slowly, giving her time to adjust. The pressure of his penetration grew with each foray. Just as she was getting used to him, he breached her maidenhead with a single thrust.

The sudden stab of pain after euphoric radiance sent her clutching at him, pushing and pulling without knowing which she wanted most.

Rafe hissed as her body seized up. "The worst is over," he promised between the tender kisses he lavished on her face.

Lorilie consciously relaxed around the invasion throbbing in the core of her body.

"That's better," he praised, raising his head until she could look into his eyes.

"How do you know?"

He chuckled softly. ''You didn't tell me I'd feel your pain as well as your pleasure when we made love.''

Had she known, she might have warned him. The new dimension carried an odd sort of satisfaction for the shared experience.

''We're going to take our time,'' he said through gritted teeth. ''Let you get used to me.''

Reverence tempered his drive to possess her. The control he exerted weakened the link between them.

''Stay with me,'' Lorilie pleaded, needing the heat of his love as much as the pulsing of his body. ''I feel whole . . . complete . . . when you give all of yourself.''

''I know.'' A low rumble released in a laugh. ''No. I didn't know. It's so good like this.''

The link regained its strength, restoring the myriad of emotions surrounding his desire.

''Amazing,'' she breathed, feeling the ache diminish.

''Yes, you are.'' He rained kisses on her face and mouth between soft praises. As though powerless to prevent it, his hips began a slow, deliberate rhythm. The long, slow, deep thrusts cajoled a quivering response. What her mind failed to grasp, her body intuited from Rafe.

''We're incredible.''

They were.

''It will get even better, sweet Lorilie.''

The hunger driving them into a communion of body and spirit promised he was right.

The growing ache for an exquisite release banished the last vestiges of pain. She was on the brink of understanding the great mystery of bonding with her life mate. Driven by desire on more levels than she could assimilate at the same time, she listened only to the pulse of their desire and the demands of her love for him.

She rose high against him, reaching for the elusive rapture he approached with enforced restraint. The greater his efforts to contain the wild hunger consuming them, the more she strove to grasp it.

"All right," he rasped. "Take it."

The tethers of his restraint vanished. Their combined passion overwhelmed her, carrying her to dizzying heights and unimaginable exhilaration.

She met him thrust for thrust, ascending the invisible spiral into rapture. It burst on her like a shower of stars. He clutched the rounded flesh of her hip and molded himself to her. The low, rumbling groan of his release followed her cry of delight. He was hers. His heart, his love, his body. They were bound in love as part of their inescapable destiny.

They clung to one another, prolonging the afterglow until the chill of the night warned an end. Reluctantly, he released her and she allowed it.

She dressed, laughing softly.

"What do you find amusing?" He laced his boots, grinning at her with a new tenderness in his eyes.

"All the nights we would have found Craig and Marica's company a welcome diversion. Now I believe privacy a bygone." She gazed across the river into the darkness. "As many things will soon be."

"You're right. There is an ironic twist there." He stood and gathered her in a warm embrace. "Are you all right?"

Heart singing, she locked her arms around his neck and kissed him lightly. "I have never been happier than tonight. Thank you."

"Jeezus, Lorilie, I hurt you." As though to shelter her from further pain, he tucked her close and held her.

"Next time, it will be only pleasure."

"I promise," he said into her ear.

"And I may touch and explore and . . ." Her voice trailed off with the realization of his growing desire against her abdomen.

"Ignore that." He kissed her, then released her. "Let's go home while we still have one."

*   *   *

"Go soak in the spring," Rafe told her as they approached the fortress. "I'll wash up in the basin." He squeezed her shoulder. "I don't think I could be naked with you and not make love."

Lorilie grinned at the idea of mating in the hot spring. "I would like that."

"Tomorrow. Let's give your body a chance to recover."

They shared a kiss before she left him at the basin and went to the bathing pool.

He was right. Strange she had not noticed the little aches coming to life while they mated. Lorilie lingered in the hot spring, hoping the three of them were asleep by the time she emerged. Before leaving the mountain, there was something she had to do.

Luck favored her. Rafe, Marica, and Craig slept soundly in the main chamber.

Lorilie left the fortress and joined Loner. It was a gray summer morning, the kind that promised rain and never delivered. The subdued sky was appropriate for her mood. The low, lazy clouds reflected her regret over leaving her mountain.

Of course they had to leave—for many reasons. If the Ketchums did not force them out now, the horde of gold seekers Craig spoke of posed an even greater hazard.

Too exhausted to run, and savoring the ethereal afterglow of bonding with her life mate, she sauntered and occasionally jogged beside the energetic wolf. As she ate blackberries, her gaze roamed the trees, seeking to memorize every leaf and pine needle in the forest. She touched rocks and stroked the brush in a final farewell.

At first glance, the Ramey homestead appeared unchanged from her last visit. The weeds in the garden had won the final battle for territory and flourished in triumph. When she neared the house, she noticed the glass in the windows was gone. If the Ketchums could have dismantled the house itself, they probably would have. A superstitious lot, they had stopped short of usurping the stalwart house of a man they had murdered.

Regardless of their reasons, Lorilie found comfort that they had not taken over all her childhood memories.

She drank from the well for the last time and rehung the dipper out of habit.

She gathered the wildflowers blooming along the side of the house, then went to the graveyard. With painstaking reverence, she arranged a bouquet on each of the graves. At Joseph Ramey's toppled headstone, she knelt and bowed her head.

"The time has come to leave the mountain, Grandfather. Not because I want to. Because I must. I came to say good-bye. I know you're not really here, but I feel like you might hear me better in this place we loved.

"I miss you all. Especially you, Grandfather. You taught me so much.

"I chose a life mate. I believe him the Guardian you said I should seek. How this happened . . . I cannot say. He came through time for me and I believe he is Gifted, but does not know it. There are many things he is just now allowing himself to discover.

"I love him, Grandfather, with all my heart, enough to let him go if that is what he wishes. Rafe is a predator and would die in a cage, even one of his own making. If he stayed with me out of obligation, I fear he would become an angry and bitter man. He deserves better." Detritus she brushed from the headstone clung to her fingertips.

"Everything is changing so fast. Tomorrow we leave, but you are forever in my heart, just as Rafe is regardless where he goes."

She sat in silence, drinking in the sound of the morning birds and the occasional rustle of the grasses when the fickle breeze swept along the ground. In a final act of straightening her affairs, she pushed on Grandfather's tombstone. It should be upright. After tomorrow, it no longer mattered if the Ketchums saw the signs of her farewell visit.

Pushing with all her might barely budged the marker. She tried again. Something beneath the headstone snapped. A whirring noise whipped the air and sent the birds scattering from the branches overhead. A flurry of leaves and grass formed a racing whirlwind across the graveyard. Without warning, the ground beneath her writhed like a bed of snakes. In the blink of an eye, it collected in on itself and carried her into the air. She tumbled head over heels jerked upward in a wild, swaying arc.

When she recovered enough of her wits to look around, she screamed in frustration. Tightly woven ropes netted her well above the graveyard.

Panic set in. This could not happen now. Not when they were so close to escaping. She tore at the net and rocked her body in an effort to snap the branch holding her.

She fought it until exhaustion overtook her.

This could not, would not happen now. Freedom lay only a day away.

With forced calm, she summoned the scarred cougar. The old cat's sharp teeth and claws would make short work of the rope holding her cage.

Beneath her, Loner paced the ground. Agitation heightened his confusion. Again and again he leaped, trying to catch the horrible confines of her prison.

Unable to bear his turmoil, she sent him into the forest. The Ketchums had laid their trap well. They would check it.

She ceased struggling and waited for the cougar.

The sounds of morning returned with the birds nesting in the surrounding trees. The hum of the breeze played in the branches.

As she knew he would, the cougar came. He bounded

effortlessly up the tree. When he encountered the rope, he tore at it with fangs and claws.

Lorilie laced her fingers through the netting and gathered her feet beneath her. The strict confines allowed only a hunched crouch in preparation for the fall to freedom.

A shot rang out.

For an instant, everything stilled.

The cougar tumbled from the branch and landed on the ground. A trickle of blood ran from below his scarred ear.

When the gruesome reality of what she was looking at struck, a scream of outrage ripped from Lorilie's lungs. Her keening wail pierced the trees and sent birds into flight.

"Well, well, well. Look what we caught for lunch. Where's your big troublemakin' friend?" Satisfaction twisted Hal Ketchum's grin into a sneer.

Lorilie glared at him. Hatred dripped from his taunts. She reined in the pain and anger threatening to pull her apart. Rafe had done it many times; she could do it now and deny her enemy further triumph. While schooling her heartbreak into a cracked mask of detachment, fear slithered through her stomach.

"I'm talkin' to you, girl. Answer me! Where's your friend?"

Four more Ketchums joined Hal.

"Hot damn, we got her!" hollered old man Ketchum.

"Watch for her friend. He may be out there, or he may be gone," Hal warned. "She ain't sayin'."

"She will," old man Ketchum promised, pulling his rifle from its scabbard. "Check your rifles, boys. If you see any of her critters or Hal's giant, shoot 'em. If you even think you see anything move, shoot it."

Instinctively, Lorilie focused on the threat of more death and warned her friends away. Within minutes, even the birds fled the trees and an eerie silence descended.

"Damn witch," Hal muttered.

"Cut her down and tie her up before you let her out of

the net. Fine idea, Clyde. Damn fine,'' old man Ketchum crowed, then clapped Clyde on the shoulder.

"Easy,'' Clyde shouted at Bobby and Hal heading for the tree holding the net. "Let her down easy or you'll break her neck.''

The rope lowered her, then snapped. She tumbled amid the ropes and hit the ground hard. Her head spun and her vision narrowed. Her last thought was of Rafe.

Chapter 23

RAFE BOLTED UPRIGHT. The knife he kept beside his pallet filled his hand, ready to defend against life-threatening danger.

Loner stood just out of reach, his head lifted in a mournful, ear-splitting howl.

Rafe was alone on the pallet. How the hell had he fallen asleep? "Lorilie!"

Driven by a fear greater than he'd ever experienced, Rafe bounded from the quilts. In the dank light of the cavern, his gaze rapidly scoured every nook and cranny.

"What the hell—" Craig was on his feet looking for something to shoot with the gun in his hand. Marica leaped up behind him.

The wolf continued howling.

"Check the hot spring, Craig." Genuine terror ripped through Rafe. He sheathed his knife and pulled on his clothing. "Check it now!"

Clad only in his shorts, Craig ran.

The wolf quieted. The baleful howl echoed inside Rafe's head as he laced his boots.

"She's not there," Craig said, reaching for his pants. "I'll go with you."

"No. You'll slow me down." He grabbed the arrows, dropped them into the quiver, then ducked his head and shoulder though the strap.

"How long has she been gone?" Marica stood with the quilt wrapped around her.

"I don't know. She went to bathe and I fell asleep." He picked up the bow. In two strides he reached Craig.

"I'll go with you, Rafe. It'll even the odds."

"No. Marica, show him where the Ketchums live. If they have her, that's where they'll take her. Keep the gun, Craig. You might need it. All bets are off. Shoot to kill."

Rafe scurried through the passage, the wolf just ahead. Once outside the fortress, they ran. Unconcerned about leaving a trail for his enemy's discovery, he concentrated on the terrain.

Twice movement in the brush distracted him. Each time, wolves from the pack joined him. Their common bond forged an easy alliance. Soon dread piled onto his fear. The wolf led him toward the most dangerous place on the mountain, the one place Lorilie was most likely to go and find the Ketchums waiting. Why the hell didn't she tell him she wanted to visit the Ramey homestead a final time?

Bathed in perspiration, he relied on the adrenaline rush when his lungs burned. Fear for Lorilie prevented his pacing himself over the four miles of hills and valleys that seemed like forty.

He stopped on the rise overlooking the serene ruins of the Ramey homestead. While catching his breath, he sidled through the brush, scoping out the quiet ground below.

If Lorilie or the Ketchums were here earlier, they had left.

Loner became a gray flash racing down the hillside and across the open yard.

Rafe followed at a slower pace, scanning the shadows for a sign of Lorilie or the Ketchums.

The sight of the slain cougar and the devastated grave-yard told him as much as the frayed rope dangling from the branch and the maze of shod horses' tracks.

Swearing under his breath, he wasted no time. Years of training fortified him. Yet the detachment he sought for total concentration eluded him. Fear hovered, building an agitated urgency he couldn't afford.

Trailed by the wolves, he followed the tracks. Besides the horses, he found footprints. Lorilie's. The staggered pattern halted. A swath of bare earth cut the trail where they had dragged her. Outrage welled inside of him. He clamped his teeth and held the voluminous anger to a growl that sent the wolves retreating several steps.

The Ketchums deserved execution.

He ran along the trail until certain of their destination. The steely determination of the predator asserted itself enough to moderate his pace through the forest.

He had to put the images of all the despicable atrocities the Ketchums were capable of out of his mind and rely on his instincts and training. There were eight Ketchums and one of him.

They moved too fast for Lorilie's rubbery legs. The spinning in her head blurred her vision. Her feet got in the way of one another. She stumbled and fell.

"Let her rest," Clyde ordered.

"All right," old man Ketchum agreed. "She ain't no good to us dead."

She could not die, not when she had just discovered how sweet life could be, not while Rafe remained in her time.

Rafe.

Anguish twisted her heart.

When he awakened and found her gone, he would come for her in all his deadly fury. Nothing would stop him until bullets from the Ketchums' guns lodged in his chest.

Every muscle in her body ached. By sheer force of will, she pushed into a sitting position. The pounding in her head grew stronger with each movement. She rested her forehead on her bound fists. Somehow, some way she had to escape.

The rope biting into her wrists jerked. Her bonds were too tight to pull free of easily.

"You ready, girl?"

She shook her head. She would never be ready for whatever they had in mind.

They wanted gold. They wanted the intimacies she'd shared with Rafe. They would get neither if she could stop them.

Mentally, she prepared for the ordeal ahead. When it was over, she would be dead. Most likely, so would Rafe. Knowing he would come was a bittersweet realization.

He loved her.

He would come.

He would die.

Rafe slaked his thirst at a stream, then ascended the hill overlooking the Ketchum stronghold. An eerie silence filled the forest. Even the gray clouds lingered as though waiting. The animals once belonging to Joseph Ramey cowered near the ramshackle barn; their heads rose toward the slope.

Old man Ketchum and his clan had not arrived yet.

The wolves flanked Rafe in the trees.

He crept down the hill.

The tracks of five horses were evident on the trail with Lorilie. That left three Ketchums in or around the stronghold.

He changed course around the side of the hill. Several minutes later, he spotted his first quarry panning for gold in a swift, wide creek.

Hunkered at the water's edge, the expanse of Cyrus Ketchum's back provided a perfect target.

Rafe whipped an arrow from his quiver, notched it, then drew the bow string.

And hesitated.

Lorilie's elfin face flashed through his mind. He'd promised her and Marica he wouldn't kill. Although circumstances had changed drastically, he'd keep his word as long as possible.

He lowered the bow and pulled his knife.

Cyrus remained unaware of Rafe's presence until a shadow fell over the pan he swished above the creek. A quick glance changed Cyrus's gap-toothed grin into startlement, then fear.

Rafe delivered a single blow to the side of Cyrus's neck. The pan fell into the creek, followed by Cyrus.

With quick, calculated motions, Rafe cut swaths of material from Cyrus's trousers, then bound and gagged him.

After dragging Cyrus's rotund carcass into the brush, he headed down the path leading to the back of the Ketchums' stronghold.

He found Bart boiling laundry behind the house.

Rafe waited and watched, and felt the minutes ticking away.

Opportunity knocked when Bart went into the house. Rafe darted across the clearing, snatching up a piece of firewood along the way.

When Bart came outside with another pile of laundry, he caught the full impact of the log low on his hips. The fist to his jaw knocked him out.

Rafe caught the man over his shoulder as he toppled, then scurried into the trees trailing laundry as he went. With deft motions, he bound Bart to a tree, then gagged him by stuffing a dirty sock into his gaping mouth.

He collected the laundry trail, tossed it into the fire beneath the boiling vat, and approached the house.

One more.

Slowing his breathing, Rafe crept along the sheltered side of the house. In the trees, the wolves watched, a silent cheering section. Their restraint bespoke Lorilie's benevolence. They watched, but did not attack. Darkly, he realized how thoroughly her influence protected the Ketchums.

They didn't deserve it.

A whisper of breeze rustled the grass. Rafe inhaled deeply. Bobby. Unmistakably Bobby.

Rafe crept toward Bobby's domain, the barn. He approached at an angle.

In the dank interior, Bobby shoveled manure into a wheelbarrow.

Rafe slipped inside. He moved quickly. Bobby smelled as though he'd died last week and was in desperate need of cremation. Anything less posed a biohazard.

With the stealth of a cougar, Rafe approached from behind. He pinched the nerves at the juncture of Bobby's neck and shoulder. The shovel clattered against the wheelbarrow. Manure flew in all directions.

The knife at Bobby's back made Rafe's point that struggle was useless. "Slowly put your hands on your head and lace your fingers."

Bobby raised his right arm and placed his hand squarely on his head. "My arm won't work. Yer killin' it."

Rafe adjusted his hold. "Do it now."

Bobby's trembling arm rose. He laced his fingers as instructed.

Together they left the barn and walked into the woods. "Pa ain't gonna like this. Where ya takin' me?"

Rafe released the painful hold on Bobby's nerve endings. In the same motion, he whipped Bobby's sidearm from the holster. What kind of idiot shoveled manure and mucked a barn while wearing a revolver? The slob had a total disregard for weapons. Judging by his foul body odor, Bobby had just as much disdain for his own cleanliness.

"Keep walking. You say another word and I'll carve out your kidneys."

Bobby continued toward the brush. He faltered when they penetrated the dense treeline and the wolves closed around them. His body trembled and his steps grew more unsteady.

"You're shaking, Bobby. Thinking of running? These guys love a good chase," Rafe whispered next to Bobby's ear, then chuckled.

Bobby's head shook in vehement denial.

Rafe prodded him deep into the forest before gagging him and tying him to a tree. The thought of fetid Bobby Ketchum within ten feet of Lorilie turned his stomach.

Killing the Ketchums would have been more expedient. Each time his thoughts turned in that direction, he remembered Lorilie on her knees pleading for Hal's miserable life.

Lorilie collapsed in the center of the Ketchums' yard. The blessed numbness in her hands spread up her arms and pervaded her body. Even the throbbing in her head waned. The grotesque distance between her dreams of love with Rafe and the surrounding reality yawned wider.

"Bobby! Get her some water," Clyde called.

Steeped in physical exhaustion, fear sharpened her senses. Her nostrils filled with the familiar smells of a barnyard. Sounds registered slowly. The clop of horses' hooves on hard-packed earth came from near the barn. All around, male voices muttered unintelligible complaints. Beyond the barn a hen squawked.

"Bobby! Where the hell are you?" old man Ketchum hollered.

Lorilie kept her head bowed and swallowed the grit in her mouth. Eventually, she would see more of Bobby Ketchum than she ever wanted. She drew a steadying breath. If she did not escape soon, Rafe would awaken and search for her. The predator in him would not rest until he extracted his form of justice from the men endangering the woman he vowed to protect.

He would come. And at the moment, she did not care if he killed any of the Ketchums as long as he stayed alive.

"Where'd those boys take off to?" Hal called from the barn. "They ain't finished their chores."

"Abner, go look for 'em. Hal, you and Clyde sink that there pole. We're gonna make sure she don't escape again."

Old man Ketchum's shadow loomed over Lorilie. A rough hand yanked her unraveling braid, jerking her head back.

Hatred gleamed in his dark eyes. "You ain't getting away this time, girl. You're ours. If you're smart, you'll keep them wolves away. We got traps out for 'em. You know we'll shoot them damn beasts on sight. We got more bullets than you got wolves or any other critters."

Lorilie said nothing and hoped her eyes didn't reveal her fear.

"Perty damn quiet now, ain't ya?" He pulled on her hair until she bit her lip to keep from crying out in pain. "That'll change. I'm damn tired of eking out a living on this mountain."

The pounding in her head returned with fresh vigor when he released her hair. She wanted to curl up and hide.

A steady thunk of picks biting into the hard earth drew her gaze. Hal and Clyde took alternate swings at enlarging a hole in the ground.

Gut-twisting fury knifed through Rafe when he saw old man Ketchum torturing Lorilie. With strong discipline, he quashed the desperate urge to go to her. Acting out of anger wasn't the way to rescue her. It would get them both killed.

Crouched beside the wolves, the metal jaws of a trap protruded from a clump of pine needles. In his hyperalert state of mind, it was easy to see and difficult to understand why he'd missed it earlier.

He picked up a heavy stick and waved it in front of the wolves. When he had their attention, he waited for the sound of pick and shovels below. In unison, he plunged the stick into the trap. The metal jaws snapped shut. The stick shattered.

Uneasy, the wolves milled around him, aware of the danger.

Rafe watched the ground closely. He sprang six traps and retrieved the last two.

In the distance, someone approached the creek calling the three missing Ketchums. A malevolent snarl curled Rafe's lips.

He sprinted ahead, quickly laying the traps in the path worn down to the creek, then camouflaged them with grass and leaves.

Moments later, from behind a tree less than six feet away, Rafe watched his prey.

Irritation marked Abner Ketchum's strident calls. He traveled the path with long strides, missing the first trap. The second snapped around his ankle.

He collapsed, then scooted in a circle, trying to pry the trap's jaws apart with his hands and free foot.

Rafe stepped out from behind the tree and silenced him with a quick blow to the head. The trap snapped shut again.

"Four down and four to go," he told Loner. "Let's see if Craig is here yet."

The wolf soon outdistanced him. With an eye peeled for traps and the events in the yard below, Rafe trekked along the hillside.

He found Craig and Marica with Loner.

"I see four," Craig said.

"That's all that's left."

"You killed them?" Marica gasped, her hazel eyes widening in horror.

"No, I didn't—but don't fool yourself into thinking they wouldn't kill me or Craig if they had the chance. Look at Lorilie. Look what they've done to her, Marica. Look at that stake they're going to tie her to, and the fire they're building beside it. Then tell me how much they deserve to live. Those are branding irons they're heating in that fire." No emotion touched his evenly spoken words. He had neither compassion, nor disdain for the pacifism she embraced without reservation.

"Where do you want me, Capt'n?" Craig asked.

How easily they reverted into comfortable roles. "Take up a position with a clear line of sight on the post. Shoot any man who picks up a hot iron." He started down the hill with Loner at his side. "I'll give you five minutes. But don't wait if it gets dicey."

"Where are you going?" Marica asked, starting after him.

"Down there."

"Rafe, be careful. She loves you. She'll trade her life for yours."

Rafe's composure faltered and he paused. "That's unsat, Marica." Seeking equanimity, he proceeded toward his objective.

"What does that mean? Unsat?"

"Unsatisfactory," Craig said. "Not an option."

Rafe continued walking, with an air of unflappable calm.

He was ready for battle.

Hal jerked on the rope, forcing Lorilie to her feet. The sudden movement accelerated the throbbing in her head. A cramp in her left calf knotted painfully. She limped forward.

"You can make it easy on yourself by telling us where the gold is, girl." Old man Ketchum tugged at his stained hat.

She eyed the branding irons heating in the blazing fire.

Fear made her legs unsteady. She could not pull her gaze from the irons. She wanted to be brave, but she was not. Terror lodged in her throat, throttling the scream gathering force in her lungs.

"You better be afraid, girl. I'm done chasing you through these mountains and being stalked by your critters."

His fingers clamped on her jaw and jerked her head around. Her eyes barely focused on his hate-twisted face. Her heart pounded loudly in her chest. Terror pulsed in her temples until the top of her head felt ready to explode.

"Where's the old man's gold? This is the last time I'm askin'. Tell me, or you're gonna beg me to listen later. Which way's it gonna be?"

Realizing she might buy a moment, she tried to speak. The words came slow and halting. "I—I never looked for gold . . . never needed it. G-Grandfather . . . he went to the creek. On the other side of the swale behind your house. He took what he needed whenever he left the mountain for supplies." Praying he believed her, she met his dark glare, and knew he did not.

The fear caved in on itself. Regardless of what she told them, it would not matter. Just as there would never be enough gold. Nothing would save her from the hot irons. Not the truth and not a mountain of gold. He wanted to hurt her.

"He had a stash. Where is it?"

"He died with his secrets," she said without flinching. How easily the deception left her lips when the truth jeopardized those she loved sleeping beside the gold.

"I don't believe you, witch." Old man Ketchum lifted his hat, smoothed his silver hair, then replaced the hat. "Tie her up."

"It makes no difference whether I know or not, does it?"

Hal yanked on the rope.

"It'll be a pleasure having you scream while your flesh

burns under a branding iron. You know, and you'll tell me. Count on it,'' old man Ketchum sneered. ''Tie her tight.''

There would be no escape this time. She longed for the secret place Rafe spoke of where nothing in the physical realm penetrated.

Hal pushed her against the post and gave each loop of the rope he fastened around her an extra tug. The coarse hemp bit into her skin through her shirt and trousers.

Terror festered, quickening her breath and heartbeat. She might not be brave but she was stubborn.

Exhaling in resignation, her head bowed in submission to the inevitable, but never to the Ketchums.

The presence of the wolves anxiously prowling the trees intruded. As their leader, she was the steward of their welfare. The fear bubbling in her veins disallowed calming them. When she tried, she encountered the presence of a formidable predator, one so cunning and confident the hairs at the back of her neck prickled.

Rafe.

During the brief connection, he touched the core of her Gift with serenity. Fear melted into unnatural calm.

He was here.

He shut her out as quickly as he revealed his presence. Her senses whirled. Serenity vanished. Her wild gaze raked the trees, but found no sign of his presence. She reached out, searching, desperate to warn him away.

And found only the wind.

''Where the hell did Abner go?'' Old man Ketchum peered toward the outhouse.

''He went lookin' for Bobby, Bart, and Cyrus,'' Hal said from the barn door. ''I don't like this, Pa. We ain't seen hide nor hair of the big man.''

Resigned that their fate rested on Rafe's shoulders, the fight went out of her. Bleak despair filled the void. Better that Rafe killed them all rather than risk himself.

Drawn by an impression from Loner, she turned her head to the left.

Rifle in hand, Clyde walked along the side of the house and watched the tree line. When he reached the rear, his feet left the ground. He disappeared.

Lorilie blinked hard, unsure of what she saw, or if she really saw it.

Rafe?

The life mate she accepted with her heart and body was also a predator beyond her comprehension. He had stalked the Ketchums in their own den. Now he attacked them, one at a time, just as he had forewarned.

"We're not waitin' any longer," old man Ketchum said from beside the fire. The muffled clank of the irons bespoke his preparations. "Get over here, Hank."

"What the hell is going on? What happened to Abner?" Hank demanded from behind her. The sound of his boots on the hard dirt shuffled toward the fire.

"It's the big man." Hal sounded nervous. "I tell you, it's him. I know it. You don't hear him comin'. He's just there."

Lorilie turned her head to the right and studied the three men. They watched one another, yet never made eye contact.

Hal perspired heavily.

Old man Ketchum adjusted his hat again. Not a good sign.

Only Hank seemed calm.

"What sort of idiot would take on eight men in broad daylight?" demanded old man Ketchum.

"I only see three of us," Hank said. "Just in case Hal's right, I'm getting my rifle."

"Bring mine," Hal said. "I left it on my saddle."

"Mine, too." Old man Ketchum wheeled on Lorilie. "Where is he?"

Lorilie shook her head.

"He says he's the Angel of Death," Hal grumbled.

Old man Ketchum released the branding iron. "I thought you folks didn't believe in killin'."

"He does," Hal interjected, uneasily studying the trees.

"I'm talkin' to her." He straightened, leaving the branding iron in the fire. "Where is he, girl?"

For a fleeting instant, she savored the triumph of holding the upper hand. Her chin rose in defiance. "How would I know? I have been with you."

Old man Ketchum shook his head and stared at the ground for a moment. "Bobby's gonna be mighty disappointed you got yourself a man before him."

"Bobby has the pigs. He has no need of me," she murmured, biting back a shiver of revulsion.

A whizzing, followed by a thwapping thud, sounded behind her. Hank shouted in pain.

"Goddamn—" Hal whipped his revolver from his holster.

Another whizzing sound passed close behind her head. An arrow penetrated Hal's gun arm and pinned it to his ribs. The revolver bounced on the ground. The barrel came to rest atop the branding irons.

Then Lorilie was staring into old man Ketchum's fear-ridden face. His foul breath filled her nostrils and permeated her soul. His fingers tightened around her throat.

Lorilie fought for air.

"I'll kill her. So help me, I'll kill the bitch!"

Lorilie craned her neck, struggling for breath. A burning in her lungs built the pressure in her chest. The scope of her vision narrowed. Old man Ketchum's fingers clamped tighter and tighter, crushing her throat. Everything turned red, then black. The ringing in her ears exploded as old man Ketchum's fingers tightened a final time.

Chapter 24

RAFE FELT LORILIE'S neck for a pulse. The tension in him eased a notch when he found a strong, steady rhythm. The imprint of old man Ketchum's fingers on her throat already darkened on her pale skin.

"Move and you're a dead man," he told Hal, silently begging for a reason to carry out his promise.

Clutching his arm against his side, Hal lowered his head onto his crushed hat. His gun lay out of reach, the barrel heating on top of the branding irons.

Rafe cut through the ropes binding Lorilie to the post. Her limp body crumpled in his arms.

He fought to suppress the emotions raging within him, unwilling to jeopardize the tenuous détente he imposed on the Ketchums.

"Is she all right, Capt'n?"

"I don't know." He looked over his shoulder. Craig held the gun on Hal as he closed the distance between them. Ashen and wild-eyed, Marica followed. "Marica, I need you here. Craig, secure the area."

Tears pooled in the healer's eyes at the sight of Lorilie.

Seeing his worries reflected in Marica's stricken features cracked Rafe's internal armor. The detachment essential for restraining his rage wavered.

Marica rested her fingers on Lorilie's bruised throat. Tears spilled down her cheeks. For moments that seemed an eternity to Rafe, she stroked Lorilie's dusty hair.

Lorilie's eyes moved beneath her lids. Thick lashes lying like soot on lavender half-moons fluttered open. The terror in her wild green eyes sent waves of fury through Rafe. She gasped for air as if her life depended on a deep breath. Her gaze met his, and widened in disbelief, then softened. Tears pooled, then spilled across her temples, leaving clean streaks on her dirt-crusted skin.

"She will recover. I can help her more . . . ." Marica's hazel eyes darted toward Hal. "Later."

Lorilie turned her head and stared out at the yard where Hal lay beside the fire, an arrow protruding from his side and through his arm. Old man Ketchum lay dead at his feet, an arrow in his neck, a bullet hole in his back. Beyond them, Hank lay curled around an arrow extending from the lower right side of his chest.

When she looked back at Rafe, the tears flowed faster. The whisper of his name left her lips like a sad kiss. The profound sorrow filling her watery eyes pierced his soul.

Rafe barely breathed until she mercifully shut her eyes and the window on her gentle spirit. He gathered her close, smelling her fear mingled with dirt and perspiration.

Straightening, he scrutinized the Ketchum place with the experience of a Ranger. For the moment, the enemy was neutralized. His training demanded complete neutralization. But today he was not a Ranger, just a man protecting the innocent lying in his arms.

"Let's move out." Anxious to get Lorilie into the comfort and privacy of the fortress, Rafe met Marica's teary eyes. "The mule in the barn, was it Joseph Ramey's?"

He wanted nothing of the Ketchums near Lorilie.

"Yes," Marica answered, tucking the ends of Lorilie's torn shirt around her upper chest. "Shall I get it?"

Rafe shook his head. "Sergeant!"

"Yo. Got it." Craig headed for the barn. "Is the one over here, dead?"

"Not yet. If either one of them makes a move, shoot him in the groin." He scowled, glaring at Hal who had not budged since the first warning. With grim approval, Rafe watched Craig lead the mule from the barn, then collect the scattered rifles and relieve Hank of his sidearm. Craig tossed the weapons into the fire.

The wolves began howling in the trees. Their keening lament mourned Lorilie's battered condition almost as much as Rafe did. His instincts insisted that he slay the remaining Ketchums. Dead enemies posed no threat.

He denied the retribution he craved with every breath, and forced one foot in front of the other. Not until they entered the trees did he risk a glance at Lorilie. Her torn clothes were little more than rags hanging from her thin frame. Scraped from being dragged behind the horses, fresh blood oozed from dirt-crusted scabs on her elbows and knees. As pathetic as the abrasions were, they were safer to look at than her face. Each time he saw the bruised, pale evidence of her suffering, the war within him escalated.

He wanted to kill the Ketchums. Every one of them. Slowly. Painfully. Making them experience the terror Lorilie knew when she realized the branding irons were for her. Let them feel the agony of the white-hot irons.

"Lorilie, Lorilie. What the hell is happening to me?" he whispered.

He had forsaken his training, ignored his instincts, and acquiesced to her pacifist beliefs. The specter of all he'd worked for promised that he would regret walking away from the Ketchums.

*   *   *

Lorilie drifted, content that Rafe was unharmed. Cradled on his chest with her ear pressed to the strong, sure beat of his heart, the aches in her limbs diminished.

He was safe, but like her, he was not undamaged. The predator in him had sustained grievous wounds. His raw conflict seeped unrestrained into her awareness. Lost within the mire of human emotions beyond the insight of her Gift, he bled silently.

Even if she had the strength, soothing his turmoil was out of the question. Such a violation constituted a broken promise.

While in the Ketchum stronghold, she had feared he would come for her. And the Ketchums would kill him when he did. Losing him would be one loss too many, and far more than she could endure.

Had it been within her power, she would have traded all of the Ketchums' lives, and her own, for his.

She had given him her love and bonded with him as a life mate with her body. The ecstatic beauty they found with each other they would find with no other.

But she did not know him. He had revealed his nature in a variety of ways, but she had not comprehended the awesome power of his lethal Gift. He truly was the Angel of Death, filled with vengeance and fury.

"She's very still." Rafe slowed his quick pace for Marica to catch up.

"That is as it should be, Rafe. Her body is already healing. She feels no pain." As though assuring him, Marica rested her hand on Lorilie's forehead and temple. "I will wake her when we reach the fortress."

His long strides carried them swiftly over the rough terrain. The distance between the fortress and the Ketchums had served as an insulator. Now it seemed doubly long. Loner kept pace beside him. The wolf pack darted in the brush. Nervous. Vigilant. Each glance Rafe stole at

Lorilie widened the crevices disintegrating his hard-won fight for emotional detachment.

Grim reality bit heavier into Rafe as he climbed along a steep rise. Of all the bizarre occurrences since awakening in Lorilie's fortress, falling in love took the prize. He wasn't any good at love. They had nothing in common, not ideology, and certainly not history. But when he looked at Lorilie, none of the incongruities of their lives mattered. He loved her, and he had damn near lost her.

The image of her struggling for breath, her slender body lashed to the post, her feet kicking feebly, remained. Rafe had seen it all, and continued seeing it in his mind's eye like a loop of videotape playing endlessly.

Now Rafe detoured along an old deer trail on the downhill side of the rise. His long strides ate up the distance. He chose the safer, longer route, and took no chances.

He tightened his hold on the precious burden he carried. She was alive. And he loved her more than he thought possible for a man to love a woman and survive. The goodness in her burned as bright as the sun. It illuminated the dank corners and moldering cobwebs of his spirit, forcing him into the light, then gently coaxing his blind eyes open on the beauty around him. She was the beauty. She was the light.

How the hell would he live without her?

And how on God's green earth could he leave her? After today, he was no longer sure where duty left off and life began, only that there was a line as fine as a spiderweb filament. It was there. Somewhere. Waiting for him to cross it.

All his determination to find the Gifted man who would send him home fled. A mountain of despair settled on his heart. He didn't want such a man to exist. If he did, he'd have to decide whether to answer the call of duty hammered into him over the years, or remain with Lorilie.

The solution switched sides with each turn of his complex thoughts.

He could not take Lorilie into his world.

Who would protect her if he left? Clearly, she needed someone. She needed the predator in him to stave off the vultures soon to fill these mountains in search of gold. How could he leave when she needed him and didn't even know it?

He loved her. He'd have to find a way.

"Can you hear me, Lorilie?"

Though softly spoken, the yearning in his voice touched her heart. She struggled to open her eyes. Her head throbbed and her bones lacked substance.

"We're home. I'm going to wash you up, okay?"

She felt a tug at her feet as her boots slipped off. With great effort, she opened her eyes. "My head," she croaked.

"Keep the lanterns turned low," Marica ordered, scurrying around the neatly packed bundles of her medicines. "Carry her into the spring. I'll be right there."

"Welcome back, wolf woman." Craig brushed the back of his fingers over her cheek.

Lorilie tried to smile and ease the worry she saw in his dark eyes. A weak twitch was all she managed.

Craig winked at her, then ducked out of sight.

"Rafe . . ." She swallowed, her throat dry from the dust.

"Shhhhh. Your throat may be sore for a while."

"Thirsty."

"We'll give you something to drink in a minute."

"Not green," she pleaded.

"Trust me, the green stuff will do you good. It'll put hair on your chest," Craig teased.

Lorilie met Rafe's searching gaze. The only hair she wanted near her chest was his, with his warm flesh and strong heartbeat promising life. Though she fought it, her eyelids closed.

"Stay awake. Please." His plea forced her eyes open. "Stay with me, Lorilie."

Given a choice, she would never leave him but would spend the rest of her life trying to understand him and his terrible Gift. Her eyelashes turned into weights pulling her eyelids down. It was so peaceful in his arms with the rhythmic thud of his heart the only sound. The serenity of the moment allowed her to block out everything except his next heartbeat.

The peace was short-lived. He moved. Moments later, they descended into warm water and he sat her upright.

"Drink this." Marica's no-nonsense command forced her eyes open.

Lorilie drank. The awful taste sparked a grain of resistance. With a feeble effort, she stayed Marica's hand, but only long enough to swallow. Resisting required more strength than she possessed. She drank until Marica removed the container.

Soon Marica's marvelous, healing hands rested on her head. Lorilie gratefully embraced the power probing and mending the abrasions and contusions incurred when the Ketchums dragged her through the forest. Gradually, the pain in her head subsided and her throat no longer felt scorched. A glimmer of strength returned to her limbs, as did the reality of her ordeal.

"We need food, and she needs sleep." Marica's fingers lingered at her cheek, a sign the healing session was over.

"Thank you." Lorilie turned her head and kissed Marica's hand.

Marica kissed Lorilie's forehead, then climbed out of the water and wrung out the ends of her skirt. "I'll see what Craig has found for us to eat. He tells me he can cook. We shall see."

When they were alone, Rafe collected her in a gentle but firm embrace. He said nothing, merely held her, rocking slightly. His barriers were intact, denying even a glimpse of the predator within.

She savored the solid bastion of his arms protecting her. Though the threat of pain and death was over, the phantom of fear lingered. Judging by the way he held her, his turmoil was also waning slowly. "I was afraid you would come when you awakened and found me gone. So afraid they would hurt you. Kill you. I had no idea what you could do." She held him, savoring his closeness.

"That makes two of us. I had no idea I'd let any of them live when I found the cougar and realized they'd taken you." His fingers stopped separating the tangles in her hair floating in the water.

"You are the Angel of Death. That is your Gift." As the words left her lips, acceptance settled in her soul.

"No, sweet Lorilie, I have no Gift, and I'm not the Angel of Death. Not any longer. The only one who died was old man Ketchum, and I couldn't tell you for sure which one of us killed him, me or Craig." The rasp of his whiskers gently moving across her temple consoled her worry.

"I promised Hal he'd die if he touched you. I hope the bastard dies a slow death from the arrow I shot into him. There are some promises a man must keep."

Sensing the depth of a wound in him she did not understand, she let the matter rest. Though she loathed the taking of life, all things considered, she could not lament the loss of old man Ketchum.

"Later, after you've eaten and slept, we'll debrief . . . talk about what happened. Meanwhile, let's get you cleaned up." He helped her out of her ragged shirt.

Relief that he did not press for an accounting relaxed her. Time and rest might soothe her rawness. "I would like to leave tomorrow, as we planned. It will never be the same here."

"The Ketchums are picking up the pieces. We need to get the hell out of here. But we're not going anywhere until you're physically up to traveling. I won't risk you again.''

''You're very accustomed to giving orders. Does everyone always follow them?''

''Everyone. Except you.''

Surprised, she allowed him to worry her clinging trousers off her calves. ''I disobeyed no edicts.''

He became silent, barely moving in the water.

She draped her ruined trousers over the water's edge, then touched his shoulder. ''Rafe?''

''Where were the wolves?'' he asked softly, as though in pain. ''Why didn't you know the Ketchums were coming?''

''They watched all night. I . . .'' She had grown overconfident and weary. ''I . . .''

''You, what, Lorilie?''

''Holding the link for so long takes a great toll. I was too tired. It broke.''

''I would've taken you to the graves.'' His tone bespoke his disappointment that she had not asked.

''Saying good-bye is something best done alone.'' Unable to endure the perplexity narrowing his eyes and furrowing his brow, she lowered her gaze. ''It seems I misjudged everything.''

''Regrets already?''

His air of disappointment quickly lifted her head. ''No! Not about mating.''

He winced. ''About what, then?''

''People. Even if I had given old man Ketchum Grandfather's gold, he would have hurt me, and enjoyed it. While I fail to understand why, I know it is truth.''

''And you didn't want me to come?''

''Perhaps I would have if I had truly understood how you do what you do. . . . You are my life mate. I love you beyond anything or anyone else.''

In the low light of the lantern gleaming off the mica facets, she saw his throat work, but he remained silent.

Small muscles in the shadows of his face flinched at an inner thought he did not share with her.

He released his trousers, then whipped his shirt over his head. A few quick motions left him as naked as she.

Lorilie leaned toward him, intent on pressing their bodies together so tightly that they would never separate.

The ghost of an apologetic smile touched Rafe's mouth. Gently gripping her shoulders, he turned her around. She allowed him to wash the lingering traces of the Ketchum ordeal from her body. Watching, experiencing the gentleness of his big hands on her made her feel worshipped.

The gentle but thorough way his fingertips massaged her sensitive scalp brought tears to her eyes. His hands bespoke the truth his lips could not, would not utter. He loved her.

When she dunked to rinse her hair, she rose facing him. She brushed water from her face and opened her stinging eyes. He was exquisite. Water glistened on his body and dripped from his silken chest hair. With a life of their own, her fingers scored the wet pelt. Curious, she bent her head slightly and rimmed his tight nipple with her tongue.

Gently, Rafe's big hands closed around her shoulders. His retreat startled her. "Ah, sweet Lorilie, we're not going there today."

The proof of his desire prodded her belly. "We wish to mate."

"But we're not going to. Making love won't take away what's happened. You need food and rest." He placed a wistful kiss on her forehead and reached for his trousers. "Do you think you could call it something other than mating? Like, making love?"

Slipping her arms around his waist, she rested her cheek against his chest. As long as she held on to him, she thought only of the moment. ''Is that what it is? What we do? Make love?''

''Yeah,'' he exhaled slowly. ''I'm afraid so.'' The resignation in his voice and the slump of his shoulders puzzled her. But then, many things about him did.

Chapter 25

THEY LOADED THE raft early the following morning. Marica concurred wholeheartedly with the tasks Rafe assigned Lorilie: keeping the mule compliant, and eating. Apparently, he considered her too thin. Though Lorilie assured them she would regain some weight when she no longer maintained tight, frequent links with the mountain denizens, all three ignored her.

"I'm a large man," Rafe had explained while urging another piece of pheasant breast at her. "When we make love I don't want to worry about breaking you."

The tantalizing inducement increased her appetite immediately. Once they boarded the raft and she settled the mule, she held on to the cart lashed to the logs.

Craig and Rafe cut the ropes securing the raft to the riverbank. The current caught it immediately. Rafe took the tiller, his feet braced, arms straining to guide the raft into the middle of the wide river.

Loath to abandon his companions, Loner trailed the raft along the riverbank. When the land rose or the rocks grew difficult, he moved inland and reappeared downriver.

She had not thought she would be glad to leave the roots her family had carved deep into the granite. But yesterday had changed everything. Like the great flocks of migratory birds, Lorilie was ready for a less hostile clime.

"I thought the mule would have bolted by now," Craig said, holding on to the cart while checking the lashings.

"He was young when Grandfather brought him home. In time, he grew accustomed to me." She stroked the short hair between the mule's eyes.

Craig settled beside her, his dark eyes squinting against the sunlight glinting off the water. "One thing bothers me."

Lorilie smiled. "Only one?"

Craig returned her smile. "How come you didn't send the Ketchums' horses running when they found you?"

"They are not wild. Taming a horse changes it. Very few have a real sense of loyalty since their masters are anyone who puts a saddle on their back and tells them where to go." She scratched the mule's left ear. "Mules are stubborn critters. Grandfather bought this one because of his stubborn streak. He suspected the mule would listen to me."

"Apparently without a qualm."

"He trusts me."

"Craig," Rafe called. "Rough water ahead. Give me a hand."

"Yo." Craig closed the distance to the tiller.

In the clear light of day, her attention focused on Rafe standing at the tiller; his feet planted wide on the logs; his arms flexing as he worked the raft through the current and around obstacles; his vigilant gaze assessing the shoreline and the next hazard in the river.

Marica crawled beside her and settled against the cart built from their heirlooms. "You look troubled. Would it help to speak about it?"

Lorilie shook her head and averted her gaze from her

concerned friend. Sometimes, like Rafe, Marica saw too deeply into her soul. "I was so wrong about so much."

"You were right about much, too. There are things you cannot know until you've had more contact with Outsiders. I can tell you of my own experiences, but it is not the same." Her fingers folded around Lorilie's. "Pretending it is over does not change the fact that it happened. Soon we may have to go among Outsiders. They are not all like the Ketchums."

"I pray not."

"Do not hide from them within yourself, Lorilie. Do not hide from us. You were a hair's breadth from dying. That violence, that fear will not fade easily."

"There are some things I must resolve alone. Neither you, Rafe, nor Craig can help me. When I have done so, there will be no reason to speak of yesterday again." Besides, it was impossible to put into words what she barely understood. How did one explain the inexplicable shadow forming at the back of her thoughts? It revealed neither a name nor a face, merely hovered like a great bird of prey in the night. The only way of coping with its intrusive presence was denying its power and ignoring it.

Lorilie squeezed her friend's hand and leaned close. "However, there is something I seek from your knowledge. It is a private matter and I believe you may help me with it."

Marica gave her a nod.

She barely knew how to phrase her question. After a moment of thought, she spoke in a near whisper. "When a Gifted mates . . . makes love, with an Outsider, is there a sharing of feelings? Of the great desire and the almost painful joy . . . the bliss that burns with the fire of the sun when his seed is released?"

"You mean, feeling one another's desire? The emotion of each other's release?"

Thank heaven for Marica's insight. What started out as awkward became a sharing between friends. "Exactly."

"I can only speak from my experience." A tenderness softened Marica's gentle features when her warm hazel eyes rested on Craig at the rear of the raft with Rafe. They exchanged a knowing smile, which became a grin lighting Craig's face.

"And?" Lorilie prodded, anxious for the answer.

"If the Gift is powerful and the Outsider exceedingly trusting, what you describe can happen occasionally. It requires great concentration on the part of the Gifted, and sometimes almost saintly patience and unfettered desire on the part of the Outsider."

Lorilie's brow furrowed with confusion.

Marica reluctantly drew her gaze from Craig. "Is that what you seek with Rafe?"

"I do not have to seek it, Marica. When he kisses me, at some indefinable point, it comes whether we want it or not."

"Spontaneously?"

"Yes. It has been a problem."

Marica's eyes darted toward Rafe, then to Lorilie. "Lorilie, dear Lorilie. That is not a problem. That's called a blessing."

Since she had no basis of comparison, she accepted Marica's proclamation. "But Rafe swears he cannot possibly be Gifted."

"Perhaps his Gift is knowing how to preserve lives," Marica mused. "I think that would be a very difficult Gift to master."

"I cannot fathom a Gift for killing." Confused, she squeezed Marica's hand. "Yesterday, before the arrows flew . . . I felt Rafe, the predator in him, the part I can sense when he allows it. It was as if he wanted to assure me all would be well. I could not help looking toward where I sensed him. Then Clyde vanished."

"He didn't vanish. Rafe pulled him around the back of the house." Marica shook her head. "He and Craig are trained in warfare beyond anything we can imagine, Lorilie. It is an art they have perfected in the time they came from."

"Do not equate conditioning with being Gifted."

"A blind woman could see he is your life mate. Unless he is Gifted, neither of you should be able to do what you describe."

"So it may be possible he is Gifted and does not realize it?"

Marica studied Rafe as though she might make the determination visually. "He could be. Your Gift is strong. Stronger than mine, which is not surprising since both of your parents were Gifted. Although you have mastered it, I doubt your control is errant enough for a bonding exchange without your intent."

"More rough water," Rafe called out. "Hold on to the ropes."

The raft pitched sideways and dipped into a watery valley. Lorilie and Marica held each other and the ropes fixed to the logs. Icy river water splashed their backs. The raft straightened for a moment, then skidded around a deep roil.

Lorilie watched the riverbank and wondered how long before they found peaceful waters.

They rode the river until the long evening shadows made the rapids too dangerous. Rafe insisted on making camp, then went hunting with Loner. Using the bow, he bagged half a dozen grouse the wolf flushed from the grass.

Lorilie and Marica's harvest of berries and greens turned the meal into a feast.

Rafe watched Lorilie closely throughout the day with growing trepidation. Outwardly, her behavior remained unchanged, as though the terror she experienced and her close encounter with death had never happened.

"We are safe here," Lorilie said with a yawn. The ghosts of exhaustion and fear lingered as circles under her eyes. The tea Marica brewed would ease her into a much-needed sleep. "Even if the Ketchums knew we left and gave chase, we have traveled too far for their horses to catch us."

In the concern Rafe saw in Marica's gaze he found an ally sharing his worry. He had no experience with women in combat, but he knew the price victims of torment paid. He wished he had killed Hal Ketchum. *Cut off the head of the dragon and the claws are useless*, a voice reminded him. Instead, the dragon grew another head just as ugly and mean as the first.

As long as Hal drew a breath, he'd stalk Lorilie. Rafe knew it, and so did she.

"I'm tired." Lorilie handed the empty cup to Marica, then rose and went to the bedroll she and Rafe shared.

Rafe nodded at Craig and Marica, and joined Lorilie. She drifted into sleep nestled against his chest. Her fingers laced tightly with his as though he was an anchor.

In a shallow level of sleep where his body rested and his mind remained alert, Rafe waited for her first nightmare. When it came, her entire body shook against him.

"Better all of them dead," came her whispered growl.

The small hairs on the nape of Rafe's neck rippled. The venom of her fear, her anger, reached deep.

"Not Rafe," she whimpered. "Please, God, not Rafe. I'm sorry."

"It's all right, sweet Lorilie. I'm here." He turned her until she faced him. Kissing her temples, her face, he whispered assurances. She clutched at him with more strength than he thought remained in her frail body.

As quickly as the nightmare seized her, it fled, leaving her limp in sleep.

Rafe held her close, unable to let go. The demon she refused to speak of had a far more insidious character than the outrage of being afraid and powerless, or the anger she denied.

He stroked her hair and cherished the feel of her sleeping quietly in his arms. The depth of her love humbled him as nothing else could. She had put him first without realizing the cost to her tender, generous spirit.

In a weak moment of desperation, Lorilie had compromised her beliefs and it tore at her on a primal level. He had not asked for the concession. He'd never considered it. She had done it because she loved him and revered his life above anything she held sacred, including her own.

The realization burned him.

How did a man like him wind up with the unselfish, steadfast love of such a woman? While he had no answer, he knew he was the luckiest bastard ever to pull on a pair of boots.

How the hell could he leave her? Given a choice, how could he stay?

The battle within him clarified. The opponents vying for his allegiance were no longer love and duty. They wore the badges of uncertain, ever-changing life and familiar death.

Tucking the quilt around Lorilie's shoulder, he protected her from the chill he felt. Pondering the chaos robbing him of sleep, he held Lorilie securely through her nightmares.

At the first hint of dawn, she awakened and returned his embrace.

"There's something I want you to know. Something important." He placed his mouth close to her ear. "When we're afraid, when all seems lost, and we're powerless in the face of terror, the mind seizes any and every thing it can to protect us. Sometimes we rail at a God we don't believe in or haven't acknowledged since the last time we were in a bind. Sometimes, when the terror is so great we think . . . we hope . . . we'll die before we have to take another breath, we'll say or do anything. Anything, Lorilie. Sell our souls.

"That's not who we are. It's fear. How we act in the face of that fear is who we are." When she pushed in protest, he held her tighter and kissed her ear.

"Whatever went through your mind when the Ketchums took you doesn't matter one hoot in hell. If you had really wanted them dead at any time, you would have made it happen. I know this, Lorilie. It's an irrefutable truth. I won't ask you to accept it. Not today, anyway. Just think about it."

When she pushed again, he eased his hold. "I won't ask questions. When you're ready to speak about your nightmares, you will." He kissed her forehead, then slipped from beneath the quilt.

"Stay under there while I feed the fire." After tying his boots, he tucked the quilt around her.

"Of all the gifts bestowed on me, you are the most wondrous gift of all, Rafe. I will love you forever."

He kissed her lightly. If he lingered, he'd make love to her. While the notion offered tremendous appeal, she needed every iota of energy for healing.

By noon the next day, they reached the waterfalls where they abandoned the raft. With the mule carrying most of the burden, they made steady progress through the mountains. Rafe's assertions concerning the effects of fear occasionally needled Lorilie into thinking about the unthinkable. The wall of black emotion threatening to consume her stopped her from delving too deep.

The evening of their third day trekking through the rugged mountains, she caught herself glancing over her shoulder.

The vigilant animals warned of no other presence, yet she felt hunted in a way vastly more threatening than when she actually ran from the Ketchums.

She made no protest when Craig and Rafe decided on sleeping in shifts. Alone on the pallet she shared with Rafe, Lorilie admitted that her Guardian's unorthodox skills provided a feeling of safety. The realization rankled her.

Sleep eluded her. She listened when Rafe returned from

his watch post in the trees and awakened Craig to take his turn.

Moments later, he slipped beneath their quilt and gathered her against his chest.

She snuggled and stifled a yawn.

"You should be sleeping," he chided softly.

"I am tired, but it seems I cannot fall asleep when you are not beside me." She scooted onto her back and turned her head to him. "Perhaps I should have accepted Marica's offer of sleeping tea." The smoothness of his cheek from his afterdinner shave made her smile. She traced his facial bones, starting under his right eye, along his cheek, down his jaw and over his chin, then completed the journey on the left side.

"Touching your skin is like touching your mind. You have so many textures, so many facets, a single lifetime is not enough to explore them all. You know things beyond the tiny sphere of my comprehension. Will you tell me about your life? Before you came here?"

He hesitated, as though revealing anything about himself required an inner battle. "What do you want to know?"

"Tell me of your family."

Rafe shook his head. "There isn't much to tell. No brothers or sisters. My parents had me late in life, long after they'd given up on having kids. They were doctors." A wistful half smile lit his face. "Hell, they were more like missionaries. They worked all the places no one wanted. They specialized in world ghetto medicine.

"Shortly after my father died, my mother followed. Recently I've begun to understand she actually died when my father drew his last breath."

"She loved him very much, then."

"It would have been the same if she had died first." He lowered his head and kissed the finger she trailed over his chin. "When I was a kid, I didn't get away with anything. There were times I thought they read my mind, and each other's. But there wasn't anything special. They had seen most of the world, and worked with a lot of kids. Nothing I did was new to them, just to me. I was a hellion and tried it all.''

She loved the way his chest pulsed when he chuckled softly and the play of the firelight on his chiseled features. Laughter softened him and lingered in his eyes. ''How old were you when they died?''

''Nineteen. I was in college. The year after I lost them was tough. One day, an army recruiter got hold of me and changed everything. Once I signed on the dotted line, I had a home again.'' His head angled sideways, inviting a wider range of exploration. ''Not a home like we usually think of with parents and siblings, but a place where I belonged.''

''Belonging somewhere is important to you?''

''It was. Once. The thing about belonging someplace is the obligations you incur. They come to depend on you. You hate to let them down.''

''And do everything in your power to protect them,'' she added.

He grew serious. The flicker of the firelight reflected in his eyes. ''Failure for me is losing a man during a mission. It's like losing a piece of myself. The hardest part is knowing some of the families will never know what happened to their sons. Some of them bury an empty casket. Occasionally, I'm allowed to attend the funerals. I'd stand beside their graves and feel the accusing stares of their families. They think I killed their son, or got him killed. They don't say it. They don't have to. I know it.

''When they fold the flag draped over the coffin and present it to a widow or a mother, I know it's a hollow consolation. The guns fire a salute, and it feels like a firing squad.''

She wanted to weep for him. He showed the world what they expected, what duty demanded. She realized the tremendous Gift he gave her by revealing the rest of himself now. "Ah, Rafe, I feared death was your only companion. It is not. Who knows of the gentle side of your heart?"

"You. Just you."

Awed that he trusted her with the secrets of his heart, her finger ceased moving along his ear. "I will hold your truths sacred and never reveal the fact that you are not the Angel of Death you wish others to believe you are."

His head lowered until his lips brushed her. "Not anymore. Living for a purpose is a helluva lot harder, and I suspect more rewarding, than being ready to die for one."

Her heart quickened with the promise of a kiss. His warm breath smelled of the tea Marica had brewed and left simmering for the men. "Life is always better than death," she murmured.

"Not always." He ended the conversation with a tender kiss. "Lorilie, sweet Lorilie."

Her arms slipped around his neck and pulled him closer. The affirmation of holding her life mate against her heart banished the night shadows.

"Get some sleep."

"I prefer making love with you." The heat of desire revived her tired body.

"Temptress."

"You want me." The slight motion of her thigh against him prodded a response.

"All the time." He kissed her nose. "But I also want you rested and strong tomorrow. We both need sleep. It will be dawn in a few hours."

Recalling his iron will in the small shelter, she sighed in resignation, then yawned. With his help, she curled onto her side with her back against his chest. The comfort of his arm tucking her close shut out the rest of the world. Within minutes the rigors of the day took their toll. Her eyelids grew heavy, then closed in sleep.

When the horrific nightmares returned, Rafe's soothing assurances lulled her back to sleep.

*   *   *

"Let's go, folks. Time to pack up. I spotted movement on the ridge." Craig folded his and Marica's blankets as he approached. "They're carrying torches."

Instantly awake, Lorilie reached for Rafe.

He kissed her lightly, then spun into a sitting position and began lacing his boots on.

Swiftly, she forged a link with the territorial predators. "Four men. Ketchums." Would only death end their hunt for her? "I believe I am learning how to hate." She levered herself to her feet by taking Rafe's hand.

"They won't take you from me, Lorilie. I promise."

"Can you promise me they won't take you, either?"

He stood, hauling the quilt with him, and started folding it. "That's a given. They'd have to catch me first."

She wanted to believe him.

Chapter 26

THEY TRAVELED AT a steady pace. The silent communication between Rafe and Craig afforded Lorilie glimpses of their true warrior natures. Their efficiency amazed her. Between them, they scouted ahead, kept track of the Ketchums behind, yet one of them always remained with her and Marica.

Lorilie monitored their pursuers through the animal domain. The links with the territorial denizens required intense concentration. While they did not know her the way those near her abandoned home had, they accepted her dominance without hesitation.

Loner remained a constant companion throughout the day. Alternately, Lorilie prodded Marica and cajoled the mule. The Ketchums were on horseback, less than a day behind.

At dusk, Rafe called a halt beside a stream. Marica and Craig made camp while Lorilie fished for their dinner.

The tension of being hunted again frayed her nerves. Twice, she lost a good-sized trout.

She carried the trout stringer to the fire. "Where is Rafe?"

Craig inclined his head toward the darkness of the trees. "Meditating."

Stepping away from the bright fire, she closed her eyes long enough for her vision to adjust, then peered into the darkness. Rafe sat on the ground facing the fire, his legs crossed, his hands on his knees, palms up. She had seen him sit in that position numerous times. Until now, she had not known his statue stillness had a purpose.

Craig started filleting the fish. "He can go days without sleep and never miss a beat as long as he can meditate."

"Amazing," Marica said.

Craig shrugged. "He once told me twenty minutes of a kind of meditation he does"—his head jerked in Rafe's direction—"was the equivalent of four hours' sleep for him. I figure he's up to about six hours right now."

Every time Lorilie turned around she bumped into another complex dimension of her life mate. Watching Rafe, she wondered again if he was Gifted. If he could bend time within his body and turn twenty minutes into four hours, surely he was. A flicker of hope ignited. Perhaps the Gifted man Rafe sought to send him home was himself. If so, he might master the Gift and return to her. Often. Perhaps give her a child.

Daydreams and wishes.

Turning to more practical matters, she fashioned several twigs into a curry comb and tended the mule.

After washing up for dinner, she returned to the fire. Rafe spoke with Craig in the shadows. Briefly, her gaze met Rafe's. He appeared refreshed and at peace. She envied his ability to transform weariness into vigor.

Marica put a fork in Lorilie's hand. "Even if the Ketchums were not chasing us, I am glad we did not have to make this journey alone." Marica lifted the fish from the fire.

Lorilie agreed. They would not have had the advantage of the raft. They had thought of it, but lacked the brawn necessary to build it. "I've felt quite useless since we left. Rafe and Craig are so . . . competent."

"You are not useless. What you are is exhausted, Lorilie. Right now, eat." Marica shoved a plate of food at her.

"This is a great amount of food."

"Eat it all." Marica set down the plate and put her hands on her hips. "You think I don't know you were monitoring the impressions of the wolves, bears, and anything else on four legs all day? I know what kind of toll that takes. Do not even think of arguing with me. Eat. Then you will drink the sleeping tea I'm brewing and go to bed."

"Marica—"

"I wish I had a mirror." Marica rolled her eyes in exasperation. "I would put it in front of you so you could see what I see. The circles under your eyes are the only color on your face, Lorilie. What you are doing is dangerous." The pinch of her brow implored Lorilie to listen. The bite of frustration ebbed from her voice when she continued.

"Trust in Providence. Trust in your Guardian, and in mine. For reasons none of us understand, they are here for us now. You are no longer alone. Unless you choose to be."

Her appetite gone, Lorilie set down the plate. "I was alone before Rafe came. I will be alone after he is gone. Knowing that, it is irresponsible to abdicate my vigilance. To my great regret, I have already fallen prey to apathy and overconfidence. I should have sensed the trap in the graveyard. I should have known the Ketchums were coming." The red ball of emotion gained power with each confession.

"There is no way you could have known the net was there." Rafe approached the fire. "They laid the trap some time ago, probably when they tilted the headstone."

Hated memories battered the black wall threatening to

topple her defenses. She refused to think about what happened with the Ketchums. It was over. Done. Why did it linger like a ghost and attack during the vulnerable hours of sleep?

With shaking hands, Lorilie retrieved her plate. She summoned Loner and found a place in the shadows away from the glare of the fire.

Rafe joined her minutes later. They ate in silence, their surreptitious glances meeting, then darting to their plates.

When she finished, Rafe took her empty plate. "I won't be with you tonight."

A stone fell on her heart. "You intend to spy on the Ketchums?"

"We need to know which ones are following. We can gauge their determination by the weight of their provisions. Once I find out, I'll lay a false trail. With a little luck, they'll follow it in the morning. That'll allow us more distance, more time to decide."

"Decide what?"

"On our destination. Your father's valley may no longer be inhabited. If it is, we'll tell them what's coming down the pike. What we don't want to do is lead the Ketchums into the last known stronghold of the Gifted."

Lorilie drew her knees up and folded her arms across them. She should have realized the danger. The last few days, simple things eluded her. "You are right," she breathed.

"Do you trust me, Lorilie?"

With her whole heart. She nodded.

"I'll be watching over you. When the nightmares come, trust in me. The Ketchums are not coming tonight." He carried their plates to the fire. When he returned, he offered his hand.

He gathered her in a loose embrace when she stood. "I'll be back before sunrise." As though hating to leave her, his arms tightened.

Instinctively, she leaned against him, savoring the solidity of his strength and the steady thud of his heart against her chin. "The wolves will warn—"

"I hope not," he whispered. "I hope you'll be asleep. Please, Lorilie, drink the tea Marica made and sleep."

"I do not need—"

"Do this for my peace of mind. I need a clear head for what I'm doing."

"You want me to sleep knowing you are sneaking around men who wish to kill you?"

Rafe's head rocked against hers. "Suppose I compromise with you."

"How?"

"I'll take Loner with me."

Hearing his name, the wolf stood and shook himself.

For a long moment, she held on to Rafe and reveled in the gentle stroking of his hands over her back and shoulders. Thinking required more effort than feeling. Heavens, she was tired, and Loner would warn Rafe of danger.

"All right." The concession slipped out and she released him. He might have total control of his body, but as much as she wanted control, too, she did not have it. The longer she stood propped against him, the heavier her limbs grew. Fatigue was winning.

With her arm around Rafe's waist, she returned to the fire where Marica poured a cup of tea. The steam reminded her of the nightmares waiting to pounce.

Later, when she awakened in a cold sweat with a scream lodged in her throat, only the moon watched over her. Thoughts of Rafe calmed her.

"The Ketchums will not come tonight," she whispered, then closed her eyes. "They will not come tonight."

"It appears you thought the Ketchums had too many provisions." Lorilie held up a sack of coffee beans Rafe liberated from their pursuers. Any man capable of capturing such a rare prize from the heart of his enemy's camp was truly amazing and far too brazen.

"I found it." Craig tossed the coffee grinder to Rafe.

"I can't believe you stole coffee beans from them," Marica said, taking the grinder.

"Let's say I traded for them. I left something in exchange."

"What did you leave them?" Refreshed from her sleep, Lorilie's curiosity perked up for the first time in days.

"They'll be very surprised and more cautious, if they understand the meaning." Rafe shook out their bedroll.

"Tell me," Lorilie insisted.

He tied off the quilts, then tossed them to Craig. "A voodoo doll made from leaves, twigs, and pine needles. It had a bib-type necklace cut from Hal's hat. I propped it against his saddle horn."

Lorilie's heart skipped a beat, then raced. "Taunting them is unnecessary. And dangerous."

"Invading their camp undetected gives us a psychological advantage. When they realize I've been there, they'll be angry. Most of all, they'll be afraid because they'll know I could have killed them. They'll make mistakes."

"It is dangerous," she repeated.

"Psychological warfare is an old but effective tactic," Rafe continued. "At it's best, the enemy defeats himself without a shot being fired."

In a bizarre way, using fear as a weapon made sense. If she had awakened with a memento from the Ketchums near her bedroll, she would have run as far and fast as possible. Of course, they would probably leave a white-hot branding iron. Yes, fear was a viable weapon.

She turned away, not wanting to hear more, and forged links with the forest animals.

"The Ketchums. They split up," she said a few moments later, staring into the distance. The impressions solidified. "Two followed your false trail, Rafe. The other two are tracking us."

Rafe cursed under his breath. "How far to the valley, Lorilie?"

"Another two, maybe three days. The snow is still melting on the peaks. If the creeks are swollen, we'll have to find crossings the mule can navigate." She broke the links, content that she interpreted the impressions correctly. "First we have to climb. There is a pass the Ketchums will not find unless we leave a trail. The slope is rocky." She pointed at the ridge rising above the distant trees.

"We'll vacuum and dust after the mule," Craig said. "They won't see our trail, just the ones we create in different directions."

"Once we find a good pass, Craig, you take the women and the mule into the valley. I'll detain the Ketchums and make sure they don't follow." Rafe poured coffee into the waiting cups.

Lorilie rummaged through her bag of treasures. She tore the back flyleaf from her favorite book, found a pencil, and retreated into the trees for privacy. A short time later, she emerged prepared for the hard journey.

The sun beat down relentlessly. Summer heat gripped the mountains in a sweltering fist. They reached the base of the ridge at midafternoon. A creek gurgled down a swath cut into the terrain by seasonal drainage. In another month, the stream bed would dry out.

"If memory serves correctly, there is a rock formation suitable for shelter a mile or so downstream," Lorilie said, studying the foot of the steep slope. "It points the way to the pass."

Without waiting for comment, she led the mule along the stream and crossed at the shallowest point. A sense of satisfaction fortified her when she rounded a bend and the rock formation came into view.

"This is a good place to part," Rafe said, unloading a few things from the mule. "I won't need much."

"*We* won't need much," Lorilie said softly. "I am staying with you." She retrieved from her pocket the map she had drawn earlier on the flyleaf and gave it to Craig.

"Take Marica and go. If you travel steadily, you can make the pass before nightfall. A short way over the crest, the cliff forms a natural shelter. The mule will balk in anything short of full daylight. He dislikes heights, but will go where you want as long as he can see the path."

"Lorilie, you must come with us," Marica protested. "I cannot seek safety and leave you here."

She met her friend's worried hazel eyes, then shook her head. "No. What I have to do is stop running. I have jeopardized you. All of you. No more. Rafe and I will join you in the valley when it is done."

"The Ketchums—"

"This isn't about the Ketchums, Marica." Rafe rested his hand on Lorilie's shoulder. His knowing gaze held a sadness. "You picked a lousy time to face your demons, sweet Lorilie."

"I am not discussing the matter further." Her mind was set. Taking a stand bolstered her courage. "This is my decision."

"So be it," Rafe said, then squeezed her shoulder. "Let's repack the mule. We're burning daylight."

"I expected you to argue with me about staying," Lorilie said when Craig and Marica started their trek up the slope with the mule.

"Would it have accomplished anything?"

"No."

"I didn't think so." He picked up a fallen pine branch and stripped off the branchlets. "I'll check the rocks for snakes, then gather wood while you set up camp."

He was taking it awfully well, perhaps too well. She contemplated his lack of protest for the rest of the afternoon.

They doubled back far enough to erase their footprints from beside the stream and lay another false trail.

They worked well together, each comfortable with the other's skills in the forest. Without time-consuming explanation, the diversions they laid were subtle but detectable. The Ketchums would believe they had passed through and suspect their destination as Sutter's Mill.

"Let's scrounge up dinner."

Lorilie gathered berries, careful to eliminate any sign of their presence. "Marica left us the rice." She popped a berry into Rafe's mouth. "There are fish in the stream."

"Guess that'll have to do."

"What more could you want?"

Rafe chuckled and dropped a handful of berries into her cache. "A cold beer and a hot pizza."

"Pizza?"

"Come, sweet Lorilie. While we fish, I'll educate you in the gourmet treats of the twentieth century."

"I would rather learn how to meditate so I would not have to sleep."

"Teaching you that would take years, not the couple of hours we have before I check on the Ketchums." He added another handful of berries. "You'd still have to sleep."

"Years," she murmured. That was fine with her.

The choking fear of the nightmare ebbed. It worked. Amazing. She had not thought it possible to sleep. The relaxation technique he explained as they fished had helped. While they ate, they had explored a variety of scenes and situations conducive to her inner harmony.

The jubilation of her successful attempt at finding a calm deep enough for sleep made her smile in spite of the aftermath of the nightmare. The joy from the simple accomplishment left her wide awake. Unsure of how much of the night had passed, she sat and pulled on her boots.

Loner stood at the edge of the circle of firelight. The remnants of a large log crackled, then split into embers. Overhead, the moon dipped low on its journey across the stars in a cloudless sky.

She tossed a log into the fire, then settled on a rock a short distance away. Loner joined her, nudging her thigh for the attention she lavished by scratching his head. An owl hooted across the stream. On the slope leading to the ridge, a deer crashed through the scrub.

"Did you sleep at all?"

Startled, Lorilie jumped. Hackles rose along the ridge of Loner's spine. Clutching her chest, she leaped to her feet and whirled in the direction of Rafe's voice.

"I didn't mean to frighten you."

"How can a man as big as you be so quiet?" She drew a long, calming breath and squinted. Not until he moved could she make him out in the shadowy darkness.

"I brought a present for you."

"Pizza?"

Rafe chuckled and dug something from his trouser pocket while approaching the fire. "Not pizza. A couple of pieces of saddle cinches." The leather strips and rings dangled from his outstretched hand. "They either get creative and find a way to hold the saddles on their horses, or they ride bareback. Whichever way they choose makes it harder for them."

No wonder the shadows hid him so well. In the firelight, he looked as if he had wallowed in black mud. "Who is following us?"

"That's the bad news. Hal and Clyde. The good news is that Hal is hurting from the arrow I shot into him." Rafe dropped the cut cinches and unstrapped his knife sheath. "The man has more greed, fear, and hate than he has good sense."

Lorilie took the knife sheath and absently cleaned the dried mud from the pliable belt. "What do you mean?"

Rafe unlaced his boots and glanced up at her. The whites of his eyes fairly glowed in the flaking mud darkening his face. "It wasn't a lethal wound when I shot him. But now I suspect he's looking harder for Marica than you."

"She is out of his reach." Lorilie gazed up the dark slope.

"Yeah, well, apparently he's not taking care of the wound too well by himself. Of course, riding most of the day in the heat isn't helping his cause." He banged the soles of his boots together. Dried mud clods flew in all directions. "He's going to die. Not tomorrow. The bastard may take several days. But it's going to happen. The wound is infected. I can smell it. So can the wolves. They're waiting, and he knows it."

The same detachment in which she had accepted old man Ketchum's death coated her emotions. Though it seemed wrong, she could not summon up the sorrow that accompanied the loss of a life from anything other than natural causes.

She had changed, and in the process lost a precious part of herself.

"He chose his path, and ultimately his death, Lorilie."

"I know." She went to the edge of the stream and crouched. Using her shirttail as a rag, she cleaned the mud from Rafe's knife sheath and belt. "Perhaps, in the end, we all do, even if we are unaware of it at the time."

Chapter 27

LORILIE ABANDONED THE contradiction between her feelings and beliefs as Rafe stripped off his clothing. She almost forgot his knife when she stood.

The lure of her life mate wading naked into the cold stream enticed her the way the firelight drew unsuspecting insects. She set the knife next to the cut saddle cinches near the fire. With each step closer to Rafe, her heart beat a little faster.

The center of the stream dropped into a hole. Water lapped his waist. He disappeared below the surface. When he stood, muddy water sluiced over his shoulders, back, and chest.

Lorilie removed her right boot, then loosened and walked out of the left.

Rafe dunked again, popped up, and shook his head. Glistening water beads sprayed in all directions, then he sank below the surface again.

Her gaze riveted on the disturbances of Rafe's washing beneath the swift running water. She unfastened the thong at the end of her braid. Fingering her hair free one-handed, she released the buttons on her shirt.

The cool caress of the night air on her warm skin formed ripples of expectation and awakened the butterflies in her stomach.

Not a trace of mud remained when Rafe straightened this time. His big hands covered his face, then rose and pushed the water through his hair.

Lorilie dropped her shirt.

The motion caught Rafe's attention. Like a statue planted in the center of the stream, his hands froze at the back of his head. He stared.

Relishing the hungry gleam in his eyes, she unfastened her trousers and stepped out of them at the water's edge. Basking in the heat of his appreciating gaze, she barely noticed the chilly water sloshing around her ankles.

Slowly, his arms lowered. The hand he extended bid her to join him. She waded to the edge of the deeper water. Instead of helping her down, his hands closed around her hips and he lifted her against him. Reflexively, she sought the brace of his shoulders.

The glide of her hips down his torso created a frisson like lightning. The wet, silken texture of his chest hair dampening her pubic mound, and sliding along the soft, tender flesh of her belly, took her breath away.

The erotic journey down the hard wall of his abdomen halted. The rigid evidence of his desire nestled in the juncture of her legs. Her suspended toes wiggled in the water, but found no hold. The motion brought the pleasure spot Rafe had demonstrated last time they made love into delicious contact with the hard flesh blocking her descent. He held her in place with one arm. The slow, sinuous ascent of his other hand along the curve of her spine brought her breasts against his chest.

The firelight reflected as a torrid blaze in his eyes. She saw desire in the gray flames. Tenderness and concern shone even brighter. She leaned into him, her arms flowing over his shoulders. The need to enfold him within her spirit brought her legs up. Her ankles locked around his thighs.

He nuzzled the hollow of her neck and shoulder. The enticement proved too much. Seeking the nectar of his mouth, her cheek pressed against his.

A sudden, fanatical burst of desire mushroomed. Heads moving side to side, their hungry mouths met and parted, only to come together again with growing impatience. Rafe wrapped her hair around his hand and caught the back of her head. The bold thrust of his tongue claimed her as a deep growl rumbled in his chest.

The more he demanded, the more she gave. She yielded to the sensory delight of his tongue delving into the recesses of her mouth. He tempered his urgency for exploring every secret she harbored. The tip of his tongue prodded hers, teasing her to join the delicious skirmish.

The bond of life mates burst on them with a jolt. She cried out, breaking their kiss, reveling in the heady waves of combined desire. When she found his mouth again, she invaded without hesitation. As his free hand scoured her back and skimmed the side of her breast, she explored the ever-changing contours of his muscles bunching and stretching along his back and shoulders. The sleekness of the water heating on his skin allowed her ravenous hands quick motion.

The next thing she knew, she was underwater. Instinctively, she released him, pushed back and found the ground. Astonished, she came up sputtering, the bond of shared desire shattered.

"What . . . Why did you do that?" she demanded, flinging her hair from her face.

"Another minute, and I'd have taken you right here. Now we're cooled off." He caught her face in his hands and brushed away her wet hair. "For the moment."

"What is wrong with here?"

Rafe chuckled. "Haven't you noticed it's cold?"

Now that he mentioned it, her feet did feel like ice

blocks. ''I guess it is. However, since I'm here, I may as well take a bath.''

''You better hurry.''

She bent her knees and dipped below the surface. Using his legs as pillars, she arched her breasts against his thighs and slowly pushed upward. Head back, her face broke the surface. Her lashes lifted.

The intensity of his expression grew painful as her breasts cradled his erection.

Lorilie pressed the sides of her breasts and rose slowly. The effect of an envelope of soft flesh rising along his erection seemed to virtually paralyze him. A slight smile betrayed her sense of playful power. Her languid rise continued. The contact of her aroused nipples along the changing textures of his abdomen, then his chest, promised the fire she played with would soon consume her.

She hoped so.

His response came in a whirling swish of water. In a smooth, swift motion, Rafe levered himself out of the depression. Without straightening, he reached down and caught her by the shoulders. Her feet barely touched the stream bed before he swept her up and carried her to the shelter.

''Did you sleep?'' he demanded, ducking below the canted rock slab serving as a partial roof.

''Yes. Make love with me, Rafe.'' Giving him no opportunity for another question, she assumed the role of the aggressor by capturing his face in her hands and kissing him repeatedly.

His progress toward the pallet onshore slowed. When he reached it, he laid her down gently, then kissed her in earnest. Passion flared between them.

For this island in time, they shared an all-consuming union. Nothing beyond the moment mattered within the cocoon of scintillating desire burning them both. In a burst of clarity, she realized their precious Gift of sharing went beyond the mating instinct. Their blended desire had melded on a spiritual as well as physical plane. It was indeed making love. Her love, like her desire, flourished with each heated breath.

"How the hell did I ever find you?" Rafe murmured. He angled his body to one side and lifted his head. Amazement softened the chiseled planes of his features and widened his eyes.

"With great difficulty, or so it seems." Her fingers coasted along his ribs. The narrowing of his waist gave way to the hard line of his hip.

"I feel this thing we share down to the soles of my feet. But I still have trouble believing it." Callused fingertips created fiery trails along her collarbone before exploring the swell of her breasts.

She loved touching him. The way he tilted on his side invited greater exploration.

"You have no inhibitions, no guile." His hand wrapped around her breast and squeezed gently. "You are a carnal creature."

"Is that good or bad?" The back of her fingers stroked his abdomen, daring lower with each pass.

"It's so incredibly good the way you want me. No pretense." A hum of appreciation sounded as he lowered his mouth to her breast. The tip of his tongue circled the pink areola bordering her nipple. "And you taste so good." He drew her nipple between the edges of his teeth.

The intense pleasure sent her arching upward. A long, deep breath filled her lungs. Her fingers rose to his neck, caressing him against her breast, savoring the endless dimensions of pleasure unfolding through her.

"Rafe. Rafe," she murmured, "I love this. What I feel when you do this."

He worshipped her breasts with his mouth and hands. His roaming hand drifted lower, caressing her ribs.

"I want you," she breathed.

"Oh, God. You have me, Lorilie." He shifted, his mouth and hands became fire on her flesh. "So sweet."

The murmur from his lips at her navel vibrated the ache growing stronger in her lower abdomen.

Gently, he parted her thighs and settled into the nest of her greatest pleasure center. His chin grazed her hairline in slow circles.

"Like spun gold," he whispered, raising her knees.

Though unsure of his intent, she shared his growing excitement. The fire of his tongue on the pleasure spot wrung a small cry from her. Each brush of his tongue, nibble of his lips was an intimate, exciting experience turning her blood to bubbling honey.

Rafe took his time teasing, tasting, hurtling her toward the brink of ecstasy. The exhilaration in her passion-blurred mind defied comprehension. He wove an exquisitely tender, bold yet reverent magic through her body. Just when she thought she would die of wanting, Rafe loomed over her.

"Touch me. Put me inside you." His body arched over her, his mouth lowered to hers.

She felt the head of his erection poised at her entrance. Her hand reached down and closed around him. Heeding the plea of her own burgeoning desire, she drew him inside, and ascended higher.

"Lorilie," he breathed into her mouth. Slowly, he eased his hips forward.

The pressure of his fullness brought no pain this time, only an odd, quaking pleasure and the quivering of expectation.

"You're so tight." The retreat of his erection sent her grasping.

"Rafe?" Her fingers dug into the granite swell of his buttocks. She groaned in relief when he moved deeper into her and did not stop until he had no more to give. "Yes. I want all of you."

"You don't." Dark, dilated, and dangerous, his gaze met hers.

"I do. Open for me. Let me all the way inside."

"In a moment." The sinuous rhythm of his hips met her eager response. "Let me kiss you first."

The control he exerted became an aphrodisiac. His slow thrusts brought the delicious frenzy tumbling through her veins. She could scarcely think, and did not care. The bliss he showered on her felt like a kiss from the sun.

A languid euphoria accompanied her floating descent from paradise. "It is magic."

"It most definitely is." He nipped her ear, then caught her lobe between his teeth.

"We are life mates, Rafe. There is no deception, no hiding when we make love." She stroked his thigh with the arch of her foot. "Teach me all you know." She traced his ear with her fingertip. "I want to learn everything."

Rafe groaned. His movements took on a quicker pace.

"I want—" The possessive kiss claiming her mouth banished the rest of her thought. True to his word, he unleashed the beast in his nature. The magnitude of his ravaging desire swept through her.

She embraced the new dimension of their ferocious passion with wild elation. In the back of her consciousness, she understood that a man could not want a woman with the totality of his being unless he loved her.

She reveled in his adoration and the mounting passion seeking release that he brought them close to again and again, tempting, delaying, seeking the pinnacle of conjoined bliss.

Though he spoke not a word, she knew when the predator in him snapped his leash. He claimed her reverently. For an instant, she felt holy. With her next breath, she reached their special paradise.

When the sun burst on her again, it burned hotter and brighter. Rafe was with her in the rapture she would never tire of experiencing.

He rolled them onto their sides. For a long time they

held one another, stroking, caressing, and exchanging tender kisses in the dark.

The awesome commingling of desires and sensation experienced when making love with Lorilie weren't a fluke. She got it right the first time—it was magic. Fan-damntastic magic the world would need a separate language to describe. The kind a man couldn't explain, but would sell his very soul for. He'd fight armies bare-handed. Sacrifice every belief and principle he held dear. The kind of mystical miracle a man would live for and cherish.

"I love you, Rafe." The soft press of her lips on his chest formed an arrow of pleasure aimed straight at his heart. "Making love with you is a sacrament."

It was more than a sacrament. Making love with her was a life-altering experience. In the aftermath, the elusive answers he had fiercely pursued stood as shiny and naked as the morning sun in a cloudless sky.

"You've changed me." He shook his head. "No, I've changed me."

Lorilie laughed sadly. "We have both changed. I do not know if it is good or bad. Perhaps it does not matter. In coming together as life mates even for a short while, we gain more than we lose."

"I can't imagine making love with any woman but you again." The confession slipped out. Instantly, he wished for it back.

Lorilie rose on her elbow. "And I will not imagine you wanting to if you found a way back to your old life. Do not make me the reason for regrets later, Rafe."

"Celibacy is not my long suit." He'd opened the door, and might as well march through. "The most I've ever managed was nineteen months and six days." A tilt of his head and a half smile offered an apology. "It was a long, dry season."

Lorilie drew back, perplexed. "What kind of man counts the days between mating?"

"A horny one. But you've got the terminology right

this time. Definitely mating. Sex. Biology with a little chemistry thrown in during the selection process.'' He rolled onto his back. Sex. He was thirty-two years old and couldn't count the number of women he'd slept with. Other than Jennifer, none had mattered enough to remember. Until the wood nymph at his side gave him her virginity, her passion, and the essence of her spirit, he'd never given enough of himself to really make love. Now he'd settle for nothing less than the miracle he shared with Lorilie.

''When I got here, I was a confused puppy. Not about sex, just everything else. I wasn't confused about sex until that night in the small shelter.'' Belatedly he acknowledged that he'd sought to protect himself by denying them both.

She spread her hands on his chest and rested her chin atop them. The red skies of dawn filtering through the rocky crags cast a fiery halo in her disheveled hair.

''I doubt I would have fared as well as you have if I found myself in your time.''

Unable to resist touching her for long, he stroked the smooth valley of her spine. ''You scared the hell out of me. You broke me the first day, Lorilie, and didn't even know it.

''Oh, I fought you. I fought myself. That's over. We're coming down to the wire.''

''What wire?''

His laughter jostled her, but she remained perched on his chest. ''Just an expression. It means decision time.'' He was not the same man who called an air strike in the Bolivian jungle. Today, he was more, yet somehow less. Mulling over the changes, he discovered he was close to renewing a balance that had fallen out of whack thirteen years earlier with the death of his parents.

''I thought you had made your decision. It is possible someone in the valley can send you back, or show you how to take yourself back.''

"What do you mean, take myself back?" The woman threw more curves than a major league pitcher.

Her brow furrowed as though she searched for the right words. "I believe you are Gifted, Rafe. You fold time when you meditate, do you not?"

"That isn't the same thing." Meditation created time travel as effectively as touching a toad gave you warts.

"Perhaps. Perhaps not. What we share when we make love does not happen spontaneously between a Gifted and an Outsider."

She had his attention now.

He sat up, taking her with him. "How do you know? Is there a written history I could read or is your source lore handed down through the generations?"

She shrugged. "I asked Marica."

Rafe shook his head in disbelief. Discussing anything so personal with Craig, let alone Marica, never crossed his mind. And never would. "I don't think that's the case. Maybe we're . . . in tune with one another. I'm not Gifted. What I am is in love with you."

"I know." An angelic smile lit her face.

"You know," he said flatly. How could she know? He'd only admitted the earth-shattering truth to himself a short time ago. Even then, he'd needed to get used to it.

"Yes. However, I did not know if you knew you love me. Now that I do, perhaps I will miss you less when you go."

"Your logic escapes me." Lorilie's train of thought reminded him of railroad tracks stretching into the distance and appearing to converge on the horizon.

She folded her legs Indian style and faced him. "Now that we both know you love me, we will celebrate whatever time we may have together without reservation. If you return to your time, I will not wish for your love. It is already mine and will grow forever in my heart."

Gazing at her, he sensed the proverbial wire at his chest. Echoes of a simpler time in his old life grew louder.

"When I was fifteen, my folks took me to Washington, D.C. We visited the monuments erected to honor those who died in the country's wars. In this time, those wars haven't happened yet, but they will, Lorilie.

"I was a reader as a kid, and filled with questions. Maybe because I regarded my parents as ancient, I looked to them for answers. They had some good ones."

"Books can tell us so much," she agreed.

"Anyway, I stood at the Tomb of the Unknown Soldier and thought about all the crosses and the long lists of names carved into the stone monuments. I thought about the men a few years older than me and how they'd never have another birthday. I'd discovered girls by then and wondered how many of the dead had to make a choice between love and duty. I asked my father how a man made such a difficult decision." He paused, recalling the conversation as though it happened yesterday.

"What did he say?"

The morning sun poked a finger of light into the shelter. The curiosity burning in her green eyes regarded him with unabashed honesty. "My father said the greatest duty a man had was to protect and take care of those he loves. Whatever that takes, that's what he does.

"At the time, I didn't think he understood the question." He exhaled sharply, amazed by the narrow view of his youth. "At fifteen, I didn't know enough to understand the answer."

He gathered her hands and pressed her fingers to his lips. "I love you, Lorilie. Will you marry me? Will you stay beside me until one of us draws our last breath? I swear by all that's sacred, I'll protect you and cherish you. I'll do my damnedest to make you glad you're my wife everyday."

"We are bound together as life mates, Rafe. There is nothing stronger. If you wish a formal acknowledgment for the rest of the world, we will have a ceremony. I will go wherever you go, even through time."

Her simple logic and open acceptance humbled him. "Where I come from . . . it would be in conflict with your Gift, with the harmony you cherish and thrive on. We aren't going through time, Lorilie. We're staying here."

Confusion pinched her eyebrows. "But you want to go back. What if you decide it was a mistake to stay with me here? I could not endure being the cause of regret when it turned into bitterness."

"I told you I've changed, but I didn't realize just how much until now. I don't fit into my old life anymore. Hell, I was good at my job because I didn't have anything to lose. I never let emotion out of its cage. Well, the door is wide open. Now I have something to lose.

"My father's answer makes sense. I love you. My duty—my life—is here. With you. The woman I pledged my loyalty to in exchange for Craig's life." The irony made him chuckle in disbelief at the man he had been. "The Ranger who surrendered without a fight to a pacifist without a weapon."

"I am awed by the depth of your love, Rafe. The sacrifice you are willing—"

"Believe me, sweet Lorilie, this isn't a sacrifice. Damn, I've never felt so free." He gathered her into his arms. The choice was not between love and duty, but life with Lorilie and death without her. "Let's make love."

"I believe it is my turn for exploring."

Holding her chin, his mouth hovered over hers. "I believe you're right."

Chapter 28

STIFLING HEAT SHIMMERED in the midafternoon
air. Perspiration trickled down the side of Lorilie's face
and neck.

Rafe had left to watch the Ketchums over an hour ago.

Downstream, the trees stirred with a promise of relief.
She let the firewood she gathered fall and faced the direction of the sound. A gust of hot wind fanned her damp
clothing. Arms spread, she greeted the respite gladly. The
breeze prickled her sweat-dampened scalp, tempting her
to release her hair and let it fly. The dry heat carried on
the wind sapped the moisture from her clothing and body.

Lorilie resumed gathering wood and kept an eye on the
line of heavy clouds rolling in from the northwest. Summer storms were usually volatile when the heat soaked
the great valley at the foot of the mountains. Once the
peaks snagged the clouds, rain would cleanse the dust
from the forest and cool the ground.

She arranged firewood on pedestals in a sheltered rock
cranny. After the storm passed she and Rafe would be
warm and somewhat dry—when he returned. If Hal was

as ill as Rafe suspected, he and Clyde would have to seek shelter, too.

Listless, she worked steadily, stopping when she realized there was enough wood for several days. Considering the steady progress of the Ketchums, Bobby and Hank would reach the stream no later than this time tomorrow. By then, she and Rafe would be farther east. The rugged high country was the great equalizer. The steep, rocky terrain undercut the benefit gained from the Ketchums' horses.

She picked up the cut saddle cinches and marveled at Rafe's daring, rivaled only by his ingenuity. What was he doing now?

Lorilie concentrated on the wolves roaming the forest. Fleet of foot, intelligent, and accustomed to acknowledging the dominance of a superior, the wolves were her easiest and most reliable allies. Because they traveled in packs, she could gather a variety of impressions by skipping among them, honing the bond. The wolves' innate interest in the men worked to her benefit. By indulging their curious nature, she kept the advantage of proximity.

It was not surprising the wolves recognized Rafe as a deadly predator. With a little coaxing, they deemed him one of their own, the mate of the one they served without question. They followed him with special interest.

The wind gusted, bending the heavy tree boughs until they groaned. Lorilie set a half-burned, flaming log aside, then doused the fire. A few wild embers would set the entire mountain ablaze. She carried the smoldering log into the shelter and lit the kindling nestled in the rock structure she had built against a boulder. The loose formation allowed the eddies of wind through. At the moment, none were strong enough to carry away an ember.

As the storm approached, she regarded the lightning flashes in the west with apprehension. A strike would ignite the blankets of golden-brown grasses dotting the lower slopes like the pattern in a patchwork quilt.

Where was Rafe? Did he see the storm?

Unable to sit still, she poked at the dead fire. Loner nudged her, begging for an ear scratch. She dug her fingers into his thick fur and appeased him.

"This storm is not a good thing right now," she murmured, distracted by the lighting flashes and the churning storm clouds. Pine needles, flower petals, and leaves swirled over the open ground. The wind scudded against the current of the stream. Foamy whitecaps formed on the miniature rapids.

"Go find Rafe," she told Loner. "Watch over him for me." She scuffed the area behind his ears. "Be my eyes, Loner."

The wolf bounded across the stream and hit full stride at the far bank.

He would find Rafe.

When Loner disappeared into the forest, she could think of nothing else to do but wait and watch.

Lorilie settled on a rock. The grumble of distant thunder heightened her unease. As a consolation, she sought Loner.

Rafe recognized the danger in the storm's fury. The temperature drop in the wind registered sharply on his sweat-soaked skin.

He spotted Clyde and Hal crossing the adjacent ridge on horseback. Even from this distance, Hal appeared in bad shape.

Lorilie was right. Hate and fear governed Hal. Seeing him sway in the saddle, Rafe doubted Hal's common sense would fill a doll's thimble.

Squinting, he saw Clyde dismount and adjust the makeshift saddle cinch. Rafe grinned. The tactic hadn't stopped them, but it did slow them down considerably. Most of the day had passed and the Ketchums had made less than three miles.

This was good. Definitely good. Tonight he'd take their horses.

While part of him enjoyed the extemporaneous torment of the Ketchums, he wanted to end it. Life with Lorilie as his wife awaited. The only sure thing about their future was that it would never be boring.

He grit his teeth into the wind.

Loner bounded through the brush.

Worry shot through him. Had something happened to Lorilie?

Gauging the direction of the false trail Hank and Bobby had followed, they could not have doubled back and found her. Her justifiable paranoia of being captured fostered frequent links with her allies. She wouldn't be vulnerable again—unless she was hurt.

Loner panted beside him, his tongue lolling over his fangs. The wolf gave no indication of distress and gazed at him in expectation.

"She sent you, didn't she?" He dropped onto his knees and scratched the wolf behind the ears.

Loner's eyes rolled with delight. "All right," Rafe whispered. Hell, there was no reason for her to worry.

He lowered his defenses, unsure how, or if, she'd sense him at this distance. Now seemed as good a time as any for trying. The absolute calm in him rippled as though a feather wafted across his forehead. The eeriness unsettled him.

Despite what they shared while making love, he doubted he'd ever be comfortable with letting her prowl the mood of his predatory nature. Reflexively, his defenses rose.

In terms of sheer physical power, without question, he was the stronger. He was also the more knowledgeable and experienced partner in their relationship. But regardless what the future held for them, he recognized Lorilie as the dominant force. She commanded the tides of his emotion with love. Unlike Loner and the rest of the forest denizens, he could keep her out if she chose to attempt entry. But like them, he accepted the mistress of his heart as dominant.

Damn, but love made a man crazy.

He and Loner marked the Ketchums' progress. As the wind gathered strength and the sky darkened with heavy clouds, Rafe kept expecting the Ketchums to seek shelter.

Several times Clyde halted as if to do so. Hal continued, determined to reap the reward he sought around the next copse of trees or in the next swale.

"Push yourself right into your own grave." Rafe watched a little longer before abandoning the low mound hiding him from their sight.

Lightning forked overhead. Thunder shook the ground as Rafe sprinted through the trees on a half-circle route that would bring him out ahead of the Ketchums. If he hurried, he'd have time to lay another false trail into a box canyon. They wouldn't find the dead end for a day or two, maybe more at the slow rate of their progress. After tonight, they'd be on foot. Yes, he liked the idea more every minute.

Around him, branches whipped and groaned. Leaves and pine needles slapped him with the wind.

The sky lit with a dazzling flash. Rafe staggered, momentarily blinded. Deafening thunder rattled his bones. What felt like the fist of God struck him.

Lorilie bolted to her feet.

Something was wrong. Very wrong.

Confusion and fear seized Loner. His disorientation registered in the marrow of her bones.

The wolf was digging, but she could not discern the reason.

She vacillated for a moment as worry blossomed into fear. Tentatively, she sought the predator in Rafe.

And found nothing. Not even the wall of his defenses.

Panicked, she began running. The angry stream pushed

at her knees, trying to wash her into the growing fury of the wind. She stumbled across, heedless of the water sloshing in her boots.

Had the Ketchums found Rafe? Had they shot him?

Half-crazed, she formed links among her allies. The forest came alive with creatures forced from their safe hiding places and into the violent storm. All searched for Rafe, and Loner, who remained at his side.

Incessant lightning and thunder charged the air with urgency. Branches whipped at Lorilie as she followed the impressions flooding her mind.

Twice the rugged terrain forced a change of direction. Each precious minute of a detour seemed an hour. Ignoring the stitch in her side, she ran, catching branches and scrub on the steepest slopes to pull up or keep her from tumbling.

Wolves howled in the lapses of thunder. The growing clarity reassured her direction. She was close.

She scrambled up a heavily forested swale and saw Loner. Her heart plunged into her wet boots. The wolf dug frantically at something trapped under a fallen tree.

Rafe.

"Oh, God, Rafe." She ran, summoning help from the denizens.

Kicking and tugging, she stripped away branches until she found him. Blood oozed from a knot on his forehead. He breathed as though asleep.

"Rafe. Rafe. Wake up." She stroked his face, begging for a response.

He groaned, then slowly opened his eyes. They flew wide at the sight of her. The pinch of his eyebrows and furrow of his brow conveyed his confusion.

"Can you move?" Silently, she prayed the tree had not impaled him.

Dazed, his gray eyes reflected the clouds overhead. A grimace twisted his mouth and narrowed his eyes when he flexed his limbs. He tried to rise against the tree trunk lying across his ribs. Despite his efforts, it remained solid. "I'm trapped."

"We can get this off you." At the shattered top of the tree, her minions of wolves gathered. The weight of the trunk rested heavily on two broken pine branches. The heavy trunk pinned Rafe beneath the arching branches. Somehow or another, they had to lift the tree off of him.

"Lorilie." He wormed a hand free, snapping branches on the way.

She caught it and brought his fingers to her lips. "I'm here, and we are going to get you out from under there."

With the eye of a problem solver, he scrutinized his situation. Testing the weight of the tree, pushing at the branches did not budge the trunk. He rested his head on the rise supporting him and the tree. "Can you reach my knife?"

Parting the branches, turning her face away from the prickly pine needles slapping at her with the wind, she groped along his thighs. "Lift and twist your hips toward me if you can."

He did, but not much. She grappled with the debris until she loosened the strap holding his knife in its sheath. "Be still. I have it."

"Trust me. I won't move. Angle the blade away from me."

"I like you whole, too." Broken branches thwarted her. She returned it to the sheath and worked bare-handed at creating the necessary space to free the knife.

"When you get the knife out, leave. Hell, we're right in the path of the Ketchums. Hal hasn't got enough sense to stop."

"Lift and twist a little more. I think I've made a path." Using both hands, she freed the knife, then crouched on her heels as she gave it to him. Lightning cracked to her right. "I am not going anywhere without you," she hollered over the thunder.

Loner resumed digging beside Rafe's shoulder.

Rafe swore under his breath. "We haven't got time to argue." One-handed, he hacked at the branches around his head and shoulders. Grunting, he gingerly wiggled onto his side.

"There has to be a way to lift this off you." Lorilie straightened, squinting against the wind and lightning, and searching for leverage points.

"If we try to lift it and it falls, it might not land on these branches. I'd prefer not to have a stake driven through any part of my anatomy. I'll have to dig out." Oddly contorted, his back pressed against the splintered branches, he used the knife as a digging tool. He widened the indentation Loner started and let the wolf scrape away the dirt.

Lorilie brought in the wolf pack. "Scoot down as far as you can and cover your head. You want a trench, they will give you one."

Dubious, Rafe tucked the knife away and did as she asked.

"I told ya! Follow those goddamn wolves and we'd find her."

Heart leaping into her throat, Lorilie whirled toward the hate-filled voice behind her. Bile rose in her throat. She swallowed frantically to keep it down.

Twenty feet away on the side slope, the wind battered Hal Ketchum. A bandanna tied his ragged hat to his head. The low brim could not hide his rheumy eyes or his ashen pallor.

"Yeah, Hal. You were right." Clyde's horse tossed his head nervously in the presence of wolves and the roll of thunder. Stroking the horse's neck, he gazed at his brother. "Now what do you want to do?"

Lorilie fought the wolves' natural instinct. The threat they perceived was very real. Her heart hammered as loudly as the thunder growling overhead. Facing Hal brought her nightmares to life. Fear weakened her knees.

Her breath came in gasps. All she could think about was getting them away from Rafe.

"Fetch her. If one of them wolves makes a move, shoot it." Left-handed, Hal fumbled a revolver from the belt in his trousers. "I got you figured out, girl. Them wolves ain't gonna come after us. You know we'll kill 'em, and you don't want that, now, do you?"

Any response she might have found died in her throat. She heard Rafe and the wolves tearing at the ground behind her. Paralyzed by fear, she gaped at Hal. The waking nightmare embodied bullets instead of branding irons, but death cared little for the manner it claimed its own. Hal's hatred allowed only one option.

"I'm not getting off my horse. Damn it, she's surrounded by wolves." Clyde's horse danced nervously, his eyes rolling with terror.

"Yes, you are. You're gonna do it while I put a bullet in that bastard's brain." Hal urged his frightened mount closer.

"No!" The scream ripped from Lorilie's throat. The anger she denied while awake had festered in nightmares. It surged toward freedom with a long, silent scream. Regardless of the cost, she would not allow Hal to shoot Rafe.

"You ain't gonna stop us, bitch. You're ours." He edged closer. The wind swirled the stench of his infection over her. Like his heart, his untreated wounds exuded a malevolent poison.

Wild with outrage, bolstered by determination, she focused on Hal's mount. With a perforce of will, she projected images of the wolves viciously tearing the horse apart.

The terrified animal reared in wild-eyed panic. Hal's gun sailed into the brush as he grappled for the saddle horn one-handed. The gyrations of the horse broke his tenuous hold. Shouting, he toppled off the fleeing horse. He bounced against a tree, then landed hard and immediately curled protectively around his injured arm and ribs. While he screamed in agony, the horse fled.

Clyde soothed his mount and held the bit tight in the horse's mouth. The horse backed away, fighting the bit and the command keeping him near the wolves.

Gradually, Lorilie became aware of the scraping and digging sounds behind her. Rafe and the wolves worked relentlessly. The fallen tree shuddered and shook from their frenetic efforts.

"You will not hurt him." The anger seething in her flourished with no end in sight. The stranglehold of fear clutched at her throat with the horrific memory of old man Ketchum's choking fingers.

Hal groaned and curled tighter onto his injured side. "Kill the bastard," he wheezed. "Take her."

Lorilie positioned herself between Clyde and Rafe. "I have endured your hatred. Your fear. Your greed. Even your torture. Through it all I did not retaliate.

"I have had enough!" Her shout stilled the wolves.

Rafe continued digging and prying himself from under the heavy trunk.

"You think I will go without a fight? You are wrong. I will not go at all. Nor will I allow you to harm Rafe."

"Clyde . . ." Hal started.

Clyde dismounted, then tied his horse securely to a tree and withdrew his rifle. "Stand aside, Lorilie. I have no wish to kill you."

"I promise you this, Clyde, you will have to. And if you do shoot me, the wolves will attack you and every Ketchum in the mountains. They know you on sight. As a pack and alone, they will hunt you as you have hunted me. They will torment you night and day. It will be a slow, painful death since I won't be around to control them." She took another step closer, making sure the rifle remained pointed at her.

"Ahhh, Lorilie McCaully, you can't do that. It's against your people's beliefs."

Fury calmed her when she met Clyde's mocking stare. "Beliefs can be changed. I would trade my life, my very soul for Rafe, so what possible regard could I have for any of you?" Disdainful, she sneered at Hal groping the bushes for his gun.

Loner broke ranks with the wolves behind her. She pointed at Hal. Obedient, Loner approached his target with a growl, his fangs bared, the hackles on his back rippling in the wind. "Do you seek to test the depth of my convictions?"

"Shoot it, Clyde," Hal whimpered.

That was their answer to anything in their way: kill it, hurt it, wring the last ounce of will from it until they got what they wanted. A coldness swept through her. Committed to her unfurling anger, she persisted. "If you shoot him, I will turn the rest loose on you. They will not kill you. Not right away." She took another step. "I may vacillate, and let you live long enough to heal, then send them after you again. And again. Just as you did to me and Grandfather."

Her eyes narrowed with the realization she was not helpless unless she allowed them to make her so. She sneered at him. "Hal isn't worth wasting time on. He lies dying as we speak. I smell it. So can you." Her head inclined toward the wolves. "So do they. His stench is as rancid as his soul. They regard him as carrion."

Clyde's eyes widened and the rifle barrel shifted. The wolves gathered around her.

She risked a backward glance. Covered with dirt and sappy pine needles, Rafe shimmied out from under the tree.

Clyde swore under his breath and raised the rifle.

"I always keep my promises," Lorilie said, moving closer and blocking his line of sight.

"Lorilie." Rafe came to stand behind her. Dirt-crusted fingers closed around her shoulders.

The Ketchums were her demons. Rafe would not intervene again. The rage pulsing through her flashed at the predator in him, then focused on Clyde.

"He could have killed you any number of times. Take a good look at him, Clyde. Does he appear submissive, docile?" Another step brought her within reach of the rifle. "He knows ways of tormenting and taking a man's life you have never thought of. Yet he let you live. Instead of being grateful for the gift of your life, all you want to do is kill."

"Why?" Clyde eyed Rafe nervously.

"Why what?" she snapped, inching a little closer.

"Why didn't you kill us when you had the chance?"

"She asked me not to," Rafe said from beside her. "Are you going to do something stupid and make us all regret it as much as I regret not killing old man Ketchum before I did?"

"Kill 'em." Hal coughed and shivered under Loner's dripping fangs.

Lorilie met Clyde's uncertain gaze and placed her hand on the end of the rifle barrel. "For what purpose? Gold you will not find? Fear of those who helped instead of harmed you? Or for the satisfaction of the hate festering in Hal's heart?"

Lightning struck a tree on the adjacent ridge. Thunder mingled with the explosive sound of the sap igniting. Tendrils of smoke laced the gusty wind whipping and snapping the trees around them.

Waiting for an answer, Lorilie's anger abated. Her demons were flesh and blood. Like her, they could live or die. Refusing them the nourishment of helpless fear starved their life force.

Clyde took a hard look at Hal. Slowly, he lowered the rifle. "There's no reason to kill them." Decisive, he turned away. He patted the horse's neck in reassurance and angled his rifle into the saddle holster. "You don't suppose Marica would consider helping Hal, do you?"

"She's gone," Rafe said.

"Ungrateful bitch." Hal rocked in pain.

"Come on, Hal. Let's go home."

"You ain't no kin of mine," he hissed, breathing rapidly. "If you were, you'da shot that bastard and this wolf. You'da made her scream. Like her ma."

The chill of revulsion rode Lorilie's skin. "Take him and leave before I lose my temper," Lorilie said quietly, then approached Hal. "You will not goad me into the favor of taking your life. Your fate is in your own hands. We each chose our paths."

"I'll see you in hell." Hal clutched his wounded arm against his chest. "I'll catch you there."

"She won't be there, but I will. And I'll be looking for you, Ketchum," Rafe said softly.

"Come on, Hal. We're leaving." Clyde helped his brother stand on shaky legs. Not a sound escaped as Clyde lifted and pushed him onto the nervous horse.

Neither sympathy nor satisfaction rippled Lorilie's awareness as she watched the personification of defeat slump in the saddle.

Clyde took the reins and started walking.

"I will not stay these wolves for more than two days, Clyde. Travel quickly."

Without turning, he raised a hand.

Fat raindrops rode nearly horizontal on the wind. By the time Clyde and the burdened horse disappeared over the edge of the slope, the rain pelted them.

Lorilie released the wolves and let the hollow of her spent anger and fear settle. She leaned into the shelter of Rafe's broad chest.

"I don't suppose it'll do any good to yell. You scared the hell out of me, Lorilie. Damn, but I hated feeling helpless when you put yourself in front of Clyde's rifle."

The reassurance of his vitality swept away the remaining cobwebs of fear. Amazement crept into her awareness. "I did not believe myself capable of such . . . violence. I would have done as I promised." The realization sent a shiver of apprehension through her.

"You damn near exploded every brain cell I have left." He drew a heavy breath and let it out slowly. "Sometimes facing a demon is the only way to exorcise it, sweet Lorilie." His protective embrace tightened in emphasis.

"I am ready to speak of my nightmares." She tilted her face upward. Rain washed dirt from his face in irregular blotches. The tender understanding in his eyes regarded her with undisguised love. "But perhaps we should get off this ridge."

He kissed the tip of her nose, then nodded. "No perhaps about it. If we don't get across the stream soon, it'll be too swollen to cross."

She released him with a smile. "Are you always so practical?"

"Afraid so."

She skirted the fallen tree, then paused and squinted at him through the rain. "You will not see Hal in hell, Rafe."

"You think not?" He caught her hand and followed Loner through the driving rain.

"No," she called over the wind. "I will not allow it."

Chapter 29

"YOUR NIGHTMARES MAY linger for a while," Rafe said above the storm thundering outside the safety of their rock shelter. He lifted his right shoulder. Whatever Lorilie had spread on the punctures had the bite of a wasp stinger. "They'll come back, but they lose their punch with time."

"Spoken by a man of experience." She kissed his shoulder. "One miracle at a time is sufficient. I can endure the nightmares now that I have faced Hal."

"He's a stubborn customer. Judging by the stench of his wounds, I give him three days at the most." He picked slivers from his hands with a needle. "You pegged him well. He wanted you to take his life. In his eyes, that brought you down to his level, and put him out of his suffering."

Lorilie rested her cheek against his back. "His death does not sadden me in any way."

"You were wrong about me, Lorilie. I'm not Gifted. I have no ability to bend time. If I did, we wouldn't be here."

With one finger, she applied the stinging salve to another puncture wound. "Did you try to leave?"

Rafe snorted. "That's an understatement. I wanted us anywhere but there. I tried concentrating. I tried resignation. Hell, I even tried acceptance. You notice we didn't go anywhere?"

"In one way, that was good. I was not ready to leave. Hal filled me with fear. And anger. I was angry because I was afraid, and afraid because I was so very angry. If you had whisked us off to another time, I would not have confronted him or my fears."

"Look, Lorilie, what I'm telling you is—"

"There may be someone in the valley to explain why you could not use your Gift."

Rafe pushed the needle into the cardboard he kept in his small first-aid kit and dropped it in his pack. "Lorilie." Turning, he pulled her around to face him. The openness of her heart shone in the green depths of her adoring eyes. "I am not Gifted. Don't make me something I'm not."

"I will not, nor will I pretend you are anything other than what you are."

"Exactly what I am remains to be determined." The only Gift he had was the green-eyed wonder he loved. She was the only one he needed. "I'm just beginning to discover my potential."

"Let's discover it together. There is much we can learn from one another if we have the patience." A coy smile accompanied her finger making counterclockwise circles against the swirls of hair on his chest. Carefully, she avoided the multitude of scratches and scrapes from the fallen tree. "I already know the depth of your self-discipline concerning lovemaking. Perhaps you can teach me some, but not too much."

Hungrily, he found her mouth. She tasted of life and everything good in the world.

He drew her across his lap, and deepened their kiss.

A mischievous glint lit her eyes. It spread into a seductive smile filled with secret warning.

"What's behind that look, Lorilie?"

"I was thinking."

"About me, I hope." He intended her to think of nothing else for the next several hours.

"What else would I think of while kissing you?"

"Yeah. What else?" He lowered his mouth to make sure.

Lorilie pulled back slightly, her enigmatic smile teasing him. "I was thinking, we will know without question if you are Gifted even if the valley is deserted."

"We will?" He straightened. "How?"

"Not how, Rafe. When."

"All right, when?"

"When we have our first child." She drew his head down and placed a kiss on his clean-shaven cheek.

"What happens then?" Her breast fit his hand as though made for him. "I get religion?" He kissed her slowly, letting the passion build. A leisurely exploration of her delicious mouth and inviting body gave all the response he needed.

"You get to share in the miracle of life we created. I want many children, Rafe."

He kissed her repeatedly, unable to quench his ravenous appetite for her. He was parched with thirst and she was the oasis of everything he craved. "We'll have ten if you want. All at once or one at a time."

Shimmering blond tresses rippled against his chest. Laughter bubbled from the core of her. "Ten? All at once?"

He nuzzled the hollow of her throat, savoring the unique taste of her clean skin. "However, whenever you want."

"Really. May we have ten children? Few Gifted men want more than two."

"I'm not Gifted." A flicker of shared passion ignited.

Open, uninhibited, she tested every level of control with her eagerness and genuine sexual curiosity.

"And if you are? May I still have ten?"

"Ten. Twelve. As many as you can stand."

"Oh, Rafe, you are truly the most marvelous, brave, unselfish life mate ever." Her arms twined around his neck, and she covered his face with wild kisses.

"What did I just agree to?" he asked, confused.

"If you are not Gifted, to be the father of my children."

"Oh." The interruption over, he resumed kissing her.

Her hand pushed at his shoulder. "If you are Gifted, you will experience childbirth with me. We will share all of it."

The storm had broken the back of the summer heat. Cool evening breezes provided a respite from the sunny afternoon warmth. Lorilie and Rafe lingered at the stream for two days. True to her word, Lorilie restrained the wolves. Hal died the evening of the second day. The wolves had watched Clyde dig a deep grave. Her demons buried, her stalkers thwarted, Lorilie was eager for the adventure ahead.

They left the makeshift rock shelter beside the stream the morning after Hal died. Late in the afternoon, they paused on a ridge offering an obstructed view of their destination.

"Nice setting," Rafe said scanning the horizon.

"It is beautiful. Look at the meadows. In the spring and early summer, they are filled with flowers. The creek meandering through the heart of the valley is a small river then. And . . ." She gazed up at him, puzzled. "Why are you laughing?"

"I don't need a sales pitch, sweet Lorilie. Not only do I see all the places an enemy might hide or lay a trap, I can see the beauty of the place. Now." He tugged her braid and planted a quick kiss on her lips. "Nothing in this world is as beautiful as you." A slow survey of her tattered clothes caused her to glance down. Rips flapped the knees of her trousers. The shirt gaped, exposing the tops of her breasts. When she met his gaze, he winked. "It's probably the stylish outfit you're wearing that turns me on."

"The buttons are gone."

Rafe removed his holey shirt and handed it to her. "What you have on is fine for me, but I'd appreciate it if you covered up before we enter the valley. I'll wear my jacket."

Lorilie donned his shirt over hers. "I suppose we could use some fresh clothing."

"You suppose?" Rich, bass laughter boomed over the valley.

The sound of his mirth made her grin. "Will you carry this?" She gestured at the packs she had toted over the pass.

"Sure." He gathered their belongings and balanced the load on his shoulders. "Ready?"

"I'll race you." Turning sideways, she sidestepped over the lip of the ridge.

"You're kidding." He started after her.

She stayed ahead of him down the steepest portion of the slope. Her mistake was looking over her shoulder. The packs flapped like bat wings on his shoulders as he side-slipped from tree to tree. Running, catching the brush, with Loner prancing at her heels, Lorilie started laughing.

Rafe caught her quickly. "Never let it be said chivalry is dead." He darted around a tree and halted her uncon-trolled descent. "Neither is female trickery."

"I should apologize." The laughter spilled unchecked. Happy down to the soles of her feet, she let it flow.

"For what, my free-spirited wood nymph?"

"Tricking you."

"You can make it up to me later." A quick brush of his mouth on hers quelled her laughter. "Right now we'd better keep moving. I spotted Marica near the cabins above the creek.''

The impulse to kiss him won out. One merely whetted her appetite. The fires of desire ignited instantly.

''Shall I go away, or do you want to meet the rest of the natives?'' Craig asked, trudging along the slope.

Lorilie reluctantly relinquished her life mate.

''Any trouble?'' Craig relieved Rafe of half the packs.

''Nothing Lorilie couldn't handle.''

Including Marica and Craig, eight people occupied the valley. Unlike the widely spread settlement Lorilie came from, people built family cabins within sight of one another. The settlement made use of common areas that included a central well, a blacksmith forge, and a barn.

Craig and Marica had taken up residence in an abandoned cabin.

''Only the elders remain. The rest have left since your last visit, Lorilie,'' Marica told them after hearing the fate of the Ketchums. ''They cannot stay here.''

''We're in the heart of the gold-rush country,'' Craig said. ''These old folks won't survive what's coming. The early forty-niners were like locusts. They stripped every board and plank they could find for sluice boxes and used the seasoned logs for shelters and firewood.''

''If the remaining Gifted want to come with us, we'll take them.'' Rafe removed his jacket for Marica's examination of his back. ''They have wagons. Animals. Are any of them too frail for the journey to the coast?''

''They are strong enough—although leaving here will sadden them greatly,'' Marica said.

Lorilie folded Rafe's jacket over her arm. ''I will speak with them of the Ketchums, of the wages of greed, and of my grandfather.'' Empathy for the elders' plight dampened the joyful reunion with her friends.

''We found clothes for you.'' Marica adjusted a lantern

for a better look at Rafe's back. "You have two punctures with signs of infection."

"Do they have anything like a bathtub and hot water? Lorilie and I could use it." He took the jacket from Lorilie and pulled it on.

"Come with me, Capt'n. They have just the ticket."

"My turn next."

"You may go first, Lorilie," Rafe offered.

"Thank you, no. Marica and I will prepare dinner." She refreshed her tea. "Your turn to cook tomorrow."

Rafe kissed her forehead. "Got yourself a deal."

After dinner and dressed in clean clothes with all the necessary buttons and without any holes, Lorilie and Rafe joined the valley residents gathered at the largest home.

A distinguished, silver-haired man introduced simply as Albert acted as spokesman. Clear brown eyes, set in a leathery face conditioned by years and the elements, missed nothing. His broad shoulders and slight paunch seemed incongruous on his tall, willowy frame.

Albert concluded the brief round of introductions. "We have expected you for several years."

Surprised, Lorilie looked hard at Albert, then at the remaining Gifted elders. As she did each time she had visited the valley, she searched for a hint of familiarity reminiscent of her father.

"Years?" she asked softly.

"Yes." A sinewy hand gestured an odd arrangement of chairs brought from the kitchen into the small parlor area. "We were visited by Gifted journeying from your mountain shortly after the Ketchums entered your midst."

Lorilie sat beside Rafe. The aura of comfortable belonging piqued her curiosity.

"The remaining Ketchums have the mountain and little else now. I doubt they'll stay long with the old man and Hal gone." Rafe took Lorilie's hand.

She laced her fingers through his.

"We have discussed what lies ahead." Albert settled

into a rocking chair even older than he. Absently, he rocked in a slow, even motion. "Craig has convinced us of the necessity of leaving the homes we cherish, and seeking a place where we can live relatively undisturbed for our remaining years.

"What of you, Captain Rafe Stricter? It is clear Lorilie has chosen you as her life mate. Yet I understand you wish the Gifted to return you to your time."

"Is it possible?"

The anticipation seizing Rafe squeezed Lorilie's heart. The bleak possibility that he would change his mind if directly confronted by the opportunity to return raised its head sooner than she had anticipated.

"Yes, for the man with the Gift to do so."

The ladder-back chair creaked under Rafe's weight as he shifted. "Who is that man? Is he still here?"

Albert's gray eyebrows rose in amusement. "You discovered your Gift late in life, Rafe Stricter. From what I understand, you and Craig had accepted death in your time. Only you know what went through your mind in those moments. The catalyst lies there."

Rafe slumped forward and rested his head in his hand, his elbow braced on his knee. "I didn't think about anything . . . except . . . Craig didn't deserve to die so young. . . . If I had one wish, it would be for a second chance for him.

"We felt the mountain shake.

"The next thing I knew, we were in Lorilie's fortress and I ached like I'd lost a bar fight with a platoon of marines."

"Ahhhh." Albert stopped rocking.

The silence stretched.

Rafe lifted his head. "Would you mind elaborating?"

Albert shrugged. "It takes a powerful Gift and tremendous physical endurance to bend time. I surmise your wish for your friend was greater than the barriers hiding your Gift."

"I know myself pretty well, Albert. I'd have known . . . would know if I had such a capability. For the sake of argument, why would I have picked here? Now? Instead of some other time and place?"

"This is where your life mate awaited. Your Gift is untamed. 'Tis only natural you would seek her, your counterpart, knowingly or not." Albert grinned. "To a man with the Gift to bend time, even untamed time, the place and years are nothing more than crossing a room when his life mate is his destiny."

"How would I have known where she was?"

"How does the wind know when to blow? She drew you, albeit unknowingly, because of the danger she faced. What puzzles me is why you did not recognize her."

"I think . . . maybe I did, but I sure as hell didn't want to," Rafe mused. "When I first arrived, there were times . . . flashes, really, when it seemed I should know her . . . but they came and went so fast. After a while, they stopped."

Albert began rocking again. "It seems you did not just rescue your friend and yourself from death but found the path to life. A wise man knows the difference between escaping from something and going to something. Are you a wise man, Rafe?"

"Getting wiser by the moment."

"You have to be Gifted, Capt'n. How else could we have gotten here? Maybe you had Gifted ancestors and you're a throwback. Maybe it's a genetic lottery and you wound up with the winning ticket."

"I'm not Gifted. If I were, I'd have been able to get us off the ridge when Clyde and Hal caught up to us." The finality of his statement clamped Craig's jaw shut. "I don't know how we got here. Neither one of us is going back, so it doesn't really matter, does it?"

Rafe straightened and squeezed Lorilie's hand. "Do you have anyone left who can marry Lorilie and me?"

"We would like a formal ceremony," Lorilie explained.

"I would be honored," Albert said. "Marica, Craig, do you also want this?"

"We do," Craig answered.

"So be it. Tomorrow. Now, let us discuss the long journey ahead."

Harmony pervaded Lorilie's being. Confident that wherever they settled Rafe would be with her, she prayed a silent prayer of thanksgiving for Rafe's Gift of untamed time.

SANTA CRUZ MOUNTAINS, NORTH OF
MONTEREY, CALIFORNIA, 1872

From the parlor doorway, Lorilie observed Rafe and Craig arrange chairs around the long dining table set to accommodate the entire Blackstone and Stricter families. The celebration marked the engagement of Joseph Stricter, the eldest of the brood, with Claire Blackstone, the second of the three Blackstone children and only daughter.

"Do you ever miss the life we had at their age?" Craig asked.

"The only time I missed anything from our time was when Lorilie went into labor. Then I wanted a modern hospital. Specialists. Anesthesiologists, preferably two or three."

Lorilie smiled when Rafe shuddered at the memory of their five offspring entering the world.

"How the hell women keep on having kids without morphine or sodium pentothal is beyond me."

"Marica says the pain goes away when she holds the baby." Craig looked around for more chairs.

"So does Lorilie." He aligned the chairs with the place

settings. "They lie, Craig. It's like having a bullet cut out of the most sensitive place in your body."

"Is that why you ended up with five instead of ten kids?"

"Maybe. Pregnancy takes a helluva toll on a woman's body. All things considered, we've been lucky five times."

"There are extra chairs in the sewing room." Lorilie smoothed her skirts as she entered the dining room.

"Eavesdropping?" Rafe asked.

"Sure, she was. I'll get the rest of the chairs," Craig said with a wink.

"I am guilty." She slipped beneath his beckoning arm. "Do I understand you do not want more children? Surely, you have recovered from Angela's birth. It has been ten years."

"Five children are enough. If we have any more, we'll need a bigger table."

Lorilie laughed and hugged him. After twenty-five years, he still sidestepped any direct question he did not wish to answer. "Five is plenty. They are growing up so fast. In a few years, we'll have grandchildren."

"Speaking of the kids, I'm concerned about Roric."

Of course he was. Rafe was always concerned about Roric, the most precocious of their brood. "He's twenty-two and experimenting."

"One day, he'll find his life mate and not return."

"It if happens, it will not matter if you are ready for him to leave, Rafe. He will go. He is so much like you. Is that why you worry about him more than the rest of the children?"

Both knew the answer. Roric had inherited the Gift of time travel from his father. While Rafe had found the key only once, Roric had already tested the boundaries twice.

Lorilie smiled at him. "I love you, Mother Hen. Roric will do as his heart commands. As will we. Speaking of which, let's play war games tonight. The moon is full."

A chuckle vibrated Rafe's chest. "You want to play with the wolf pack and make love beside the creek. I'd call those love games."

"Then let's play love games after everyone goes to sleep tonight."

"There's nothing I'd enjoy more."

That night, while the Stricter children slept, a warm summer breeze whispered the story of the lovers who roamed the mountainside with the wolves and made love by the light of the moon. The trees sighed over the free spirit who fell in love with a warrior and how together, they tamed time and the world around them.